W9-CNN-817

HOW TO START A FIRE

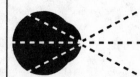

This Large Print Book carries the
Seal of Approval of N.A.V.H.

HOW TO START A FIRE

LISA LUTZ

WHEELER PUBLISHING
A part of Gale, Cengage Learning

GALE
CENGAGE Learning·

Farmington Hills, Mich • San Francisco • New York • Waterville, Maine
Meriden, Conn • Mason, Ohio • Chicago

Wheeler Publishing, a part of Gale, Cengage Learning.

LIBRARY OF CONGRESS CATALOGING-IN-PUBLICATION DATA

Lutz, Lisa.
   How to start a fire / Lisa Lutz. — Large print edition.
     pages cm. — (Wheeler Publishing large print hardcover)
     ISBN 978-1-4104-8181-8 (hardback) — ISBN 1-4104-8181-6 (hardcover)
   1. Female friendship—Fiction. 2. Life change events—Fiction. 3. Large type books. I. Title.
   PS3612.U897H69 2015b
   813'.6—dc23
                                        2015016168

Published in 2015 by arrangement with Houghton Mifflin Harcourt Publishing Company

To my two favorite Julies:
Julie Shiroishi
and
Julie Ulmer

PART I

All good things are wild and free.
— Henry David Thoreau

2005

LINCOLN, NEBRASKA

"Are you lost?" the man asked.

"No," she said.

"Where are you headed?"

"Don't know."

"Seat taken?" he asked.

"As you can see, it's empty," she said.

He sat down across the table. A road map of the lower forty-eight states separated the man and woman. It also joined them in a way.

"Wasn't an invitation," she said, not pleasantly. Not unpleasantly.

He ignored the comment. He ate lunch in this diner every day at noon. It felt kind of like home. He didn't need an invitation to sit down in his own dining room.

"So, let me get this straight. You don't know where you're going, but you're not lost."

"That's the gist of it."

"On a road trip?"

9

"Something like that."

"You picked a good place to begin a journey. We're practically smack in the middle of the country."

"And the middle of nowhere," she said.

He couldn't argue with that and nodded in agreement. "My name's Bill."

"Hello, Bill."

"You got a name?"

"Everyone has a name."

Bill waited. He was expecting a name. She wasn't sure which one to use.

"Kate," she said. It felt odd saying her real name again.

"That's a nice, simple name."

"I guess so."

"You should be careful, Kate. A woman alone on the road. Never a great idea," Bill said.

"I can take care of myself," she said.

"Some people, you just don't know. You don't know what they're capable of."

"I think I do."

"I've been around awhile," Bill said.

She couldn't argue with him about that. The lines were etched deep on his forehead like a maze of estuaries, with his hair running from the shore. He'd managed to avoid the middle-aged spread, but his gut still seemed a little soft. She knew he meant well. She also knew he'd keep talking because he was tired of hanging on to all that wisdom.

"I'm sure you have. Can I get the check, please?" she asked the waitress.

"A woman shouldn't be traveling alone," Bill continued. "Especially if she's got no particular destination. I know you think I'm just an old man prattling on and I should mind my own business. But I got a daughter about your age and I would tell her the same thing."

"Has your daughter ever killed a man?" she asked.

"Excuse me?"

Kate leaned in and spoke in a whisper so as not to disturb the other patrons. "Has your daughter ever killed a man?"

"Of course not," Bill said.

"I didn't mean for it to happen, but it did."

Kate said it to silence him. She was surprised how well it worked. It slipped off her tongue so easily this time. She wondered why that was.

Bill placed his hands on the map and traced the Continental Divide.

Kate paid the check and carefully folded up the map. She smiled warmly at Bill, just to ease the tension.

"Excuse me. I have to be somewhere."

1993

SANTA CRUZ, CALIFORNIA

"Eighteen is the age of emancipation. Now you're free to do whatever you want except rent a car, run for president, and drink legally, but that's what fake IDs are for," Anna Fury said.

She was lying flat on a dewy lawn, staring up at a starless sky. Soon the moisture from the grass would seep through her thick pea coat and she'd announce that it was time to go. When she was uncomfortable.

Kate Smirnoff, next to her, clutching her legs in a shivering ball, was already uncomfortable. But she liked the challenge of seeing what she could endure. She had on an old man's suit coat. Her father's coat, which she wore less out of sentimentality and more for reasons of cost and comfort. Most of Kate's wardrobe had previously been inhabited by other souls. Her father's coat, unlike Anna's navy-surplus purchase, was far too big and made Kate look even younger than she was. At midnight she'd turned eighteen, but she still looked fifteen. Much of it you could blame on her small frame, just over five feet and barely ninety pounds. But the pageboy haircut and the giant blue toddler eyes didn't help. Neither did clothes that needed to be belted or pinned to stay on — they made her look like a child playing a very drab game of dress-up.

Anna looked like an intellectual in a French art film — a boyish silhouette offset by long, neglected brown hair. She'd take a scissors to it only when she encountered a stubborn tangle. Anna was pretty in a plain way, the kind of pretty that had been thought beautiful in the seventies, but not anymore. Her features were all too standard. Except her eyes, which slanted downward and always gave the subjects of her gaze the sense that they were being studied.

Nirvana's *In Utero* was blasting on a loop in the rundown Craftsman house on Storey Street. That's why they'd left. Kate was afraid overexposure would cause her to loathe something she loved. So they'd taken their pints and retired to a neighbor's lawn, where Anna was now pontificating about the age of emancipation.

"How does it feel to be free?" Anna asked.

13

"I don't feel any different," Kate said.

"Now I'm cold," Anna said, jumping to her feet and shaking the wet grass from her coat. Next to Kate, Anna felt like a giant, even though she was just a scrape more than five four.

They walked along the lit side of the road at Kate's behest. Clothed all in black, they wouldn't stand a chance if a car careened around the corner. Kate thought of such things; Anna didn't.

"Nobody can tell you what to do anymore," Anna said.

About four months earlier, when Anna had turned eighteen, she'd stopped at a gas station, bought a pack of cigarettes, and smoked one on the porch while her mother barked her disapproval. Anna didn't smoke, but she had to deliver the message loud and clear: *I'm free.* Although she'd soon realized she wasn't.

"Turning eighteen was the happiest day of my life," Anna continued. "I bet twenty-one will be pretty good too."

"Do you see that?" Kate asked.

Across the street a woman was sleeping under a willow tree. It was the light flesh of her thigh set against the dark landscape that caught Kate's eye. They approached. The motionless woman was wearing a short black dress hiked up high on her almost comically long, well-toned legs. The smell of vomit was in the vicinity. Her only source of warmth was a short denim jacket.

"What do you think she's doing out here?" Kate asked.

"I think she got tanked at the party and went outside to barf," Anna said authoritatively.

"It's forty degrees out. Why would she wear something like that?"

Anna knelt down and tried to shake the woman awake.

"Wake up! It's time to go home."

"I'm sleeping," the woman slurred.

"I know her," said Kate. "She's in my biology class. I think she's on the women's basketball team. She's always wearing sweats and coming in with wet hair after practice. Plus, she's really tall."

Anna shook the woman more vigorously, but each time, she got little more than garbled words and an adjustment in sleep posture.

"Maybe we can carry her," Anna said.

"No," said Kate. "You can't carry dead weight. You see it in movies all the time, but it's almost impossible. For once, I'd like to see a film that accurately reflects that challenge."

"We're not leaving her," Anna said.

"How did I get here?" the tall woman asked.

"We brought you here last night," Kate said.

"Where am I?" she said.

"Porter College. Where do you live?"

"Stevenson," the tall woman said.

Kate held her tongue. There were subcultures in the UC Santa Cruz residential colleges, and it was well known that Stevenson was where all the Republicans lived — not that there were many of them at the decidedly left-wing university.

The room was disconcertingly familiar to the tall woman, as if someone had redecorated badly while she'd been sleeping. The walls were the same dirty beige, and the bland chipboard furniture was battered similarly, just in different places. There were two of everything: two twin beds that contained storage compartments beneath, two four-drawer dressers with mirrors on top, two wardrobe closets. The red velvet comforter was most definitely not hers. In her eye line was a poster of a malnourished-looking man holding a microphone. His jeans were partially undone.

"Who are you?" the tall woman asked.

16

"Kate Smirnoff. Like the vodka." Kate extended her hand in a formal businesslike gesture.

"Hi," the confused guest said, accepting the handshake.

"And you're Georgianna Leoni," Kate said, tripping a bit over the name.

"How do you know?"

Kate handed her guest a small clutch purse. "We found this under your body. Your ID was inside. Should I call you Georgianna?"

"George."

"Good. That's better in an emergency. 'George, call 911,' as opposed to 'Georgianna, call 911.' "

"What happened?" George asked.

"We were at a party on Storey Street last night. You were probably at the same one. We found you passed out under a willow tree. After you'd vomited, most likely. We decided we'd better move you because there were lots of really drunk men at the party. Do you want some water?"

"Yes, please."

Kate filled a purple plastic tumbler from the in-room sink.

"I don't remember coming back here."

"Not surprising," Kate said. "Anna slapped your face a few times to wake you

up. We got you to your feet and walked you maybe half a block, like coaches and trainers do with football players who get injured on the field. But then you stopped moving on your own, and you're heavier than you look."

"Then what happened?" George asked, because stories about things you did that you don't remember are always particularly compelling.

"Then we found the shopping cart," Kate explained. "Getting you inside was a whole other hassle. I won't go into the details, but if you have any unexplained bruising, suffice it to say, that was the cause. Sorry. We tried. But you really do weigh more than you appear to."

"And then what?"

"We carted you to the shuttle stop. The shuttle driver was kind enough to help you onboard. It was late, and we didn't know where you lived, so we just took you back here. The RA helped us get you inside. After he left, Anna took your dress because it still had vomit on it. The rest is history."

George lifted the covers and noticed she was wearing a Banana Slugs T-shirt and underwear. She scanned the room for her clothes, but it was hard to spot anything amid the chaos.

"Where is my dress?" George asked.

"Anna's washing it. She should be back any minute."

As if on cue, Anna Fury entered the room, carrying a laundry basket and a can of Dr Pepper.

Anna smiled and said with the air of someone who knows, "I bet *you're* hungover."

She dropped the laundry basket on the floor and handed the soda to George. "This should help — that's why it's called *Dr* Pepper. But what you really need is a greasy breakfast."

George cracked the soda and took a sip. It helped. She crawled out of bed and glanced in the mirror.

"I look like shit," she said.

Anna rolled her eyes. George was the kind of woman who could do nothing to shake her beauty. The old T-shirt, matted brown hair, and mascara migrating down her face only added to her attractiveness. She had a perfect olive complexion and freakishly high cheekbones and eyes that were a green-gray color Anna realized, when she finally got a good look at them, she had never seen before. George was on the cusp of being too tall. All legs, but useful legs, not decorative sticks. The kind of legs that could send a person places, like into the air for a perfect lay-up. Looking at George, Anna felt a stab of envy. But she understood from watching her mother that there was a cost to beauty — you were chained to it for years, and when it finally released you, you didn't know who you were anymore.

George put on her dress from the night before, a form-fitting jersey that had clearly shrunk in the wash.

"Thank you for . . ." George said.

"You're welcome," Anna said. She turned to Kate. "I figured out what we should do today," she said with the expression of a scientist who has just found solid proof of his career-making theorem.

"What?" Kate said.

"Go camping," Anna said.

"Where?" Kate asked.

"I think it's time you saw the Stratosphere Giant," Anna said.

George must have looked confused, so Anna explained. "Kate is prone to desultory and passing obsessions. When I first met her, it was the actor Lon Chaney. Now she's really into the California redwoods. The giant ones. Not your average redwoods."

George stared blankly. Kate misunderstood the expression, interpreting it as information-seeking rather than the slow

20

uptake of the hung-over.

"Some of those trees grow to over three hundred and fifty feet. That's longer than a football field. You can even drive your car through one of them. Probably not a truck," Kate said.

Anna turned to George and said, "You should come too. That's exactly what you need: fresh air, enormous trees, a dip in a cold pond, s'mores, and sleeping under the stars."

It wasn't like George to participate in spur-of-the-moment activities, but Anna seemed so sure of her plan. When people have a certainty that you lack, being swayed feels less like a sharp turn than a slow arc in the road. George returned to her dorm, showered, and changed into practical clothes. She washed the makeup from her face and scrubbed a phone number off her forearm. His name was Doug, or maybe Don. She had left the party with him — that she could remember. What she couldn't recall was why he'd left her passed out on the lawn.

Attending Santa Cruz was not unlike going to college in a campground. You walked through the woods to class, and there were miles of trails where you could avoid even seeing a campus structure. But Anna firmly believed that adventures could not exist at one's door. They required travel. She was using Kate's obsession as an excuse to take a road trip. Her car was already loaded with off-season clothing, neglected schoolbooks, a myriad of empty soda cans and candy wrappers, and camping gear. Kate, always more practical, brought food, water, and emergency flares for the six-and-a-half-hour journey.

It was decided that George should take the back seat so she could stretch out her legs. For the first hour of the drive, George listened to Kate and Anna's conversations as if she were tuned in to a radio show. Their back-and-forth had a speed and rhythm she couldn't match. George's hangover was still quietly vibrating, so she just watched and listened. After a while she realized that she had never seen two women so patently different be so at ease with each other.

Kate and Anna had met only three and a half months earlier. They were thrown together not by the careful dorm-room pairings that the housing administrators prided themselves on but simply because they were late applicants in a pond of already-paired fish.

"I have a theory," said Anna now. "They

try to match roommates based on common interests and similar backgrounds and areas of study. But from my observation, that breeds competition. What truly matters in a congenial cohabiting situation are sleep habits, taste in music, and levels of cleanliness. Kate and I have all three in common — basically, we're sloppy insomniacs who loathe pop music. But in everything else, we're like night and day. See, I'm a biology major; Kate, business. I have two parents, still married. Both of Kate's are dead. Car crash when she was eight. I've never held a job. Kate has worked in her grandfather's diner since she was twelve. I grew up in Boston. Kate was raised right here in Santa Cruz. She's never even left California. Can you believe that?"

"We won't be far from Oregon," said Kate, who didn't seem to mind having her life summarized solely in terms of how it differed from Anna's.

"Maybe we'll just dip inside," Anna said, "so you can say you've been there."

As Anna shattered the speed limit on Highway 101, the landscape turned a lusher green. Dark clouds pushed their way into the sky as headlights started to blink on. Anna interrogated her new friend with a series of seemingly random but actually premeditated questions. *What song would your torturers play to drive you mad?* "It's a Small World." *How many hard-boiled eggs can you eat in one sitting?* Five. (Anna was impressed; most people couldn't answer that question.) *Who would you save in a fire, Keith Richards or Pete Townshend?*

"I don't know," George answered, indifferent to both men.

"The answer is Pete Townshend. A fire wouldn't kill Keith Richards," Anna said.

Kate asked the pedestrian kinds of questions and learned that George was a midwestern girl, raised in Chicago. An only child. Still-married parents. Italian American father. WASPy mother. She had several male cousins who'd taught her how to fight and play basketball. She had had a four-inch growth spurt when she was thirteen and played on the boys' team until high school. Her major: undecided.

A few hours into the road trip, Kate posed a question that spurred a rapid-fire conversation George found hard to follow; it was like listening to actors in a 1940s radio show.

KATE: Did you check the weather?
ANNA: No. I thought you were going to do that.

KATE: Did you tell me to do that?

ANNA: No.

KATE: Then why did you think I would?

ANNA: Because you're more practical than
I am.

KATE: It's going to start raining soon.

ANNA: You don't know that.

KATE: I do.

ANNA: No, you don't.

Small droplets of water dotted the windshield. Then the drizzle turned to rain, forcing Anna to turn on the windshield wipers.

KATE: What more proof do you need?

ANNA: What's a little rain?

KATE: We can't go camping in the rain.

ANNA: Why not?

KATE: You can't start a fire in the rain.

ANNA: So we won't have a fire.

KATE: If we don't have a fire, then we don't
have s'mores.

ANNA: So?

KATE: Camping isn't camping without
s'mores. We can't have other cooked
food either.

ANNA: We can have potato chips, beef
jerky, and beer.

KATE: Maybe you should slow down.

ANNA: What does that sign say?

KATE: Make the wipers go faster.

ANNA: That's as fast as they go.

GEORGE: I think you should pull off the road.

ANNA: Good idea. We'll find a place to bunk for the night.

KATE: A Motel 6 or something.

ANNA: Not a Motel 6. Some place that sounds more rustic.

KATE: Like what, the Rustic Inn?

ANNA: It can't be a chain motel and it has to have the word *Lodge* in the name.

GEORGE: What was that?

The car swerved back and forth across two lanes with a rhythmic thumping sound. Anna slowed the car, turned on her emergency blinkers, and pulled onto the shoulder of the road.

ANNA: I'm not an expert, but I think we have a flat tire.

KATE: I second that opinion.

ANNA: Don't worry. I'm going to take care of everything.

GEORGE: Do you know how to change a tire?

ANNA: No.

GEORGE: I can do it. My dad showed me

like a year ago.

ANNA: Good to know. For future reference.

KATE: Uh-oh.

GEORGE: You don't have a jack, do you?

ANNA: Nope. But it wouldn't do us any good anyway.

GEORGE: Why not?

ANNA: A jack is useful only if you have a spare tire.

GEORGE: You don't have a spare?

KATE: She used to.

ANNA: I took it out a while back. Wanted to see if I got better mileage without the extra weight.

GEORGE: Oh my God.

ANNA: Relax. Everything is under control.

Anna donned a yellow rain slicker that she found under a waffle iron in the trunk. George didn't ask about the waffle iron — or the toolbox, or the snowshoes, or any of the other items that together easily exceeded the weight of a spare tire. Several minutes elapsed as Anna attempted to flag down passing vehicles, only to be drenched by their splash. Eventually, a Ford truck pulled over a little way up the road.

Anna ran the fifty-yard dash to the truck. Kate and George watched her gesture to whoever was sitting in the passenger seat.

An objective observer would have thought the tale she was weaving was far more complicated than a simple flat tire. Then Anna turned around to face her travel companions, gave the thumbs-up sign, and casually walked back to the VW.

Anna opened the car door. "Just grab your coats and whatever you need for the night. They'll drop us in town. We'll get the car fixed in the morning. Oh, and Kate, you're a foreign exchange student from the former Yugoslavia."

Anna insisted on buying Charlie Ames and Greg Wilkes, Humboldt County loggers and longtime residents, dinner for their trouble. At least that's what she said, but really it was to prolong Kate's impersonation of an Eastern European exchange student. Charlie and Greg had never met anyone from a country that no longer existed. They were intrigued. They also wanted to present their country in a flattering light, and they tried to include Kate in all conversation.

"So, Katia, how are you liking your visit so far?" Charlie asked, enunciating each syllable with careful precision.

"Oh, America iz very nice," said Kate in a perfect Czech accent. That was the only accent Kate could do; she figured the men wouldn't know the difference.

"And where were you headed before your tire blew?"

"Avenue of the Giants," Anna said. "That's all we came for. Katia and I have been pen pals for almost ten years now. She read about the giant redwoods in school. Heard there was a tree you could drive your car through and just had to see it. Isn't that true, Katia?"

"Yes," Kate said. "I have grrret luf fur de big trees."

George dropped her napkin under the table and searched for it until she could get her laughter under control. This took a long time and made Charlie and Greg either suspicious or uncomfortable, which broke up Kate, who covered for her sudden, inexplicable laughter by picking up a saltshaker and saying, "Look, iz so funny. We don' haf in my country."

Anna, however, was the master of her invented game. She never cracked, not during the meal or the ten-mile drive to the Redwood Lodge or even when she retold her invented tale to the motel clerk.

"I just feel terrible. This is her first time in America and we get a flat tire."

In room 15 of the Redwood Lodge — which looked about as rustic as a Motel 6, with the exception of the faux-pine finish on the dresser — George and Anna passed a bottle of cheap whiskey back and forth, repeating their favorite Katia quotes of the night.

"My home is no more der and dat make me sad."

"Who doesn't vant to dance on Stalin's grafe?"

"In my country, lipstick is fur whores and men who vant to be vomen."

"Television is de best ting about your country. And Pop-Tarts."

"Americans are wasteful. Ve can feed a family fur a week on a pot of borscht."

George was awed by Kate's ability to play Anna's game. What George didn't know was that Kate was always playing Anna's games. Maybe that was why she wasn't laughing.

The rain never relented. The tent was never pitched. The following morning, Anna had her car towed to a gas station, where the tire was replaced. Kate insisted that Anna also purchase a spare, knowing that money was not an object. A stranger wouldn't have guessed that Anna was a rich girl, mostly because Anna was hell-bent on avoiding that label.

After taking a vote, the women decided to

continue their rain-soaked adventure. They drove through the Avenue of the Giants, the massive trees looming above. George had never seen anything more beautiful. Kate studied her map, trying to pinpoint the location of the Stratosphere Giant, currently the tallest tree in the world — although that statistic was debatable, since not all trees had been measured.

Despite the weather, Kate demanded they go on a hike. It was then she and Anna learned that George was on the track team as well as the basketball team. Her pace was brutal. George was so awestruck that she barely noticed her companions huffing and puffing in her wake. Kate struggled to match George's speed while offering morsels of information she had gathered over the past few months.

"The oldest coastal redwood is over two thousand years old. Can you imagine that?"

"Which one is it?" George asked.

Kate looked around. "Don't know," she said. "But many are at least six hundred years old. Take your pick."

George stopped in her tracks and craned her neck to try to see the top of a tree. As she continued along the trail, she found a white anomaly among the green brush.

"What is this?" George asked.

"It's an albino redwood. A mutant," Kate said. "They can't manufacture chlorophyll, so they're white. They survive as parasites, linking their root system with normal trees and getting nutrients from them. They can grow to only about sixty feet. But aren't they cool?"

"They're amazing," George said.

Kate's obsession had been sated. She had seen in real life what she had only read about in books. But it seemed she'd passed her obsession on to George, as if it were a physical object that could be handed off.

Anna liked the trees and all. She didn't mind the hike, but her internal experience was far milder than the other girls'. Anna slowly caught up with George and Kate, pulled out a joint, and lit up, smoking among the greenery.

"How can you smoke in a place so beautiful?" George asked.

"It makes it *more* beautiful," Anna said.

They stayed in the Redwood Lodge one more night and made s'mores on their camping stove in their room, which meant flattening them on a skillet. Kate shook her head in disappointment; this was not how it was done. She missed the smell of burned marshmallow and wanted the musty, used odor of the motel room to disappear. Anna lit a joint, even though George pointed at the No Smoking sign.

"That only refers to cigarettes," Anna said.

The scent of marijuana overpowered the various odors of past occupants that seemed layered in the room. Anna passed the joint to Kate, who lately, after months of rejecting the offer, had found herself giving in now and again. She took a drag and suffered a brutal coughing fit.

George shook her head in the manner of people who don't partake.

Kate said, when she could speak again, "It will make the s'mores taste better."

George, being the guest, was served first. The chocolate and marshmallow dripped onto her fingers, stinging them with their heat. She took a bite and thought, *Why does it need to taste better?*

The next day, Anna drove thirty minutes north on the 101 and crossed the Oregon border.

"Welcome to Oregon," Anna said, as if she were a representative of the state. "You have now officially been to two states," she said to Kate. "How do you feel?"

"I think I like Oregon. It's definitely my second-favorite state," Kate said.

"Excellent," said Anna as she began looking for an exit so that they could start their journey home.

After forty-eight hours of constant chatter, the trio drifted into silence. It wasn't the tense silence of those who'd had their fill of one another, just an unspoken sparing of words. They knew when to speak and when to stop.

"I'm hungry," George announced as the mileage signs to Santa Cruz dipped into double digits.

"I know a place," Kate said.

An hour later, they were sitting in Smirnoff's Diner on Church Street, devouring an assortment of pies and French fries. Ivan, Kate's grandfather, guardian, and the owner of the establishment, approached the table and scoffed dramatically at the victuals selected from his very own menu. Had he taken their order instead of Louise, he would have insisted on the turkey dinner or meatloaf or something that had been a square meal back in his day.

He kissed his granddaughter on the cheek and then turned to Anna.

"Are you behayfing yussef?" he said as he bent down to kiss her forehead.

"Always," Anna said, insincerely.

34

"Meet George," said Kate. "She's our new friend."

"Is gut to make new frens," Ivan said.

George noted that Ivan's accent was an exact replica of the one Kate used with the loggers.

He shook George's hand. "George, you say?"

"Short for Georgianna," she said.

"I call you Georgianna," Ivan said.

"Okay," George said.

"Why did you order dis junk?" Ivan asked.

"We were hungry," Anna said, not exactly answering the question.

"I bring you someting with protein," Ivan said, still staring at the table and the young women around it.

"I'm a vegetarian now," Anna said.

"You ate hamburger here last veek," Ivan said.

"That was last week," Anna said. "Things change."

Ivan turned to George and gestured in the direction of Anna. "Watch out for dis one. She's got the devil in her."

Ivan winked at Anna, but he wasn't joking. Not exactly. He patted his granddaughter on the head and said, "I get back to the bookkeepings. I see you Monday."

Anna explained more of Kate's story to

George: Kate had been raised by her grandfather from the age of eight. She'd lived with him until she was eighteen, when he insisted that she move into the dormitory, even though she was going to college only a few miles from his residence. She still worked at the diner three days a week for pocket money.

What Anna didn't mention to George was that Kate planned on taking over the diner. Anna didn't mention it because she couldn't fathom anyone wanting something so ordinary out of life. Kate had tried to explain it to her. It wasn't just about the familiarity of the diner and how it tied her to her family. She wanted something that was hers completely. A tiny kingdom to rule as a benevolent dictator. She didn't have Anna's gift for becoming a dictator in any situation.

Anna pulled up in front of Stevenson College. As George slipped out into the soft, drizzly air, Anna said, "Let's do this again sometime. And when I say *this,* I mean something completely different."

Not knowing what that something might be, George said, "That sounds fun."

"Don't be a stranger," Kate said.

2011
SAN FRANCISCO, CALIFORNIA

"Who are you, Anna Fury?"

"I have no idea," Anna said.

"Tell me something about yourself," Jeff Fisher said, squinting earnestly. Jeff had various go-to expressions for a set list of situations. He reserved the squint for probing for personal details. The squint came in handy on dates. At least, dates with women who couldn't see the squint for what it was — a schooled expression, formed with intent.

"What do you want to know?" Anna said.

"What makes you tick? That's what I want to know."

"I think it might be my watch."

It had been six months since Anna was hired as a paralegal for Jeff Fisher, an intellectual property litigator. Jeff was the golden-haired boy of the office, an ex-fraternity president with plastic good looks and a suspiciously even tan. Jeff was accustomed to women responding to him — a quick laugh at one of his playground jokes, a smile in reaction to his Crest-white grin. Anna hid her growing distaste for him behind a veil of professionalism. She was respectful and prompt, giving Jeff no cause for complaint. But the smile he would demand on occasion — with the not-so-subtle "How about a smile today, Anna?" — would be answered with a broad, fake grin that she would drop the moment she turned away.

Matthew Bloom, Jeff's colleague, had more of a detective's eye and saw something else. Everything about Anna spoke of extreme discipline. Her collars were always starched, her skirts neatly pressed and appropriately conservative, and yet Matthew was convinced it was a disguise. She arrived exactly fifteen minutes early for work every single day, her face flushed — he suspected from an early-morning run. She participated in minimal chit-chat, made almost no personal calls, typed well below average with hands that, he'd noted, were ringless. She left work at exactly 6:00. She made it clear that overtime didn't interest her and would agree to it only under extreme duress.

Matthew and Jeff were sitting in Jeff's office consuming deli sandwiches and reviewing a shared case when Anna entered and placed a piece of letterhead on Jeff's desk.

"Sign," she said, adding "please" at the last second, aware that her directive would offend Jeff's notion of the chain of command.

Jeff reviewed and signed the letter. "I'd like that to go out today," he said.

"That's why it has today's date," Anna said.

"Thank you," Jeff responded in an elevated tone. "That will be all."

Anna departed even before his "thank you" was complete.

Ever since Anna began working at Blackman and Blackman LLP, rumors had bubbled, as they usually did in the absence of hard facts. Some of her coworkers said she had lived on a commune for five years. Others claimed she came from money and had suddenly been cut off. Because of her age, the precise figure unknown, marriage theories were followed by bitter-divorce theories. But Matthew never believed anything unless it was substantiated by solid evidence.

"So, how's it working out?" Matthew asked Jeff when Anna was out of earshot.

"She's not really my type," Jeff said.

"She doesn't have to be. She's your colleague," said Matthew.

"Employee," Jeff corrected. "Something is wrong with her, you know? She's incapable of having a normal conversation. I asked if she had any brothers and sisters. She said, 'Yes.' That's all. I asked her what she did for fun. She said, 'Not work.' I asked her what she'd done before coming to Blackman and Blackman, and she said, 'Something completely different.' I even made the mistake of inquiring about the scar on her forehead. It's not like she tries to hide it or anything. Told me she got it in a prison knife fight. Sometimes her only response to a question is 'I don't plan to answer that.' "

"Do you want to swap?" Matthew asked before he could seriously contemplate the offer. Carla Gomez had begun working for him a year ago, after Grace Henderson retired. Matthew had adored Grace, a career legal assistant who'd memorized both volumes of *Civil Procedure Before Trial*. Plainspoken and good at her job, she ordered Matthew around with an authoritarian air. Grace was a bit maternal in her bossiness, but it suited him. There was nothing wrong with Carla other than the fact that she wasn't Grace.

Once the idea was mentioned, plans to

make it happen were immediately set in motion. The only hitch was convincing Anna Fury.

Anna gazed at Matthew without comment for an uncomfortably long time before she responded to his offer.

"A paralegal swap? Is that like a wife swap? We switch back and forth depending on your mood?"

"No. It would be permanent, so long as everyone was happy. Is this something you can live with?"

Anna shrugged and said, "Why not?"

She and Carla spent the rest of the afternoon switching desks.

Two months later, Matthew had acquired exactly four new scraps of information about Anna: she didn't own a cell phone; she read mostly crime novels, at least two a week; she ran four miles every morning except Sunday; and she was about to turn thirty-six. Matthew had extracted that last bit of data from Janet in Human Resources, and not without some difficulty. Although all personnel files were confidential, Anna's seemed to be locked away in a vault somewhere. Even Janet had trouble tracking it down. But Matthew persisted and promised that he would use discretion.

On the morning of Anna's birthday, Matthew buzzed her on the intercom. In a brusque, professional voice, he asked Anna to come into his office and shut the door behind her. She did, and then she sat down across from Matthew and awaited his petty complaint about the growing stack of papers on her desk. At least, that had been the purpose whenever Jeff summoned her.

Anna had almost managed to forget her birthday until Matthew slid a small, pink cardboard box across his desk. She looked down at the box and up at her boss.

"Open it," he said.

She lifted the lid and found a single chocolate cupcake with white frosting. Matthew pulled a candle out of his breast pocket, leaned over the desk, stabbed it into the baked good, swiftly took out a book of matches, and lit the candle. Anna watched him curiously.

"Make a wish," he said.

Anna said, "World peace," and blew out the candle.

Matthew laughed at the lie and wondered what she'd really wished for. He would have been disappointed to know that she hadn't made a wish, having learned some years ago that wanting things seemed to make them less attainable.

"Want some?" Anna asked as she pulled the candle out of the cupcake.

"It's all yours."

"Good," she said and devoured the cupcake in four bites. "Thank you," Anna said as she got to her feet. "I trust you to keep my secret."

"Of course."

Anna nodded her head and exited the office. She felt uneasy but couldn't say why. Sometimes she thought of herself as a poorly knit sweater; if someone pulled on one snag, she'd unravel.

Max Blackman, the boss of Anna's boss and the only surviving Blackman of the firm's name, was giving his customary tour of the fourth floor to a potential new client, Harold Sibley, co-owner of S&R Properties, a commercial real estate management group.

When Blackman passed Anna in the hallway, he took her arm and drew her to his side.

"Anna, I'd like you to meet Harold Sibley. His company is based in Boston, but they're opening a branch out west. Mr. Sibley and your father went to college together. Harold, this is Donald Fury's daughter."

Anna saw a click of recognition when Harold realized who she was. He cleared his throat, probably buying time, trying to figure out what to say. Anna could only assume that he'd heard all about her.

"Donald," Harold said with a half smile. "He's got a great chip shot. But putting isn't his strong suit."

"No, it isn't," Anna said agreeably, even though she had never played golf with her father.

Anna extended her hand to the older gentleman. He gripped it weakly and looked at his arm as if it were an inanimate object. Anna studied his face. There was a slight droop to the left side. Maybe the weakness and the droop weren't new. But maybe they were. Anna didn't want to take any chances.

"I need to speak to both of you in your office," Anna said to Max. Then she briskly strolled into her boss's office and waited for the men to follow her.

The side of Harold's face that still clocked expression revealed impatience. Anna closed the door and spoke quickly, without concern for how her words might alarm him.

"Mr. Sibley, have you had a stroke recently?"

"Of course not."

"Will you try to smile for me?"

"Max, what is the meaning of this?" Harold said, sliding too hard on the final *s* sound.

"I think you might be having a stroke. Can you raise both arms over your head?"

He raised his arms over his head. Anna and Max saw the right arm drift downward.

"Max, call 911. *Now.*"

Max reached for his phone and dialed. With authority, he demanded an ambulance, but he stumbled when the 911 operator began asking questions.

"Have a seat," Anna said calmly to Harold. She pulled over a chair from Max's desk. "When did your symptoms begin?"

"I don't know. During lunch my face felt a little numb. I had some trouble with the fork."

"So lunch was about an hour ago?"

"Yes."

"Relax," Anna said. "You should be fine."

There was a short window of time to begin fibrinolytic therapy, Anna knew. If Sibley's symptoms had really started only an hour or so ago, he was still in that window. But what if his symptoms had started earlier?

Max paced back and forth as far as his phone cord would stretch. He checked his watch. Only five minutes had passed.

45

Several employees began casually loitering outside of Mr. Blackman's office, peering at the scene through the open blinds. Matthew, too curious to restrain himself, knocked on the door and stepped inside.

"Goddamn it, where is the ambulance?" Blackman shouted.

"Max, you need to chill out," Anna said, "or we'll be sending two people to the hospital."

"Is everything all right?" Matthew asked.

"Matthew, go outside and wait for the ambulance. I don't want the paramedics to get lost on the way up," Blackman said. Nothing about Blackman's tone invited further questions.

The EMTs arrived in the office, checked Harold Sibley's vitals, and put him on a gurney. Max and Anna followed them out, Anna reporting the onset and duration of symptoms and her findings on physical exam. When they reached the ambulance, Max said to Anna, "Go with them. Make sure he gets the best doctor and the best course of treatment. I'll take my car and meet you there."

Through his office window, Matthew watched Anna climb into the ambulance.

A few hours later, Anna and Mr. Blackman

returned to the office. The steady sound-track of gossip and conjecture quieted upon their arrival, but questions remained, nonetheless. Matthew had more than anyone. Did Anna know Mr. Sibley? Why did she call Blackman by his first name, and where did that familiarity come from?

"Harold is going to be fine," Mr. Blackman said to the throng of employees who had congregated in the hall. "Back to work."

Anna headed over to her desk, but Mr. Blackman called to her from the doorway of his office. Matthew carefully observed them through his open door.

Max Blackman placed his index and middle fingers on his carotid artery. Anna walked over to him, pulled his hand away from his neck, and took his wrist in her hand. She checked her watch, taking his pulse. One hundred beats per minute, a little fast, but she could feel it slowing down.

"You might consider going for a walk now and again. Or cutting back on red meat."

"Heard it all before," he said.

"I'm sure you have," she said.

"Thank you." Max smiled warmly at Anna and drew her into a close embrace. "You're doing great. You know that, right?"

"Right."

Anna noticed eyes peering through the

slats in his blinds. She pulled away.

"People will talk," she said.

"Let them talk. I don't care."

"I do," Anna said.

"So, how are things going with the new guy?" he said, nodding in the general direction of Matthew's office.

"Better than with the old guy," Anna said.

Max chuckled. "It was fun while it lasted," he said.

"I always wondered about that," Anna said. "Who were you trying to rattle, me or Jeff?"

"Both, I think," Blackman said as he strode over to his desk and removed an envelope from the center drawer. He folded it and tucked it into the pocket of Anna's blazer. "Happy birthday."

"I can't accept this."

"You will or I'll fire you."

"I never should have taken this job."

"But you did," Blackman said. "Now get back to work."

2002

BOSTON, MASSACHUSETTS

"What are you doing here?" the patient asked.

"I work here," Anna said. "Do you know where you are?"

"I'm in the hospital," Mrs. Pearl said as she took in her surroundings.

"We met last night when you were admitted. Do you remember?"

"I'm sorry. I don't remember," Mrs. Pearl said.

"That's okay. We don't need to remember everything. I'm Dr. Fury. Do you know why you're here?"

Anna studied her patient's chart. Edith Pearl had been suffering from chronic kidney failure for two years. Her treatment consisted of dialysis three times a week and a strict diet protocol, by which Mrs. Pearl was clearly not abiding.

"The same reason I'm always here," Mrs. Pearl said in a whisper.

Anna found herself speaking in hushed tones, as if her voice could shatter another's. "You had excess fluid buildup and we needed to do dialysis. This was only twenty-four hours after your previous dialysis. Have you been keeping track of your fluid intake?"

"I used to drink four cups of coffee a day. Then water or soda, and then a cocktail before dinner. Now you tell me to chew on ice chips and eat food that has no flavor. I can live without the food, I guess . . . I was playing bridge with my girlfriends, and Lucy made the most delicious lemonade, and I drank a glass and then another glass."

"Unfortunately," Anna said, "you can't do that anymore. If too much fluid builds up in your body, it stresses your heart and makes it hard for you to breathe."

"I know."

"I have to remind you."

"What if I wanted to stop?" Mrs. Pearl asked.

"Stop dialysis?" Anna asked.

"Yes."

"Have you talked to your family about this?"

"This is my decision, right?"

"It is. But you should talk to your family."

"What would happen if I stopped treatment?"

"Toxins would build up. That would cause problems with your heart rhythm."

"And then I would die?"

"Yes."

"How long would it take?"

"Not very long. A week. Maybe less."

"Would it hurt?"

"The pain could be managed."

Mrs. Pearl diverted her attention to her failing manicure. "Would you look at this?" she said, pointing out a chip in the cotton-candy-pink polish. "I just had them done three days ago."

"They still look nice," Anna said.

"What would you do?" Mrs. Pearl asked, her voice eggshell thin.

"I don't know," Anna said. Lying.

"How do you make a decision like that?"

"It's a difficult decision."

"I'm always thirsty."

"I understand," Anna said.

TO: Anna Fury
FROM: Kate Smirnoff
RE: Bloodletting

I've been reading about this phlebotomy business. What I don't get is how a procedure that was practiced for three thousand years could have no pal-

51

liative advantages. So far, I can find none. Sure, I get that the early bloodletting was a crazy religious practice at first and then that it was used to restore the balance of bodily humors. I'm sure you had to be there for that to make sense. But when men of science, capable of some deductive reasoning, got involved, how come they didn't notice that draining someone's blood never made him feel any better? The only use for it that makes sense to me is, say, if there was an area that was swollen. I guess if I knew nothing about the human body and was practicing medicine in ancient times, I might find a logical reason to let blood out of a swollen body part. I suppose it's not that different from lancing a boil.

You know what else is really funny? That barbers were surgeons way back when. Did you know that the red-and-white barbershop signpost was also the sign for a surgeon? I'm sure they teach all that crap in medical school. Even now, a barber must have steady hands and is trusted with a very sharp blade. If I were a man, I'd never let a barber give me a straight-razor shave. I always hate that procedure when I see it in movies.

You'd think there'd be more barbershop murders than there are.

How are you doing? And please let me know if you can think of any condition in which bloodletting made sense.

Kate

TO: Kate Smirnoff
FROM: Anna Fury
RE: Bloodletting

Hi. Your new obsession is intriguingly macabre. Most ancient medicinal practices were more likely to kill you than heal you. Then again, some ghastly measures, like leeching, turned out to be rather useful. Hirudotherapy (the fancy word for the medical use of leeches) made a comeback recently because it can aid postoperative patients who run the risk of blood clots from venous congestion. I'm not sure why bloodletting lasted so long, but there are surely things we are doing right now that one day might seem barbaric. I'd like to say it's inserting bags of silicone into the chest wall. But I think big tits (or *proportional breasts,* as they were described in my plastics rotation) are here for the duration.

Enough about medieval medicine. Have you thought about my offer? Why don't you come for a visit and you'll see.

Anna

After medical school in St. Louis, Anna was accepted into a residency program in Boston, and so she returned to the cold embrace of her family. Colin was there, which helped, but it wasn't like she ever saw him. Within six months, she met a man who'd come into the ED after being bitten by his girlfriend's dog. She looked at his chart. Nick Charles was the name he gave. He must have shown ID and proof of insurance at registration, but she still didn't believe it.

"Nick Charles. Really?" she asked.

"My sister's name is Nora."

"No."

"Yes."

"Were you teased in high school?" Anna asked.

"Only by teachers," Nick said as Anna examined the dog bite.

"I would have teased you."

She treated Nick's wound and gave him a tetanus shot, and he returned a few days later with flowers and asked her out. It was considered highly unethical for physicians to date patients, and she told him so. Two weeks later, when the wound was a ghost of its former self, he was waiting outside the hospital after Anna's shift (and he couldn't have learned her schedule without dedicated effort). He asked her out again, this time adding that he was no longer anyone's patient. She asked about the girlfriend and the dog. He had dumped both shortly after the bite. He reminded her that life was short. Anna didn't particularly like this ploy, the constant allusions to 9/11 by people who hadn't been touched by it at all. But Anna liked his name and so she said yes, although whenever anyone asked how they'd met, she'd say they began chatting at the local farmers' market (even though she couldn't remember the last time she'd bought fresh produce). The appeal of Nick Charles was simple: he was nice and he wasn't a doctor or a lawyer, which somehow seemed important, at least in terms of disappointing her mother. Nick Charles did something with computers, but Anna never asked enough questions to really understand his career. (If Kate had met him, she would have found out that he worked on a compiling team that transformed source code into another programming language, and then she'd be able to explain what that meant.)

Nick didn't mind Anna's lack of interest in his job. Most people, other than his colleagues, lacked interest in it. After they'd been dating for six months, Nick thought they should move in together, but Anna put him off. He couldn't understand, since she had a two-bedroom apartment and was hardly ever home.

Anna had never felt right about leaving Kate behind. She couldn't leave her in Santa Cruz after what happened, but then, after she'd dragged her to St. Louis, she didn't want to leave her in St. Louis, because it was St. Louis. Kate was twenty-seven, alone in the Midwest with just a handful of friends, or acquaintances, depending on how you looked at it. She was on a career track to become the manager of a coffeehouse. Anna couldn't help but feel responsible. That extra room in Anna's apartment was for Kate. She wasn't taking in anyone else.

TO: Anna
FROM: Kate
RE: Bloodletting

I don't know what it is, but modern medicine holds no interest for me. I talked to George the other day on the

56

phone. Well, sort of talked to her. Carter was crying and she put the phone down for five minutes. Once she did it for ten, so I decided that five minutes was my absolute maximum hold time. She should play music or something.

I've thought about it. But I really like it here. I'd miss the City Museum. I like the slides a lot and I know the layout. Plus, I have a car now, and I hear it's really, really hard to park in Boston. As you recall, parallel parking is my weak spot.

Kate

GEORGE: Hi, Anna.

ANNA: I hate caller ID. I miss hearing the inquisitive "Hello?"

GEORGE: Hello?

ANNA: Hi, George, it's Anna.

GEORGE: What's up?

ANNA: I need you to help me convince Kate to come to Boston for a visit.

GEORGE: Just a visit?

ANNA: Once she visits, it will be easier to convince her to move here.

GEORGE: I'm not sure it's a great idea. You two living together again.

ANNA: I'm an upstanding citizen these days. Besides, Kate's nearing her three-year anniversary at her café job. Maybe if she moved, she might find a more ambitious career goal beyond master barista.

GEORGE: You may have a point there. During our last conversation, she pontificated for ten minutes on optimal coffee temperatures. Apparently, French press is the only way to go. What does she talk to you about?

ANNA: Bloodletting.

GEORGE: At least you have something in common. Don't wake up. Please don't wake up.

ANNA: Excuse me?

GEORGE: The baby didn't sleep at all last night. I don't know what I'm going to do. The crying drives Mitch crazy. He hasn't been the same since 9/11. I think he has PTSD. He doesn't like noise.

ANNA: Are you sure he liked noise before 9/11?

GEORGE: I'm not sure what he likes anymore.

ANNA: Is everything okay?

GEORGE: No. Mitch hasn't been home in three days. He said he was staying in a hotel so he can sleep, but I don't know which hotel. That's fucked up, right?

ANNA: Well, I'm not married, so I'm not an

expert on these things.

GEORGE: You can be honest.

ANNA: You should know that's fucked up without even asking.

GEORGE: I've called him at least twenty times and he doesn't pick up.

ANNA: Are you sure he wasn't in an accident or something?

GEORGE: I wish.

ANNA: Has this happened before?

GEORGE: Yes.

ANNA: Many times?

GEORGE: He's seeing someone, isn't he?

ANNA: May I continue being honest or have you had enough honesty?

GEORGE: Continue.

ANNA: He's probably seeing someone. Or, if you're lucky, he's just got a serious gambling problem. Have you checked his phone?

GEORGE: Impossible. He guards that thing as if it contains nuclear launch codes.

ANNA: Have you ever asked him?

GEORGE: Please, please, don't cry.

ANNA: We need a transitional code word so I know if you're talking to me or the baby.

GEORGE: The baby is crying again.

ANNA: Babies cry, George. Relax.

GEORGE: Can you come visit me?

ANNA: I'm sorry. I don't know if I can get away for a while.

GEORGE: I have to go. I'll talk to you later.

KATE: Hello?

GEORGE: It's George.

KATE: I know. Did you get my postcard?

GEORGE: Yes, thank you. There's something you should know. I can't read your writing. The postcard had a giraffe and the St. Louis Zoo logo on it, but other than that, I got nothing.

KATE: They have a baby elephant named Clementine, but that's not why you've called.

GEORGE: I've been dispatched by Anna to convince you to visit her in Boston. So, you should visit her in Boston.

KATE: Is that your entire sales pitch?

GEORGE: I'm revising the pitch. Forget Boston. Visit me in New York.

Kate couldn't refuse once she'd heard the details of the offer: an all-expenses-paid trip to New York City with free rein for Kate to prove that Mitch was the louse she'd always said he was. The visit was entirely undercover. George booked the flight and a hotel room just around the corner from her apartment. When Mitch was convincingly alibied in his office, George and Kate roamed a chilly late-fall Manhattan. When his whereabouts were less certain, Kate tailed him like a private detective. She wore an old pea coat and skullcap as a disguise, though she doubted he would recognize her in any case. He'd hardly seemed to register her presence the few times they'd met.

On a Wednesday afternoon when Mitch was supposedly at a business lunch, Kate followed him from his office to his mistress's apartment at Eighty-Second and Fifth. Kate snapped photos of the duo with a tiny digital camera as they emerged from the woman's apartment, walked down the street hand in hand, and kissed on the corner while they waited for the light to change. She followed him again the next day to establish a pattern. Mitch emerged from his office at lunch and took a taxi to his gym at Lexington and Sixty-Third. Kate sat on a bench reading the newspaper, watching the most well-dressed people she had ever seen in her life enter and exit the sports club, until Mitch emerged an hour and a half later with a different woman, a shockingly underweight but well-toned brunette, on his arm. She followed them six blocks and one avenue to the Four Seasons hotel. Snapped a photo of the couple entering the grand revolving doors. It looked like a shot from a magazine spread.

Kate transferred the images to George's computer and played the slide show. She was surprised by George's stillness as she took inventory of her husband's infidelities. George sighed once, turned off the computer, and retreated to the kitchen.

"That was just two days, so there may be more," Kate said.

"I'm sure," George said.

"What are you going to do?" Kate asked.

"I'm going to have a drink."

"After the drink?"

"I'm going to do what needs to be done," George said.

The next time Mitch returned home after an unexplained and long absence, George didn't ask him where he had been. She greeted him politely, like the person working the counter at an airline. Within five minutes of Mitch's return, George left with a simple "Mrs. Klinger is with Carter; I'll be back." Two hours later, George came home, sweaty from a pickup basketball game at the gym. She was a member of a different kind of gym than Mitch's. She acknowledged Mitch with an atypical grunt, walked into the kitchen, and foraged through the refrigerator, savoring the blast of cold air. George chugged straight from a gallon of milk. A string of white liquid trailed a line down her chin to her neck. She wiped it away on the sleeve of her sweatshirt. She cracked open a bag of potato chips, lay down on the couch, and turned on the television. She found the channel that played all of those nature programs that were like horror films for her husband. Mitch watched his wife as if she were a 3-D hologram at a science museum. He circled her on the couch, noted her shoes resting on a white throw pillow, and watched crumbs of potato chips spill onto her sweatshirt as she stared in a daze at the television.

"Don't you want to take a shower?" Mitch asked.

"Not right now."

"Do you mind taking off your shoes?"

George kicked her shoes off and onto the floor.

"What should we do about dinner?"

"Sorry, I've been bogarting the chips," George said, tossing the bag in Mitch's general direction. The bag fell at his feet.

Mrs. Klinger surfaced from Carter's bedroom, wearing her coat and clutching her handbag.

63

"He's asleep," she whispered.

George walked her to the door.

"Thank you, Mrs. Klinger. See you Monday?"

"Yes, dear," she said.

After George shut the door, she sniffed her armpit and said, "I guess I'll take that shower now."

George spotted a daddy longlegs crawling along the edge of the tub. Her shower ritual often involved the dispatching of any creatures that had found their way into the apartment. Spiders were a particular problem. Mitch had once knocked himself unconscious when he'd tripped over the tub trying to escape a brown house spider. This time, though, George relocated the spider to the glass on the sink. She took a shower, reached for the razor out of habit, then changed her mind. She had a moment more blissful than any she could remember in the entire marriage when she realized that now that it was over, she could do exactly what she wanted. Nothing mattered anymore. Of course George knew that divorce and attorneys and moving out of the apartment and fighting were inevitable, but she decided she'd live in this state of I-don't-give-a-fuck for a little while longer. Long enough to enjoy it.

After she toweled off, she returned the spider to the exact location where she'd found it.

After five days in New York, Kate took the shuttle to Boston. Anna picked her up at the airport. Kate shoved her luggage into the trunk of Anna's old Volvo, which contained, much to Kate's pleasure, a spare tire, among Anna's other incongruous nonessentials: ice skates, hockey puck, throw pillow, toolbox, and an old-fashioned coffee mill.

Kate slipped into the passenger seat and slammed the door.

"Was your mission successful?" Anna asked.

"I believe it was. We have photographic evidence and everything."

"It always seemed like such a waste," Anna said.

"What part?"

"She was *one* year into her career and she gave it all up for him. What was the point of getting an education if she wasn't going to use it?" Anna said.

"So there's no point in being informed, having an area of expertise, if you don't use it? That's ridiculous. I know all sorts of things that I don't need to know when I'm steaming milk. And not once have I wished that I hadn't learned those things."

"You know what I mean," Anna said.

"I do," Kate said. "I just don't agree with it. She quit her job to get married and have a child, and there's nothing wrong with that. What's wrong is that she gave it all up for *that* guy."

"Agreed. So how is she?"

"Look, I've suffered through almost a week of domestic purgatory," Kate said, "in which I've revisited in excruciating detail every aspect of George's married life. I want to talk about the weather, global warming, rising tides, I want to talk about how sad I am that Marty Feldman is dead —"

"He's been dead a long time, you know."

"I'm still sad about it. Also, I want to talk about the one billion birds that die every year by flying into windows and why we're not doing anything to stop it. And I want to talk about those whacked-out people who want to amputate perfectly healthy limbs."

"You really want to talk about that?"

"I want to talk about anything but men."

Anna reached into the back seat and dropped a textbook on Kate's lap.

"Hemochromatosis," Anna said. "The page is marked."

"I know that word," said Kate.

"That's what I forgot in my last e-mail. It's a condition where too much iron builds up in your organs. The treatment is phlebotomy and chelation therapy. The disease is extremely rare, but in medieval times, if you had it, and your barber practiced bloodletting, you'd be in good shape."

Anna pulled her car into the airport traffic, cutting off an SUV.

"That's so awesome. How rare is the condition?"

"Extremely rare."

"Got a number off the top of your head?"

"I don't have your recall. Must come in handy with all those drink orders."

"More useful when I waitress. There are a limited number of caffeinated beverages. Sometimes you can just look at a person and know what she'll order."

"Your birthday is in two days. What do you want?"

"Nothing."

"Pick something or I'll assume you want a Saint Bernard puppy."

"There *is* a new book on the plague out."

"More plague? Haven't you learned everything there is to learn?" Anna asked.

"There wasn't just one plague, you know."

1999

ST. LOUIS, MISSOURI

"Did you know that the Great Plague killed an estimated twenty percent of the population of London?" Kate said to the nameless man in her kitchen.

Kate didn't bother introducing herself, since she wasn't likely to meet him again. She couldn't even be sure that Anna knew his name. Why should she learn it? Anna was conveniently long gone, leaving Kate to deal with the detritus from her night out. This wasn't the first time, nor would it be the last. Kate's current method of ridding herself of these human pests was blathering on about pestilence.

"You must be the roommate," Nameless Man said.

"You must be the guy who spent the night with Anna," said Kate.

"Darren."

She'd preferred not knowing. It made them more human.

"Twenty percent of London at the time was approximately one hundred thousand people. *Dead* within the year," Kate continued.

"That sounds horrible. Mind if I get a cup of coffee?"

I would be most grateful if you left, she wanted to say, but instead she went with "Help yourself. I recently cleaned the coffeemaker, so it might taste a little bit like vinegar."

This statement was false, but Kate was just as interested in the power of suggestion as she was in the Great Plague. She'd often try minor experiments on Anna's lingering guests. As expected, Darren poured a mug of coffee and scrunched up his nose before he even took a sip.

"It would kill around fifty percent of the infected individuals within a week's time. A horrible death. Enlarged lymph nodes, nausea, fever, vomiting, diarrhea, petechiae. That means broken blood vessels, in case you didn't know. How's the coffee?"

"It's okay. Do you have any sugar?"

"We're out."

"Why do you know so much about the plague?" Darren asked.

"I'm writing my dissertation on it. Do you want to see pictures?" Kate said, picking up her one reference book, which she'd found at a used-book store for five dollars.

"No, thanks," Darren said. "I better run."

"See you around," Kate said, confident that she would not.

"Did you know that Pythagoras founded a religion of which the major tenets were the transmigration of the soul and not eating beans?" Kate said to the nameless man in her kitchen.

"Is that coffee?" the nameless man said, eyeing what was clearly a pot of freshly brewed coffee.

"Decaf," Kate lied. She wished she had chosen a more macabre topic, but she was on a new book and couldn't resist sharing this morsel of information.

The nameless man scoured the cabinets until he found a mug and then helped himself. He sat down across from Kate.

"Pythagoras? The triangle guy?"

"The Pythagorean theory guy. He didn't invent triangles or anything."

"You the roommate?"

"Yes. Anna's gone, you know."

"Yeah, I figured that out when I woke up and she wasn't here."

"Do you have to go to work?" Kate asked.

"Not today. Do you?"

"No."

"What do you do?" he asked.

"I'm currently unemployed," Kate said. She then realized her strategy was all wrong. If she pretended to dress for work, she could usher the stranger out as she left and return thereafter.

"I'm Shayne."

"Hello."

"Do you have a name?"

"Um, yes. It's Sarah," Kate said. She had already given the stranger too much information.

"What do you do with all your free time?"

"Stuff," Kate said.

Shayne drained his coffee and poured himself another cup. He searched the refrigerator and began plucking out items and placing them on the counter. After he was done, he turned to Kate and said, "Mind if I make breakfast?"

She did. Especially since every food item he had chosen came from Kate's fist-tight budget.

"Excuse me," she said, and she ducked into her room and dialed Anna's pager. While she waited for her to call, she put on a pair of old blue jeans and threw a sweater over her pajama top. When Anna didn't respond right away, Kate returned to the kitchen.

"I just remembered I have a doctor's appointment," Kate said. "I have to go."

"Okay," Shayne said, setting the plate on the table and taking a seat.

"So maybe I can put that in a container and you can take it to go."

"Or I'll just eat it here."

"I bet you can finish that in like five minutes," Kate said, rocking on the heels of her slippers. She noticed her footwear and returned to her bedroom for a pair of sneakers.

"I was thinking of taking a shower after this," Shayne said when she came back.

"I don't mean to be rude. But I have to lock up."

"No worries. I can lock up myself when I leave."

"Oh," Kate said.

Shayne flipped open the newspaper and consumed his egg-and-bacon breakfast like a suited family man in a vintage film.

"Um. Well, goodbye."

Kate's hand hovered over the doorknob for a spell as she tried to concoct another plan. But she was at a loss. She opened the door and closed it behind her. She strolled down the hall and found a corner on the stairwell, where she tucked herself out of view. As soon as Shayne left, she could return. She opened her library book on Pythagoras and the Pythagoreans and tried to focus on the text.

"Can I help you?"

Kate lurched awake like a car screeching to a sudden stop.

"I didn't mean to startle you," the man with a hook for a right hand said.

Kate looked at the man as she gathered herself. She must have nodded off on the stairwell. The man stood in front of apartment 3B. Cans of paint and brushes waited at his feet.

"Do you live here?" the man asked.

"Yes," Kate said. "Not in the stairwell. Just in the building. 3E."

"I'm James Lazar. Your neighbor. 3B."

"Kate . . . Smirnoff."

"Like the vodka?"

"Yes."

"Are you locked out?"

"No. I, um, there's someone in my apartment. I'm waiting for him to leave."

"Your boyfriend?"

"No. I don't know him. I have a first name, but that's it."

"There's a strange man in your apartment?" James asked.

73

"Yes."

"Have you called the police?"

"My friend invited him over. But she's not home. I don't think it's a police matter."

"Did you ask him to leave?" James asked.

"I strongly suggested he leave. He didn't pick up on the subtext."

"Men kind of like direct communication."

"Good to know."

"Do you want me to ask him to leave?"

"If you think it will get a better result," Kate said skeptically.

James walked down the hall with Kate on his heels. When he reached the door of 3E, Kate passed him the key. James opened the door and found Shayne sprawled on the couch with the television playing backup to his hiccupped snoring. James picked up the newspaper and smacked Shayne's legs with it.

"Buddy, wake up."

Shayne slowly came to. "What's up?"

"It's checkout time. Get your shoes and go."

Kate closely studied James's technique. No hesitation. Clear, concise language that was not open to interpretation. She also noted that while Shayne appeared disgruntled, there was no danger in the situation. He responded predictably.

"Whatever, dude," Shayne said as he slipped on his shoes and ambled out the door.

An hour later, Kate, wearing her grandfather's old dress shirt and some battered denims, knocked on the door of 3B.

James opened it, wiping his beige-paint-streaked hand on his shirt. Plastic tarps covered his living room from one end to the next. Paint fumes traveled into the hallway.

"Hi, Kate."

"I noticed you were painting today," she said.

"How'd you figure that out?" James asked.

"Deductive reasoning and now direct observation," she said.

"I'm impressed."

"I thought maybe you could use a hand," Kate said. And then she realized what she'd said. "Sorry. That came out wrong."

"Don't worry about it."

"I brought a paintbrush," Kate said, holding up an old synthetic wall brush containing the memory of a blood-red kitchen backsplash. Anna's idea.

"You want to help me paint?" James asked. When he smiled, Kate noticed that his two front teeth looked like they were at odds with each other. Almost like an old-fashioned boxing photo. Only they were teeth.

"It seemed like the neighborly thing to do, and I owe you."

"It's not necessary," James said.

Some offers were merely gestures. James had learned this distinction after his accident. It was a shift in the eyes that usually gave it away, the person searching for an exit. Kate's offer was not a gesture. She entered his apartment without invitation.

"Why don't I start on the baseboards, since I'm short?"

James poured a layer of paint into a pan and passed Kate a trim brush.

"I know what I'm doing," Kate said. "In case you were worried."

"I wasn't," James said.

Kate and James painted for three hours. Since moving to St. Louis, Kate hadn't made any new friends. She liked chatting with the woman at the library, and there was a homeless man she talked to sometimes at Black Forest Park, and she really liked a docent at the City Museum. But Anna was her only real friend in St. Louis, and Anna was always absent. Friendships had never come that easily to Kate. She refused to cover unpleasant silences and yet would share her opinions at the most inappropriate moments. This was what Anna had always liked about her — there was no subtext. Anna never had to read meaning into Kate's words, which meant she could trust her. But even Anna had to admit that Kate asked too many questions. They grew in Kate's mind like weeds.

During what James would later describe as a friendly interrogation, Kate culled the following information:

James was recently divorced. He had one daughter, who lived with his ex-wife two miles away in Creve Coeur. He was an electrician by trade but was currently reconsidering his options. He had a sister, Mary, recently diagnosed with MS. He rode his bike everywhere. He had a special prosthetic for gripping the handlebars. He wore the hook because when he met someone new, he wanted the person to know right away so he could dispense with the awkwardness of discovery. He wanted to see whether someone avoided eye contact or swelled with pity. James had been in the military some years ago, was a veteran of the Gulf War; the irony was that he'd lost his hand riding a motorcycle a week after his return. A drunk driver.

There was a zigzag rhythm to Kate's inquiries, like the sharp sierras of a lie-

77

detector readout. James eventually managed to sneak in one question of his own.

"What brought you to St. Louis?"

"I was abducted," Kate said.

James thought Kate was joking, but it was practically the truth. No one used any other word to describe the event. Anna was moving to St. Louis for medical school and wanted Kate to move with her. Anna devised a shockingly manipulative and well-laid plan to make that happen. Despite aiding in the abduction, George didn't necessarily believe that Anna's company was the best option for Kate. But it was superior to Kate's remaining alone in Santa Cruz in that house.

"You moved to St. Louis against your will?" James asked.

"As a matter of fact, yes," said Kate. "My roommate abducted all of my things and so I had to follow my stuff."

"Are you staying here against your will?"

"No. But I'd never have moved if left to my own devices."

"So maybe your roommate did you a favor."

"I wouldn't go that far. I finished the baseboards. Can I start prepping the windows?" Kate asked.

"Uh, sure. Don't you have someplace to be?"

"No."

Kate shoved the window open and scraped buckling paint from another era off the pane.

"Were you left-handed or right-handed?" Kate asked.

"I was left-handed. Still am," James said, flashing his good hand.

"That was a lucky break," Kate said. "Only ten percent of the world's population is left-handed."

James was glad she didn't try to put some God-was-looking-out-for-you spin on it like everyone else.

"You ask a lot of questions, Kate."

"I have a lot of questions."

"You should have been a cop."

"I don't know about that. But I should have been something."

Kate sat at her kitchen table sipping coffee and reading the paper. A shirtless male entered the room, rubbing sleep from his eyes.

"Morning," the shirtless male said.

"Morning," Kate said.

"Any coffee?" the shirtless male asked,

79

even though the aroma wafted through the room.

"This isn't a B & B," Kate said. "This is a shitty, rundown motel on the side of the highway. There is no continental breakfast, and it's checkout time."

1990

BOSTON, MASSACHUSETTS

"Anna, it's time to leave," Lena Fury, wearing a Jackie Onassis suit with the requisite pearls, said as she knocked on her daughter's bedroom door.

While she waited for Anna to surface, Lena checked herself in the hallway mirror. Her highlighted blond hair was in an elegant upsweep, revealing her long ballerina neck — one of her more attractive features, although she had never been a dancer. Lena's face was perfectly proportioned. That was a compliment she'd received from a plastic surgeon a week ago as they'd discussed options for stopping time. People used to tell her she was beautiful. Now she was told she was perfectly proportioned. She obsessed over her skin and every new mark of age that seemed to surface overnight. Her evening ritual involved a gentle face scrub, a prescription retinol cream, and a moisturizer with ingredients

81

that, one day, would be deemed hazardous to the water supply.

Lena knocked on the door again, thinking about whether she could blame the permanent equal sign between her brows on her fifteen-year-old daughter.

"For God's sake, Anna, open up."

Anna had a lock on her door. Every time Lena and Donald had it removed, Anna would install it again. She'd checked out a DIY book at the library and purchased a two-dollar screwdriver. Lena lost so many fights with Anna that she had to choose her battles carefully, since they were almost invariably followed by defeats. Lena reached for the knob and it turned, to her surprise. The bed was made and the room was empty. Lena hurried downstairs.

"Where's Anna?" Lena asked her husband.

"Probably still sleeping," Donald said, eyes on his newspaper.

"I just checked her room. She's not there."

"We have many rooms," Donald said. "Perhaps she's in one of the others."

"Martha," Lena said to the Fury housekeeper, "can you check her usual haunts and remind her that she was supposed to be ready by eleven and dressed appropriately?"

"Yes, ma'am," Martha said, a tiny smirk passing over her face.

Donald chuckled to himself, eyes still focused on the newsprint.

"Something funny?" Lena asked.

"With Anna, you can't use words that are open to interpretation."

"Excuse me?" Lena said.

Donald finally tore his eyes away from the headlines.

"Remember when you forced Anna to take ballet class? You bought her pink tights and a tutu and when it was time to leave, you ordered her upstairs and told her to dress appropriately."

"I don't remember," Lena said.

She did remember, vaguely, but it had been an event that so alarmed her sensibilities, she refused to let herself think of it too often. Besides, it was years ago.

"She wore her field hockey uniform," Donald said. "When you reprimanded her for her inappropriate attire, she reminded you that you had said, 'Dress appropriately,' but you never specified for what occasion."

Lena joined Martha on her manhunt. Thirty minutes later, when the entire Fury house and grounds had been inspected, the obvious conclusion was drawn.

"She's not here," Martha said.

Not even a flash of panic interrupted Lena's determined poise. She was disappointed, but mostly in herself. She should have known that Anna wouldn't go quietly to lunch.

Anna had attended her first ladies' lunch when she was ten. Her powder-blue dress was overstarched, puff sleeved, and trimmed with lace. Her dainty, pristine white anklets were in sharp relief to the spatter of scabs and bruises on her shins and knees. Everything itched, Anna remembered, and there was nothing to draw her attention away from her stiff, ridiculous outfit. Lunch was a poached fish that was so bland it was hard to imagine it was ever a living creature. The conversations were muted and meaningless. How could clothing be the topic of three hours of discussion when the goal of the gathering was to raise money for impoverished inner-city schools? Anna's mind wandered into adventures that didn't require good posture. She imagined being a hobo. In her closet was a bindle made from an old blanket and her field hockey stick. She even had train schedules hidden on the underside of her desk. She stashed extra cash in a smelly sneaker — a place she knew her mother would never look. Anna had always lived like a convict, even as a child, perpetually preparing for her next breakout.

She had escaped a few times before but was invariably caught, wearing rags, carrying her bindle, strolling down her quiet Beacon Hill street, where a child in hobo gear could not go unnoticed. A neighbor would call. A BMW or Mercedes would pull up next to her, and some adult would tell her to get into the car. When she refused, a litany of threats would follow. Eventually, one of them would induce cooperation.

At fifteen, Anna had planned a more sophisticated escape. She stuffed her school bag with a change of clothes, a toothbrush (no toothpaste, since she assumed that where she was going, she'd find it in abundance), and a few pairs of underwear. She had enough cash on hand for a proper vacation, which was how she saw the whole thing. She'd climbed out of her window at 8:00 a.m. after calling a cab from the phone line in her father's office. The cab took her to the train station. She bought a ticket, boarded the train, and read Salinger's *Nine Stories,* a gift from her brother last Christmas. She transferred trains and read "A Perfect Day for Bananafish." She laughed convulsively when Seymour had his outburst on the elevator, accusing a woman of staring at his feet. Other passengers stared at Anna. At the end of the story, she thought she might cry, could feel that half second in which she could lose control. She turned it off like a spigot. She was prouder of that talent than she should have been.

Nine hours and two buses later, she was in Princeton, New Jersey. Anna had visited before, with her parents, so she knew where to find her brother. But she needed to wait and then find him later at night, when no one would be willing or able to drive her home.

She found a café where she could sit and read until she finished the book and could see her own reflection in the glass. Then she used the battered map her brother had given her on a family tour of the university and tracked down his dormitory. Outside the dorm, Anna applied lipstick and pulled her hair into a knotty college-girl bun. She looked remotely like an underdeveloped coed. She circled the dormitory, looking for those telling Saturday-night lights that signified a party. Her best guess was that it was simmering somewhere on the third floor. Anna climbed the stairs and heard the distinctive hum of humans congregating. From the end of the hall, it was simply a collage of sounds, the common cackles and squeals in an inebriated orchestra. But then the notes in the symphony, the individual instruments, made their claim on Anna's eardrums.

We need more beer.

I need more vodka.

Where's Sandy?

Vomiting in the bathroom.

What kind of crazy motherfucker reads Ayn Rand?

How'd you do on the physics test?

Fucked up.

Where are you going for the holidays?

I heard Jamie lost his scholarship.

The problem isn't reading Ayn Rand, it's liking her.

Anna slipped through the door unnoticed. She reached into a giant bucket of ice and fished around until the throbbing in her arm radiated up to her neck. She retreated and waited until her circulation returned. A blond guy in a polo shirt approached, sank his arm into the ice bath, and eventually surfaced with a beer. The last beer, he informed her as he uncapped it, barehanded, and gallantly passed it to her.

"Have we met?" he asked.

"Nope," Anna said.

"Hunter Stevens," Hunter Stevens said.

"Anna," Anna said, deliberately skipping her last name.

"What dorm are you in?"

"Clearly I'm in this one," said Anna.

"Oh, you're funny," Hunter said. She could tell he didn't like the funny ones.

"Thank you."

"Where do you live?" Hunter asked.

"Far, far away."

"Who invited you?"

"No one."

"So you're crashing?"

"Don't tell," Anna said, and she fought her way through the crowd and out of the eye line of Hunter Stevens (Hunter Stevens III, she would learn years later).

Anna drank her beer and leaned against the wall. She knew how to shed that cloak of self-consciousness. The beer helped, but it was more the role she played — she was an anthropologist, objectively studying her subjects. Usually they were overdressed women with too much time on their hands. Tonight they were casually dressed college students numbing their stress through alcohol, maybe drugs, and the hope of sex.

Her beer empty, she tossed the bottle in a grocery bag brimming with others of its kind. More booze arrived, and another unfamiliar face passed her a plastic cup filled with vodka and cranberry juice.

"Thanks," Anna said.

When she was halfway through her drink and feeling a warm buzz, a hand reached out from the mass of bodies and pulled her away like a rip tide. Red liquid splashed from her cup and she found herself face to face with Malcolm Davis.

She noticed his eyebrows first, black and severe and completely at odds with his warm brown eyes. Anna also liked Malcolm's nose, which veered just slightly to the right. (She always figured he'd gotten it from a fight but had never had her theory confirmed. Anna's mother once described Malcolm as Jewish-looking. Later, in school, one of Anna's classmates asked her what her type was. "Jewish," she'd said.)

"Come with me," Malcolm said, brusquely ushering her out of the party.

Silently he dragged her through the hallway, down a flight of stairs, and into the dorm room he shared with her brother. While Malcolm's expression was an exact replica of the scowl of disappointment that Anna had come to see as normal in grown-ups, it looked funny on a nineteen-year-old male.

"Your parents phoned Colin five hours ago after an exhaustive search in Boston. Where have you been?"

"It takes a long time to get from Boston

to Princeton. Did you know there are no direct trains?"

"This isn't funny, Anna. Nobody knew what happened to you."

"Ah, that's what I forgot. I should have left a note," Anna said, as if she had forgotten to buy a gallon of milk on her way home.

Malcolm picked up the phone and beat numbers into the handset. Anna thought about tackling him to the floor, but she knew he'd still find a way to make contact with the furious Furys, so she raided the minifridge, uncapped a beer, and sat down on her brother's bed.

"Hi, Donald, it's Malcolm. She's here. I would drive her home myself, but I let a friend borrow my car for the weekend. Colin is on his way to Boston. Maybe he'll call from the road so he doesn't have to make a full trip. I'll put her on a train tomorrow morning. Do you want to speak to her?"

Malcolm extended the phone to Anna while trying to confiscate her beer. She shook her head no. Malcolm covered the mouthpiece and whispered, "I'll let you have the beer if you talk to him."

"Hi, Dad," Anna said. "I'm sorry about that. I just needed to get away. You know how that is."

Malcolm could hear Donald yelling all the way from Boston. Anna moved the phone away from her ear. When her father quieted, Anna spoke again.

"Tell Mom I'm sorry. Tell her if she really wants to punish me, she must *never* invite me to lunch again."

With that, the phone call ended. As far as Malcolm could tell, Donald had hung up on his daughter. Anna wasn't one to fret over future punishments. She had learned long ago that punishments would always be in her future. She took another swig of beer and smiled at Malcolm.

"How should we celebrate?" she asked.

"What are we celebrating?" Malcolm said.

"My last night of freedom. After this I'll be kept under lock and key for at least the next few months."

"Why do you do this, Anna? It only causes trouble for you and your family."

"Sometimes I just need to breathe fresh air," Anna said.

A stranger wouldn't know what she was talking about, but Malcolm did. After his first visit to the Fury home, he'd described it to his stepfather as being like a smoky bar: the air was always thick, and you couldn't see anyone too clearly.

"Come on," Malcolm said to Anna. "I'll

buy you an ice cream."

"That wasn't what I had in mind," Anna said.

"Too bad."

It was too late for any ice cream parlors to be open, so Anna and Malcolm walked to a corner shop and studied options in the freezer case.

"Butter rum," Anna said.

"You know there's no rum to speak of in there," Malcolm said.

Later, after an hour of negotiations, Anna finally agreed to stay in bed on the condition that Malcolm tuck her in and read her a story. Malcolm sat on top of the covers next to Anna and opened a well-worn paperback.

" 'The New Music,' by Donald Barthelme. Have you heard of him?" Malcolm asked.

"Nope."

" 'What did you do today?' "

"I escaped," Anna said.

"Shhh, I'm reading," Malcolm said and continued. " 'What did you do today?'

" '— Went to the grocery store and Xeroxed a box of English muffins, two pounds of ground veal and an apple. In flagrant violation of the Copyright Act —' "

"This is the best story ever," Anna said.

"Shhh," Malcolm hissed and continued.

" 'You had your nap, I remember that —'

" 'I had my nap.'

" 'Lunch, I remember that, there was lunch —' "

"There was no lunch," Anna said, interrupting for the very last time.

Colin Fury returned to his dorm after driving four hours in one direction, stopping for gas, making a phone call in which he discovered his sister's whereabouts, and then driving four more hours in the other direction. It was 4:00 a.m. when he rolled his sister off his bed. She landed with a thump on the floor, which jarred her out of a deep sleep.

"Sorry," Anna said after she'd worked out her current situation. She realized she needed a pillow and a blanket and asked for them politely. Colin wrapped his bedding tightly around his body so that it couldn't be stolen in the night and clutched both pillows as if they were family heirlooms and he were in a roomful of thieves. Malcolm took pity and gave Anna the blankets and one pillow from his bed after Colin was asleep.

Later that morning, Colin drove his sister to the train station, bought her a ticket, and waited with her on the platform until the train arrived. Standing side by side, the two were unmistakably siblings. Colin just got more of the good DNA, Anna thought. Anna's Roman nose dominated her face, but on Colin, it appeared elegant. Their eyes had the same downward slant. On Anna, they looked exacting; on Colin, mysterious. He also got better hair, darker and thicker. Just a year ago, when Anna realized she had reached her full height, she'd said to her brother, "Two of your inches. They should be mine."

Colin had given her twenty bucks and suggested they call it even.

When it was time for Anna to board the train, Colin hugged his sister, mussed up her hair, and said, "For now, suck it up. In three years you'll never have to live there again."

2006

BOSTON, MASSACHUSETTS

Lena stood on the threshold of Anna's bedroom, or the bedroom that Anna had once inhabited and was now inhabiting again, though it had been redone as a guest room. Unlike the first time she'd occupied the space, the room showed little evidence of the person who lived there. The guest-room walls, set off by a flowery duvet, were painted white with pastel trim. Anna thought the white was a statement beyond a preference for white. When Anna was sixteen, while her parents spent a weekend in Vermont, she had found a shade of red like the blood from a fresh wound and painted three of her four walls with it. A wild standoff ensued, which Anna naturally won. Two years later, on the very afternoon Anna departed for college, Lena had those blood-red walls sandblasted.

Lena no longer ventured over the threshold, Anna noticed, although she couldn't remember when she'd first noticed it. Anna looked at the clock. It was eleven fifteen at night.

"What are you doing tomorrow?" Lena asked.

"I'll start with a long nap," Anna said. "Maybe eight hours."

"You should get some air. Do something outside," her mother said.

"Are you having a luncheon?" Anna asked.

The last time she'd been asked to leave the house, her mother was entertaining. Anna was no longer the type of daughter a mother could show off. Not that she was ever that type, but for a few years there, on paper, Anna could spark the occasional daughter-envy in the luncheon set, if you didn't have too deep a conversation about her. But those days were long gone. Anna was now thirty-one years old, living at home, doing virtually nothing at all. Well, not exactly nothing.

"I am having a few people over from the committee," Lena said.

There was always a committee. Anna never pressed her for details.

"What time will they be arriving?"

"Around eleven thirty."

"I will be long gone by then."

"Susan will be sorry she missed you,"

Lena said, without irony. She hovered in the doorway. Lena was the sort of woman who found questions beyond the banal — *Where did you get those gorgeous shoes?* — rude or intrusive. But her daughter had never made any sense to her. Now more than ever. And after what happened, well, Lena had begun asking more questions because that sort of thing could not happen again. Lena wouldn't stand for it.

"What do you do with your days?" Lena asked.

"I go to meetings."

"Besides meetings."

"I read. I take walks. I drink coffee. I think about what I'm going to be when I grow up."

"Well? Have you come to any conclusions?" Lena asked, folding her arms in a defensive posture.

"No," Anna said.

"I hope this is something you've been discussing with Dr. Stein."

"Mom, he's a psychiatrist, not a career counselor."

"For two hundred dollars an hour, he should be both."

"I can move out, if you'd like," Anna said. She wished her quiet threat had more power. Anna's medical school debt and dismal job prospects had left her in the red. She had some small savings from her trust fund, most of which had been blown on medical school and drugs. She had only what her parents gave her, and that left her at their mercy.

"I don't want you to move out, dear. But if you could keep me apprised of your schedule, I'd appreciate that."

"Of course," Anna said.

"I was once a Supreme Court justice. I made a single bad decision on, um, what was it again? *Weston v. the State of Kentucky.* I have since fallen from grace. Forgive my appearance. I used to wear suits designed by what's his name," said the man in the library.

Anna had seen him there before. He smelled better than he looked like he'd smell, so Anna didn't mind when he struck up a conversation.

"I don't know," Anna said.

"You know. The suit designer."

"There's more than one."

"No. *The* one."

"Um, Hugo Boss," Anna said, because those were the suits her brother wore.

"Hugo who?" the fallen justice said.

"Armani?"

"Yes. Ar-man-i. He used to make suits just for me. I'd call him up and tell him what colors and what fabrics, and two days later, they would be on my doorstep."

"That's a very fast turnaround."

"I believe he had help," the justice said.

"I'm sure he did."

"If you're important, you have help."

"I suppose that's true."

"Do you have help?"

"No."

"You must not be important."

"I'm not," Anna said.

A librarian approached the table and knocked twice on the cherry-wood corner to get the justice's attention. She raised an eyebrow, and a silent exchange passed between them. The justice got to his feet, dusted off his jacket, and adjusted the bandanna he wore around his neck as if it were a cravat.

"Pardon me," the justice said to Anna. "I have a meeting downtown in twenty minutes." He glanced at the invisible watch on his bare wrist, tipped an imaginary hat, and departed.

Other than rare conversations with Supreme Court justices, Anna's days were differentiated only by appointments. Monday,

Wednesday, and Friday, meetings started at 7:00 p.m.; Tuesday and Thursday, she had Dr. Stein at 3:00 p.m. Mornings were spent in the library, the park, sometimes the museum, other times a café, where she brought a hefty book to guard herself against the other patrons. Thursday, Anna's brother always asked her to lunch. Sometimes she said yes.

Every Wednesday, Anna handwrote a letter to Kate. This was after her telephone and then e-mail attempts to make contact had failed. Anna recalled Kate saying once that e-mail would kill the letter, and it did. But Anna knew how much Kate preferred the older form of communication and thought that by resurrecting it, she might lure Kate back into an exchange. Anna wrote to Kate six times before she received a reply. She never knew when Kate would get the letters, since her address was a PO box in Colorado, from which her mail would be forwarded to whatever part of the country she was currently passing through. After a while Anna stopped thinking of her letters as one side of an even exchange. Things weren't even between the two of them. Nor did they feel even between George and Anna, but communicating with

George was simpler, if ultimately less satisfying.

After leaving a few voice-mail messages that went unanswered, Anna sent George an e-mail, because she knew George didn't hold any romantic notions about the long-lost letter.

TO: George Leoni
FROM: Anna Fury

George,

I'm sure you know enough about recovery that you could probably see this part coming. Maybe that's why you didn't return any of my calls. I don't want this apology to hurt you or dredge up memories that you'd rather forget, but some things no one will forget.

I don't remember that night, but I know it happened because I was careless. I am more sorry for that than anything else I did, and I did so many things I regret. I'm also sorry that it took me eight years to say something. I'm not sure which is worse. There's more, I know. But most things I can't remember. I hope that doesn't sound like an excuse. I own every mistake I made.

I know this is insufficient, as apologies

go. I've got far better apologies up my sleeve; just say the word. I'm happy to provide them for you at any time and in any form you like — in person, by telephone, theatrical performance, PowerPoint presentation. I know that nothing will ever be enough, but I can do better than this. I hope you can forgive me for some of these things.

Love,
Anna

During their entire friendship, George often felt like Anna owed her an apology, but mostly for crimes so small she would have felt foolish asking for one. Anna rarely took out the trash, she never returned a CD to its case, and she *always* left just an inch of milk in the carton. There was something about this particular apology that was too big and sweeping for George. She began to wonder about Anna's other transgressions, the ones she didn't know about. She figured there were plenty. Still, Anna was certainly paying for her mistakes.

TO: Anna Fury
FROM: George Leoni

A,
Thanks for the note. It matters. But it was all a long time ago. It would be nice to try to forget.
Here's a picture of my oldest animal.

G

George included a photo of Carter, now four, hanging precariously from a tree branch. George wrote to Kate right after she responded to Anna.

TO: Kate Smirnoff
FROM: George Leoni

K,
I guess Anna is at some step of recovery that involves making amends. I think she's really trying this time. And the apology I've hoped for has seemed to change over the years.
Have you heard from her? When are you coming home? This road trip of yours, I don't like it.

G

Kate no longer attempted any longhand

correspondence with George, who insisted that there was no point in communicating with someone if you could not actually decipher the communication. So their exchanges were reduced to telegram-length communiqués.

TO: George Leoni
FROM: Kate Smirnoff

George,
   Yes, I have heard from her. I haven't replied yet, but I'll get around to it. I do think this time is different.
   As for my road trip, I'll be back when my business is done.

Kate

It was George's e-mail that finally prompted Kate to respond to Anna. She was waiting for Anna to figure out the one apology that mattered, but maybe Anna would never uncover it on her own. Anna saw her life before recovery as one big error and she'd apologized for all of it. If Kate wanted a specific apology, she would have to ask.
When Anna got the letter from Kate, it was the first time she'd heard from her in almost six months. The postmark on the envelope was Bismarck, North Dakota, and

the note was written on stale stationery from a Motel 6. If Anna had one gripe about hearing from her, it was the same gripe everyone had: Kate's unruly script made her letters as comprehensible as redacted government documents.

Anna,

I got your letters. And thanks. I was tthrslnfl for a while, but I'm jhkemmn now. I know it's part of your iewrnc to kwejreoiej the past. But do we need to ojerfg? I hope you're doing okay. And that living with your qwewq isn't werhwje your khwevv. It would pkloij with mine. Seems like there has to be vcffhgj way. Let me know how you're doing. How you fill your days.

Have you heard about the hhumsltond of the wekjrlg Bkersg? I, for one, am kerqpmm. How do you go your whole life being a slwwsf and then, suddenly, you're not a slwwsf anymore. Correction: ewjrop. What does that even mean? I see an msqqprm taking lllqwec. Five, ten years from now, when someone gets wkppmvma or wjeojroj his or her job, people will say, "He was looenowejn." "Are you lejworjmv me?" someone will say when witnessing a kihywghf. "That was some olejpwejr, wasn't it?" Hmm, I'm not sure about the ppajkkd of the last one, but I think you get the yurjs.

Do you think I should write NASA?

I've been hearing things about the Nriierh mwp and I've been thinking I should see that, just so I can be that person who tells you one wlero isn't so different from the next. I might kwerk and seek ewrkpwer. I'll write more soon.

Kate

Anna pored over Kate's letter for at least an hour, but the fading ink of the ballpoint pen turned Kate's already almost indecipherable script into a cipher. Anna could confidently glean only a few simple facts: Kate had received Anna's letters; she wanted to know how Anna was doing; she was thinking about writing NASA; and she would write again. Anna saw this as a door cracking open and promptly sent a two-page reply describing her dishonorable return to the Fury homestead.

Anna heard from Kate again just a few weeks later, a longer letter including tales from her journey, but just the postcard-worthy bits. The two of them continued communicating solely by the United States Postal Service. Anna felt a rush of excitement whenever she received a letter and recalled afternoons at summer camp when the mail was delivered, holding the promise of stickers and candy and mix tapes.

Kate had been sitting in her car for four hours, minus two bathroom breaks and a short trip to the coffee shop — which she fully acknowledged was a bad idea during a stakeout — when Colin phoned. She picked up out of boredom and then she regretted it.

"Where are you?" he said.

"I don't know." It was less of a lie when they both knew it was a lie.

The day before, she'd driven for over twelve hours on I-70 from St. Louis to Stratton, Colorado. She could have stopped overnight in Kansas, but the pancake-flat prairie land, tumbleweeds, and messages from God on billboards made her soldier on. She held her bladder until she crossed the Colorado border, then she stopped at the first Motel 6.

At dawn, she'd driven along the same highway, which suddenly become a tangled, twisty, and breathtakingly beautiful mountain road. She pulled into a gas station and got directions to the address Mr. White had given her for a Leanne Hicks in

Boulder, Colorado. A light blanket of snow covered the brown lawn. The ranch-style home needed painting and a junk truck to haul away forgotten chairs and TVs and other things that apparently no longer had to be inside. Kate rang the doorbell. No answer. She'd returned to her car and waited. Then Colin had called.

"We need to discuss your corporate finances," he said.

"I don't think that's necessary."

"Who are Janet Gray and Leanne Olmstead, and why did you have me write them checks totaling over ten thousand dollars?"

"Because I owed them money. A good business pays its debts."

"Why did you owe them money?"

"For services rendered."

"What is the business model of Golden Retrieval Inc.?"

"I'm still working out the details."

"Work harder. What is it about these people that makes you feel like giving them all your money? Are they special?"

They weren't.

"Did I ever congratulate you on your wedding?" Kate asked.

"Yes. And thank you . . . for the rock."

"It's a geode, a dragon stone. I was told it's pretty rare. Although I'm not a rock expert, so it would be fairly easy to pull the wool over my eyes."

"As your lawyer, I need to advise you to stop this, whatever it is. Now."

"I don't think of you as my lawyer. More as my accountant or bookkeeper, but if it's a title you're after, we can work on it."

"Kate, the money is going to run out. And then what will you do?"

"Get a job. I have to go. My client just arrived."

Kate disconnected the call as a green pickup truck pulled into the driveway. The woman behind the wheel had two inches of roots in her bleached-blond shoulder-length hair, which left a black trail down her center part. Since she was carrying groceries, Kate waited exactly ten minutes for her to put them away.

"Are you Leanne Olmstead, formerly Hicks?" Kate asked when the woman answered the door with an impatient scowl.

"Who are you?"

"My name is Sarah Lake," Kate said.

"What do you want?"

"I wanted to talk to you about your deceased brother's estate."

"He owed me fifty dollars when he died. There's no way he had an estate."

"I work for Golden Retrieval Inc., an

asset-recovery firm based in Boston. Sometimes individuals purchase stocks or bonds and lose track of their investments. It appears that your late brother made a few small investments in some mutual funds in the early nineties. What I do is help distribute that money to the family."

"Please, come in."

Kate sat in Leanne's living room for the next two hours drinking stale coffee and waiting for Ms. Olmstead's tongue to loosen. Kate knew that each relative would claim to be the sole living heir, so she sat back, drank the viscous brew, and listened patiently. That was what had happened with the aunt in Memphis — she didn't start talking until after she'd poured herself her third hot toddy. Kate had waited her out; people always told you too much if you gave them enough time. Nobody kept secrets anymore. Although Kate was pretty good at it.

"He was a mean son of a bitch, but every once in a while, you saw his sweet side," Leanne said as she got to reminiscing about her brother. "When I was ten I outgrew my ice skates and begged and begged for a new pair for Christmas. But Santa decided I needed socks and underwear. I cried for an hour after I unwrapped my gifts and then I was sent to my room without supper. We were broke back then. I should have known better. A few days after Christmas, I found a pair of used figure skates outside my bedroom door. They were wrapped in a brown paper bag with a bow that he probably took out of the neighbor's trash. One size too big, but I got some wear out of them. Later at school, I heard Jennifer Glass had a pair of skates stolen from the rink just a few days after Christmas. I put two and two together. I even thought about giving them back to her, but a week after that, I saw her at the rink with a shiny new pair. Even nicer than what I had."

"Did your brother have many girlfriends?"

"He went through an awkward stage. Lots of acne, too skinny. No girl would give him the time of day way back when. But when he got older, his skin cleared up, and he filled out a bit. The last time I saw him, he was almost handsome. You could see some girls looking at him."

"You remember any of his girlfriends?"

"I met a few, but I only remember the one that stuck. Audrey."

"Who was Audrey?" Kate asked.

"His wife. His ex-wife."

"Where is she now?"

"I think she died a few years ago."

"I'm sorry to hear that."

Kate had a check ready in the amount of $4,352.24. She remembered jotting down numbers again and again, searching for that perfect note of randomness.

"This is for you. We have a complicated process for calculating distributions. But I hope it helps."

"Thank you," Leanne said.

"Now, where can I find your niece?" Kate said.

Kate phoned Mr. White from the Motel 6 and provided all the information she had on Evelyn Baker, formerly of Sunriver, Oregon. White said he'd get back to her as quickly as he could. Kate paid for another night in the motel. After toggling through the depressing television options, she turned off the TV and returned to a biography of Winston Churchill that she'd purchased from a used-book sale at the library. She'd been looking for transcriptions of his speeches but instead found this biography written by his nephew, who mentioned that Churchill did a mean gorilla imitation.

In the morning, Mr. White called.

"Got an address for you. Butte, Montana."

Kate gave herself three days to reach Butte,

Montana. Yellowstone National Park beckoned. She felt like she was cheating on Anna and George by visiting the national park alone; it had been on the list she and Anna had made in college of places they wanted to go. Kate always wondered where she would have gone without Anna whispering adventures in her ear. She had to admit feeling a bit aimless traveling without her. Kate bought a guidebook and followed the outer loop of the park, starting in Gardiner, Montana. It was like an Old West town. She found a saloon and ordered a root beer. Then she drove under the Roosevelt Arch. She remembered Anna at a party years ago blaming the past president for all of the current forest fires. *You know whose fault it is? Fucking Teddy Roosevelt's.* She had to slow her car as bison and deer crossed the road, and she caught a glimpse of orange sheep. She took a brief tour of Fort Yellowstone and decided she didn't need to see any more forts in her life. She hiked briefly among the hoodoo rocks, found a hot spring hidden from other tourists, quickly disrobed, and jumped into the water.

She traveled on to Upper Geyser Basin, whose namesake geyser refused to perform. She almost willed it not to. She didn't want to have a once-in-a-lifetime experience alone. She bought postcards but never sent them. She figured this was a trip she probably wouldn't reminisce about.

Evelyn lived in a four-unit brick building off Broadway.

"Are you Evelyn Baker?" Kate asked when a young woman with long brown hair and eyes like her father's, minus years of resentment, answered the door.

"Who are you?"

"I'm Sarah Lake. I work for Golden Retrieval Inc., an asset-recovery firm based in Boston," Kate said. "I have some very good news for you."

The next letter that Anna received had a return address in Prairie Basin, Montana. Colin told Anna that Kate was planning on staying there awhile. Anna knew no more than Colin or George about Kate's ill-conceived business. Although it was quite possible, with all of the holes in her letters, that she had simply missed that part.

Anna,

I know I could write an e-mail and you'd receive it as soon as I clicked the Send button, but there's something about that format that insists on brevity and the reckless use of abbreviations, like sxhtyh and wehrih. Of course, sending a letter to your parents' house comes fraught with different pqpepj. I picture it like prison, the guards reading your mail and literally cutting out the inappropriate parts. I think I saw that in a movie from the eighties. Lwerojo of Pwerw. Did you see it? The letter is carefully sealed, so if you notice any wejkrbz, you should assume your mother has tampered with it. Hi, Lena.

So far small-town life is agreeing with me. I've made a few friends. Not in my tppy, but there aren't too many people in my tppy here and those usually have several children and are suspicious of women without their own brood. I got a part-time job at the Prairie Basin Reporter — PBR, for short, which is sometimes confusing, since PBR is what the whole town drinks. It pays fifty dollars a week. I write fluff pieces on the high school ieurutkw and the obits. I asked for the crime blotter, but Rkrwlke, the boss, says there isn't enough crime to warrant one. I'm almost positive someone nicked a wrench from my toolbox, so I respectfully disagreed. It's qqaedkb I misplaced it. But unless I can drum up some criminal activity, I'm stuck with the dead and the undead. (That vampire shit has made it into the sticks too; it's all over the high school.) Fridays I go to high school football games. Wednesdays I play bingo. And when somebody dies, I usually attend the funeral.

As I serwle in the last letter I also work part-time shelving books at the library. Last Thursday when I meenrn, Mrs. Uwelkn was dead. At first I thought she was taking a nap on the floor, but she's not the nap-on-the-floor kind of woman. Not too many people are, I guess. You, maybe. Or you used to be. Is it okay to say that? Anyway, Mrs. Uwelkn was totally dead. I didn't want to bbejbawoe the crime scene, so I went next door to the oiepe and told them to call 911. But they don't call 911 in Prairie Basin. Mrs. Indbwsed (the postmistress — that's what they call her) phoned Sheriff Bleeker from the next town because we don't have a sheriff. He was in the middle of lunch, so he jajsedj ham and cheese and drove over.

The sheriff walked into the library, turned Mrs. Uwelkn over, and then picked up the phone on her desk and called the morgue. There was no investigation, which is good for him since he totally cccdd up the crime scene. I don't suspect foul play, but she was on the young side. At least for death. The funeral was kfdec. I wrote her obit, of course; if I were working at a big paper, they'd say it was a conflict of interest. But this is PBR. I hope I don't die like her.

What's the zsdlwerj amount of time to wait until I ask for her job?

One last thing: I wanted to tell you about the sky. I stepped out of the PBR office at sunset. There was a fhew of clouds like those ropy doughnuts, twisted up with reds and blues with an aiiei slate backdrop, in an endless drifting motion. A ytebajw so complex it doesn't seem natural. If we lived in ancient Greece and knew nothing of the world, we would be saying that the gods were at war. It was a violent, beautiful sky. It was better than any sky I've ever seen.

I wish you could have seen it.

Love,
Kate

Kate,

Thanks for the letter; I grabbed it directly from the mailbox so the gatekeeper would have no chance to tamper with the seal. Although I wouldn't put it past Lena to "accidentally" open my mail. There used to be a lock on my bedroom door, but when I moved back, it was mysteriously gone. Sometimes I think she's stuck in the past, still playing a game of cat-and-mouse with her adolescent daughter. She's upped her game, or I've lost mine. I would like to be able to open my bedroom window at night without setting off the alarm. She never talks about what I did. She just calls it "the legal matter." And occasionally implements a new security measure. I offered to explain it to her as best I could. But she thought we should just put the past behind us. I'm living at home. I can't fucking escape the past.

My life isn't as exciting as yours — dead librarians and brilliant sunsets. I did just meet a fallen Supreme Court justice or a man with delusions of grandeur. You decide. I'm not one to judge. I'm adjusting to most of the stuff. Living at home is the hardest part, but right now I don't know what else to do. I'm broke. The legal fees took the last of the trust fund. My brother keeps asking me why I did what I did. It seems so obvious. Doesn't everyone want to escape sometimes?

Speaking of escapes, is that what you're doing? I hope you find more than death and sunsets. Unless that's all you're looking for.

Love,
Anna

2000

OLD FORGE, NEW YORK

It was a moonless sky, riddled with stars arranged like holiday decorations hung in haste, the beauty in their chaos. Too many to count, although George often tried. Kate mumbled the constellations. Anna slunk away. She dipped her hand in the icy water of the creek and pulled out a beer from the makeshift cooler that she'd brainstormed earlier in the day by loading a twelve-pack into a fisherman's net, submerging it in the water, and securing it with a bowline knot to a tent stake. Anna twisted off the cap with her numbed palm and sat down on the tarp, slipping between George and Kate for warmth.

There was a house, the Fury weekend home, just a mile away. But George insisted that they find a place to camp out for the night, that they make use of the acreage Lena ignored. It reminded her of her childhood vacations at her father's lake cabin in

Michigan. Although that was just a cabin, not like Lena's four-thousand-square-foot refurbished barn. George always felt cut off from nature inside the Fury vacation home — it was too civilized for all that ungroomed land. George made sure they hiked far enough away from the property that you could pretend it wasn't there. After a year of working as a forest ranger, George couldn't remember the last time she'd sat under the stars without feeling responsible for the earth beneath her. Tonight she was free.

George built the fire while Kate and Anna pitched the tent. Those roles had been established years ago, after numerous fire-building competitions, which George always won, her fire often ablaze several minutes before Anna or Kate could get the kindling started. George had learned at her father's cabin — the only heat was from his wood stove. Her system was second nature to her, and she had an eye for those perfect dry sticks that never disappointed. After two seasons of losing the fire battle, Anna and Kate decided to step up their game. Kate read books on fires and learned about soft- and hardwood and gathered her kindling ahead of time, hiding it in her backpack. Anna went to a hardware store and purchased a small paraffin-and-sawdust fire starter that supposedly blazed for fifteen minutes, giving your fire ample time to catch. Both girls lost yet again that year.

George added another piece of wood to the fire and returned her gaze to the endless sky.

"Won't you miss it?" Kate asked.

"It will always be here," George said.

"But not every night. You'll have to go looking for it."

"People give up all sorts of things for love," Anna said, having only a theoretical knowledge of that subject.

"You're changing your whole life for a guy you met on an airplane," Kate said.

"And one day you might change your whole life for a guy you meet at a bus stop," George said.

As the story went, George Leoni met Mitch Misenti in first class on a flight from San Francisco to Chicago. George was flying home for the holidays and, as usual, was running late. The airplane doors were about to close as George dashed to her gate, a coat and carry-on bag rising and falling like wings in her wake. The flight attendant gave her a sharp scowl as she pegged George as one of those pretty girls who thought they could get away with anything. George, winded and apologetic, wove an intricate lie about not being able to find her cat before she left. George had no cat. But the flight attendant did, and although she'd been about to give the one remaining first-class seat to some almost-lucky frequent flier in coach, it was simpler to assign it to George.

The seat was 2C. An aisle. George rushed down the jet bridge, tossed her bag in the overhead compartment, and slipped into her seat, managing to avoid all the disapproving eyes. As soon as she buckled her seat belt, she was offered a glass of champagne, cementing in her mind a causal relationship between being late and getting pleasant surprises.

The champagne went down easy, and then exhaustion set in. George could sleep anywhere. Within moments of takeoff she was drifting into slumber, her head lolling to the side and eventually resting on the shoulder of the rather attractive stranger in 2D.

This was not the first time a fellow passenger had fallen asleep on Mitch Misenti. He traveled often for work (he was an investment consultant, always on the prowl for businesses that were underperforming) and had sat next to an incongruous variety of humanity. Some slept upright; some dozed on and off; some worked straight through; some chatted politely; some prattled on, baring their souls without invitation; just a few fell into a sound sleep and slouched over onto Mitch, and only one was allowed to stay asleep. Passenger 2C.

George woke with a start as the dinner service began.

"I'm so sorry. How long was I out?"

"About an hour."

"Was I sleeping on you the whole time?"

"Most of it," Mitch said pleasantly.

"Why didn't you wake me?"

"You looked like you needed the rest."

"I'd buy you a drink for your trouble, but they're free here," George said.

"Since you slept on me and all, it seems like I should know your name."

"George. George Leoni."

"Nice to meet you, George. I'm Mitch Misenti."

During that first encounter, it seemed that Mitch asked all the questions. Later, when the flight was over, George knew very little about the man. Mitch, however, never missed an opportunity to arm himself with information.

"What do you do?" he asked.

"I'm a forest ranger."

"Are you really?" Mitch said, amused. Most attractive women he met were in sales; a disproportionate number were pharmaceutical reps. There was the occasional model or actress or model/actress. And once he'd met a woman who was an aspiring television host, a mutation of the model/actress that was new to him. But most of the women he encountered on the road and sometimes passed a layover with were under that vague umbrella of the corporate work force with job titles no one had ever thought of in kindergarten when dreaming of what they would be when they grew up. No five-year-old ever said she wanted to become a search strategist for a global technology conglomerate.

George Leoni, forest ranger. It was so preposterous he had to choke back a laugh when she said it. It suited her, though. Something about her seemed meant for the wild. It might have just been the untamed eyebrows. He wasn't used to the natural look. Most women he knew had been plucked and waxed and sprayed the color of something vaguely resembling a suntan. George had a natural tan that was a mix of geometric shapes and shades layered across her body like papier-mâché.

"What would possess you to become a forest ranger?" There was a slight hint of horror in Mitch's voice.

"Humans weren't meant to live their lives indoors in windowless cubicles under fluorescent lights breathing recycled air."

"That's one way to look at it."

"Anyway, when I discovered there was a job where you could spend all day at a campsite, I knew it was for me."

"So what does a forest ranger do?"

"There's a broad spectrum," George said. "I work for the state forestry service. I haven't been out of school that long, so I man a campsite in the Russian River Valley. I keep the peace. I'm occasionally charged with pulling soil samples for research, surveying, determining fire risks."

"Have you ever had a run-in with a bear?"

"I have."

"What do you do?"

"First, I try to reason with it. If that doesn't work, I shoot it."

"Shoot to kill?"

"No, with a tranquilizer gun."

George would at times attempt to maneuver the conversation back to Mitch, but his replies were abrupt and final, as if he were hiding something. She learned that he lived in New York and was on an extended business trip. San Francisco, then

Chicago. He owned a company that invested in Internet startups. When George asked for further details, Mitch asked George yet another question about her life. He wasn't actually hiding anything, at least not at that point. It was all part of his game plan, finessed over years of careful scrutiny of the opposite sex. Mitch had a particular way with women — a formula of giving and withholding that almost always managed to hook them. Getting them to talk about themselves was the first step; remaining enigmatic was the second. There were other steps, but he used only the first two during that encounter.

Mitch got George on the subject of forest fires, and their conversation didn't end until the plane landed. That summer in California, fires had raged for months; just when one was quenched, another blazed. The newscasters called it a phenomenon of the drought, but every summer was the same. George took those fires personally, as if they were set by someone seeking revenge against her. She could pontificate for hours on the subject but had abbreviated her speech over the years.

"In nature, lightning strikes occasionally cause small, localized fires that burn away the underbrush. The policy has been to put out those fires. So now there's plenty of underbrush, which is the perfect fuel for massive destruction. Hundreds and thousands of acres have been destroyed, lives lost, because we didn't trust nature to do its job."

Actually, the policy began with nature lover Teddy Roosevelt. George used to single him out in her impromptu lectures on the subject, but she'd quit when it seemed that Anna had extrapolated only that one bit of information: "All these forest fires. You know whose fault it is?" Anna once asked some drunk student she had cornered at a party. "Fucking Teddy Roosevelt's fault."

As George and Mitch deplaned, the intimacy of their in-flight exchange faded into the polite surface conversation of virtual strangers.

"It was nice meeting you, George," Mitch said.

"Yes, really nice talking to you too," George said after a brief pause. She was expecting their parting to be accompanied by an invitation.

They walked down the terminal together in silence. Almost as an afterthought, Mitch handed George his business card.

"I come to San Francisco at least once a month. If you'd like to have dinner sometime, give me a call."

George phoned Mitch a week later, after she'd returned to San Francisco. Mitch called her back two weeks after that, just as he was about to board the aircraft on his way to San Francisco. He invited her to dinner that night. George said yes and scrambled to finish her paperwork, find an appropriate dress, and drive to the city. She was half an hour late. Mitch waited impatiently at the restaurant. By the time George got there, he had already put away half a bottle of wine.

George was, once again, winded and apologetic when she arrived. Mitch slowly put his napkin on the table, got to his feet, and kissed her on the cheek. He leaned in and whispered in her ear.

"I think I'm going to buy you a watch."

They began a long-distance relationship that was long distance mostly for George, who had to endure the brief weekend trips to New York City, red-eye flights in coach that left her spent and jet-lagged at least half the month but were, generously, bankrolled by Mitch. By then, George's lack of timeliness had landed several rungs down on their ladder of arguments. Sex and housekeeping were at the top, although only the housekeeping arguments were voiced. Mitch would find a glass of water on the nightstand in the bedroom, an old coffee cup on the kitchen counter — a flagrant disregard for the use of coasters. He'd take George by the shoulders and march her over to the spot, as if she were a child being taught a lesson. At first, the message was patiently delivered.

"Have you finished drinking that?" Mitch would ask, and George would sweep up the mug and promptly stow it away in the dishwasher. Later, when she'd hear the key in the door, she'd scramble through the house looking for anything amiss. And a few times, she'd drink stale tea or coffee as if it had just been brewed. Every man had his quirks, and this was Mitch's. She told herself that this was certainly superior to living with a slob. Although there were moments when she questioned that. When Mitch ceased voicing his reprimands, he would pick up her beverage and angrily clank around the kitchen, tidying up the invisible mess. She caught him once in the bathroom collecting her bleached-blond hairs off the floor. George tried to explain that you could lose up to a hundred hairs a day. How was she supposed to keep track of them all? Mitch kissed her on the forehead and suggested she brush her hair more often.

The sex arguments were silent. If Mitch returned home to a mess (a few crumbs on the counter), he'd refuse to touch George that night. Her only recourse for affection would be a blowjob, an unspoken apology. Otherwise, sex was always according to Mitch's desires; if George initiated, Mitch would roll her onto her side, kiss her on the cheek, and say a firm good night. There was never a reciprocal refusal from her. Anytime Mitch wanted her, he could have her. There was something sick about her desire, George knew. Once, just thinking about him being inside of her, she felt nauseated and saw spots in the air. No one had ever had that effect on her.

Chatting with Kate on the phone, George said, "He just owns me in bed. You know what I mean?"

"No," Kate flatly said. Kate wasn't as experienced with men as Anna and George, but she'd had a boyfriend in high school and a few in college and not once had she felt owned by them.

George often felt that Kate and Anna were judging her, even during conversations about sex that the other two women thought were hypothetical. In college, George had had a boyfriend who could come only when he was being blown, and so she asked Kate and Anna how many blowjobs a week was normal.

"I have no idea," said Kate. "When I was nine and I first learned that people did that, I promised myself I'd never give a blowjob ever."

"How'd that work out for you?" George asked.

"My nine-year-old self would be very disappointed in my adult self," said Kate.

Anna, the scientist, gave George a range of numbers. "Zero to three. Unless you're talking about a sex worker. Then we're talking double digits, at least. What's your average?"

"I haven't counted. Just curious," said George.

Oh, she had counted. Ten in one week. Sex-worker terrain. But that was the last time she consulted with Kate or Anna about normal sexual behavior. Although she did break up with the ten-blowjob-a-week guy after she started to hear a clicking sound in her jaw.

George felt ashamed of her suffocating desire for Mitch. She told Anna during one drunken phone call that when she had sex with Mitch, she stopped thinking. Anna said, "Huh," which George interpreted as criticism, although in fact Anna was thinking that that sounded nice. Anna couldn't recall ever having sex without a nonstop sportscaster-like commentary running in her head.

There was no sex talk the night of the girls' New York camping trip, even though it was often on George's mind. Eventually George got lost in the sky and stopped thinking about Mitch's penis. It was Anna who tired of nature first. She thought of another beer and the sleeping bag. Anna uncapped the bottle and retired for the evening.

In the morning, Kate gathered wood for the fire while George started the kindling. Anna woke to a blazing fire. She had promised herself that she would go camping alone someday so that she could have all the jobs to herself, but she never did. Truth was, nature didn't do it for her anymore. She missed the convenience of the city, the neon lights, the bed and the sheets and the blackout window shades that let you believe it was night all day long.

Anna got the first cup of coffee even though she had had no part in the chore of making it. It was just how it had always been. She needed it most. George warmed her hands by the fire as she sipped the brew. Anna and Kate admired her expression of repose. She looked so at home. You'd never know that they were in Anna's domain. George had found the spot yesterday and insisted they carry their supplies half a mile through untracked land.

A few hours into sunlight, the earth began to hold the heat. Anna led Kate and George on a short trail to a private swimming hole beneath a thirty-foot waterfall. George tilted her head back and let the sun beat down on her face. She bent down to feel the water.

"It's warm enough," George said, stripping down to nothing. "You guys coming in?"

"What happened to your pubic hair?" Kate asked.

"Some woman named Olga took it," George said.

"You look like a ten-year-old girl," Kate said.

"With a twelve-year-old's tits," Anna added.

"It's called grooming," George said, padding along the rocks, looking for a place to dive.

"You have no hair. Anywhere. Other than

134

your head. And eyebrows," Kate said.

"Might be the best case of alopecia I've ever seen," Anna said.

"I don't get it," Kate said, baffled. "All of it is gone."

"My body, Kate. I get to do with it what I want." George dove into the frigid water, blotting out the conversation.

"Twenty bucks that it wasn't her idea," Kate said to Anna.

"That's a sucker bet," Anna said. She stripped down, revealing a triangle of semi-groomed hair that Kate found reassuring.

Anna took in a deep breath, knowing that the cold water would knock it out of her. She followed George with a more tentative dive.

"How is it?" Kate asked from the shore.

"Just keep moving. You won't notice a thing," Anna said in short, gasping breaths.

"That's your answer for everything," Kate said.

George flicked on the light switch in the entryway, then glanced around, hunting for the remote — the control panel for the entire apartment. She found it, pressed a button, and the blinds were drawn, revealing a blue sky and an expansive view of skyscrapers with the Hudson River as a backdrop.

"Holy shit," Anna said, stealing the remote from George.

Kate methodically scrutinized the conspicuous consumption, silently noting the glare of chrome and glass amid the tar-colored wood floors and the leather everything else. It was the most masculine home Kate had ever seen, other than in a movie about a rich banker/serial killer she had accidentally watched on cable. Kate gave the stereo console a white-glove test with the bottom edge of her white T-shirt. Came up clean. At least, she was pretty sure that the smudge on her shirt had been there before.

While Kate tried to acquire some evidence that her friend lived in this three-bedroom Manhattan apartment, Anna pretended she was in an interactive museum and went crazy with the remote control, brightening and dimming the track lighting, raising and lowering the blinds, igniting the fireplace, and, with the press of a button and a magician's hand flourish, making the fire disappear. When she tired of the fireplace, Anna plopped down on the bed-size sectional sofa, turned on the fifty-seven-inch TV, and channel-surfed with the rhythm of a metronome, erasing all complicated thoughts from her mind.

"Can I live here?" Anna asked.

"Where's the bathroom?" Kate asked.

While infomercials, cop dramas, telenovelas, game shows, and sitcoms blared in the background at varying decibels, Kate searched through the bathroom looking for George. That was where she found her, in moisturizers, fragrant salon shampoos, and a brush with her DNA all over it. She took a peek in the closet and saw the meager quarters for George's clothes. She was about to take a closer look at a small row of cocktail dresses, a few still with price tags dangling, when she heard the television noise mute and a man's voice in its place.

"Anna, finally we meet," Mitch said, giving her a kiss on the right and then left cheek. "I've heard some stories about you." He winked expertly.

"All lies," Anna said.

"George said you'd deny everything. This must be Kate," he said, turning around and offering a warm smile in her direction.

Kate held out her hand as she approached. Mitch understood the signal and shook it.

"Welcome to my home. Our home. Sorry, old habits. Did you have a nice trip?"

"It was wonderful," George said. "Perfect

time of year."

"Good," Mitch said, putting his arm around her waist. "Glad you got it out of your system."

George explained, "Mitch hates camping."

"Maybe you'll grow to like it," Kate said.

"Not gonna happen," Mitch said with a nervous edge in his voice.

George looked at her shoes. A puzzled expression took up residence on Kate's face, and Anna returned her energy to the remote. A silence that begged for breaking set in.

"Just tell them," Mitch said to George, who responded with an impish grin.

"Mitch has some phobias," George said, "that pretty much exempt him from any kind of outdoorsy activities."

"I play basketball," Mitch said, correcting her.

"Indoors. At the Y," George noted.

"What kind of phobias?" Kate asked.

"Nature," George said.

"Huh?" said Kate.

"Mitch has a pathological fear of most things one would find in the wild. Insects, squirrels, legless creatures," George said.

"Snakes mostly," Mitch said.

"And worms," George added. "He can't even look at those things on television."

"I usually just watch sports," Mitch said.

"To a lesser extent, he's afraid of rodents, wolves, bears, hyenas, mountain lions, and giraffes, which I really don't get."

"The long neck," Mitch said, as if it were obvious.

To the casual observer, it might have appeared that Anna had tuned out the conversation, but then she briefly lifted her eyes from the mesmerizing remote. "Where do you stand on trees?"

"I like trees," Mitch said. "And I don't mind birds. The nice ones. Not pigeons or vultures. But nobody likes pigeons or vultures."

"I love vultures," Anna said.

"It's kind of funny how a forest ranger and a guy who hates nature end up together," Kate said, not in a finding-it-funny way.

"Opposites attract," Mitch said. That was his cue to them that the nature conversation was over. It was a friendly transition but one that made it obvious to everyone that the subject was not to be mentioned again. "So, can I get anyone a drink?"

Anna raised her hand as if she were in the third grade.

"What'll it be?" Mitch asked.

"Doesn't matter," Kate said. "She'll drink

anything."

"Let me make you my specialty."

While Mitch peacocked his mixology skills, Kate noted without having any feelings of attraction that she might never have seen a more attractive man in real life. His home, his hair, even what passed as his casualwear, seemed magazine-worthy. And his small talk was impressive. He managed to put a pleasant spin on Kate's career inertia.

"So, Kate, George tells me you're a student of the world."

"I'm a barista," Kate said.

"Oh my God!" Anna shouted, pressing a button on the remote. *This thing makes rain.*

A shower of water cascaded over the terrace outside. Anna approached the window and put her hand on the glass, as if she were visiting rain in prison. She watched the window waterfalls with rapt attention.

"It waters plants," Kate said, taking possession of the remote and pressing the Off switch. She turned on the stereo. The first phrase of *Kind of Blue* encased the room. *So predictable,* Kate thought, even though she liked it too. Charles Mingus would have surprised her. If Sun Ra's *Space Is the Place* had suddenly blasted from the speaker

140

system, she would have changed her mind about Mitch completely. But now her opinion was as immovable as the Sierras.

"What do you think?" Kate whispered to Anna.

"I try not to think," Anna said, taking back the remote and turning on the rain again.

2010

BOSTON, MASSACHUSETTS

"Who are you?" Anna's father asked as she stood over his bed.

Anna used to think of her father as the boss of everyone. Now Donald Fury was just a shrunken old man in too-large pajamas. She wondered why her mother hadn't bought him a new pair.

"It's me, Anna. Your daughter."

"I know," Don said impatiently. "When did you get here?" His voice hadn't lost as much weight as his body.

"I flew in yesterday," Anna said. "Do you want me to fix the pillows?"

Don slept propped up. An invalid angle, as he called it, to ease his sleep apnea. The pillows had shifted during his slumber and left him bowed precariously on the side of the bed.

"No, I want to get up."

"Should I get Alvita?" Anna asked.

Alvita Bailey was the full-time nurse

Anna's mother had hired the moment Donald took ill. Her father had fallen the week before, and Anna had been cautioned not to let him move on his own. A painter's palette of a bruise had overtaken his forearm and splattered onto his cheek.

"I don't need Alvita's permission to sit on my own couch," Donald Fury said with the air of authority that he once owned.

"Of course not," Anna said.

As Don stirred in bed, Anna opted against annoying her father further by calling for help. She assisted him to the couch, surprised by his lightness, the hard edge of bones barely contained in his paper-thin skin. It would have been simpler to pick him up and carry him, but Don would always cling to dignity, no matter how much was taken from him. Once he was safely seated, she adjusted the pillows on the couch until her father slapped her hands away.

"Just sit down and talk to me," he said.

Anna complied. He didn't used to have time to talk to her. Now that he did, most of their conversations were built around a lie.

"How's work?" Don asked.

"Can't complain."

"How are the patients treating you?"

"They have good days and bad days. Just

like anyone else."

"Have you made chief resident yet?"

"No. I haven't."

"Why not?"

"Somebody else was better."

"Then you should work harder."

"Okay."

The industrial-size clock flipped to 6:00.

"Anna, dear, would you get me a bourbon and soda."

"I don't think you're supposed to drink today," Anna said.

Alcohol interfered with his medication, so he was never supposed to drink, but Anna thought making the comment temporary would lessen the effect.

"Then you have one for me."

"No, thank you."

"I've never known you to turn down a drink."

"I'm just tired after traveling," Anna said.

"Suit yourself."

Don then reached out and gently held Anna's hand, something he never would have done before. When she was young, he would pat her on the head, especially when she amused him. Sometimes he'd give her a quick hug, but the release was so immediate, Anna never felt much comfort in it. Now Anna internally recoiled at the feel of her father's skin. It had a reptilian dryness, which made the oddness of their physical contact even more pronounced. She patted his hand once, stood abruptly, and fetched him a glass of water.

"I'm not thirsty," he said.

"Drink it anyway," she said.

"How's your husband? What's his name again?"

"Dad, I'm not married."

"I just went to your wedding."

"No. Maybe you're thinking of Colin's wedding."

"Really?"

"Yes."

"Does he get married often?"

"Yes."

"You should get married sometime, Anna."

"We'll see."

"You don't want to be alone, do you?"

"There are worse things one can be."

Anna took in a deep breath as she closed the door to her father's room. She hadn't noticed the hospital smell until she was inhaling the potpourried air of the rest of the house. Her mother sat in the enclosed porch, sipping iced tea and reading a biography of a dead woman who'd lived in more mannered times. Lena looked tired and years older than she had six months before, when Anna had seen her last. When Lena turned seventy, Anna noticed, she had surrendered to age. While she still dressed impeccably, styled her hair into an immovable upsweep, darkened her eyes, and reddened her lips, she'd stopped waging a full-scale battle with her skin. Her dermatologist remained in the Rolodex for cancer checks and unsightly rashes, but he no longer performed a quarterly tune-up of injections, lasers, and peels.

Anna liked seeing her mother's forehead furrow again, although it seemed from the shelf of creases that her skin was trying to make up for lost time.

"You didn't argue with him, did you?" Lena asked.

"I told him I wasn't married, but the other thing I stayed quiet about."

"It's for the best," Lena said. "Remember what happened last time?"

"I do."

Anna found her brother in the basement, scavenging through the rubble of decaying boxes. Lena's idea of spring cleaning involved ridding the house of memories. She'd even had her bedroom redecorated now that her husband no longer slept there. If Donald were capable of climbing stairs and finding his way to his old abode, no one could ever have convinced him he'd once slept there. Even without the rosy palette, the bedroom was aggressively feminine.

"Should I be ruthless or sentimental?" Colin asked. He was paging through a file folder of yellowed papers littered with typewriter ink and whiteout. "High school essays. Do I need this?" he asked.

"Your biographer might," Anna said, shoving a box with her name on it out of the way and taking a seat on the stain-resistant gray rug.

Colin put the folder in a trash bag. He uncovered a photo album in the box and set it aside.

"Let me see that," Anna said, stretching out her arms.

"No," Colin said.

"I want to see the photo album," she said.

"You have five boxes with your name on them and one hour until dinner. Get to work."

"Just a quick peek," Anna said.

"No," Colin flatly said. "It will make you sad."

"It's okay to be sad," she said.

"Deal with your own past first," he said, pointing at a box marked *Anna*.

Anna and Colin heard the distinct creak that came when someone stepped on the third stair down from the landing, and both twitched out of habit. All their adolescent vices had been nurtured in the basement.

Lena took the stairs at a cautious pace. Hand on the railing, one step at a time. She had too many friends who had broken a wrist or a hip out of sheer carelessness. She had never used a bedpan in her life and hoped to die before she had to subject herself to such an indignity.

When Lena reached the bottom step, Colin and Anna sat frozen, as if they had been caught smoking weed.

"Anna, you haven't opened any of your boxes."

"I was just about to get started," Anna said.

"Anything you don't take will get tossed. It's shocking how much stuff a person can acquire over a lifetime, and it all means nothing."

Lena ascended the stairs without another word. Anna and Colin both exhaled. Long ago, Anna had noticed that she breathed less when her mother was around. Sometimes, she'd even find herself light-headed after a long interlude with Lena.

"How was Dad?" Colin asked as he studied an old swim-team medal that was slated for landfill.

"Fairly lucid, although he seemed to think he attended *my* wedding six months ago. And he said the funniest thing: 'Does Colin get married often?' I said, 'Yes, yes, he does.' "

"I'm glad you were amused."

Twenty minutes later, he had reduced his ancient swag to a single box and dusted off his hands with the satisfaction earned from a day of hard labor. Anna opened one of her boxes, which was loaded with school papers, report cards, and old letters. She closed the box and decided that she had lived more than twenty years without whatever was in that box. She could last the duration.

"Let's get out of here," Colin said.

"Do you think we'll ever be down here again?" Anna asked.

"Maybe after dinner, if Mom insists on an inspection."

"I need to show you something."

The basement had been unfinished until Colin and Anna were adolescents. Lena's living room was always off-limits to the children, and the den was Donald's domain.

The dining room was the dining room, and sometimes Lena simply couldn't keep Anna and Colin contained in their bedrooms. Turning the basement into a young-adult playroom was her solution.

Anna strolled down the galley-shaped corridor to the far end of the basement, where the washer and dryer sat beneath a window providing a ground-level view of the backyard.

To the left of the washer and dryer was a crawlspace for workers, should they require access to the utility hub of the home. Anna pushed against the door with her knee and it popped open. She got down on all fours and crawled inside.

"I've been in there before, Anna," Colin said, remaining on his feet.

"Get a flashlight," Anna said, ignoring him.

A Maglite rested in a basket by the back door. Colin grabbed the flashlight and followed his sister into the crawlspace. Cobwebs hung from the beams. Anna stole the flashlight from her brother and shone it along the right-side wall. A tiny lever jutted out from the baseboard. Anna clicked the lever to the side, and another small door, about four feet high and three feet wide, clicked open. Anna swung open the tiny door and slipped inside yet another crawl-space, this one about six feet by four feet, with a ceiling just high enough for Anna to stand.

Colin, on hands and aching knees, followed his sister into the secret cavern and took a seat against the opposite wall. On the floor was the same gray basement carpet, along with a mattress from one of the outside lounge chairs that had mysteriously gone missing years ago, a sleeping bag, a wooden crate filled with books, and a night lamp adjacent to a working electrical outlet.

Anna pulled the string on the lamp, illuminating the room. The interior was painted light blue, and the walls were covered with pictures from art books and Emily Dickinson poems. Malcolm had given her the poet's collected works when she'd turned fifteen. She'd cracked the spine only when he'd told her that you could sing "Because I could not stop for Death" to the tune of the Coke song.

"What is this place?"

"My secret room," Anna said. She could almost smell the incense she'd burned to mask the musty odor that stuck in the basement after heavy rains.

"Someone made this for you," Colin said.

It was something between a question and a statement.

"When Mom decided to refinish the basement, there was a contractor who worked down here. He was homeless. I caught him sleeping in the utility room one morning. He asked me not to tell. I wasn't going to. But then later, I thought how perfect it would be to have this place where I could escape in my own home. I squirreled money back then. Had something against banks. I had seven hundred and sixty dollars. His name was . . . Cesar. I told Cesar what I wanted. Electricity and a secret latch was my priority. I wanted it black. He painted it light blue. We argued over the color, but in the end, he was right. Too small a space to go dark. You wouldn't believe the number of hours I spent in here."

After what Lena called the legal matter, Colin had thought there was nothing left that Anna could tell him or do that would surprise him. But, once again, he was proven wrong.

"You kept this secret for twenty years?" he asked.

"If you haven't noticed, I'm kind of good at keeping secrets," Anna said.

Geography, family, and work were the

excuses George had found for not seeing Kate and Anna for the past few years. They spoke on occasion and exchanged e-mails, but George's simmering resentments kept the tone distant and polite. When Anna began to make amends, George was wary about inviting her old friend back into her life. But past gripes didn't thrive under current conditions. It helped that Anna was now in an entirely unenviable position. For the first time in the relationship, George couldn't possibly feel insecure, even about being thrice-divorced, alone, and middle-aged. But what really brought their friendship back was Anna's persistence. At the time, she was more present and engaging than anyone else in George's life. George's friends in Chicago were more like acquaintances with the commonality of children. They never incensed her the way that Kate and, especially, Anna could, but they also bored her. George could complain for hours in therapy about Anna and Kate (and she did) but they had always offered something more. Jeremy once asked George to describe Kate and Anna, and she first, ungenerously, said, "They're weird." Then she added, "But they're also alive. More than most people."

After a long day of ignored alarms, meetings at the principal's office, massive cooking spills, arguments over video games, and three hard-core negotiations over bedtime, George got a phone call from Anna at what had become her usual time, eight o'clock. George told Anna about the mouse that had escaped its cage and terrorized the housekeeper all morning. George had thought it all quite hilarious until she'd mentioned it to the mother of Miller's classmate, who had asked what the mouse's name was, and George said that they'd decided not to name the mice anymore since they fed them to Carter's snakes. She was fairly certain Miller and Owen's next playdate was canceled.

Anna suggested that George needed some time away from laundry and frozen meals and video games and mothers who didn't understand that you can't feed a Western rat snake a salad. George jumped at the idea and suggested they meet at her father's cabin on Lake Huron. These days, it was mostly a rental, her father's belongings having long since been removed. Now it contained the leftovers of previous inhabitants.

George pawned off her boys on their respective fathers. Anna took a day off, and Kate didn't need an excuse to spend a weekend at a rustic cabin in the woods. No one would admit it, but all three women were grateful that it was winter and they could sleep in soft, warm beds. George and Kate shared the bedroom. Anna was happy sleeping on the couch in the living room.

Inside, a glowing amber fire burned in the living room, and everything smelled like pine or chocolate or marshmallows. The scents were intoxicating. Outside, snow blanketed the entire world. During the day, icicles would drip and grow; at night, they'd refreeze, and in the morning they'd start the process again. One ice dagger on a shingle had grown to almost two feet long.

"That's the perfect murder weapon," Kate commented when she saw it.

"I need to build a snowman," Anna declared.

Bundled up and in hats and scarves and waterproof gloves, they all went to it. Anna rolled the base of the snowman, because she was the expert. She and Colin had perfected the craft when they were children. Muscle memory kicked in as she packed together an ambitiously large base in record time. When Anna was satisfied with it, she assigned Kate the second layer. Finally, she and George molded the head to perfection.

Kate stole a knit cap and scarf from a

drawer of discarded items in the house. Two buttons extracted from what was most likely a deliberately forgotten reindeer sweater made for mismatched eyes. George thought a mushroom would be the perfect nose; Anna and Kate found it disturbing. They swapped the mushroom for a rock, against great protest. George dotted raisins across the lower region of the head to make a smile. Three grown women stood back to admire their team effort.

KATE: It's missing something.

George gathered two small branches from under a tree. She stabbed one into either side of the middle snowball.

GEORGE: Those are arms.
ANNA: We would have figured it out eventually.

George took a picture with her phone and texted it to her sons. Kate knit her brow and shook her head.

KATE: It's still missing something.

Kate pulled a twig from one of the snowman's branch arms and stuck it in his mouth.

KATE: That's better.

George was unconvinced that the twig improved his appearance.

GEORGE: What's that supposed to be?
KATE: A cigarette?
GEORGE: It looks more like a toothpick.
KATE: Traditionally, a pipe is used, but I searched the house and couldn't find one.
GEORGE: It's a nonsmoking house.
ANNA: You know what would be awesome?
GEORGE: What?
ANNA: A crack pipe.
KATE: That *would* be great.
GEORGE: Now we have to name him.

Silence.

KATE: Edgar.
GEORGE: Edgar?
KATE: You remember him, don't you?
GEORGE: Of course.
KATE: What happened to him?
GEORGE: I don't know.
ANNA: Who are you talking about?
KATE: You don't remember Edgar?
ANNA: I don't remember a lot of things.
KATE: Edgar. Apartment 3A.

1994

SANTA CRUZ, CALIFORNIA

Scraps of paper folded into quarters were dropped into a plastic pumpkin. Halloween was still a not-so-distant memory. Anna reached her hand into the orange bucket, stirred the pot with her fingers just to be fair. She hand-picked a single scrap from the mass of confetti.

" 'Kresge. Apartment 3A,' " she read aloud. "Who takes point?"

"Should we draw straws again?" George asked.

"Rock, paper, scissors," Kate suggested. She suggested it because it gave her a fighting chance. To lose, that was.

"Fine by me," Anna said, aiming her fist at George.

Anna won. She picked up a bottle of whiskey and turned back to her cohorts.

"Give me ten minutes," she said. "And then you can bring the ice."

■ ■ ■ ■

Anna walked through the Porter College quad into Kresge. Each side of the drive was flanked by student apartments, the bottom floors with giant windows that at night were lit inside, creating a fishbowl view of collegiate life. The curtains on the third window were closed but backlit by a cheap fluorescent lamp. Anna listened at the door. Inside, nothing was stirring. In fact, the silence was such that Anna thought they might have to go back to the pumpkin and draw another room. She knocked, waited, and knocked again. Eventually she heard feet padding toward the door. It swung open, and a tall sophomore who would take ten more years to fill out his emaciated frame stood before her.

"Hello?" he said.

"Apartment 3A?" Anna said, looking at the door.

"Uh, yes."

"Oh, good," Anna said, stealthily slipping through the doorway. "I thought I had the wrong room for a minute."

"Jack's not here, if that's who you're looking for."

"Where is he?"

"At the library."

"I guess we'll have to start without him."

"Start what?"

"Do you have a name?" Anna asked.

"Yes."

"What is it?"

"Edgar."

"Edgar?"

"Yes."

"I like it."

"What are you doing here?" Edgar asked.

"Do you have any glasses?"

"Do we know each other?"

"Forget it. I have some in my bag."

Anna pulled a stack of plastic cups from her backpack and poured Edgar and herself each a healthy serving of whiskey. She handed Edgar his drink.

"Bottoms up," she said, tapping his cup with hers and taking a sip.

Edgar held his drink aloft, still confounded by the surprise visit from this stranger. An attractive woman mysteriously shows up in his apartment with free booze. Surely this was some kind of cruel prank. Cautious by nature, a lover of all things that could be logically explained, Edgar was not quite willing to play along with this game, whatever it was.

In truth, it had a name, and it had been

played at least half a dozen times in the past year. The party con, as the creator was known to call it. News of it had traveled across campus but had not yet reached Edgar, who took his studies seriously and was also too shy to earn the inside line on school gossip.

"Who are you?" he said, still keeping his drink at arm's length.

"Where are my manners?" Anna asked. "Forgive me. I'm Natasha Navarone. Nice to meet you, Edgar."

Anna extended her hand. Edgar, polite by nature, shook it.

"Is there something wrong with your whiskey? Are you a bourbon man?" Anna asked.

"Um, what?"

"Your drink. Is it okay?"

"I was studying."

"Would you like some ice?" Anna asked, going to their freezer. As she'd suspected, the ice trays were empty. "How difficult is it to fill an empty ice tray?" Anna asked.

"I was studying," Edgar repeated.

"Edgar, it's Saturday."

Anna drew the curtains open. The whole point of having the party in the fishbowl was the implicit invitation. She sat down on the couch and patted the seat next to her.

Edgar warily accepted her silent request. Exactly ten minutes from the time Anna had knocked on Edgar's door, there was a second knock — or two knocks, to be precise.

"Don't get up. I'll get it," Anna said.

Anna opened the door just as Kate was taping a watercolor *Party!* sign to it. George lugged the five-pound bag of ice. On the way to their destination, George and Kate had shoved sloppy party invitations under random doors. Then they'd made a run for it. The plan was now in full swing. Within an hour, Edgar's (and Jack's and Heath's and Tree's — yes, that was his name, although he was gone for the night) place would be swarming with revelers, students spilling out onto the steps. The final exchange between Anna and Edgar occurred when she tossed a couple ice cubes into his drink.

"Now try it," she said.

That was the point of no return for Edgar. He gave up and gave in. That night would be a series of firsts for him — his first house party, his first joint, and the first time he fell in love.

Within two hours, Edgar's entire apartment had been overtaken by complete strangers.

He tried to escape to his bedroom, but soon that also was invaded by revelers. He retreated to his bed and made his last stand on his mattress.

Kate often found herself drawn to the victims of Anna's party con. To alleviate their sense of helplessness and confusion, Kate would distract them with conversation, trying to make them feel at home in their own homes. Kate had always been partial to the socially awkward intellectuals.

Without disrupting Edgar's study material, Kate sat on the corner of his bed. Rather than ask the customary questions (*Sophomore? Junior?* They were both sophomores), she used a statement of fact to begin their conversation.

"So, you're a physics major."

"How'd you guess?"

"I deduced."

"Are you a philosophy major?" he asked.

"No. Business."

"Really?"

"Yes," Kate said. Usually when she mentioned her major, the conversation dried up. She veered off the topic with her typical lack of elegance. "Lately I've been really into mushrooms."

"Taking them?"

"No. Studying them. People think

163

mushrooms just equal fungus, but as far as fungi are concerned, the range is beautifully broad and complex, from the edible and medicinal to the toxic and psychoactive mushrooms. Did you know that some mushrooms, identified as tinder fungi, can be used to start fires?"

"Have you ever started a fire with a mushroom?" Edgar asked.

"I wish," Kate said.

Unlike the other coeds with whom Kate had shared her mushroom obsession, Edgar was genuinely interested. She sketched a few pictures so that Edgar could, if necessary, distinguish a toadstool from other fungi, although she cautioned against eating any mushrooms one found in the wild, which Edgar thought was stating the obvious. Her current favorite mushroom was *Amanita muscaria,* also known as fly agaric. It was bright red and mottled with white spots. Kate thought it the most beautiful of all the mushrooms, even though it was poisonous and had psychoactive properties. Still, her readings had informed her, it was unlikely to kill you. Some cultures consumed it as food after it was properly cooked. Kate had drawn a picture of one from a library book and hung it on her wall.

With Kate, Edgar lost that feeling he often

had of always being in the wrong place. Kate broke the ice with her mushroom data, but soon their conversation shifted into warring questions, because they both had more of a need to understand than to be understood.

EDGAR: Tell me the truth. Is this some kind of game?

KATE: We pulled your apartment out of a pumpkin head. Do you mind?

EDGAR: Not anymore.

KATE: Where's home?

EDGAR: Duluth, Minnesota.

KATE: Seriously.

EDGAR: Yes. Have you been?

KATE: I've been almost nowhere.

EDGAR: Where are you from?

KATE: I've lived my whole life in Santa Cruz.

EDGAR: What do your parents do?

KATE: They're dead.

EDGAR: I'm sorry.

KATE: It was a long time ago. Do you have parents?

EDGAR: Yes.

KATE: What do they do?

EDGAR: My mother is a homemaker and my father is a minister.

KATE: A minister? Unbelievable.

EDGAR: It happens on occasion.

KATE: Did your father want you to become a minister?

EDGAR: My brother is taking on that role, so I'm off the hook.

KATE: How does your father feel about you being a physics major?

EDGAR: Are you asking whether our religion conflicts with science?

KATE: I guess so.

EDGAR: We were taught Darwinism at school, and my father believes in the rational world. He doesn't see it in conflict with God.

KATE: So are you very religious?

EDGAR: I'm agnostic, but I pretend for my dad.

KATE: That's nice of you.

EDGAR: It's no trouble and it makes him happy. Who raised you?

KATE: My grandfather. He has a diner in town.

EDGAR: Is he a mycophagist?

KATE: I hope not. What does that mean?

EDGAR: Sorry. I wasn't showing off. I just figured a mushroom enthusiast would know the word.

KATE: I don't. So what does it mean?

EDGAR: A mushroom enthusiast.

KATE: I only got enthused about them last

166

Tuesday.

EDGAR: I see. That changes everything.

KATE: I have to pee now. You can explain yourself when I return.

Even minor events such as using the bathroom can change one's fate. Had Kate not drunk two glasses of water before the party and two vodkas with cranberry juice upon arrival, what happened next might not have happened next. Edgar was unaccustomed to the attentions of women. Kate could see who he would become once he sloughed off that skin of discomfiture. She imagined a caterpillar-like conversion, and she wasn't wrong.

Edgar was on a freshly paved road to a crush. Once his wariness passed, and he became certain that Kate's interest in him wasn't part of yet another con game, he could feel his hands start to sweat. Edgar hung on to his drink, thawing the ice with his heat. She intrigued him. Being around her made him feel something that had no appropriate scientific name, and he felt that that something had the potential to be reciprocated.

After Kate departed, he sat alone, but not truly alone, since bodies elbowed and jostled him as if he were on a crowded subway. Once again, the feeling that he was in the wrong place washed over him.

"Can I get you another drink?" George came in and asked.

She had noted earlier that Edgar was the silent host. Now he was trapped in a corner of his own bedroom clutching an empty cup. She thought she'd help. However, her primary interest was in keeping as much distance as possible between herself and the groping lug who loitered by the doorway. George stepped over several bodies on the floor to reach Edgar. She wedged herself between him and a semiconscious girl in a skirt too short for her semiconscious state. George tugged at the skirt's stretchy fabric, trying to cover up the white panties that were on display. She noted a sneer from across the room from a guy who'd been enjoying the view.

"Show's over, motherfucker," George said.

The dude identified as the motherfucker slunk away when he realized all eyes were on him. Eventually George's heart rate slowed. She returned her attention to Edgar, who had, in the midst of all the chaos, focused his attention on George's legs. Long, tanned, and muscular. He'd seen great legs as defined by the cultural consensus — the long, bony, runway variety. But George's legs were more complicated than that, sinewy and strong, bruised and scarred, war wounds that she proudly displayed. Her knees got most of Edgar's attention. An array of new and fading scars in the shape of scythes convened around the joints. Edgar saw art in the shadow of injuries. He wanted to hear the story behind each one and was intrigued by the fact that she wouldn't hide them. He could never admit something so utterly preposterous, but Edgar was now in love. He was mostly in love with a set of legs, obsessed with a pair of knees, but the legs were attached to a body and mind, and the sudden, heady emotion washed over everything connected to those limbs. There was definitely no scientific name for what he was feeling at that moment.

"Do you want to get out of here?" George asked. "I need to go for a walk or something."

"Yes," Edgar said. He would have said yes to anything she'd asked.

The pair traversed a jungle of bodies to make their escape. Once they reached the door, George overheard Anna describing in great detail the ankle break that had destroyed her figure-skating career.

"See you later, Natasha," George said,

closing the door to apartment 3A.

A month later, Edgar was a habitual visitor to the tiny Fury/Smirnoff/Leoni dorm room at Porter College. For the first few weeks, Anna always screwed up his name — Ernest was the most common error, because *earnest* was the word that described him best. Years later, Edgar had scarcely any memories of talking to Anna (he eventually learned her real name), and when they did speak, their conversations were always rather superficial.

Once, when Edgar knocked on the girls' dorm-room door, Anna opened it and asked him, "What does this building remind you of?"

"I don't know," Edgar said.

"Think about it," Anna said.

"A college dorm?"

Anna motioned for Edgar to gaze down the long hall.

"Now do you see it?"

"The hallway?"

Anna grew impatient and gave him the answer she'd been trying to extract. "Very institutional. Don't you think?"

"I guess so."

"The architects designed prisons. That's what they were known for."

This was an exaggeration based on a shred of truth. After Anna had imparted her bit of misinformation, she left, an attempt to facilitate his budding romance with the roommate she thought he was courting. She assumed the object of his affection was Kate, since Edgar and Kate were an obvious pairing. The fact that George was always in class or at basketball practice while Kate was present for Edgar's visits supported that notion. And Kate too began to think the visits were for her. But Edgar assumed he and Kate were forging a friendship. He had few female confidantes and found comfort in the idea that one day he might be able to tell Kate everything.

An hour after one of Kate and Edgar's study sessions had begun, George returned from basketball practice. What Kate hadn't yet deduced, George already knew. She had seen that look before, but behind Edgar's harmless eyes, there was no threat, and so she let his emotions take form without doing anything deliberate to lead him on. George never knew that Kate had met Edgar first and that she thought of him in ways George never would. Had she known, she would have discouraged him at every turn. Instead, she maintained a level of friendliness that could easily be misinterpreted as encouragement by someone inclined to misinterpret.

"Turn around, Edgar," George said as she proceeded to disrobe.

Edgar looked away, stared at the poster of the gaunt man with his jeans partially undone, and tried to control his sudden erection. That was the tell that Kate did not miss. After George wrapped a towel around herself and headed for the showers, Kate decided to test her instincts.

"I think I need to go to the library. You in?" she said, gathering her books.

"No. I'm almost done with the assignment. I think I'll head back," Edgar said.

They collected their respective study materials and departed in unison. Only Kate noticed that Edgar had left one of his physics books behind. Kate had grown accustomed to being invisible to men when in George's company, but she'd always thought that Edgar saw her. Discovering otherwise hit Kate hard, although no one would see it. Kate thought that pining over a guy was the ultimate indignity. She went to the library to wait out whatever was going to transpire at Porter College. She tried to lose herself in a book on Morse code.

As it turned out, nothing transpired. George returned to the room, put on her pajamas, and studied for a biology exam. Edgar knocked on the door exactly twenty minutes after he'd left and inquired as to whether she had seen his physics book. George retrieved the physics book and handed it to him as he stood outside the door.

"See you later, Edgar," George said.

" 'Look in the closet' or 'There is no Santa Claus,' " Anna said, reading off strips of paper once again culled from the basin of a plastic pumpkin.

George would have liked to attend a party without a mission, but Kate was so used to missions and games and plots that it never occurred to her to protest. And this was one game she liked.

"The first one," Kate said.

"Whatever," George said.

"Do you need to write it down?" Anna asked.

George was prone to forgetting the code phrase, or so she claimed. Reluctantly, she took the slip of paper from Anna and stuffed it in her pocket.

This party was a legitimate one, not a con. It took place in a three-bed-room off-campus apartment that belonged to grad students in the English lit department. Anna had recently begun a friendship/flirtation with her American lit TA. She frequented his office hours, always in an attempt to get a grade changed. She managed this approximately 30 percent of the time, according to her notes. Reed Bannister, PhD candidate, had moral codes — he stood by his grades, and he didn't date students. Anna, however, was good at cracking codes.

"When you were a child, were you afraid of monsters?" Kate asked the first person she encountered at the party. It happened to be Lane Smith, a theater major who was never seen without a colorful scarf around her neck and wild, wayward hair that appeared unstyled but took hours to fashion.

"No, but I had an imaginary friend named Lucy," Lane said.

"Where did Lucy live?" Kate asked.

"With me."

"She didn't hang out in any particular part of your bedroom?"

"No."

"You never had to go look for her or anything?"

"No."

"I see," Kate said. "How about ghosts? Did you have any ghosts in your house?"

Anna tried a different tack. She approached the preppiest male in the room.

"Do you play golf?" she asked.

"Sometimes," Preppy Male said.

"If you were to instruct someone on how to find your golf clubs, what would you say?"

"Look in the trunk of my car."

"No, that's not it," Anna said, meandering away.

The triumvirate settled around the keg, refilled their cups, and shared notes.

"I'm getting nowhere with the monsters-as-a-child method," said Kate.

"For future reference, if you ask a stranger to borrow his clothes, he finds it suspect," George said.

"Back to the drawing board," Anna said.

"I have an idea," said George. "Why don't we just enjoy the party?"

"Now, where's the fun in that?" Anna said.

"What's the game, Anna?" her TA asked, approaching the group with an empty glass.

"What game?" Anna said, playing innocent.

"Your friends are asking my friends ridiculous questions."

"My friends can be ridiculous at times."

"You are a very strange woman," Reed Bannister said to Anna.

"Thanks," said Anna. Had he told her she had the manners of a truck driver or the ethics of a bank robber, she would have replied in the same tone. Anna maintained a thick skin by never being inside it.

Meanwhile, George was ready for the game to end. She instructed Kate to hide in the closet so that she could ask someone where Kate went.

"That seems like a shortcut," Kate said.

"That's the point," said George. "Now, please, get in the closet."

Reed Bannister came closer to Anna and whispered, "In fifteen minutes, meet me outside."

"I don't think so," Anna said, but they both knew she was bluffing.

Reed departed just as Edgar stepped across the threshold. He scanned the room nervously. Not even a minute passed before he felt out of place. Anna saw him turn around abruptly as if he were about to make a run for it.

"Edgar! Get back in here," she shouted.

Edgar followed her instructions, as most people did.

"Glad you could make it," she said.

Edgar searched the room, looking for the woman he was always looking for. "I'm not sure I can stay," Edgar said when he couldn't find her.

"You need to tell her," Anna said.

"Excuse me?"

"You know what I'm talking about," Anna said. Although Anna was talking about Kate, and Edgar was thinking about George. "I know her. She won't say anything until you do. You have to tell her how you feel and you have to do it tonight."

Edgar summoned courage from some mysterious recess in his mind.

"Where is she?" he asked.

Anna answered, reluctantly ending her own game.

1998

SANTA CRUZ, CALIFORNIA

"Did you know there's a woman sleeping in our closet?" George asked.

"She moved in a few days ago," Kate said, coating her toast with a thick layer of butter. "I've been meaning to introduce you, but you haven't been around."

"Who is she?"

"Sarah Lake."

"Where did she come from?" George asked.

"Do you mean what city and state? Humboldt is where she was last living. I'm not sure where she was born. I can ask her when she wakes up," Kate said.

"Why is she here?" George said.

"She needed a place to stay. And the hall closet is big enough to sleep in. Anna always said we should turn it into a guest room."

"How long is she staying?"

"I don't know. But she's paying rent."

"What? So it's permanent?"

178

"I don't think any of us are staying here permanently."

George checked her watch, unhitched a banana from its bunch, and poured a cup of coffee into a commuter mug.

"She's not staying," George said. "This is a whole human being. It's not like a stray cat."

"You didn't let me keep the cat," Kate said. She had never argued about the cat, which only fueled her resentment. It was short-haired, and there were shots, and some people just got over cat allergies. All points she'd made in her head when she carried the Abyssinian mix in a pillowcase to the pound.

"I have allergies!" George snapped.

"Now you have a human allergy?" Kate asked.

"You can't just invite people to move in here."

"Before you rush to a decision, maybe you should meet her first," Kate said.

It was, in fact, Anna who'd first met Sarah Lake, the closeted houseguest. But later she would not recall their introduction.

For two weeks straight, Anna had lived in the library, studying for her organic chemistry final. She was barely passing the

179

class going into the final exam. Sometimes Anna would study with Kate, making 3-D molecular models. But Kate always managed to digest the material in a fraction of the time it took Anna, assembling her model like a child playing with Legos.

Anna was living on caffeine and Ritalin and gummy bears and beef jerky. In the library, it was hard to miss the pajama-clad woman with an overcoat and matted hair. She was afraid to stop, like the driver of a car with a recently jump-started battery. Her skin took on a blue-yellow tone. Her hands had a Parkinson's tremor; she couldn't trust that she hadn't accidentally stabbed an extra electron on the Lewis dot structure. Sometimes merely looking at a hydrocarbon chain would bring her close to tears. Nucleotides went down easy. DNA, RNA, their relevance to medicine, the human body, shook her awake. But the snaky polymers and peptides, those fucking endless impenetrable carbon chains, made her forget everything she'd learned. She scratched her neck until it bled. Kate put a bandage on Anna's scratches and covered her fingers in sports tape. One night, Anna entered the front door, sat down on the floor to remove her shoes, and fell asleep in the foyer.

Kate woke her early the next morning and fed her coffee, and the cycle started all over again.

The final exam was on Tuesday from ten to noon. When the TA collected Anna's Scantron, he raised his eyebrow with an unspoken question. Anna shrugged. She refused to predict her performance, having surprised herself too many times with abysmal test results on exams she'd thought she had aced. Anna left the physical sciences building at 12:05 p.m. with other bleary-eyed students. While many congregated for an exam postmortem, Anna was done, like an assembly-line worker clocking out for the day. There was no need to revisit any of it. She walked, with no destination in mind, just away.

A winking neon sign beckoned her. She could have sworn she witnessed a letter die, like an old square flashbulb. Now the sign said Pet E ra. Anna decided then that if she ever opened a bar, she'd call it Pet Era. She even wrote the name on her forearm so she wouldn't forget. She opened the door. Inside, it smelled of whiskey and beer and bleach; that was good enough for her. She entered the tavern. Darkness had never been so inviting.

"What's your poison?" an unusually tall woman with dirty-blond hair and white-girl dreads asked with a touch of irony.

"Whiskey, with a beer back," Anna said.

Two men, regulars, chatted at the edge of the bar, griping over politics, the economy, the End of Days. Anna listened only so she could blot out the battling formulas and compounds that dusted her brain, like a chalkboard haphazardly erased between lessons. The whiskey helped, and so did the beer. She knew how this day would end. That familiar sensation would return — the need to do something wrong. Anna ordered another round and thought about calling Kate or George as a preemptive strike, but she knew they'd show up too soon. Anna scratched her home number on the back of a coaster and called the bartender over.

"When it's time for me to go, will you call this number? Ask for Kate."

The bartender looked at the coaster and then returned her gaze to the young woman, already on her second round before one in the afternoon.

"You got a name?" she asked. "I figure I better be able to identify you to whoever I'm calling."

"Anna."

"I'm Sarah. Nice to meet you."

"Can I get another round?"

Sarah put a bowl of salted nuts in front of Anna. "Eat the nuts and then we'll talk."

Four hours later, Anna was slumped in a booth with a dodgy-looking guy wearing a trucker hat and sunglasses and sporting a Fu Manchu mustache. Happy hour was in full swing. Sarah knew the man's look was most likely just the result of a series of bad fashion choices, but it came off as a sketchy disguise, and Sarah began to feel uneasy, having time to clock Anna only occasionally out of the corner of her eye.

Sarah picked up the phone and dialed the number.

"Is there a Kate there? Hi, I'm a bartender at Pete's Emerald. It's on Pacific Avenue and Water Street. You should pick up your friend Anna. She's had a few and, uh, is currently keeping some questionable company."

Anna's plan to drink her studies into oblivion had backfired. Her final exam clung to her like a remora. She exhausted the disguised man as she droned on explaining organic chemistry to him, though she could barely explain it to herself anymore. His eyes darted about the room in search of another diversion.

Kate arrived half an hour later. When

Anna saw her, she had a sudden recollection of a series of mnemonics that Kate had contrived to help her on an anatomy test. Anna had no knack for mnemonics, so she'd gladly relinquished the job. Kate dove into the assignment with great aplomb, but Anna managed to recall them only because of their sheer preposterousness.

"Sammy Likes Taking Paul's Teeth To Charlie's House. Scaphoid, lunate, triquetrum, pisiform, trapezium, trapezoid, capitate, hamate.

"Tom Creates Nuclear Missiles Inside Locust Caves. Talus, calcaneus, navicular, medial cuneiform, intermediate cuneiform, lateral cuneiform, cuboid."

The disguised man wrapped his arm around her waist and whispered in sour-beef-and-cheap-beer breath, "Shut the fuck up."

"I can't," Anna whispered back. She couldn't.

Kate stood in front of the table with her arms folded in disappointment. "Did you come here right after the test?"

"Hello, little girl," the disguised man said.

"I thought I told you not to talk to strangers," Kate said to Anna.

"Why don't you take a seat, sweetheart?"

"Why don't you take a hike, mister?" Kate

184

said. She was usually incapable of that kind of bold retort but was buoyed by the public space and Anna's presence, as if Kate could somehow own part of Anna's powerful persona when that part was missing from Anna herself. Not unlike the way atoms share electrons.

"You don't have to be like that," the man said in a sly, reptilian voice.

Sarah watched the proceedings cautiously. The disguised man was a regular. Never caused any trouble. But men and booze and someone interfering with a potential fuck were a combustible mixture. Sarah finished wiping dishwasher spots off a glass and approached the trio.

"I think this one has had enough," she said.

"I think she'd like to stay for another round," the disguised man said.

"Yes! One more round," Anna slurred.

"I'm afraid I'm going to have to refuse service," Sarah said.

A guy in denim and layers of cotton and polyester with carefully coifed bedhead who appeared to be somebody important (at least in the hierarchy of Pete's Emerald) entered the bar. He approached the tense congregation, took one look at Anna, and said, "Get her out of here."

Kate helped Anna to her feet. Anna broke free and cut a switchback to the door, then shouted "Serpentine!" in a weak Peter Falk impression. "I want to see that movie again," she said to no one in particular.

Sarah and Kate followed Anna outside in a straight line.

"Where's your car?" Sarah asked.

"What car?" Kate said.

Ten minutes later, Kate and Sarah loaded Anna into a pristine 1972 charcoal-gray Mercedes two-door. Anna was encouraged to hang her head out of the window like a dog on a road trip.

"Don't even think about vomiting." Sarah put the key in the ignition and started the car. She adjusted the seat, turned the windshield wipers on and off, and pulled onto the road.

"Thank you," Kate said. "That was going to be one long walk home."

"You couldn't borrow a car?"

"I could. But I couldn't drive it."

"How do you live in California without knowing how to drive?"

"Buses. And hitching rides. It's easier than you'd think, and I don't have the responsibility of a vehicle."

"You should learn how to drive," Sarah

Lake said.

"That's what people tell me."

"Does your friend always drink like that?" Sarah asked.

"It's a little early in the day for her. At least, it was when she got started. But it's finals week. She hasn't been herself lately."

Sarah and Kate propped Anna's arms over their shoulders, walked her through the front door and up the stairs to her bedroom, tossed her on the bed, and tipped her onto her side. Kate removed Anna's shoes and socks and threw a blanket over her. Later, Kate would force her to consume three glasses of water, a liter of Gatorade, and four slices of toast. But for now she let Anna sleep.

Kate walked the Good Samaritan to the door and said, "If you ever need anything, you know where to find us."

The next day, accompanied by a wicked hangover, Anna flew back east for a short visit with her family. Colin had a new girlfriend to be vetted; she was the same as all the other girlfriends, Anna thought after she met her. Over dinner one night at the Union Oyster House, Anna said, "Does Pet Era mean anything to you?" She turned away from her parents' blank look to her brother and his date. The woman's name she would remember as Tanya, but really it was Anya.

"No," Colin said, sucking down his sixth shuck of the night.

"Is it a band?" Anna asked.

"I don't know. Did you look it up on the Internet?"

"It takes forever. Nothing came up but pet stores."

"Maybe it is a pet store," Colin said.

"Why would I write the name of a pet store on my arm?" Anna said.

"Can we please change the subject," Lena said, which brought all conversation to a halt.

"You said if I ever needed anything," Sarah said, standing in the doorway of the High Street house on a Saturday night. Kate was home alone and had had no plans until Sarah arrived.

An hour later, Kate was perched on a fire escape outside the window of Sarah's apartment building, the center block of three neglected brick squares. Laundry hung on lines stretching to the next building, and television noise vied for airspace, creating a cacophony of jingles, laugh tracks, and screams.

"What happened to your key?" Kate asked.

"I've got it somewhere," Sarah said from inside the apartment. She leaned her head out the window and passed a brown grocery bag brimming with clothes to Kate.

"This would be a lot easier if you found your key."

"Not really. The key doesn't work."

"Huh?"

"Manager changed the locks. Asshole."

"Why?"

"I stopped paying rent when I saw the mouse."

"I see."

"Do you want to come inside? I think the gas is still on. I can make you a cup of tea while I'm packing."

Kate could hear the three admonishments her *deda* had repeated in broken English many times over the course of ten years. "Tree tings you remember: One, you a citizen, you vote. Two, don't vaste your money on nonsense. Tree, don't break laws. American prisons like summer camp compared to my country, but you still shouldn't break laws."

"I guess I'll just stay out here," Kate said.

Sarah dropped a suitcase and five grocery bags off the fire escape. She climbed down after Kate. They gathered Sarah's most valued possessions and lugged them in the shadows to a late-model Cadillac with fuzzy dice and a pine-tree air freshener hanging from the rearview mirror.

"What happened to your other car, the Mercedes?" Kate asked.

"That wasn't my car."

The High Street house was empty when Kate and Sarah got there. George had a date with a man who washed and waxed his Porsche in their driveway every weekend. Kate never bothered to learn his name. She called him Spyder, after his car.

Kate found a bottle of bourbon that she had hidden from Anna pre-finals. She poured Sarah a double on ice (what Anna drank) and two fingers for herself (her *deda*'s allotted nightcap).

Over the course of the evening, as they drank and Sarah created a decent pasta dish culled from canned and packaged goods, Kate heard the *Reader's Digest* version of Sarah's life — that obligatory download of information that happens when two strangers are in a confined space.

Sarah had been raised in the foster-care system in Oakland, California, her father unknown, her mother dead of a drug overdose when Sarah was eight. A string of households followed, ranked from acceptable to terrifying; some molestation was mentioned in passing, and a few brushes with the law (nothing too serious, theft mostly); she spent some time in juvie and then was emancipated from the state. Homeless for a year. Then she found a job waiting tables, got an apartment, quit smoking pot all day long, and met her girlfriend. She and Sonia had moved to Humboldt County six months ago. They broke up a month after they arrived. Sonia fell in love with someone else. Sarah hitched a ride to Santa Cruz, talked her way into the Pete's Emerald job and an apartment without a security deposit, and she'd been there ever since.

Kate was certain her life paled by comparison, but she provided the brush-strokes of it anyway. She told Sarah about her parents' deaths and about being raised by her *deda.* She talked about her plans to take over the diner, a goal Sarah found far more reasonable than Anna or George did. And she mentioned her current obsession: nineteenth-century prison slang.

"It was called flash language," Kate said.

"Huh. Give me an example," said Sarah.

"There are three different words that all

mean 'shoes.' *Crabshells, hopper-dockers,* and *stamps.* My favorite word for 'shirt' is *flesh bag.* The slang for 'tanked' is *floored,* like on the floor. Also, if I handed you a knife and told you to cheese it, that meant stow it."

Kate talked about flash language for another ten minutes, until it became clear her audience was bored. Sarah asked about the missing roommates.

"What's Anna like when she's not floored?"

"Anna always tries to make things bigger, more exciting than they are. She can turn a trip to the grocery store into an event. That can sometimes get old. But she also makes you do things you'd never think of doing."

"And George?"

"George has your back. I was at this party off campus and this guy was bothering me, asking for my ID, calling me a little girl. He was standing way too close, breathing his vile beer breath on me, and I kept telling him to back off but he wouldn't listen. George came over, told him to step away. He didn't. She warned him one more time, didn't really wait for it to register, and then punched him in the nose. Hurt her hand and couldn't play basketball for a week. She's a regular flibbing gloak. That means 'pugilist.' "

Kate and Sarah ate dinner and drank and then Kate gave her a brief tour of the house. Sarah lingered in rooms and opened cupboards as if she were surveying real estate for purchase. It was then that Sarah found the enormous walk-in closet in the entryway. Five minutes later, they were negotiating a deal. Kate didn't see a downside. They used the closet only for coats, and Kate had always thought it would make a nice bedroom. Kate's cut of the two hundred dollars a month was enough to feed her for two weeks and two days, if she didn't go out to dinner.

Sarah had been living in the closet for three days before George noticed she had a new roommate. This was the argument that Kate presented to Anna once she returned home to play tiebreaker.

Anna, weary from the six-hour flight and the seventy-two hours with her family, was not unmoved by the fact that Sarah had saved her from the disguised man in the bar or that she had grown up in the foster-care system or that she had done time.

"She goes or I go," George said.

"Sorry, Kate," Anna said. "Give her three days to find another place."

Kate shot dagger eyes at George, who returned the look with an icy stare.

"Do you want me to tell her?" Anna asked.

"No," Kate said. "I'll do it."

Kate walked the 1.8 miles to Pete's Emerald. Behind the counter was a man who looked like a Pete, or like the kind of guy who opened a bar with his name on it.

"Is Sarah working tonight?"

The man Kate believed to be Pete shook his head and chuckled grimly. He raised an eyebrow and revealed his right incisor with a snarl. "Nope. She's not working tonight or any other night."

"Did you fire her?"

"What's it to you, sweetheart?"

"She was living with me," Kate said.

"Well, I'd check my silverware drawers if I were you."

"Excuse me?"

"She cleaned out the cash register two nights ago. Haven't seen her since."

As Kate ran home in the rain, she thought that this would be a really good time to know how to drive. Once inside, she tracked water through the hallway and opened the closet. It was empty except for a sleeping bag rolled up in a tight fist in the corner. On the floor was an old weathered postcard. A standard shot of the Golden Gate Bridge.

Kate flipped over the card and read the single line written in rushed script.

I was never one for goodbyes.

SL

2001

BOSTON, MASSACHUSETTS

"Hello, darling. Where have you been hiding?" Hunter Stevens III asked as he parked himself in a silver Chiavari chair next to Anna.

"In plain view," Anna said. She was hard to miss, she thought, dressed in coral pink punctuating a room decorated in white and silver.

"What are you doing later?" Hunter asked.

"I suppose I'll get another drink," Anna said, staring down at her empty glass.

"And then what?" Hunter asked.

"Then . . . then I'm getting out of this fucking dress," Anna said.

"If you need any help, let me know."

Anna was thinking that his parents had named him perfectly. Then she was quietly calculating how many IIIs were attending her brother's wedding. The percentage was well above average even for a tony Boston affair.

"I'll do that," Anna said dryly. A few lines of small talk with Hunter were all that Anna could stomach. She wobbled over to the bar, cursing the mandatory heels and yanking up on her strapless bridesmaid's dress. The bust was tailored for manufactured breasts, and Anna spent much of the night readjusting, at first privately, then publicly, as the booze untied the already loose knot on her social graces.

"How ladylike," Anna's mother said as they crossed paths in the ballroom. Anna rolled her eyes but didn't respond. Her mother's full-time job for the past nine months had been planning her son's wedding. Somehow Lena Fury had managed to shove aside the mother of the bride and the bride herself to become the chief operating officer of the Fury/Wentworth nuptials. Fortunately, Lena had the kind of taste that is admired by people who take weddings seriously. The consequence of the bride's loss of control was the pristine white tablecloths, white roses, white everything, with just a hint of platinum to remind people that there was a cost to the whole affair. The pink bridesmaid's dresses were an unfortunate compromise that Lena had had to accept. The bride's favorite color.

Taking in the room, Anna thought the

whole thing looked cold, but then, snow was white. And the guests had an icy way about them. It was as if everyone had emerged from a meat locker. The booze melted a few souls, but not many.

She found her brother chatting with Malcolm at the bar. She had noticed earlier that the bride and groom worked the room separately, as if they were dividing the crowd for their future divorce. When Anna approached, Colin put his arm around his sister and drew her close.

"Has Mom started enjoying herself yet?" Colin asked.

"Does she ever enjoy herself?" Anna said. "Beer, please," she said to the bartender. "No, you don't need to pour it in a glass. I'll take the bottle."

Anna took a healthy, boyish swig. Out of the corner of her eye, she could see her mother scowling at the sight of her daughter guzzling beer like she was in a biker bar.

"You're just doing that to annoy Mom," Colin said.

"What's your point?" she said.

"No point. I saw you talking to Hunter," Colin teased.

"He was talking to me."

"He was on the list."

"What list?" Malcolm asked.

"I gave Anna a list of all my friends she should stay away from tonight."

"Am I on the list?"

"Of course not," Anna said, grinning at Malcolm.

Anna had been thirteen when Malcolm came into their lives. He had witnessed her clumsy entrance into adolescence and her resistant entrance into adulthood. It would never have occurred to Colin that he couldn't trust Malcolm with his sister, though Colin should have realized that it wasn't his sister he needed to worry about. She was the predator in any scenario.

"So what happened at the bachelor party?" Anna inquired.

A tic of tension crossed Colin's face, then vanished. Colin had impressive control of his emotions. But Anna had learned to read his microexpressions.

Her question was typical Fury passive aggression. Anna was drunk and annoyed that so much of her recent life had been devoted to painful bridal showers (plural — she hadn't been able to get out of her obligatory attendance at more than one), inefficient dress fittings, and endless conversation about the upcoming nuptials. Her brother was marrying because it was time; he was thirty-one, his wife was well connected, and he'd bowed to the ultimatum that Megan gave him exactly eighteen months after they began dating. But Anna knew her brother, his proclivities. Because Colin had made an unwise decision, Anna had to suffer through the wedding. And for what? He wasn't ready. He would fuck this up. Anna was surprised only by how quickly the fucking-up had commenced.

"The bachelor party was like any other bachelor party," Colin said, giving away nothing.

"So, then, why aren't you and the bride speaking?" Anna said, taking another gulp of beer. "I should have ordered whiskey."

"You should slow down," Colin said. "Excuse me. I think I'll dance with my wife."

Malcolm shook his head at Anna. "Why don't you behave yourself?"

"Why don't you make me?" Anna said, then turned to the bartender and ordered a whiskey.

"You think that's a good idea?" Malcolm asked.

"I ordered it for you," Anna said, sliding it across the bar.

Another of Colin's college buddies slithered over.

"Anna, looking lovely as ever," Gabe said.

Her dress was slipping again, and Malcolm caught Gabe shamelessly leering before he became distracted by the stable of liquor.

"Is he on the list?" Malcolm quietly asked Anna.

"I think so," Anna said. "If not, I'll add him."

Once Gabe had his drink in hand, he turned to Anna and said, "Before the night is through, Anna, you are going to dance with me."

"I'll catch you later," Anna said. Then she looked at Malcolm. "Get me out of here."

Malcolm slugged back his whiskey, took Anna's arm, and led her out of the room as if she were an invalid. Uncomfortable heels will do that to a woman.

"You can't keep her all to yourself," Gabe slurred, although he was already scoping the white room for another pink silhouette.

"Sorry, buddy, you're on the list," Malcolm shouted over his shoulder.

"What list?"

When Anna retired to her room, she called the front desk.

"Lenox Hotel, how may I direct your call?"

"Malcolm Davis's room, please."

"One moment."

201

The phone rang twice and Malcolm picked up.

"Hello?"

"I'm in room 511," Anna said. "I need your help." She hung up the phone, knowing that Malcolm would be more likely to come if he was ignorant of the motive. Five minutes later, there was a knock. Anna swung open the door, still in pink.

"You rang?"

"I can't get this fucking dress off," Anna said.

Malcolm entered the room, turned Anna around, and tried the zipper. He tried again, with a little more effort. Still it wouldn't budge.

"Hurry up," she said, panicking.

"I'm trying," he said.

"What's the problem?"

"Something's wrong with the zipper."

"Fuck."

"Can you learn a new word?"

"Can you just get the fucking dress off?"

"I don't want to ruin the dress."

"Why not? I'll never wear it again."

Malcolm wrenched apart the back of the dress like it was a stubborn bag of potato chips. Anna threw herself out of the gown like it was a straitjacket. Malcolm quickly averted his gaze.

Anna sighed. "Why do you have to be so decent?"

Malcolm wasn't thinking decent thoughts. He was thinking that he, too, should have been on that list. He headed for the door to forestall any more trouble. Anna rushed to the door to block his exit, wearing only her underwear. Malcolm wasn't sure where to look. He stared up at the ceiling when he spoke.

"You should go to bed now, Anna."

"I'm not tired."

"Then put your pajamas on and watch TV for a while."

"That sounds so boring."

"Anna, I need to leave this room right now."

Anna tugged on Malcolm's tie, trying to release the slipknot. Malcolm put his hands over hers and kept them in place. His hands were warm and they sent a shiver through her. He finally looked at her, pleading.

"What's wrong?" she asked.

"You're drunk," he said. "Too drunk."

"So what?" Anna whispered.

Then she kissed him. He was warm and sweet and he tasted like mint toothpaste. She felt Malcolm's hands slide down her waist and rest on her hips. There they froze. He gently pushed her away.

"I'll make you a deal," he said.

"What?"

"Let's get you sobered up first. See if you change your mind."

"And what if I don't?"

"Then we'll come back here. Okay?"

"Okay."

"Now put some clothes on."

Anna threw on a pair of jeans and a sweater. Malcolm averted his gaze once again.

"Why do you have to be such a gentleman?" Anna asked.

"Just so you'll know how to identify one in a lineup."

Anna and Malcolm sat in the back booth of a diner they'd found just a few short miles from the hotel. Anna ate French fries and apple pie. Malcolm sipped on a Coke. He studied her for too long. Anna noticed.

"Something on your mind?" she asked.

"I just can't believe you're going to be a doctor," Malcolm said. Nostalgia was creeping into his conversation.

"Are you worried about the state of modern medicine?"

"No. It's just that I remember when you were *thirteen.*"

"When you saved my life?" Anna asked.

204

Her memory of the incident was a fond one. For Malcolm, it was different, uncomfortable. They were both recalling the events of a family vacation at the Furys' Adirondack cabin. Colin had met Malcolm his first year at Princeton. They lived across the hall from each other. They were different kinds of men, the differences allowing their friendship to thrive. Perhaps that was where Anna had developed her theory.

Anna had just turned thirteen. Her mother had prematurely bought her a training bra, which existed more as a threat of things to come. Then, Anna had still felt right in her body. A few months later, she'd add an extra layer of clothing as armor. But that day she was a little girl who feared only dusk, because that was when the voices would call to her, forcing her out of the water. She swam off the private beach, as she had every summer since she'd learned to swim. She had recently heard about people who could hold their breath for five, ten minutes, even longer. She once did sixty seconds, timed by her brother. She didn't believe him; she thought it was longer. For Christmas she asked for a waterproof watch so she could time herself. She dove under at the end of the pier so she could wrap herself around its wooden leg.

Forty seconds and she released all the air in her lungs; sixty seconds and she felt as if her body might explode. But she told herself that it was all in her head. If someone could do five minutes or more, surely she could manage ninety seconds. At seventy, she pushed off the bottom of the lake to get to the surface and smacked her head on the edge of the pier.

"Is she okay?" Malcolm asked when Anna was underwater and unconscious.

Colin had left his glasses inside. He couldn't see a thing. Lena barely looked up from her legs as she slathered on suntan oil.

"She's fine," Lena said.

Malcolm couldn't see anything past the pier. He got to his feet and slowly walked the planks until he saw Anna in her rainbow-colored swimsuit floating face-down on the surface. He dove into the water and wrapped his right arm around her. He pulled her onto the dock, put her on her back, and pressed on her chest wall to empty her lungs of water. Anna coughed convulsively. Malcolm's heart pounded so fiercely he had to rest on his haunches to catch his breath. When he turned to look at the beach, he found Colin racing toward them. Lena followed without any sense of urgency, cocking her head to the side as if the image of her daughter gasping for breath on the dock was just a minor hiccup in the afternoon.

After that day, Malcolm continued to be polite to Lena, but he could manage nothing more.

Inside the diner, Anna reached into her purse and put on a pair of sunglasses. The fluorescent diner lights were as blinding as the sun at high noon; perhaps the goal was to trick you into believing it was lunchtime all the time.

"You look ridiculous," Malcolm said.

"The lights are giving me a headache."

"Are you feeling better?"

"I'm feeling less drunk, which has nothing to do with feeling better."

"Good. That was the plan."

"I haven't changed my mind," Anna said.

"The night is young," Malcolm said. "Drink more water."

That was the last thing Anna would remember from that night. No more details would ever return.

What happened next she would learn secondhand, two days later, when she finally regained consciousness at Massachusetts General Hospital.

The nurse found Anna awake and called her family. The first familiar face she saw was her mother's.

"What have you done?" her mother said.

1997

SANTA CRUZ, CALIFORNIA

"What have you done?" George asked Anna as she studied the assembly of beer cans on their balcony.

"I made a castle out of beer cans," Anna said.

"It doesn't look like a castle."

"Sure it does," Anna said, admiring her architecture.

"No, it doesn't. But that's not the point."

"Does there always have to be a point?" Anna said quickly. She was talking faster than usual, which was already fast.

"Why would you make a castle out of beer cans?"

"If I didn't do it, who would?"

Anna wasn't herself, George thought, and she had been thinking that a lot lately. But now, Anna seemed so unfamiliar, George felt obligated to become acquainted with her new roommate.

"Did you study today?" George asked.

"I studied for six hours straight, went for a jog, took a shower, and made a castle out of beer cans. Now I'm going to study some more."

"You seem to have more energy than usual."

"I'd have to agree with you," Anna said. "And more focus."

Anna went inside and wiped down the kitchen countertop with a sponge. George noticed the spotless sink, a sink that was usually mountainous with used dishes and cutlery. While George was concerned, she couldn't ignore that this version of Anna was in some ways an improvement over the other.

"Did you clean the kitchen?"

"I think I did while I was trying to wrap my head around a physics problem. Physics. That's going to be my downfall. Figuratively, not literally. Although you never know."

Anna sat down at the kitchen table and opened up her battered test-prep bible. It was as if George no longer existed.

George needed to consult Kate for some answers. Kate, these days, was always easy to consult. George found her in her usual spot, downstairs in the unfinished basement. The room was outfitted with an old couch, a television, and a 1970s-style bar. There were wood beams overhead; exposed pipes lined the walls. The girls had never found mold in their many searches, but they knew it was there. It felt like the room was in a cold sweat. A single low-wattage bulb hung from the ceiling, providing just enough light so that you didn't trip over anything on your way to the couch.

Kate's gaze remained fixed on the television. George sat down next to her, crowding her into the corner next to the armrest.

"What's going on with Anna?"

"Don't know."

"Did you see what she did with those beer cans?"

"Yep," Kate said, eyes still on the idiotic television show.

"Do you know why she built it?"

"I asked. She said, 'Castles don't build themselves.' "

"Something is wrong with her."

"She's taking study pills," Kate explained.

"What are study pills?"

"I asked her what's in them and she said they're just caffeine."

"Do you believe her?" George said.

"I'm not sure. Have you seen how clean the kitchen is?" Kate asked.

It briefly occurred to George that she was living with two drug addicts — only Kate's drug was mindless television.

"What are you watching?"

"Separated at Birth."

"What's it about?"

"Just what it sounds like. Identical twin brothers separated at birth. One is raised by hippies; the other by two type A parents, a doctor and a lawyer. Then the brothers find each other and become roommates, only their differences drive each other crazy. The same actor plays both brothers, in case you were wondering."

"I wasn't," George said. "I thought studies showed that identical twins were often quite similar, even if they were separated at birth."

"They both like chocolate milk and double-knot their shoelaces, but other than that, it's an *Odd Couple* rip-off. Besides, what's the point in an actor playing dual roles if both characters are exactly the same?"

"It looks awful," George said over a blaring laugh track.

"It's badly executed but in theory a good idea. I really like studies on twins. They're the perfect control group. They should make it mandatory. All twins have to volunteer for at least one nature/nurture experiment. Of course they would be paid handsomely for their troubles, especially if something went wrong."

George picked up the remote and pressed the Mute button.

"Other than contemplating ways to take away the basic human rights of identical twins, what did you do today?"

"The usual."

"Don't you think it's about time to mix things up?"

"I'm retired."

"You're not retired."

"This is what retired people do."

"Actually, they play golf. Do you want me to book you a tee time for tomorrow? Even that would be an improvement."

"Need clubs," Kate said, retrieving the remote and unmuting the sound.

"Kate, he did you a favor. He didn't want you to have his life."

"But *I* wanted that life."

"You can have a better life," said George. "Be ambitious."

"That's so American of you."

"Your grandfather was from the old country. Not you."

"Shhh, my show is on."

■ ■ ■ ■

Three months earlier, Kate had graduated from college. Only one month after that, she announced her retirement. George's forestry degree was a five-year plan, and Anna stayed in school another year to bolster her med-school applications with a chemistry minor. While Kate's mind and body atrophied in front of the television, Anna and George went about their lives. George would on occasion remind Kate that even retired people did things. Kate argued that the point of being retired was to be free to do all of the things you couldn't do as a working stiff. What she wanted to do, she insisted, was watch television.

At first George and Anna had thought it was just a phase. A family member's death, the loss of a job, graduation, and a sudden influx of cash are bound to have a ripple effect. A few weeks of idleness, maybe a month or two, was reasonable, but George didn't see any end in sight. Kate woke up every morning, turned on the television, and stared, stopping only for a few necessary chores, bathroom breaks, food, or a summons from her roommates. When pressed about her future plans, Kate came up blank.

Her future had always been mapped out. The map was still there, but the roads had all changed, leaving Kate stranded in the middle of nowhere.

Kate liked rituals and order. Not that she was tidy, but her sense of adventure was limited to accompanying Anna when Anna's sense of adventure struck. But Anna these days was a slave to the books, in part because she had not been enough of a slave to them during the past four years.

"This is an easy one," Kate said, reading from the practice test. " 'What is the most likely side effect of a sympathetic nervous system inhibitor? (A) increased pupil diameter; (B) decreased blood supply to the skin; (C) decreased heart rate; (D) auditory exclusion;' or (E) a sudden and inexplicable need for potato chips."

"Can you stop adding option E?" Anna asked. "It just makes it harder to concentrate."

"I add option E only on the easy questions."

"How do you know what's easy or not?"

"If I know the answer, it's easy," Kate said.

"You know the answer without looking at the key?" Anna said skeptically.

"Yes."

"What is it?"

"The sympathetic nervous system is basically the fight-or-flight response, the way the body responds to stress. If a drug is an inhibitor of the sympathetic nervous system, then it would have the opposite effect of stress. The answer is C, decreased heart rate, because if you're stressed out, your heart isn't going to slow down."

Anna snatched the book out of Kate's hand. "You're learning too much. I'm going to have to cut you off. But you're right. That was any easy question. I would have gotten it, too, if you hadn't mentioned potato chips."

"I'm hungry," Kate said.

"Do we have food?"

"No."

Like a cosmic intervention, there was a ring at the front door.

Neither Kate nor Anna was expecting company. Their familiarity with the random visitors in their neighborhood had hardened them to people soliciting for magazines, children selling candy, and grownups hawking religion. Anna reached into her pocket, tossed a quarter in the air, caught it, and palmed it over the back of her hand.

"Heads or tails?"

"Tails," Kate said.

The doorbell rang again, followed by a knock. Anna lifted her hand, stuffed the quarter back in her pocket, and said, "If it's another Jehovah's Witness, I'm calling the cops."

A tall, dark-haired man with a weathered but undeniably handsome face — all bone structure and blue eyes, it seemed — was standing on the porch bearing groceries. Four bags of them, which he was struggling to keep in his arms. Anna took two of the bags and shouted over her shoulder, "Free food!"

Kate greeted the visitor by shouting his name. "Mr. Leoni! What are you doing here?"

Mr. Leoni shook his head in mock disappointment. "Always Mr. Leoni with you. You make me feel old, Kate."

"Sorry, Bruno," Kate said.

When you're raised by someone who arrived in this country on a boat, it takes a while to shed the old-world ways. Kate would never lose that knee-jerk respect for her elders. Anna had none of that.

For that all-too-brief hour before George returned home, both Anna and Kate stole whatever attention they could from Bruno. Anna showed him her beer-can castle; she didn't have to tell him it was a castle. He knew. Kate offered her assistance in the kitchen, her technique culled from hours in front of the television watching cooking shows. Bruno declared her the perfect sous-chef. As Kate was slowly and meticulously cutting onions, Bruno noticed the silence.

"It's so quiet in here. You're in college. Shouldn't your neighbors be calling the police with noise complaints?"

"Yes," Anna said enthusiastically. "They should."

She marched over to the stereo, pressed Play, and jacked up the volume, louder than it had been in months. Synthesizers shook the room. Dr. Octagon was paged.

First patient, pull out the skull remove the
    cancer
Breakin' his back chisel necks for the
    answer.

Bruno bobbed his head to the rhythm as he sweated onions in a pan.

"What is this delightful music we're listening to?"

"Dr. Octagon," said Anna. "This is my favorite album this year. I can't stop listening to it."

"It's true. She really can't."

"Dr. Octagon. Very interesting," said Bruno.

My skin is green and silver, warhead lookin'
  mean
Astronauts get played, tough like the
  ukulele.

"What kind of doctor is he?"
"He's an octagonecologist," said Anna.
"He's a time-traveling gynecologist from the planet Jupiter," said Kate, as if she were providing the credentials of the family physician.
Bruno doubled over and let out the loudest laugh Anna had ever heard from a grown man.

Earth People, New York and California
Earth People, I was born on Jupiter.

When George returned home an hour later, she heard music blaring, the hum of voices, and the clanking of cutlery and assumed Anna was throwing an impromptu party. She steeled herself for a fight. As George walked through the front door, Dr. Octagon was listing the ailments he treated.

"No," George said, looking directly at the
stereo as she kicked the power button with
her foot. If George couldn't play her music
around Anna, Anna couldn't play her music
around George. It was only fair. Even
though Anna thought she was performing a
public service by trying to guide George
away from the top-forty music to which her
tastes bent.

Everything quieted after that, as the chefs
in the kitchen waited for George to notice
the guest.

When George saw her father, she dropped
the scowl on her face, tossed her bookbag
on the floor, and threw herself into his arms.
Bruno picked his five-foot-ten daughter off
the ground and spun her in a circle. There
was a physical ease between Bruno and
George that Anna found so alien it made
her guts twist. George, twenty-one, could
still be caught sitting on her father's lap.
Donald Fury's equivalent would be a light
pat on the head — the kind of affection you
might show a dog, if you weren't a dog
person. Anna told Kate she thought it was
weird, the way they were touching all the
time. Secretly she wondered how she might

have turned out if she'd had a father who knew how to express love.

Kate was incapable of mislabeling her reaction to Bruno and George. When Kate watched them together, it evoked sadness so deep that it felt like a weed was taking root inside of her. She was young when her father died, but she remembered being smothered with hugs and kisses and unrestrained love. It was always her papa who read her bedtime stories. Sometimes for hours, long past her bedtime. Kate's mother complained that he read books beyond his daughter's reach. When he should have been reading *The Cat in the Hat,* he chose *Aesop's Fables* and the Chronicles of Narnia.

After Georgianna Theresa Leoni got home, Bruno's attentions zoomed in like a telescope on his daughter, and everyone else fell out of focus. Anna immediately poured herself a goblet of wine, and Kate chopped the parsley into dust.

"Why didn't you tell me you were coming, Dad?" George asked.

"Where's the surprise in that?" Bruno said, kissing her on the cheeks and the forehead. He took her by the shoulders and stepped back so that he could get a good look at her. "You could gain a few pounds," he said.

George gazed around the kitchen. "If you're cooking, I will."

Bruno resumed his meal prep. George stirred the assortment of simmering sauces, tasting one at a time. There was an unspoken changing of the guard.

Once Bruno finished preparing his culinary masterpiece, he called the girls to the table for their feast. There they sat for the next three hours eating a five-course meal, beginning with anchovies in oil on crostini, followed by stuffed tomatoes, pasta puttanesca, chicken parmigiana, and finishing with ricotta pie. Bruno named each plate with an overdone Sicilian accent. George rolled her eyes with mock embarrassment.

Bruno tried to make everyone feel important. He asked questions and even follow-up questions. He asked about Anna's studies and gave her a fatherly reminder about the importance of good nutrition. He gently inquired about Kate's career inertia, and when she clumsily changed the subject to discuss a documentary on moles she'd recently watched, he convincingly feigned interest.

"If a human baby grew at the same rate as

a mole, it would be one hundred and twelve pounds by the time it was a month old," said Kate.

"That's remarkable," said Bruno.

After the dinner party was properly over-nourished and saturated with red wine, Bruno turned to his daughter.

"Let's go for a walk," he said.

George and her father grabbed their coats and left.

"I'm living with two lunatics," George said after they had strolled a safe distance from the house. "Kate is now watching close to fourteen hours of television a day. And Anna, I don't even know where to start. That's not the first time she's made a construction from our recycling bin. And her music. I *hate* her music."

"I take it you're not a fan of the time-traveling gynecologist?"

"If you had to listen to him on a six-hour loop, you wouldn't be either."

"I suppose not. There's something serious we need to talk about," Bruno said.

"What?"

George stopped under a streetlamp and looked up at her father. The light shone directly on him. A bead of sweat stood out on his forehead, despite the cold night air.

"Your mom and I have separated."

223

"Why?" George asked.

"Things happen."

"Like what?" George said, impatiently awaiting a solid answer, something that could be written in a textbook.

"People grow apart, George. We've been married twenty-five years."

"Did Mom meet someone?"

"No."

"Did you?"

"That's not why we're separating."

"So you *did* meet someone?"

Bruno tried to reach out to his daughter; she danced to the left. "Yes, but —"

"You had an affair?"

"George, I'm not here to talk about that."

"Who was she?"

"It doesn't matter."

Bruno took another step closer to George; she swayed to the right.

"Of course it matters," said George.

"George, nothing will change between us."

"Are you in love with her?"

"No."

"Then why are you getting a divorce?"

"Because that's what your mother wants."

"Why did you do this? Why did you have sex with a woman you didn't love?"

"I make mistakes. I'm sorry."

"Have you made mistakes before?" George

asked, recalling the long, unexplained silences in her house growing up. Her mother would say she was angry because her father hadn't taken out the trash or replaced the floodlight. George had always thought her mother's mute punishments particularly harsh.

"We all make mistakes," Bruno said, still trying to reach out, thinking some physical contact would repair this divide.

George bobbed and weaved like a boxer.

"How many times?"

When George and her father returned to the High Street house, George silently hooked her coat on the rack and climbed the stairs to her room.

Anna sat at the kitchen table with her book splayed open. She regarded Bruno's glassy-eyed gaze as he watched his daughter head up to her bedroom. Trying to remain invisible, Anna closed her book and looked for an escape route. Her only option was going out the back door and then hoisting herself through the bathroom window. It seemed extreme under the circumstances.

Bruno poured himself a glass of wine. He turned to Anna and silently asked if she wanted one. Anna nodded her head. She was hoping tonight she would sleep. All that food and wine; it seemed possible. After four nights of insomnia, one of the many secrets she had been keeping lately, Anna was afraid of what another sleepless night would do to her.

Bruno passed her the glass of wine.

"Is she okay?" Anna asked, nodding in the general vicinity of George's bedroom.

"I don't know," Bruno said, sighing. "We'll see."

Anna wanted to respect their privacy, so she didn't ask. But often, not asking made the answers pour in.

"Her mother and I are getting a divorce."

"I'm sorry," Anna said.

"It's okay. We've been talking about it for a long time. I think George blames me."

"Why?" Anna regretted asking the question as soon as it escaped her lips.

"I'm not perfect," Bruno said.

"She'll get over it," Anna said.

"You sure about that?"

"Everybody's parents get divorced these days."

"Yours aren't," Bruno said.

"Yeah, but they should be," Anna said, biting back a laugh.

Bruno looked concerned. He had known Anna for almost four years. She was different this visit. Her hands were shaky; her eyes sometimes didn't focus. Excessive studying and sleep deprivation would explain it, but he saw something else that he didn't like.

"Are you all right?" Bruno asked.

"Better than ever," Anna said lightly. She got to her feet and stumbled toward the kitchen counter. She could feel herself fading and she liked it. Tonight she didn't want to think about anything at all. She poured herself some more red wine, filling her glass to the rim.

2003

BOSTON, MASSACHUSETTS

Anna watched the bubbles rise to the edge of the champagne glass and then collapse. Her third flute of the night of the cotton candy of spirits. It was like drinking air. Anna wondered why she bothered. Lena Fury breezed past in her full-length red evening gown and, with the grace of a ballerina or a pickpocket, stole the flute from her daughter.

"You've had enough," Lena said. "Why don't you get yourself a cup of coffee?"

"Excellent idea," Anna said.

Anna circumvented the throngs of bow ties and painted faces, acting invisible, as she had as a child. Unlike most children, playing hide-and-seek, Anna had never really wanted to be caught. It was the same now. Her presence that evening was ghostly. Many guests would later wonder if Anna had even made a showing.

Anna avoided eye contact, always a

precursor to conversation, as she navigated through the room. She brushed past yet another tuxedo, but this one reached out, gripped Anna's elbow, and drew her close.

"Anna," he said.

"Dad," she said, startled.

"Anna, you remember Paul, don't you?"

"Yes," Anna said. She didn't.

She assumed, correctly, that Paul was an investment banker who worked with her father, but she had no recollection of ever having met him.

"Nice to see you again, Anna," Paul said. Or maybe he, too, was bluffing.

Anna caught a glimpse of her brother sneaking into the kitchen. He was up to something, she'd noticed earlier. Always slipping out of the room to take a phone call, not his usual practice.

"What are you doing these days, Anna?" Paul asked.

"Anna is a doctor at Boston Medical Center."

"Impressive," Paul said.

"I know!" Anna said. Medical school had been such a challenge for Anna, she never dismissed any comment about her accomplishment.

"What line of medicine are you in?" Paul asked.

"Emergency. Although I'm thinking about switching to anesthesiology."

"Why is that?" Paul asked, genuinely interested.

Anna understood the customs of these events: a polite question was asked, and a polite answer was provided. She also knew that honesty was often the most direct path to ending a conversation.

"I think I prefer unconscious patients," Anna said. "But many doctors feel that way. That's why anesthesiology is such a competitive field."

Don patted his daughter on the head and said, "Run along now, dear."

As Anna beat a less ghostly path through the black-tie traffic into the kitchen, she wondered how many times in her life her father had said "Run along now, dear" to her. It was something he'd say whenever she made him uncomfortable. She was always happy to comply.

Anna followed her brother into the kitchen, but he was already gone.

George had been surprised when she heard the voice-mail message from Colin inviting her to his parents' anniversary party. He thought Anna could use a friendly face, he said. George reminded Colin that Kate lived in Boston, and Colin reminded George that Lena was afflicted with an extreme aversion to Kate, the origin of which no one could uncover, triggered during a Christmastime visit years ago. Anna had never seen her mother dislike someone so aggressively: if Lena was in a room with Kate, an arctic chill permeated the air. Even the most socially oblivious could feel it.

George was glad to get away and pleased that she didn't have to brainstorm any of the details. Colin bought her plane ticket and made all of the arrangements. A car service picked George up at the airport and alerted Colin when she arrived at the house.

Colin slipped out of the kitchen and through the back door, where George was waiting in the garden. He snuck her into the basement so she could change out of the jeans and sweater she'd worn on the airplane into something less comfortable.

"I'll be back to collect you in a half hour. Is that enough time?"

It wouldn't have been enough time for Colin's ex-wife.

"Fifteen minutes," George said.

When Colin returned, George was dressed in a full-length black evening gown with spaghetti straps and just a hint of sheen. It was a simple, unfussy dress, the kind of dress Colin would have chosen for her. George and Colin had met on only two previous occasions, but she was as beautiful as he remembered.

"Shall we?" Colin said, offering his arm.

George looped her arm through his as they walked upstairs to the party.

"Your ex-husband is a fucking moron," Colin whispered as they traversed the kitchen and entered the living room.

"Thank you," said George.

She had been so locked into her recent marital downfall that she had forgotten what it was like to be something other than a mother and a divorcée. She liked the way Colin looked at her, even though anyone else would have described it as a leer.

Anna was searching the room for her brother when they entered. While she was still adjusting to the surprise of seeing her old friend, the pair approached her. Anna immediately noted her brother's predatory gaze upon George.

Colin noted the slight squint in his sister's eye, always a sign of suspicion. Anna's face was rarely in calm repose. Interpreting her expressions could be exhausting; it had become easier simply not to look at her.

"Surprise," Colin said.

Anna and George embraced.

"What are you doing here?" Anna asked, trying to amp up the level of enthusiasm in her voice.

"Look what I brought you," Colin said. "A sparkly George for the entire weekend."

"You did this for me?" Anna said.

"I did," Colin said, ignoring the edge in her tone.

"You look great," Anna told George. "Divorce suits you. Or is it motherhood?"

"It must be motherhood."

"Where is Carter?"

"With his grandmother. This is the first time I've left him since he was born."

"It's really good to see you," Anna said. She meant that.

"You too," said George, wrapping her arm around Anna. "Are you getting enough sleep?"

That was the most generous comment Anna could expect. The first thing her mother had said to her when she stepped through the front door was "What happened to you?"

It had been a month since Anna had seen her mother, even though they both lived in Boston. After medical school, Anna had reluctantly returned to her hometown; her father had pulled some strings and helped get her into the Boston Medical Center emergency medicine residency program despite her unspectacular med-school transcripts. He never said anything about it.

It was true; Anna did look awful. Her skin had a grayish tone, and her hair was obviously thinning. Her teeth had yellowed from the bottomless cups of black coffee. Unlike Lena, she wasn't schooled in covering up her physical flaws, so, other than a bit of mascara and rouge, there was no camouflage.

George felt like a teenager again as the trio slunk away from the adult crowd and retired to the basement. On the way to the hideout, George watched Anna slip by the bar and steal two bottles of champagne. Downstairs, they kicked off their shoes and sat on the plush white carpet. Anna popped the cork on a bottle and took the first sip for herself. She passed it to George.

It had been a year since Anna had seen her friend. Anna and Kate had made a short trip to New York to mark the dissolution of the marriage between Mitch and George. George's spirits then had been better than they had expected. George had told them that the last few weeks of her marriage were the happiest of their union, mostly because she didn't care anymore.

The conditions of the divorce, however, were a rude awakening. George had signed a prenup that was so airtight that when Colin read it, he told his sister it was written for someone who had never planned on staying married. George had two options: she could accept her payoff money and child support as it was, or she could fight for more and risk losing what she had. She signed the divorce papers. The only thing George couldn't lose was custody of her baby. Fatherhood hadn't agreed with Mitch even before he was a father. George's pregnancy seemed to repulse him. Anna and Kate had known many unsavory details of the marriage, but George had never mentioned that by the time she reached her third trimester, Mitch could hardly look at her.

Colin had taken a seat next to George, and he put his arm around her. It had been a while since George had been so close to a man who wasn't her father. It was comforting and seductive and she wished Anna weren't there. She did, however, feel guilty for wishing that. Anna knew exactly what her friend was thinking as she watched George's body settle into the crook of Colin's arm. Anna opened the second bottle of champagne and took a gulp like an athlete swigging Gatorade.

"I was sorry to hear about your divorce," George said to Colin.

"It wasn't meant to be," Colin said.

This was one subject that Colin and Anna avoided entirely. Anna had known from the start that his marriage was doomed, but even she had to admit that she'd accelerated the process. No one wanted to think about that day — which was unfortunate for Colin and Megan, since it had been their wedding day. The marriage ended within a year. In the two years since, Colin had cycled through women as if they were ice cream flavors he wanted to sample. Anna figured George was the next flavor.

"How have you been?" Anna asked George.

"I'm okay now," George said. "I really am. Kate was right about him."

Colin stole the bottle of champagne from George and poured it into flutes.

"To Kate," George said, raising her glass. "I should have listened to her."

Colin and George clinked glasses. Anna clinked with her bottle.

"You didn't listen to her about your tits," Anna said. "But look on the bright side: they'll never droop."

George laughed, but the memory of that conversation with Mitch filled her with shame. She didn't see herself as someone who was easily swayed, and yet in that relationship, she could not recall winning a single battle. Anna, still sober enough to pick up on her discomfort, changed the subject.

"Did you notice my mom's face-lift?" Anna said.

"I thought she looked rested," said George.

"Don't you mean surprised?" said Colin.

"How's residency treating you?" George asked.

"I have good days and I have bad days."

"What's a good day?"

"When I don't kill a patient."

Anna downed the rest of her champagne, shook the empty bottle, and said, "I'll be back."

Colin used Anna's departure to whisk George away. They left the basement, found two fresh champagne flutes in the kitchen, and slipped outside into the garden.

The cold air was refreshing after the overheated Fury home. Colin gave his suit jacket to George and led her to a bench under the gazebo.

"Now that you're a free woman, what will you do with all of your time?"

"I think I'll look into environmental-consulting jobs."

"In New York?"

"Not necessarily," said George. "I suppose I could live anywhere."

"So that's where you've been hiding," Anna said as she casually approached.

"George needed some air."

"Looks like you found it," said Anna.

Anna stole her brother's champagne flute and drained the glass.

"Your liver must really hate you," Colin said.

"We're not as close as we used to be," Anna said. "I'll get you a refill," she added, quickly exiting the garden.

"I think she's suspicious," Colin said.

"Of what?"

"Of my intentions toward you. That maybe they aren't completely honorable."

"She'll never leave us alone," said George.

"Then we need to come up with a plan."

Before any plan could be put into action, Anna returned with two more glasses of champagne. She passed one glass to her brother.

"For you," she said.

"Thank you," said Colin.

Anna raised her glass. "To old friends."

George hadn't noticed Colin drinking heavily, but he must have been. It was alarming, his turn into a sloppy drunk. He began slurring his words and then he rested his head on her shoulder.

"Is he all right?" George asked.

"He started drinking early in the day," said Anna. "It must have finally caught up with him."

George thought the brother of Anna should be able to hold his liquor better.

"We should get him to bed before my mother sees him," said Anna.

George kicked off her heels, threw Colin's arm around her shoulder, and got him to his feet. George still had the strength to manage a semiconscious hundred-and-eighty-pound man. They stumbled upstairs and put Colin to bed.

"Why am I so tired?" Colin mumbled.

"It's been a long day," Anna said.

Anna helped him remove his shoes and socks while George freed him from his bow tie.

"Go to sleep," Anna said. It was an order, not a suggestion. "And lie on your side," she added, rolling him.

George kissed Colin on the forehead.

"You okay?" she said.

"I'm fine," Colin said, slurring his words. "Why don't you stay here and keep me company?"

"She's coming with me, Colin," Anna said. "We have a lot of catching up to do."

As the revelers downstairs slowly dispersed, Anna and George took over another spare bedroom and changed into their pajamas. Anna removed her dress; George noticed a patch sticking to the small of her back.

"What is that?" George asked.

"What?"

"That patch on your back. What is it?"

"Oh, that," Anna said. She paused a little too long. "A nicotine patch," she finally said. An easy lie. A patch was a patch to George. Nicotine, fentanyl, they all looked the same.

"But you don't smoke," George said.

"I took it up briefly," Anna said, buoyed by the ease of her lie. "All the stress at work. You'd be surprised how many doctors and nurses still smoke."

"I guess I would," said George.

The guest room was furnished with two twin beds. Anna called it the future-grandchildren room. It would be neglected for years. There were moments she felt sorry for her parents, but those moments passed quickly.

Anna turned off the light, and they slid into their beds. Anna thought they'd stay up for hours talking, but George drifted off within minutes. Anna remained awake the rest of the night. She had slipped into Colin's champagne the one thing that would have put her to sleep.

1989
BOSTON, MASSACHUSETTS

Malcolm Davis woke up in the guest bedroom of the Fury household with no idea where he was. This often happened to him when he slept in unfamiliar environments. This morning he was able to place himself quickly. The voices outside were so familiar. He heard Lena Fury say, "Stop that, Anna." He heard Anna say, "One more time."

Malcolm got out of bed and opened the curtains. Outside, a cloister of denuded trees stood immodestly among mounds of raked maple leaves. Anna charged at the pile of leaves and threw herself on top, a human wrecking ball.

As Anna got to her feet and brushed herself off, Lena said, "Are you done?"

"Yes, I believe I'm done," Anna said in an oddly formal tone.

The previous morning, Malcolm had looked out of his window and observed the fourteen-year-old girl with the wild, uncombed hair in the midst of an animated debate with a thirtysomething man in painter pants and a battered Red Sox T-shirt. Malcolm found the air of professionalism in their interaction disconcerting. He had seen the man around recently, painting the Fury garage. White paint over the very same white of five years ago.

The painter shook his head no; Anna nodded yes. He shook his head with less conviction. Anna swept the backyard with her emphatic yes and held out something for the man to take. A beat passed. The man in the Red Sox shirt took the thing from her hand and shoved it into his pocket. He nodded his head in defeat and spoke a few more words. The odd pair parted in the yard. There was a smirk of satisfaction on Anna's face. A familiar sight.

Colin knocked on the guest-room door and entered. Malcolm was still staring out the window.

"Your sister's up to something," Malcolm said.

"Always," Colin said.

"Do you worry about her?"

"I worry about anyone who might cross her."

■ ■ ■ ■

Anna had set her alarm for 2:00 a.m. There
were certain hours in the Fury home when
you could trust its stillness. She crept
downstairs and began collecting her provisions, contemplating items that could be
stored for weeks, maybe months. She was
always amazed at the number of things that
didn't require refrigeration. She'd already
stockpiled bottled water, nuts, cookies,
candies, and even a liter of cheap vodka. Its
absence would never be noted. She hated
the smell and taste, but a few minutes after
the slow burn down her throat, she felt as if
a soft warm blanket had been wrapped
around her.

Footfalls sounded on the staircase. Anna
closed herself in the pantry and crouched
next to a slab of empty jelly jars. Feet padded around the kitchen. The refrigerator
opened and closed. Silverware clanked. The
noises were all wrong. Anna had lurked for
years in this house; she knew the sounds of
its inmates. The whoosh of her mother's
dressing gown; the slight tap-shoe click that
her father's slippers made; the chronic
throat-clearing that Colin succumbed to in
the middle of the night. He claimed to have

allergies only in the home where he was raised; he said they mysteriously vanished in any other location. But this inmate was new, quieter than the others. Stockinged feet. Only the creak on certain floorboards hinted at a trespasser. Kitchen cabinets opened and closed in slow motion, but with unfocused frequency, as if the person didn't know what he was looking for.

It wasn't Cesar. He had moved out a week ago. He and his wife were now living in a cousin's trailer. Anna had just given him his final payment. They'd argued over the secret latch. He thought a pushbutton lock would suffice, but Anna thought that was too plain. She wanted the showy security of a secret room, even if she was the only person who would ever appreciate it. Cesar made her promise not to tell; she made Cesar promise not to tell.

As Anna crept over to the pantry door to confirm the identity of the late-night snacker, she dislodged a jelly jar from its pack. It clunked on the ground but didn't break. She could hear the feet padding toward the pantry door. She had only seconds to hatch an explanation.

Malcolm opened the pantry door and stepped backward as if a bat might take flight. When he spotted Anna, he shook his head, exasperated.

"I should have known it was you," he said.

"What are you doing up?" she asked.

"It's hot upstairs. Seeking lower ground."

"My mother is very thin, ergo, always cold. Ergo again, thermostat always set too high. I've tried to talk to her about it. It's bad for the environment. She has a remarkably sound argument: in summer, we don't turn the thermostat down as much as most people do. She claims it evens things out. Truthfully, it doesn't work out fifty-fifty, but still, she has a point."

"What are you up to?" Malcolm asked.

"Just doing some nighttime shopping."

Malcolm picked up the grocery bag at Anna's feet, placed it on the shiny granite countertop, and inventoried the contents, taking them out one by one.

"Crackers, olives, Cheez Whiz, biscotti, peanut butter sandwich cookies — my favorite."

"Help yourself. I have some storage bins for opened items."

"Caviar?"

"Just a little jar I found behind a can of sardines. They'll never notice it's gone."

"Do you even like caviar?"

"No. But I have been told that I will develop a taste for it," Anna said.

"Bottled water, soda, and . . . vodka," Malcolm continued. "This is a very strange party you're planning."

"It's not a party," Anna said, returning everything to the bag.

Except for the vodka. Malcolm held the bottle under his arm like a football.

"Then what is it?" he asked.

"Provisions."

"For what?"

"A disaster, End of Days, the usual."

"Why not leave it where it is?"

"Are you going to give me the vodka or not?"

"Not," Malcolm said.

"Whatever. I'll get it later," Anna said.

She picked up the bag, left the kitchen, circled through the den into the foyer, and went down the stairs that led to the basement. Malcolm, out of pure curiosity, followed her, and Anna did nothing to evade him. He had caught her smoking three days earlier under the gazebo and never said a word. She prided herself on her ability to spot a snitch. Malcolm wasn't a member of that breed.

Anna plucked a flashlight from a hook at the bottom of the basement stairs and illuminated the corridor that led to the laundry room.

"Where are you going?" Malcolm asked.

Anna said nothing. She opened the tiny door by the washing machine and crouched down to enter, then returned to grab the bag of groceries. Malcolm had to get on his hands and knees to crawl through the space. Inside, he caught glimpses of wooden beams, a maze of pipes, and drywall flickering in and out of view as the flashlight bounced around, carried between Anna's teeth. He missed the part where Anna slipped her finger along the baseboard to the secret latch.

Suddenly a small door opened to his right. It wasn't like the first tiny door, which had a knob and some presence. This one sat on hinges and swung inward, its seams barely visible in the dim light. Anna crawled inside. Malcolm followed after her. She flicked on an old lamp, the light dimmed by a patterned cloth over the shade.

"What is this, Anna?" Malcolm asked as he surveyed the four-by-six-foot space.

"My office."

"Who knows about this?"

"No one," Anna said. "Well, you do now. But you won't tell."

"Is it safe?" he asked, knocking on the walls and studying the architecture.

"Why wouldn't it be?"

248

"It doesn't look safe."

"You're just not used to secret rooms. They don't look like ordinary rooms."

Malcolm noted the sleeping bag, the milk-crate bookshelf, and a series of marks penciled on the wall: *I I I I.*

Anna slashed across the quartet, and Malcolm realized she was counting the days.

"It's not that bad here, Anna."

"Here? Or here?" Anna asked, the second *here* referring to her hideaway.

"Most kids would kill to live like you do."

"I am extremely aware of my good fortune," Anna said stiffly. "I do not know what I could have said to make you think otherwise. Can I offer you a complimentary snack or beverage?"

Anna served them both sandwich cookies and hot cocoa from a thermos. She wished she had brought some wine from the cellar. She had a new idea for a cocktail she wanted to try out; it involved spiking her cocoa with wine. She planned to call it *cocoa vin.*

"What do you do down here?" Malcolm asked.

"Think."

"Can't you think upstairs?"

"Not as well. Besides, I need the privacy."

"Your bedroom isn't private enough for you?"

"My mother doesn't knock, and it's searched on occasion."

"You're fourteen, Anna. What have you got to hide?"

"Not much. It can all fit in here," Anna said, sweeping the room with her hand, "and here," she added, patting a metal lock box by her side.

"I hope you have something more interesting in there than cigarettes, cash, and weed."

She had all of that and more. It was the other thing, the thing she'd found while rummaging through boxes in the basement, that she treasured the most. It had taken her a few days to recover from the discovery. Like any dark secret, it wasn't something she could be alone with. She toyed with the idea of telling Colin, but it felt as if she'd be crossing a line. Even reading the letters gave her a rush of danger, the sense that she was doing something filthy and wrong. Some girls recoiled from that feeling; Anna didn't mind it that much.

She pulled the key from the long chain around her neck and unlocked the box. Inside was the predictable contraband and a small stack of old letters, yellowed with age and wrapped in a red ribbon, a cliché of old-fashioned missives. The letters were addressed to Lena Fury. From a J. L. Who lived in Vermont.

"What have you got there?" Malcolm asked.

"Proof."

"Of what?"

"Proof that my mother doesn't love my father."

"You can't prove something like that."

"All you have to do is look at the two of them," Anna said. "Is *that* what love looks like?"

"Love looks like all sorts of things," Malcolm said.

"*This* is what love looks like," Anna said, fanning the dusty letters.

"Those letters are private, Anna."

"My mother got pregnant and had to marry my father. Whoever wrote these letters was trying to stop her. Didn't work, obviously. The funny thing is, the letters are all signed *J.* Just *J.* At first I thought Jack, John, Jim, but then I read the letters over again and I consulted a graphology book. The script is swirly and ornate. I realized that it could be Jane, Jill, Jennifer."

"Should I ever need the services of a graphology expert, I now know where to go," Malcolm said.

"J. L. was also on the field hockey team," Anna said.

"You're currently on the field hockey team."

"Because I couldn't make the basketball team. What if the love of my mother's life was a woman? Sad, isn't it? She's married to a man," Anna said.

What Anna thought was different than what she'd said. It wasn't the sadness of the idea that stoked her interest. If these letters narrated the story she'd let run wild in her mind, it changed how she saw her mother, made her more complete. She'd always seen Lena as strangely two-dimensional, like a photograph of a stern relative who had long since passed.

"Your mother has a right to privacy," Malcolm said, startled that he was defending Lena.

Malcolm also had an oddly incomplete and two-dimensional perception of Anna and Colin's mother. A stately villainess. Her chilly severity always smacked of performance. He was wildly disappointed in Anna for bleeding her mother's secrets, but mostly he didn't want Lena humanized. He realized he enjoyed the luxury of disliking the woman and not having the remotest desire to please her, since he had that need with virtually everyone else he met.

"She has no idea they're missing, if that makes you feel better."

"It doesn't. Get rid of them," Malcolm said.

"No. I need them."

"What do you need them for?"

"Leverage," Anna said flatly. "As long as I have these letters, my mother doesn't have the power she thinks she has."

Malcolm bowed his head and rubbed his eyes. It was only a year since he'd saved Anna from the lake, when he'd pulled her up and felt the violent gasp for breath in her lungs and her thrumming heartbeat. What Anna was, who she became, mattered to Malcolm, and he saw with stunning clarity that the little girl he'd saved might be turning into something ugly.

"Put the letters back. If I hear you've done anything with them, I'll tell your mother every secret I know about you and then I'll make up a few."

"You wouldn't take her side," she said, calling his bluff.

"There's some part of you, Anna, that isn't good. It worries me and it should worry you too."

Not a scratch of emotion surfaced on Anna's face, but Malcolm's disapproval struck her hard. She busied herself by unpacking her provisions. She avoided his gaze until her glassy eyes dimmed.

"Did you hear me?" Malcolm asked.

"Yes. Do you have anything to add?"

"No."

"Can I get you anything else?" she asked. "Homemade peanut brittle or liver pâté?"

"Good night, Anna."

2000
RICHMOND, VIRGINIA

"Isn't it past your bedtime?" the father of the bride asked Anna.

"I don't have a bedtime anymore," Anna said.

It was late. Anna hadn't bothered changing out of her bridesmaid's dress. But it was a "normal" dress, as George had promised — navy blue, bateau neckline, no bow or taffeta in sight. The bar at the Jefferson Hotel was finally emptying out after spillage from the wedding had taken over. Now it was just Anna and Bruno Leoni and a very cozy private couple at a back table. Anna had watched them for a while. Adulterers, she'd decided.

Bruno ordered himself a Scotch and another of whatever Anna was having.

"Unless you were leaving?" he said.

"No," Anna said. "I don't like to leave until I'm asked."

When the drinks were served, Bruno and

Anna clinked glasses.

"Congratulations," she said.

Bruno formed a smile, but it took effort. He cast his eyes about the room, as if he were looking for something to distract him. "Thank you. I couldn't be happier."

"Lovely wedding," Anna said. "It was very . . . white, wasn't it?"

"Yes," Bruno said.

"And those pillars in the ballroom were enormous."

"Indeed."

"And that was some chandelier," Anna said.

A real conversation masquerading as small talk. Anna was commenting on how utterly un-George-like the wedding was, down to the white-tiered vanilla cake. George liked chocolate cake. She always said vanilla was so vanilla.

"Why are we here?" Bruno asked.

"To drown our sorrows," Anna said, taking a sip of her drink.

"No. Why are we in Richmond, Virginia? The bride's family lives in the Midwest and the bride currently lives in New York."

"The groom and his family are from Richmond."

"I thought weddings were all about the bride," Bruno said.

"Not this one."

"My daughter once told me that when she got married, she wanted to wear a sundress and waders in the muddy yard of my lakefront cottage. Who got married today? It wasn't George."

"People change," Anna said.

"Not that much," said Bruno.

"You okay?"

"I feel old," Bruno said. "Time is slipping by so much faster than it used to."

"Is that all?" Anna said, trying to lighten things up.

"I have a slightly indelicate question I must pose. My daughter's looking a little different lately. Do you know what I'm saying?"

Anna had clocked so many differences. The even tan, the plucked eyebrows, the unnecessary weight loss. But Bruno was thinking of something more indelicate.

"You mean her boobs? Yeah. They're fake. There's no push-up bra in the world that can do that."

Bruno drained his drink and ordered another.

"I never thought she was the type to do something like that."

"She wasn't," said Anna.

For months after meeting Mitch, Anna

and Kate had believed that George would come to her senses. Then they learned of the boob job and realized that sense had flown the coop. Kate started talking plots and kidnapping and grand interventions. Anna tried to subtly slip in hints during phone calls, planting seeds of doubt in infertile soil. At the bachelorette party, Kate was relentless.

KATE: What have you done to yourself?

GEORGE: Nothing that many other women haven't done.

KATE: You were happy with your tits before you met him.

GEORGE: How do you know?

KATE: Please tell me they're saline.

Anna knew they weren't. You could get that teardrop shape only with silicone.

GEORGE: My boobs are none of your concern.

KATE: Silicone implants have been banned since 1992, and you had them put into your body. You didn't even talk to Anna about it?

GEORGE: These were fifth-generation implants and I was dealing with one of the best plastic surgeons in Manhattan.

KATE: You signed up to be a guinea pig.

GEORGE: They are safe. I'm fine. All current studies indicate that the newer silicone is not a problem.

KATE: But saline is even safer. It's also cheaper and not as high maintenance.

GEORGE: Cheap and not high maintenance isn't exactly a selling point for breasts.

KATE: That's how I'd describe my own.

Anna yanked Kate off the barstool before she could repeat her statistics on the first-generation silicone implants. Or discuss the environmental ramifications of the disposal of implants, which rarely lasted more than ten years. When Kate began her research, she'd imagined a giant landfill of discarded breast implants swollen with saline or silicone. Her research informed her that they would be treated like medical waste. So, the plastic boobs would be incinerated and the remains would rest in peace with other medical trash. Kate had planned to mention the environmental impact of burning plastic, but Anna interrupted the lecture, having heard the details over breakfast months earlier when Kate was fully ensconced in her research.

Four cocktails after the implant argument, Kate cornered George and said, "Don't marry him. You will regret it."

"You're drunk," George said and told Anna to put Kate to bed.

"Can he make my daughter happy?" Bruno asked.

"Yes," Anna said. She always felt better about single-word lies. After the fact, you could plausibly claim that you hadn't understood the question.

"If you say so," Bruno said. No part of him believed her.

"Trust me. I'm almost a doctor."

"So, Almost Dr. Fury, tell me a secret," Bruno said.

"You don't want to know my secrets."

"Of course I do," Bruno said.

"Okay, but don't tell anyone. I secretly dream of being a country music star. I've even written a few songs. Want to hear one?"

"Why do you always play games, Anna?"

"Is that a no?"

Bruno put his hand on top of Anna's and said, "Does anyone say no to you?"

It was easy to explain what happened next. The bar closed and Anna and Bruno wanted another drink. They retired to his hotel room, since it was a suite with a sitting room and a minibar. Like a living room in a hotel.

They had never been alone in an enclosed space before.

George's mother and Charles, her second husband, still seemed wildly in love. Almost four years after the wedding, Vivien's hands never seemed to leave Charles's skin. Anna found it extreme, as if Vivien were trying to keep Charles from floating away. Or maybe it was a performance for her ex-husband. Anna clung to the scientific explanations for love — pheromones, dopamine, norepinephrine, serotonin — because it made falling out of love seem so much simpler. At least when it happened to her.

"Couldn't you find a date for the wedding?" Anna asked.

"You invite a woman to a wedding, she might get some ideas."

"Do you have a woman in your life who is inclined to get ideas?"

"I know your games, Anna. It's just to keep the other person talking, to stay in control."

"No, it's not about that. I really want to know what happens with other people, inside their heads. It seems wrong or unfair or something that I only get to be in my own head."

"That's life, Anna."

"Doesn't mean I have to like it."

"You have lovely feet," Bruno said.

"That was an abrupt transition."

"I just noticed them. Only my noticing was abrupt."

"Huh."

"Say thank you when someone gives you a compliment."

Bruno reached for Anna's left foot and began gently rubbing his fingers along the high arch.

"Thank you," Anna said.

She relaxed with her foot in his hands. It seemed so natural, so easy. And certainly some chemicals were involved.

She wasn't thinking when she straddled him on the couch and kissed him. She wasn't thinking, *I'm kissing my best friend's father.* She still wasn't thinking when he got to his feet, turned her around, and unzipped her dress. It fell to the floor so quickly, you'd think it was weighted. Anna figured that was where it was meant to be all along. The only coherent thought that passed through her head as she unbuttoned Bruno's shirt was that she needed to move fast so that he wouldn't change his mind.

Bruno called room service early in the morning, anticipating the condition in which Anna might find herself. Every palliative measure was delivered: water, coffee, eggs, toast, bacon, bloody mary, Alka-Seltzer, aspirin, saltines, ginger ale, and Coke. An hour later, the nausea and pain had dimmed to the annoying flicker of a dying neon light. She would live with it for the rest of the day, but she could still function and smile and attend the brunch scheduled for out-of-town guests, which was just about all of them.

Anna slipped on her dress. Bruno zipped up the back and turned her around. He kissed her on the lips and said, "Forgive me."

Anna returned to her hotel room to shower. Kate was dressed and had even made the bed.

"The whole point of staying in a hotel is that you don't have to make your own bed."

"I'm sure there are other reasons," Kate said, in a tone that Anna couldn't peg.

Anna reached for her dress's zipper and realized she needed assistance yet again.

"Can you help me?"

Kate unzipped her dress. Once again, it dropped to the floor like it was weighted.

"I'll be quick," Anna said as she got in the shower.

She scorched her skin with hot water and then switched to cold for as long as she could tolerate it. Back to hot, then cold.

After the shower, she pulled her hair into a tight bun. There was no time to blow it dry. She dressed quickly, packing at the same time.

Kate's tiny suitcase rested by the door. Kate sat on the edge of her bed, studying Anna's unfocused efforts. The bridesmaid's dress was disrespectfully balled up and stuffed in a crevice of Anna's suitcase, as it deserved to be. Anna zipped up her bag, thinking it signaled the perfect compartmentalization of events. As if none of it had happened. Anna was starting to feel human again. Then Kate spoke.

"I went looking for you last night when you didn't come back. The bartender told me you had left with a man. He described him," Kate said. "A good police description."

Anna remained expressionless.

"One day," Kate said, "you might have the urge to come clean, to tell George what you did. When the urge comes, fight it. It won't clear your conscience and it won't do anything for her."

"It's not what you think," Anna said. The words sounded so foolish, it was as if someone else had spoken them.

"Just promise me," said Kate. "And then we'll never talk about it again."

Anna slumped against the door, leaning her head against the evacuation instructions.

"I promise."

2011

SAN FRANCISCO, CALIFORNIA

"Another Scotch and soda," Jeff Fisher said to the bow-tied bartender.

The bartender poured obligingly, having already obliged Jeff five times before. Matthew regarded his red-faced colleague with concern. Matthew was standing next to Anna under droopy streamers hung by tipsy secretaries at the office holiday party. It was as if Jeff's tongue sat unanchored in his mouth. Surely another Scotch and soda wouldn't glue it in place.

"Should I cut him off?" Matthew Bloom asked Anna.

"It'll only make him angry. Then he'll go to some dive bar down the street and pick a fight."

"I should get his keys."

"Done," Anna said, pulling the set from her pocket and twirling them around her index finger.

"When did that happen?"

266

"The third time he hugged me."

"Now I remember. It did last longer than the first two."

"Shouldn't you be bonding and scheming with your colleagues?" Anna asked.

"I thought I was," Matthew said.

Matthew had planted himself behind his desk for the first two hours of the annual Blackman and Blackman holiday bash but had surfaced an hour ago; since then, he'd drunk two cocktails and allowed Anna to provide him with a play-by-play of what he had missed, as if he were tuning in to the final quarter of a knuckle-biting football game. Unfortunately, this game was far from over.

The most compelling dramas happened under the mistletoe. Jeff had lip-locked with at least four members of the support staff, including a temp who had been employed at the firm for only two weeks. The final kiss, after Jeff's fourth jigger of Scotch, lasted for a particularly long stretch, considering the circumstances. When Jeff's hand began drifting southward, Mr. Blackman cleared his throat and launched into an improvised toast that was brief and inelegant and ended with the words "Bottoms up," which he later regretted. At the end of the toast, Mr. Blackman slipped over to his lecherous employee and mumbled something. A few minutes later, Anna spotted the two in Mr. Blackman's office, Jeff slouching in the client chair while being reprimanded by his boss. Anna knew that Jeff wouldn't remember it the next day. She also knew that Blackman didn't know the half of it. If he had, Jeff would have been axed years ago.

"Who's the idiot who brought the mistletoe?" Matthew asked.

"I did," Anna said.

While she had learned to rein in virtually all of her reckless whims, she still got a secret pleasure from watching other people lose control. However, by night's end, Anna came to agree with Matthew: the mistletoe was definitely a mistake. Jackie Greenberg pulled Anna aside and whispered in her ear that heartbreak was unfolding in the women's restroom. Anna arrived to find Carla Gomez in tears. She'd received the first kiss from Jeff and believed in its romantic potential, in part because they had been having an affair for the past four months. But then Carla watched Jeff parcel out his affections to three more women. Only then did she realize her insignificance. Sometimes it's not the truth itself but the surprise that feels like a blow.

Anna told Carla to splash her face with cold water and then helped her wipe away the raccoon eyes made of mascara and tears. Coworkers congregated in the bathroom, showing their female solidarity and offering the scathing personal commentary that typically follows caddish behavior. Anna always hated the ritual. It wasn't all Jeff's fault. Carla had made a choice. Anna said nothing and let the verbal attacks fly.

Forget about him. You can do better.

He's a dog.

He has the worst table manners I've ever seen.

I think he dyes his hair.

That's a fake tan, you know.

He's a pig.

He uses more hair product than I do.

He's compensating for a small penis.

That last statement was pure conjecture, and Carla knew it was not the case. Although he was a selfish lover.

"That is not the kind of man you cry over," Anna said, drawing the unseemly conversation to a close.

By now the boss and his very drunk employee were back in circulation. However, Jeff appeared to have been cowed by his superior's lecture, which had included a sharp reminder that as an employee of

Blackman and Blackman, Jeff Fisher was also an ambassador for the company. Max Blackman had never used the word *ambassador* in that context, and later, before bed, he would laugh uproariously as he told his wife about his pompous speech. Still, it did the trick. Fisher sullenly approached the bar, ordered a seltzer, and then joined the ranks of his male colleagues, touching on safe subjects like past or pending sporting events.

Anna saw the quizzical look on Matthew's face when she returned from the bathroom forum.

"Everything under control?" he asked.

"Of course," Anna said.

"Care to elaborate?" Matthew asked.

"Not particularly."

"You never tell me anything."

"I tell you what you need to know."

Just when Matthew was about to press Anna for more details, the boss's wife arrived. Abigail Blackman kissed her husband on the cheek, made eye contact with Anna, smiled warmly, and approached her. It had been almost six months since they'd last seen each other. An awkward dinner party, which Anna later learned was executed for the sole purpose of a romantic introduction. Abby thought Anna Fury and Wendell

Miller were perfect for each other, mostly because Wendell didn't drink either. The common denominator of sobriety was so rare in Abby's circle that it seemed like an esoteric mutual interest, akin to stamp-collecting or beekeeping.

What Abby didn't understand was that there were different types of sobriety. Anna was sober because she was a drunk; Wendell didn't drink because he didn't have a taste for it. That neither of them drank might have been the most salient similarity, but their differences were so magnificent that Anna found herself making mental notes of all the reasons he was ill suited for her. For instance, he liked smooth jazz; he had recently joined a lawn-bowling team; he drank tea, not coffee (although even Anna had to admit her distaste for that detail bordered on irrational); and his favorite book was *The Fountainhead,* by Ayn Rand. A burst of laughter escaped Anna's lips when that nail in the coffin was hammered in. As an exit strategy, she'd pretended she was choking on her soup. In the kitchen, she drank a glass of water and steeled herself for the rest of the meal. Max found Anna in the kitchen and conveyed his apologies, but Anna wasn't buying his feigned guilt. Max believed that the awkward romantic setup was one of life's many nuisances. If others could endure it, so could Anna. When the evening ended, Wendell asked for Anna's phone number. Even though she wasn't remotely interested, she might have given it to him if it were not for one simple fact: Wendell hadn't asked Anna a single question the entire night. He knew nothing about Anna other than her taste in clothing and her table manners, so why would he want to spend another night with her?

"What have I missed?" Abby asked Anna and Matthew as she joined them at the office party.

"Where to begin," Anna said.

"I couldn't tell you," Matthew said.

The boss came over and handed his wife a glass of white wine.

"I have a feeling I missed something juicy," Abby said.

There was something in the room, a feeling that, early as it was, the party had ended. The revelers were losing steam, resorting to conversations about work and plans for after the holidays. Something about the buffet table's resemblance to a battlefield after combat told you the best was in the past.

"Hold this," Abby said, passing her drink

to her husband. She rolled up her sleeve and showed Anna a dark mole on her left forearm.

"Should I worry about this?"

Anna looked over, casually, trying to hide her clinician's gaze, and studied the mole.

"You should see your dermatologist once a year for a mole check," Anna said quietly, pretending that Matthew couldn't hear her.

"But until I make it in, does it look malignant?"

"I don't think so, but it's a tad asymmetrical. You should ask your doctor."

"So you'll make an appointment tomorrow," Mr. Blackman said abruptly.

"Of course," said Abby.

Matthew stared at the trio quizzically.

"Is Anna some kind of mole expert?" Matthew asked.

"No. I am not a mole expert. Would you like another drink?"

Anna took Matthew's half-full glass of bourbon and approached the bar. She could hear the conversation about her continuing in the background.

"Is Anna an expert on other things I should know about?" Matthew asked.

"Well, she *was* a doctor," Abby said with a tinge of hostility, as if Matthew were deliberately disregarding the value of seven years of medical training.

"Anna was a doctor?" Matthew repeated.

"Yes. You didn't know that?"

Anna turned around and looked at Max, pleading for help. Her cover was partially blown, but no other details needed to be passed on this evening.

Max cut off the exchange before another piece of information could be served. "Abby, since you arrived late, you need to mingle before everyone gets too soused."

With that, Max guided his wife toward the senior partners before Matthew could launch into any follow-up questions. Anna returned and gave Matthew his fresh drink.

"What is she talking about?" he asked.

"Nothing," Anna said.

Had this information surfaced at the beginning of their working relationship, Matthew wouldn't have pressed on. But he was tired of her particular brand of reticence, and the bourbon had loosened his tongue.

"Anna, if you don't answer the question, I'll find out another way."

"Just let it go."

"No. Why is Abigail under the impression that you used to be a physician?"

"Because I was."

"If you were a doctor, what are you doing

working here?"

"If you tell anyone, I'll quit."

Matthew had never responded well to
threats. He had been a willful child,
overindulged by his mother, who felt so
bound by the shackles of adulthood herself
that she refused to rein in her son. Glynnis
Bloom disciplined Matthew only when she
was under direct observation from scornful
eyes. Because she had no tried-and-true
methods for establishing a parental dictator-
ship, she threatened only when desperate
and never followed through. Years later, she
would marvel at how reasonable her son had
become, all things considered. Then again,
she'd never had to appear against him in
court.

After the Christmas and New Year's break,
Anna returned to the office. A week passed,
and Matthew said nothing of their office-
party conversation. Anna assumed
Matthew's interest in the topic had eventually faded, just like Jeff Fisher's hangover.

As the trial date approached for a
particularly important copyright case, Anna
found herself working more hours than she
had since she was a resident. At eleven on a
Wednesday night, she and Matthew were
on the floor of his office reading through

precedent on the parody fair-use doctrine. The case involved a children's book called *Whopper,* about a whale who tells tall tales. A year after it came out, a similar children's book — this one geared more toward the adult reading the book to the child — was published: *Flibber,* about a dolphin who is a compulsive liar, his tall tales bordering on the absurd. In *Whopper,* the whale learned his lesson; Flibber learned no such lesson. Instead, he engaged in doublespeak and hyperbole, convincing his friends to invest in a subaquatic water park. Both books hit the bestseller list, but the authors of *Whopper* thought that the authors of *Flibber* had stolen their story.

Anna had read both *Flibber* and *Whopper* at least ten times. Each book featured an ornery sea otter and a pompous penguin.

"I'm worried about the penguin and the otter," Anna said. "The parody isn't clear."

"Well, the penguin is a drunk," Matthew said as he twisted his right wrist in a circular motion and studied a lump that had formed over the carpal region. "Could you come over here for a second?" he asked.

Anna crawled over to Matthew, who was sitting with his back against his desk. He held out his hand and pointed to the small protuberance.

"Should I be concerned about this?"

"Maybe you should see a doctor."

"I thought I was."

"I'm not a doctor."

"Whatever you are, you have some medical knowledge. Do you want to put my mind at ease?"

Anna took his wrist in her hands and palpated the solid but movable mass. She checked the mobility of the wrist and let go of his hand.

"You'll live," she said.

"It looks like a tumor."

"I'm sure you've investigated the condition online and already have a diagnosis," Anna said.

"Maybe you'd like to confirm my diagnosis," Matthew said.

"Why would I do that?"

"So I don't jump to the conclusion that I have cancer of the wrist."

"It's most likely a ganglion cyst. It could go away on its own or you could have it drained or surgically removed. And there's excellent anecdotal evidence supporting some unorthodox treatments."

"For instance?"

"I've heard smashing a book on it works. The Bible is best. But I'm sure a law book would do. Most people aren't capable of striking the cyst hard enough themselves, so they need someone else to do it."

"Are you offering?" Matthew asked.

"Are you asking?"

"Yes."

"Sure about that?" Anna said.

Matthew was deathly afraid of needles and medical offices and he avoided anything that might cause pain or permanent damage. But as a lawyer, he was accustomed to testing people and their limits, and he found it difficult to step away from a challenge that might enlighten him about someone's character. He set his wrist on his desk as if patiently waiting for the guillotine.

Anna surveyed the law books on his shelf, taking her time. She was going to punish him for not letting his medical line of inquiry die. When Anna pulled the copy of *California Personal Injury* from the shelf and said, "This will do," Matthew realized it was not a bluff.

"On the count of three," she said.

Matthew pulled his wrist away. "Wait, are you sure this is safe? And that it will work?"

"No. There are no formal studies on the efficacy of this procedure. The evidence is purely anecdotal."

"You're having a good time, aren't you?" Matthew asked.

"Better than usual."

"Do you want to hurt me?"

"No," said Anna. "But the dormant scientist in me wants to know if it will work."

Matthew realized that this gave him bargaining power.

"If I let you do it, will you tell me what happened?" he said.

Anna mulled over the offer. "You can ask three questions."

"Ten."

"Three."

"Seven."

"Three."

"Anna, do you understand how a negotiation works?"

"I do. I'm worried that you don't. Three."

"Give me five."

"Three. Hand on the table now or no deal."

"There's no way you can break my wrist, right?"

"Doubtful. But you could always sue me."

Matthew got on his knees and leveled his arm across the table. He turned his head away and closed his eyes. "Just do it."

"On the count of three," Anna said. "One."

She swung the book down on Matthew's wrist on the first count. A solid thud reverberated throughout the office.

"Two. Three."

1998

SANTA CRUZ, CALIFORNIA

George didn't hear the man enter the house or the footfalls on the creaky floorboards. She didn't hear the rattle and squeak as he opened her bedroom door. What woke her up was his fingers around her neck. And it woke her up fast. He didn't look familiar. He wore a blue sweatshirt under a denim jacket. Either the sweatshirt or the jacket smelled like three-day-old armpit. His hair was greasy and vaguely in the mullet category. His skin suggested years spent picking at zits. This wasn't the kind of man she would have engaged with under any circumstances. And here he was in her bedroom, choking her.

It took about three seconds for George to understand what she had to do. He was on top, straddling her body. She twisted onto her side, breaking the hold, and then rolled back over and kneed him in the groin. She screamed after he lost his grip. He moaned

281

in pain, but the knee hadn't been a debilitating blow. He punched her in the face, and his hands returned to her neck.

"Who are you?" he said, when a sliver of light from a streetlamp illuminated her face.

She wouldn't remember the question until later. She boxed his ears. Her legs thrashed beneath him.

"Bitch," he said, his fingers tightening.

You're fucking strangling me, and I'm *the bitch?*

The intruder pinned George's legs to the bed with his knees. Only her arms were free. She tried to wrench his fingers off her neck. When that failed, she landed blows to his head, but they grew weaker as the oxygen in her blood diminished.

George's scream woke Kate. She got out of bed, and as she climbed the stairs from the basement, she heard the muffled sounds of a male voice. She tiptoed over to George's bedroom door and saw the intruder.

I need a weapon, Kate thought. She rushed into the kitchen and saw the knife block, but she had heard stories about intruders wresting knives from their victims. She wasn't sure how well she'd do in a knife fight, never having seen one outside of *West Side Story.* The recycling sat by the back door. A 750-milliliter bottle of Smirnoff vodka (Anna bought only that brand, in honor of Kate) was at the top of the bin. Kate picked up the bottle and grabbed the phone. She dialed 911, told the operator there was an intruder in the house, put down the phone, and padded down the hall and into George's room.

The man didn't hear her enter or come up behind him. He noticed her only when he felt the bed bounce and tilt as Kate stepped onto the mattress. Kate held the neck of the bottle in both hands like it was a baseball bat. She told herself she had to commit to this swing. She had a tactile memory of playing softball. She had been painfully mediocre, rarely making contact with the ball, but she'd always dedicated her whole body to the swing. Kate smashed the bottle into the side of the man's head. In the movies, the bottle would have broken, but in real life, it merely slipped from her hands.

She heard the man grunt, then watched him slowly cant to the side and slip off the bed. George gasped as if she had just come up from a long dive; her breath rattled as her lungs gorged on air. When she could move again, she climbed off the bed and stood over the man. He was on the floor, a small bit of blood on his temple. Kate picked up the bottle.

"Hit him again," George said. "He might wake up."

Kate's heart was still bucking in her chest. She didn't want him to get up either. This time she swung the bottle like it was a golf club. Maybe with a little less conviction, but there was a solid thump as it made contact. The intruder still wasn't moving.

"How are you feeling?" Detective Rose Williams asked from the edge of the hospital bed.

She wore a ridiculously snug brown pantsuit with her badge clipped to the waistband. Rose had gotten married just a year before to an ex–defensive lineman who still had a lineman's appetite. She'd been gaining weight at a slow but steady pace, eating all those square meals with her husband. She had resisted buying new clothes, but feeling the pinch in her waist now, she was about to relent.

"I don't feel much of anything," George said. "They gave me some painkillers and sedatives."

Fuchsia finger marks were forming around her neck. A mottled purple bruise decorated her eye. She was under observation for a minor concussion but would go home the next day.

"Could you look at a picture for me?"

"Sure."

Detective Williams showed George a mug shot of the suspect. He had a record, so a picture was on file.

"Did you know him?" Williams asked.

George glanced at the picture and looked away. "No."

"Are you sure you've never seen him before?" Rose asked, rephrasing. There were no signs of a break-in, and her partner, Detective Russell, had said something about the girls' stories not jibing.

"I have no idea who he is," George said.

"Well, you put up a good fight," Rose said.

"Until I didn't," George said.

The drugs made George's answers sound flat and unemotional. As George was internally piecing together the events of the previous night, the detective walked her through them again.

"I can come back if you like," Rose suggested.

"I'm fine."

"What's the first thing you remember?"

"I woke up to a man strangling me."

"Did he say anything to you?"

"He said, 'Who are you?' "

"That's an odd thing to say, don't you think?"

"I did think it was strange. Although not as strange as his strangling me."

"Did you say anything to him?"

"I couldn't talk with his hands around my throat."

"Then what happened?"

"Kate hit him with the vodka bottle."

"Just once?"

"I think so."

"Tell me what happened," Detective Frank Russell said to Kate as she sat in a swivel chair by his desk. Detectives Russell and Williams had been first on the scene the night before. They'd interviewed Kate and Anna at the hospital, but the women were too distracted, and Anna had been too inebriated, to be much use, so they were questioned the next day. Detective Williams took Anna into an interrogation room. Kate — the batter, as they had dubbed her — was given a seat next to Russell's desk.

She was a little thing, Russell thought, much smaller than the two others — and most grown women. Despite Kate's childish demeanor, Russell sensed a hardness in her, as if her bones were made of titanium. You couldn't dent or scratch the surface; you also couldn't get her to sit still. The chair-swiveling drove Russell crazy. He wished he had taken her into the interrogation room, where the furniture was bolted to the floor.

Detective Russell steadied the arm of the chair and said, "You were saying?"

"George's scream woke me," Kate said.

"Where were you?"

"In the basement."

"And your other roommate, Ms. Fury. Where was she?"

"In her bedroom."

"Where's that?"

"She has the attic."

"What happened after you heard Ms. Leoni scream?"

"I got out of bed and walked upstairs into the kitchen. I picked up an empty bottle of vodka from the recycling bin and dialed 911."

"Did you plan on using it as a weapon?"

"I thought about using a knife, but the bottle seemed better."

"Then what?" Detective Russell asked.

"Then I put the phone down, even though the operator was still talking, and I went into George's bedroom."

"Was she still screaming at that point?"

"I don't remember when exactly she stopped screaming, but she'd stopped."

"What did you see?"

"He was strangling her."

"You mean the man in the blue sweatshirt, correct?"

"The same man you found at our house. I couldn't see the color of his sweatshirt in that light."

"Then what did you do?"

"I swung the bottle of vodka at his head. It didn't break. I thought it would break. He fell off of George. I could hear her gasping for breath. He was still sort of moving and I was afraid he would get up again, so I hit him again with the bottle. It still didn't break. Then he stopped moving. How is he?"

"In the hospital."

"Will he be all right?"

"He's going to prison."

"I guess that's good."

"Is there anything else you can think of?"

"No. Where's Anna?"

"She's talking to my partner right now."

"She won't be much help."

"Why?"

"Because she slept through the whole thing."

"She must be a sound sleeper," Detective Russell said.

"She is," Kate said.

The detective studied his notes. Kate studied the pattern on her pajama top — sheep blithely jumping over stiles. When the detective had asked her to come to the station, she hadn't changed, just thrown on a pair of jeans and a coat, not considering that she might want to remove the coat. It was warm in the precinct house. She felt ridiculous wearing a top covered in cheery livestock.

"It would seem that the intruder entered through the back door. Do you usually leave it open?"

"No. But sometimes we forget."

"Is it possible that the intruder had met George before?"

"That seems very unlikely," Kate said. "Especially since he was strangling her."

Detective Frank Russell scribbled Kate's answer in his notes. But something about her tone felt off.

George was released from the hospital the morning after the attack. The marks of her ordeal would take two weeks to completely fade.

She got home and found Kate in the basement watching television.

"You plan on changing out of those pajamas anytime soon?"

"I have nowhere to be, remember?" Kate said.

"I do. But you used to actually wear outside clothes even when you were inside."

"Now sometimes I wear inside clothes even when I'm outside."

"I called my mother. She wants me to come home for a few days," George said.

"I think that's a good idea," Kate said.

"Do you feel safe here?" George asked.

"I'll make sure the doors are locked and I'll keep an empty bottle by my bed."

"It won't stop you from thinking about it."

"I have many distractions."

"You have television."

"What did people do without it?" Kate asked.

"Thank you," George said. "For, you know."

"You would have done the same for me," Kate said.

"The man said, 'Who are you?' Why did he say that?"

"I don't know."

"He came in through the back door. She must have left it open again."

"George, don't tell her."

"Why not?"

Kate muted the television. "Because it

won't change anything. It will only make her feel guilty. What's the point? She didn't invite that guy into our house. She left a door open. If you tell her she did that, she'll reframe it as her hands around your neck. She'll take the blame for everything. And then she'll get worse. We should blame the person who actually committed the crime, and that wasn't her."

"Okay. If you don't want her to know," George said, still unsure what she wanted. But the sedatives and painkillers had made her more agreeable than usual.

"There are so many things I wish I didn't know," said Kate.

■ ■ ■ ■

PART II

■ ■ ■ ■

People don't realize that the future is just
now, but later.

— Russell Brand

2005
DENVER, COLORADO

"Checkout time is 11:00 a.m. Eighty-five plus tax a night and I'll need a credit card and a photo ID," Hank said. At least, *Hank* was the name embroidered on his bowling shirt.

"Can I pay cash?"

"A grown woman should have a credit card," Hank said.

"I have a credit card. I just don't want to use it," she said. "My business partner gets the bills and we're having some financial conflicts as of late."

"We need a credit card on file in case there's any damage to the room or you refuse to vacate."

"I won't do either of those things."

"Company policy," Hank said.

"Are you the proprietor, Mr. . . . Hank?"

"Hank Weathers. Yes. I am the . . . proprietor," Hank said, sounding out the last word. It had a nice ring to it. He'd use it more often.

"So, you make the policy?" Kate asked.

"Miss — I didn't get your name."

"Sarah. Sarah Lake." She said the name out of habit, immediately realizing it was a mistake. If she couldn't convince Hank to depart from policy, she'd have a hard time explaining why her credit card said Kate Smirnoff.

"That's a pretty name."

"Thank you."

"Miss Lake, I've been burned a few too many times. Now, you look honest, but it's always the honest-looking ones, so you've already got one strike against you."

"What if I left a deposit of five hundred dollars? You could inspect the room when I check out."

"Five hundred, you say?"

She pulled several bills from her stuffed wallet.

"A girl shouldn't be carrying all that cash around."

"Just a minute ago I was a grown woman."

"Be careful, 's all I'm saying."

"Do we have a deal?"

She placed the cash on the counter, right next to the bell. Hank picked up the bills, folded them in half, and put them in his pocket.

"How long will you be staying?"

"Two nights. I'll let you know tomorrow if my plans change."

"What is the nature of your visit, business or pleasure?"

"Business," she said.

Room 214 was exactly what she'd expected. Mahogany baseboards set off walls the color of creamer gone bad; tracks of luggage scrapes accented the entryway. The forest-green carpet, once a proud shag, was now almost smooth, greased down like the hair on a balding man's pate. There were also the obligatory matching pressed-wood nightstands, atop which sat gold lamps with dust-colored shades. A dresser of similar tone and design, but not part of the set, faced them. But the contents of the room were all second-class citizens, invisible really, next to the king-size bed, which was adorned with a once–bright orange comforter and a bamboo headboard.

She opened every drawer in the room to be sure the previous occupant had fully departed. Once, years ago, she was staying at a hotel — a few notches up from this one — and some glitch in the computer system put two people in the same room. Had she checked the closet, she would have seen a man's suit and luggage. But she didn't; she threw her small bag on the bed and immediately hopped into the shower. A businessman entered the room as she was blow-drying her hair. He had the common sense to call the front desk when he saw women's garments strewn across the room. If you think you're truly alone, safely locked in a twelve-by-fourteen-foot space, it's terrifying to learn otherwise. The sharp knock on the bathroom door then still shook her when she thought about it. The manager finessed the situation with profuse apologies, a decadent room-service spread, and two free nights for each inconvenienced party. Still, now she always searched the room, turned the deadbolt, and put the door chain on without fail.

After her inspection was complete, she grasped one end of the orange monstrosity and shucked it off the bed, then rolled it into an untidy ball and shoved it in the corner. She took a quick shower under a drizzle of water that barely had the power to wash out her shampoo. She wished she were staying at that other motel a few miles down the road. But it looked like the kind of establishment that wouldn't bend policy.

She sent a quick text to Colin: *I'm alive.*

He responded, *Where are you?*

In a motel, she texted back.

He would ask *Where* again, and she would turn off her phone. She wasn't sure why she didn't want him to know her precise location, and, in truth, she had grown tired of the tall tales she told. But he didn't need to know how many places she had been, places with nothing to see but crumbling blacktop and cheap motels, and since he got her credit card bills, she always paid with cash.

One month earlier, Kate had solicited the services of Marvin White, PI.

"Mr. White?"

"Call me Marvin."

Files and magazines towered over his battered wooden desk. Coffee rings dotted the surface in a halo around the blotter. White was in his sixties, but his skin hung with a few more years. He wore his clothes with an effort at professionalism. A blue pin-striped suit; a tie gone slack; a jacket that was a little too snug, so it killed most of the day on the back of his chair. Faded coffee stains spotted his beige shirt. Kate thought it was a good color for someone prone to spillage. She'd found his name in the phone book: Marvin White, PI. His logo was a silly fedora, but his credits included twenty years in the Denver PD. He never mentioned what division.

The office was a single room in an old brick building a few miles from downtown. His door had one of those prism windows with his name lettered across it, just like Sam Spade's in *The Maltese Falcon*. Kate smiled when she saw it. Her eyes darted around the room when Mr. White opened the door for her. It was so classic, it felt like a movie set. He had to clear off the chair for her to take a seat. A couple of bowling trophies tagged the corners of the room. Several framed photos were mounted on the wall: White shaking hands with presumably important people Kate didn't recognize.

"Have a seat, Ms. Smirnoff."

"Call me Kate."

She hadn't used her real name in a long while. It felt like a comfortable old coat. Kate had wanted to use a pseudonym, but that didn't seem wise when one was meeting a private investigator.

"Now, Kate, on the phone you said you were looking for a particular individual."

"I'm looking for information about a man named Roger Hicks."

"You want me to track him down?"

"That would be impossible."

"Why is that?"

"He's been dead seven years."

■ ■ ■ ■

"Kate, where are you now?" Colin asked as he answered the phone.

"Nebraska," she lied. Although if he'd asked her a week ago, it wouldn't have been a lie.

"Why Nebraska?"

"It's centrally located."

"Are you enjoying yourself?"

"Yes." Her affirmation carried no conviction.

"What have you seen?"

"I've been through six different states so far. I've seen lots of things."

"I think you should come home," Colin said.

"I don't have a home anymore," Kate said.

"Then I think you should go to a city where you know some people, or at least stop wandering."

"This was your idea, remember?" Kate said. "You practically kicked me out of Boston."

"I think that might have been a mistake."

"It wasn't. I'm being very productive."

"Kate —"

Colin, like many litigating attorneys, had a remarkable ability to speak ad hoc in the most persuasive manner. Since Kate wasn't open to persuasion, she interrupted, shutting down any chance for opposition.

"I need to start a corporation," Kate said. "If you could handle that, I'd appreciate it. I've looked into the matter and I think an S corp. is best. I want it incorporated in Delaware and I'll need you to be the treasurer so that you can write checks for me periodically. I'd like you to move seventy-five percent of the money in my personal investment accounts into the corporation. Let's call it Golden Retrieval Incorporated. How quickly can you set this up?"

"Golden Retrieval? Like the dog?"

"Yes, like the dog."

"I don't understand."

"I'll pay your usual fee."

"It's not about the money, Kate. You're not making any sense."

"I would rather not put my money and trust in the hands of a complete stranger, but I will if I have to. Can you set this up for me? My battery is about to die."

Colin's pause was perhaps one of his longest telephone pauses ever. He ran his fingers through his hair, answered another clue in the morning's crossword puzzle, took a sip of coffee, then another. He cleared his throat and finally spoke.

"If that's what you want, Kate."

"I'll send you the details in an e-mail."

"How can I get in touch with you?" he asked.

"You have my number."

"Where are you going, Kate?"

2001
BOSTON, MASSACHUSETTS

"Where am I?" Anna asked.

"You're in the hospital," the nurse said.

"How did I get here?"

"You were brought by ambulance two days ago," the nurse said.

"Two days?"

"Do you know what year it is?" the nurse asked.

"It's 2001?"

"Do you know what month it is?"

Colin's wedding had been May 19, a date that had been drilled into her head for nine months. Hadn't she just been at the wedding?

"May?" Anna said.

"Yes," said the nurse.

"What am I doing here?" Anna asked.

Consciousness had come slowly, her senses clicking in one at a time. First it was hearing. Voices, muffled, incomprehensible, layered on top of one another. The squeak, the knock, the shuffle of shoes on the linoleum floor. And the constant beeping of the heart monitor, toggling between steady and erratic. Then it was smell, the distinct antiseptic odor of a hospital. Kate used to say it was the smell of blood being drawn. The next sense that took hold was touch, specifically pain, but a disguised version, cloaked in morphine. Anna kept her eyes shut even when she knew she could open them. She listened for familiar voices but heard none; she steeled herself for what would come next.

Her inchoate memories were like camera stills. A picture of her brother dancing with his bride; he appeared beleaguered and numb, but a comic smile was plastered on his face. Of her mother traversing the room, like a mad scientist's crossbreed of a security guard and a debutante. Of her father holding court in the corner, ice clinking in his bourbon glass. And of so many privileged men in suits swilling booze, erupting in Tourette's-like noises, all desperate attempts to signify celebration. She saw an image of herself in the mirror trying to rip off a shiny pink, strapless gown, a straitjacket for a princess. Then Malcolm. Then the images dissolved, and she recalled an unshakable memory. Under the unforgiving fluorescent lights of the roadside diner, she was the happiest she had ever been. She never wanted to leave. She could have sat in that booth for the rest of her life. Malcolm. French fries and an apple pie. Fuck everything else.

Anna had opened her eyes slowly, as if her lids were weighted. She'd thought about closing them again and keeping them that way, but it was time to surface. The obstinate glare of the lights and white walls caused her eyes to tear and blink in flutters until her pupils adjusted. Several get-well-soon bouquets punctuated the bland and sterile furnishings. It wasn't until much later, after Anna noticed the lack of cards, that she learned they'd come from the patient in the adjacent room, who suffered from allergies.

Anna had tried to move, dislodging the pulse oximeter on her finger. A solid beep alerted the nurse, who'd entered the room and returned the clip to Anna's index finger. And that's when their conversation had begun.

"I've been out two days?" Anna asked again.

"You were in a lot of pain. The morphine kept you unconscious most of that time."

"Where's Malcolm?" Anna asked.

The heart monitor beeped faster, like a

306

truck backing up. The nurse looked at Anna's vitals.

"I don't know. Let me find your family. I think your mother went to the cafeteria for a cup of coffee. And I'll get the doctor."

The nurse swiftly departed. Anna took an inventory of her injuries. A bandage on her forehead suggested a concussion or a brain contusion; a broken leg, probably an ankle, since the cast stopped at her knee. A few broken ribs, based on the tightness in her chest. An IV taped to her hand delivered morphine and fluids. She could feel the Foley catheter. She would tell them to remove it as soon as possible.

A few minutes later, Lena entered the room with a cup of coffee. As a med student, Anna had spent a lot of time in hospitals witnessing the state of family members under comparable circumstances, and she was alarmed by how coifed her mother appeared. Perhaps a bit tired. But shockingly, almost disconcertingly, normal. Lena sighed, put her coffee on the end table. Her brow wrinkled — as much as it could — in disappointment.

"What have you done?" she said.

Lena was under strict instructions to phone Colin as soon as Anna regained conscious-

307

ness. She was not to tell Anna anything until he arrived at the hospital. Before he entered Anna's room, he found her doctor in the corridor and asked him if he would sedate Anna. The doctor refused. She was on morphine. That should be enough. Colin entered the room, which was Lena's cue to depart.

"What happened?" Anna asked. It seemed as if she had been asking that question from the moment she'd opened her eyes.

Colin delivered the facts as plainly as possible. At 3:46 the morning after the wedding, a man driving an SUV had had a stroke and veered into oncoming traffic, hitting Malcolm's VW at forty-five miles per hour. The VW spun in a full circle and crashed to a stop against a light pole. Malcolm had likely died on impact, although the paramedics made attempts to resuscitate him. Anna was taken to Mass. General. She'd suffered a brain contusion, a broken ankle, three broken ribs, and several lacerations, one of which had slashed open her forehead and required twenty-seven stitches to close. Lena made a scene demanding a plastic surgeon, but her demands were ignored, given Anna's critical condition.

Anna listened carefully but managed not

to hear the part of the story where Malcolm died.

"What happened to Malcolm?" Anna asked.

"He died," Colin said.

"How?"

"He died in the car accident you were in."

"We were in the car together?"

"Yes. You were together."

"No," Anna said.

"Yes."

"Malcolm's dead?" Anna asked again. She sat up, trying to figure out how many tubes and needles she would have to extract from her body before she could escape the room.

"Anna, you're severely injured. You need to stay in bed."

"I don't understand what happened," Anna said.

Her rapid heart rate made the monitor sound like a bus backing up. She shook the clip off her finger, which caused the alarm to go off. One solid beep.

"Turn it off," Anna said, pointing to the machine.

"No," Colin said. He took her hand and put the clip back on her index finger. "Please stay calm."

The beeping resumed. The sound rattled her and she tried to reach for the switch.

She felt a stabbing pain in her ribs as she righted herself.

"You need to stop that and do what they tell you, Anna. You almost died too."

Anna had no memory of the accident or of anything after sitting in the diner with Malcolm. But she knew, without a fraction of a doubt, that it was her fault. She cried for two hours straight, until Lena convinced the doctor to order a sedative. Then Anna slept for two more days.

Six days after the accident, Anna was resting uncomfortably in her childhood bedroom. Her mother had threatened to hire a nurse's aide; Anna had threatened to jump out the window if she did. Anna could change her dressings on her own and give herself a sponge bath, although she couldn't manage to wash her hair, which was matted down like an oil slick.

Colin had phoned Kate and George and delivered the news. Kate called Anna and offered to come and help, but Lena was so agitated that Anna was afraid Kate's presence would send her over the edge. Another time, Anna wouldn't have cared, but she couldn't stomach any more glares of disapproval.

"It's better if you don't come," Anna said

to Kate.

"Don't you need help?" Kate asked.

"It's better if you don't come," Anna said again, not sure how to explain it all.

"Lena, right?" Kate said. Lena had never tried to hide her opinion of Kate.

"Yes. I'm sorry," said Anna.

"I talked to George. She'll be on the next flight," said Kate.

In some ways, George was better than Kate under the circumstances. She could express sympathy in a more conventional manner, and it was easier for Anna to cry in front of George, since she'd seen George do it herself so many times. Although George was usually crying about a boy, Anna thought. Then Anna realized she was doing the same. George fetched food from the kitchen, and the women spent most of their time in Anna's childhood bedroom. Lena hardly had to see them at all, which was for the best because ever since Anna had come home from the hospital, Lena couldn't bear the sight of her.

For that, Anna forgave her mother. A wedding lasts only one day; it exists mostly as a memory. And Anna had destroyed the memory of her brother's wedding. Anna figured everyone had the right to hate her.

George arrived one day before Malcolm's

funeral. That first night, she slept on the floor of Anna's bedroom. When Anna woke in the middle of the night crying, out of pain or a sudden reminder of what had happened, George climbed into bed with Anna and put her arms around her. She performed reconnaissance missions for Anna. Lurking about, eavesdropping on family conversations, George managed to catch Colin and Lena in a heated debate about whether Anna should attend the funeral. Lena was inexorably against it. When Colin asked Anna what she wanted to do, Anna told him not to fight Lena.

She hadn't seen her brother cry yet. His face had a grayish hue; his voice was monotone and quiet, as if he were on the same sedatives as Anna. She didn't try to talk to Colin or ask his forgiveness. Anna made herself as small as possible in his presence.

The next day, as soon as the Furys left for the funeral parlor, Anna and George plotted as if they were about to pull a bank heist.

"I'm going," Anna said.

"Good," said George. "You should."

"I'll get the keys to my mother's car and you can drive."

The keys weren't in their usual spot. Anna could only surmise that her mother had anticipated this move.

"Maybe we can borrow a neighbor's car?"

"Which neighbor?" said George.

Anna knew of two neighbors: an elderly widow named Mrs. Penwright who owned a 1986 Cadillac, and Leonard Marks, a recently divorced stockbroker in his forties. Anna rightly suggested George would have more luck with the stockbroker. She was surprised only by the short amount of time it took: within five minutes of her departure, George returned with the keys to his BMW in her hand.

"What did you do?" Anna asked.

"I smiled," said George. "You need to get ready. We have an hour."

"What do you need for a funeral?" Anna asked.

"A black dress."

George took a simple black dress from Anna's closet, something she'd probably worn on a job interview once. She also found a boot that would cover up the bruises on the leg that wasn't sporting a cast.

"What else do I need to do?" Anna asked.

"You need to wash your hair," George said authoritatively.

"I can't lift my arms over my head."

Anna crouched over the bathtub with her

head under the faucet as George scrubbed her scalp.

"This is one of the most disgusting things I've ever had to do," George said, feeling a layer of oil covering her hands despite the soapy lather. She had to wash Anna's hair three times before it felt clean.

George wrung Anna's hair out with a towel and combed out clumps of hair along with a week's worth of tangles.

"What are you going to wear?" Anna asked.

"I didn't think to bring funeral clothes."

There was only one thing in Anna's closet that would fit George, a strappy black dress made of a stretchy material. On Anna, it hit well below the knee and hung like a slip. On George, it looked like something a high-end prostitute might wear.

"You got a raincoat or something?" George asked.

She borrowed a tan trench coat that her arms flooded out of by three inches. She could barely belt it enough to cover the dress.

Anna didn't bother with looking nice, only respectful. She was still adjusting to the crutches. She put her arm around George and leaned on her as she hopped down the stairs one step at a time.

Thirty minutes later, George had parked the car and helped Anna traverse a pebbly walkway with a steep incline to the door of the funeral parlor. A somber man in a black suit that he wore like a uniform handed her a pamphlet. She folded it over the hand rest on the crutch and went inside.

Anna could feel eyes boring into her as she entered the chapel. An open coffin sat ten yards away. She was already spent from the journey from the car. Mourners lined up to pay their respects or gawk. Women clutched tissues in their hands; men patted each other on the shoulder. In her peripheral vision, Anna caught a glimpse of her mother staring at her, but she refused to return her gaze. Her brother was standing by the casket, his face ruddy and wet with tears. His wife, at his side, glared at Anna.

"Take a breath," George said, putting her hand on Anna's shoulder.

"I'm okay," Anna said, swallowing hard. The sedatives helped.

Anna tramped down the alley between the warrens of folding chairs. People parted like a backward wake. A woman Anna didn't recognize was leaning over the coffin and whispering her goodbye to Malcolm. She cleared off when Anna arrived. The woman seemed to know exactly who Anna was. It was possible Anna was misreading her expression, but it didn't seem sympathetic at all.

Anna had been to funerals before. Mourners often commented on the handiwork of the mortician: *He looks so alive. They did a good job. You'd never know he fell off a building.* Maybe people had even said it here. They had hidden all evidence of the fact that Malcolm had died in a violent car crash. But Malcolm didn't look anything like Malcolm. Malcolm looked dead. Anna realized that she had come unprepared for that simple fact. She thought she had understood in the hospital when Colin told her. But it wasn't until she was there, looking at him, that she realized she would never have him to herself again.

People were still staring. She turned around in a three-part motion and plodded on her crutches, head down, a few steps toward the door; George followed after her. Max Blackman, Malcolm's stepfather, blocked Anna's path.

"You weren't going to say hello?" he asked.

Anna had met Max Blackman on a few occasions. All weddings. She'd even danced with him once. Max knew how Malcolm had felt about her, even if Malcolm himself hadn't.

"I thought I should leave," she whispered, taking a deep breath to calm herself. She had discovered just a day ago that the combination of crying and walking on crutches was impossible. "I'm sorry."

"We're all sorry, Anna."

"He wouldn't have been out if it weren't for me."

"So logic follows that he should never have gone anywhere," Blackman said, a lawyer to the core.

"I'm sorry."

"Don't say it like that," Max admonished her.

"I can't help it."

Max looked over Anna's shoulder and saw Lena wending a determined path toward them.

"Your mother's at twelve o'clock, closing in. What do you want me to do?"

"Stall her while I make a run for it."

Anna kissed Mr. Blackman on the cheek and lurched her way out of the funeral home. George ran ahead, started the car, and pulled it up right at the bottom of the walkway. Colin chased after his sister and helped her into the car.

Before he shut the door, Anna said, "I'm sorry."

Colin didn't say *It's not your fault* or *Don't*

blame yourself.
    He said, "I know."

1996
SANTA CRUZ, CALIFORNIA

"I blame the whiskey," Anna said.

Kate had been dry heaving since midnight. Now the amber shades of dawn were creeping through the window. There was nothing left to expel from her digestive tract, but her body remained committed. In between bouts of convulsions, Kate curled up in a fetal position on the bathroom floor, where she was attended by a committee of hangover experts.

"I blame the punch," said Arthur, who'd made the punch. "You should never mix your drinks."

"I blame *you,*" George said, pointing at Anna.

"How is it my fault?"

"You practically poured the drinks down her throat."

"There was no pouring."

"You told her it was a rite of passage."

"Well, it is," Anna said. "You turn twenty-one and you get drunk. Everybody knows that."

"This drunk?"

"Everybody's different. If you think about it, she didn't even drink that much."

"Compared to you, nobody drinks that much," George said.

"Shhhh," Kate said from the floor. "Shhh."

They obliged.

A few hours later, when Kate could swallow clear fluids and quiet her pounding head if everyone remained completely still, she returned to bed. She had her own room now, in a rented single-family home on High Street. There were better, cheaper apartments in Santa Cruz, but when Anna realized she could live on a street called High Street, there was no turning back. The deal was done in Anna's mind before the three women had even looked at the place. No one really cared. It was such a massive step up from sharing a dorm room that the first few months were sheer bliss. Just walking up the stairs or down the stairs, going into the basement or crawling into the attic, felt like minor adventures. Anna had called dibs on the attic bedroom before anyone had started calling dibs.

It surprised all of them that their friendship had survived sophomore year, when they had tripled up in a dorm room by choice. Three women, none of whom had ever shared a bedroom before college, in a fifteen-by-fifteen-foot space. While neither Kate nor George had siblings, it was Kate who found the constant proximity the most unnerving. George avoided solitude and never quite got the hang of the comfortable silences Kate liked since her head was always in a book. Anna saw dorm rooms as places to sleep and throw parties that spilled into the hall. Otherwise, the tiny room made her feel like a caged animal; she was constantly leaving for someplace else. George always asked where she was going, and Anna, prone to the vague excuses she'd honed in her childhood, remained enigmatic.

"You know. Out," Anna would say, mostly because she never decided where she was going until she was out the door. On school nights, if she wasn't at the library, she'd go to a movie, but she always kept the title of the film a secret, as if her viewing habits exposed something dark and twisted in her soul. More often than not, Anna watched big-budget American action films or mediocre comedies. George couldn't understand why anyone would go to a movie alone, and Anna had never quite grasped why movies were communal activities. She liked silence even before the film started, and when it was over, she wasn't much interested in what anyone else thought. It was about escaping, that's all. If the film occupied her mind for two hours, it had done its job.

Kate's absences were equally common, but she always left a note saying where she was going, as her *deda* had taught her, in case she didn't return. Sometimes Kate went to the library or the student lounge. Sometimes she stayed late after her shift at the diner and studied at a booth, drinking a shake or eating French fries. Although she did that less often, since her *deda* frequently distracted her from her studies.

Ivan found his customers' refusal to take leftovers home offensive to his frugal Eastern Bloc upbringing. Kate would cringe with embarrassment as she heard him arguing with patrons about the wasted food.

"Are you sure you don' vant to take home? Dat is at least breakvast. Maybe breakvast and lunch. You have a neighbor might vant? Dog? Do you haf dog? That vould be a lucky dog. No? Okay."

He'd then drop by Kate's table and show her the wasted food.

"Americans tink hamburgers grow on trees."

Kate didn't mention to her grandfather that many people don't like soggy hamburgers the next morning. Instead, she offered to take the food.

"I can give it to a homeless person, if you like," Kate said.

Her *deda* nodded his approval and wrapped up the leftovers. As he left them on Kate's table he said, "Give to real homeless person. Not vun of those hippie kids, okay?"

Kate often found trails and hiked, sometimes well into the night, with a flashlight in hand and flares and water in her backpack. It was the most reckless thing she was known to do, but at least she was prepared.

That was how she'd met Arthur. He'd started his hike in the afternoon and was unprepared for the sudden sunset, which left him deep in the pitch-black forest and unable to find his way out.

When he saw the flashlight, he shouted for help. The noise pierced the peaceful hum of nature and gave Kate an adrenaline rush. She spun around and started running. The woods were supposed to be empty at night.

Anyone hiding there was someone to be feared. As she ran, she heard the voice behind her pleading for help.

"Wait up. I'm lost," he shouted.

Those were harmless words, Kate thought in midrun. Probably not the words of a serial killer haunting the woods, but who, besides a serial killer, knew what words would be used? As she slowed down to rethink her escape, her foot caught under a fallen branch, and she twisted her ankle on the way to the ground. The flashlight slipped from her hand and landed a few feet away. She freed her foot and crawled toward the flashlight, feeling a heavy ache in the ankle dragging behind her. She could hear leaves crunching in the distance and then someone closing in. She turned off the flashlight to remain hidden.

"I need help," the voice said.

"I have a gun," Kate said. She had pepper spray. Neither would be much use in a pitch-black forest.

"Don't shoot," the voice said. "I'm just lost. I'm a student here."

"What college?"

"Oakes. I have my school ID on me. I can show it to you if you turn on the flashlight."

"Name three of your professors," Kate said.

"Wallace. Fernandez. Billings."

"What's Wallace's first name?" Kate asked.

"Sherman."

"Don't you love him?" Kate asked.

"He's a prick. Everybody knows that."

Kate turned on the flashlight. The voice and the crunching leaves moved closer. She flashed the light into the young, harmless-looking man's eyes. His voice was deeper than you'd expect it to be from looking at him. He was lean in the way that young men who will eventually become less lean are. He was clearly a student; it was obvious, from his battered sneakers to his threadbare and faded school shirt.

"What happened to you?" he said, kneeling down.

"I believe I'm injured."

Kate continued to shine the light in his eyes.

"Can you please stop that? I feel like the cops just caught me urinating in public."

"Strange analogy," Kate said. "Do you do that often?"

"It happened once and I was in an alley."

"Gross."

"I had to pee."

"Hold it. That's what I do," Kate said.

"Can you stand?" the voice asked.

"Not when I'm peeing," Kate snapped.

"I meant, can you stand on your leg."

"I don't know."

The young man cautiously offered his hand. Kate took it, planted her good foot on the ground, and stood upright. She tested the injured leg. Pain radiated from her ankle, causing her to stumble. The stranger steadied her.

Kate held the flashlight in one hand and put her other arm around Arthur's shoulder. They limped along for a few yards, traveling at the speed of a lethargic turtle. It would take hours to return to the dorm. Kate climbed on Arthur's back, and he gave her a piggyback ride while she navigated him through the familiar terrain with her flashlight.

"This is your fault," Kate said.

"Most things are."

Arthur dropped by the next day to check on Kate's ankle. He brought a bag of ice and a soda and a slice from Upper Crust Pizza. He asked her if she wanted to do something sometime.

"Maybe," Kate said. "We'll see."

George thought Arthur was cute. Maybe not cute enough for her, but definitely in the attractive category, and he wasn't peculiar in any way. Even as Kate hastened his departure, she appeared interested.

"What are you doing?" George asked. "Don't you like him?"

"I'm undecided."

"What would help you decide?" said George.

Kate had gone on a few dates with her lab partner six months ago, but after that, nothing. George thought an intervention was necessary.

"Do you want me to check him out, get a little history on him?"

Kate thought about it for a moment and then said, "Yeah. But it might not be the kind of history you think."

When Kate explained, it made perfect sense, but it wasn't something George would ever have considered on her own.

"If a guy likes *you*," Kate said to George, "maybe you figure you're his type. The type is tall, skinny, and gorgeous, and you can't really fault a man for liking that type. It's pretty standard. But if a guy is attracted to me because I'm his type, you have to wonder. I look sixteen with makeup on, and I've seen eleven-year-old girls with bigger chests. You see what I'm getting at?"

"You're worried he likes little girls?" George said.

"Remember Mike from freshman year?"

"The astronomy TA you went out with for a week?"

"Yes."

"What about him?"

"His previous girlfriend was a sophomore in high school. And he had some questionable pictures around his house. Nothing incriminating. But I *knew*."

"I had no idea."

"Well, now you know."

"Just because Arthur likes you doesn't mean he's a pervert. It means I need to do a little digging," said George.

A week later George had amassed a small dossier on Arthur's brief dating history. She assembled this information by making the acquaintance of one of his roommates, Lukas, who was immediately smitten with George, and then by going through Arthur's personal effects when Lukas left her alone in their dorm room.

"Good news," George said when she delivered her evidence. "His last girlfriend was on the softball team in high school. From the picture I saw, she was maybe five seven and a hundred and forty pounds. The one before that was short, but she had a rack on her."

"How big?"

"C, maybe D cup."

The next time Arthur asked Kate to do something sometime, she said yes.

"I think we should see other people," Jason said to George.

"You mean you want to break up," George said.

"No. I want to see other people."

"You want to have sex with me and have the option of having sex with other women as well," George asked, clarifying for him what seemed clear to her.

"It sounds seedy when you say it."

"It sounds indirect and cowardly when you say it."

"We're young."

"I know."

"I'm not sure I believe in monogamy."

"That's what people say when they find someone new they want to fuck. Who is she?"

"I could give you a name, but it might change in a week."

George admired women who seemed to store their emotions inside a box, pulling out only the ones required at the moment. Anna seemed an expert at this. She would meet men at parties, go home with them, and then not care if they never crossed paths again except by accident. It seemed to

George that Anna was master of her emotions. That was, of course, bullshit. These men had no effect on Anna because Anna had been pining for one man for almost ten years. Anyone else was merely a diversion.

George might have felt some envy toward Kate's practical approach to men if it weren't for the men she attracted. They were always too soft for George. There was no edge to them, nothing to fear.

George returned to the High Street house and drank Anna's whiskey. She blasted the radio to extinguish the suffocating quiet. She wanted the kind of overt distraction that only Anna could offer. She wanted a game, the threat of excitement, the idea that something good or uncomfortable could happen at any moment. She had never needed Anna so badly. And Anna was out.

George had always assumed that when they all moved into a home with room to breathe, her roommates would stick around more. But Kate still preferred studying in the library, and Anna continued to vanish without speaking of where she was going. She left brief Post-it notes on their refrigerator. *I'll be back* was all she'd write. The statement seemed so obvious that it made Kate and George wonder if one day, they wouldn't find the note, and Anna wouldn't return. Still, her unexplained absences always upset the balance in the home. While George and Kate could resent Anna on various grounds, they needed her there to resent.

On this night, George waited patiently for Kate to come home, ignoring her loneliness in anticipation of its end. At midnight Kate was still gone; her note said she was going to the library and then to Arthur's. George called Arthur's house. No answer. She drank more whiskey and cycled through the five channels on their twenty-two-inch rabbit-eared television. She phoned her mother, who chatted aimlessly for an hour about her solo holiday in Greece. She had returned just a week ago.

"I have to say this," said Vivien. "It's *so* much easier traveling without your father. Not only does he expect me to plan the entire vacation, but I'm supposed to pack his suitcase because he's incapable of that simple task — although he certainly manages for a business trip. Plus, it's nice to keep my own hours. I can get an early start on the day. It is ridiculous being in Europe and wasting most of the morning in a hotel room."

"I'm glad you had a good time," George said.

331

She didn't mention her recent heartbreak. She wondered whether that was the right word. Sometimes it was the men you felt superior to who did the most damage, the logic being, *If this motherfucker won't have me, I must be doomed.*

George felt as if she were inside an empty swimming pool, even with all the modern distractions at her fingertips. She found no solace in the television or the stereo; the dial-up Internet held no appeal. Even the refrigerator offered no comfort. She opened the doors wide to be greeted by wilted vegetables, sour milk, and ice cream with freezer burn. Whiskey was dinner, which was not usually the sort of thing George did. But it was Anna's whiskey, and she never saw Anna wallow. At least, not over a man. Anna had the gift of distraction, a catalog of ideas and plans. You had to be still to feel pain, and Anna never stopped moving. George thought all she needed was a plan, but that vague feeling of discomfort returned. None of the words for emotions seemed to apply to what she was feeling, a mixture of heartbreak and self-loathing and some secret ingredient. How could she feel flattened by a guy who called her "dude" and sometimes peed in a jar because he didn't feel like walking down the hallway in the middle of the night?

Her attraction to men had always seemed ugly to her. Maybe because when it happened, she was consumed by it. And also because she never wanted men who were decent. She felt lust when she felt off balance. She distinctly remembered hating the first man who gave her an orgasm.

More whiskey was drunk. She didn't need what's his name, who'd once accused her of having an emotional tapeworm. The image of the worm eating out her insides stuck. George refused to explore the need, assumed everyone felt it to a certain extent. Everyone was filled with holes and patched them up in different ways. Tonight, George was trying Anna's way.

Before Alexander Graham Bell, drunks were never tempted by the telephone. Sometimes they had to walk miles to satisfy what they would soon learn was only a passing urge. George picked up the phone.

"Can you come over?" George asked.

It was a seduction as clumsy as any drunken, undedicated seduction could be. George didn't try, because she didn't need to.

"Do you want a drink?" she asked, only to discover that the whiskey bottle was almost empty. *When did that happen?* She searched the cabinets for hidden booze. Kate didn't hold with the idea of an official liquor cabinet. Seeing it all in one place, she thought, was too distracting for Anna. Kate made boozing the equivalent of an Easter egg hunt. Anna never complained about the method until after she'd scavenged for hours and come up empty. Then she'd take the car to a liquor store and purchase enough to launch a speakeasy. They were currently in a drying-out phase. A bottle of vodka was hidden in the hall closet behind their winter coats, but George could find only Pernod, that licorice-tasting liqueur that turned cloudy when you added ice. Anna hated the taste of licorice and yet she always purchased Pernod when she was stockpiling. When Anna tried to cut back, she found it helpful to drink booze she didn't like.

George poured a glass for Edgar and added ice, because she liked watching the liquid turn opaque. It felt vaguely scientific. She liked being in the rational part of her brain for a brief moment, since she knew the irrational was dominating.

"Not everybody likes it. But the French sure do," George said.

"Are you drunk?" Edgar asked.

334

"I probably wouldn't pass a polygraph," George said.

"Polygraph?"

"No. That's not the word. Breathalyzer test. That's it. Those words are nothing alike."

"No," Edgar said. "Is something wrong, George?"

"Nothing is wrong," George said, sipping the remaining whiskey and putting her bare feet on Edgar's lap.

Edgar had fallen in love with George's knees first, but he was also a back-of-the-neck man, a breast man, a shoulder man, even a foot man, just not in the fetish-video kind of way. An entire woman was too overwhelming. He preferred admiring them in sections, the way one would study a map.

Edgar rubbed George's feet only after she'd kicked him and told him to do so. Their friendship until that point had remained respectful and distant, in the physical sense. George could confide intimate details of her life — whom she was screwing, whom her roommates were screwing, what friend had disappointed her the most at any given time. She would tell him when she had her period so he knew to tread cautiously, but she had always maintained approximately a foot's distance between them. If Edgar closed the gap, George always opened it. But tonight she was closing all gaps.

She took his wrist and led him into the bedroom, although she stumbled a few times and he had to steady her. An observer might not have been able to tell who was guiding whom. She disrobed in front of him, balling up each item and throwing it across the room, as if she were doing a study on the aerodynamics of various garments. Once naked, she slid under the covers. *What are you waiting for?* she asked. He was waiting for an explanation. There would be none. He disrobed more modestly and folded his jeans and T-shirt, placed them on the dresser. He slid into bed, and George crawled on top of him.

He asked once: *Are you sure?*

She replied: *Shut up.*

Edgar would remember every second of their night together, in part because he had a photographic memory. George would remember tangling limbs and too many kisses, like a mosquito buzzing around her head. She knew exactly one second after Edgar came that she had made a mistake. Edgar held her in his arms and wouldn't let go. Most guys just rolled over and started snoring. George removed herself from his grip. It was like pulling off duct tape. She put on her robe, entered the kitchen, and gulped a couple glasses of water and two aspirin. Afraid to return to her room, she slipped into Anna's room, put on Anna's pajamas, and tried to sleep in her bed. After fifteen minutes passed, Edgar grew restless and began searching for her. He checked the basement and Kate's bedroom before he finally climbed the stairs to the attic. When he cracked the door to Anna's room, George feigned sleep. Edgar knew she was faking, and she knew that Edgar knew. He wouldn't let her escape him so easily. She didn't have to sleep in the same bed with him, but he would be there in the morning.

When light broke, Edgar got out of bed and made coffee. George was already awake when the smell wafted into her room. She stared at the ceiling, trying not to cry, trying not to feel as if something was terribly wrong with her. She couldn't hide in the room any longer. She needed Edgar to leave, but, unlike Anna, she had no plan.

"Coffee?" Edgar asked.

George sat down at the table and let him serve her.

"How did you sleep?" Edgar asked.

"I didn't," George said.

"Can I make you breakfast?" he asked.

"Not hungry," she said.

"Did you drink enough water?"

"Yes."

"Milk?"

"No, thank you."

The sharp, dull responses felt to Edgar like a kick behind the knees.

"Is everything all right?" he asked.

"It's time for you to leave."

1999
ST. LOUIS, MISSOURI

"Hello," Kate said to the man sitting at her kitchen table. He had helped himself to a cup of coffee while she was brushing her teeth. "John, right?"

"Oren," he said.

"Where did I get John?" Kate said, picking up his cup of coffee and pouring it in the sink. When Kate got a good look at him, she realized he looked nothing like the John of last night.

"I don't know — um, I was drinking that."

"I'd like you to leave. Anna won't be up for hours and I don't like strangers in my home."

Oren grumbled something and shuffled to the door.

"Have a nice day," Kate said pleasantly.

Anna was out of bed only a few minutes later. After a booze-soaked night, she could pass out for a few hours, but it wasn't sleep, exactly. She couldn't remember the last time

339

she'd had a natural slumber. She'd study or work in the anatomy lab for forty-eight hours, her consciousness amplified by massive amounts of caffeine or Dexedrine, and then she'd take sleeping pills to regiment the time allotted for sleep. She hadn't had a recognizable circadian rhythm in months.

Kate poured Anna a cup of coffee.

"Thank you," Anna said, taking a seat at the table. "What happened last night?"

"You made me promise not to tell you," Kate said.

"Why would I do that?"

"Because you knew you wouldn't want to remember."

"But now I do."

"But I made you a promise," Kate said.

"You made that promise to me," Anna said. "So if I tell you it is okay to break the promise, it's okay."

"I made the promise to your drunk self. I didn't make it to your sober one," Kate said. "If your drunk self at any point withdraws the request, I'll tell you."

Anna had to go to class. Otherwise she would have poured a shot of whiskey into her coffee and gotten her drunk self to make the request.

What Anna didn't know was that no such promise had been made. Kate, having grown weary of the reckless manner in which Anna chose to blow off steam, thought she'd attempt a subtle intervention. Kate rarely accompanied Anna on her late-night tears, but this time, when Anna extended an invitation, Kate promptly agreed and readied herself in an outfit that didn't appear as if it had previously been worn by five different people. She even applied a layer of mascara and lip gloss.

Kate was a lousy wingman. In fact, George and Anna had crowned her the worst wingman in the history of wingmen, often quoting and requoting her late-night warnings.

In the morning you will notice his beady eyes.

Right now, try to remember your last hangover.

I have a strong feeling that guy has a sexually transmitted disease.

If you go home with him, might I suggest breathing through your mouth.

He's just going to ask you for a blowjob and fall asleep.

For Anna, nothing that happened that night, including the two-hour blackout, was out of the ordinary. She and Kate went to a hotel bar downtown; Anna had found it was the best place to avoid constant sporting events on big-screen televisions as well as fellow med students. Kate played her part true to form, and Anna played hers. At some point in the night, Anna had struck up a conversation with a stranger.

"Does Pet Era mean anything to you?" Anna asked.

It meant nothing to the stranger and yet Anna continued talking about what it might have been for the next half hour.

"Maybe it was a band that never made it. Or an art movement that never gained popularity. A bad translation, perhaps," Anna said.

Occasionally Anna would try to draw Kate into her conversation, but Kate was busy letting the bartender regale her with riveting tales of his at-home microbrewery and the hours of missteps it had taken for him to make the perfect ale. He'd named it after himself: Aaron's Ale. He also figured that having two *a*'s in the first name couldn't hurt if, for instance, someone shelved the beer in alphabetical order. Kate didn't mention they didn't shelve beers like books. She said, "Good thinking."

And then Anna turned to her and said, as she had so many times in the past, "Can you get home okay? I think we're going to leave."

"Why him?" Kate whispered.

"Why not him?" Anna whispered back, which Kate always thought was one of the worst reasons to go home with a man. Anna would argue it was one of the best ones.

Kate used to believe that Anna's recreational hookups were somewhat more dignified than George's, albeit more dangerous. George was perennially lonely, seeking comfort. Anna was bored, seeking an outlet, a temporary reprieve from her brain. But lately, Kate's opinion was inverting. Anna was twenty-four, in medical school, and she was doing things that the eighteen-year-old Anna wouldn't have thought of doing.

Kate watched Anna leave with some guy who said his name was John. Suddenly, Kate felt a frisson of fear. What if he was lying? If Anna didn't turn up in the morning, Kate wouldn't know what to say to the cops. *My friend left with some guy named John. Just John. He was average-looking, brown hair, brown eyes, average height.* Kate rushed out of the bar and saw Anna and John at the end of the block, waiting for the light to change. Kate raced in her wood-soled boots, making a clopping noise like a horse. It echoed through the empty streets.

"Hold up," Kate said.

The pair stopped and waited for Kate.

"Can I see some ID?" a breathless Kate said to the man.

"What?"

"I'm going to need to see some ID before I let you leave with her."

John ponied up his Missouri driver's license. John Porter, five eleven, 160 pounds, brown hair, brown eyes. Kate thought he'd lied about his height but didn't mention it. She jotted down his address and driver's license number and said, "Remember, I know where to find you."

Kate caught a cab and went home.

That's all Kate knew. But Anna's blackouts had grown so frequent she could trust that Anna knew even less. For instance, she had left the bar with a guy named John and the next morning was home with a man named Oren. Those missing frames would remain a mystery to both women, but Kate would pretend she knew.

"Tell me what happened, Kate. Seriously, you need to tell me."

"Your drunk self told me you'd say that."

A standoff ensued, which Kate eventually won. It's easy to refrain from divulging information you don't have. The method, preposterous, had a certain salubrious effect. Kate noted a marked decrease in apartment traffic over the next several weeks.

"Buckle up," James said.

"I was just about to do that," Kate said.

She was. She was also just about to do each of the things he told her to do after that. Like put the key in the ignition, move the seat forward, adjust the rear- and side-view mirrors, start the car, put it in Drive, not Drive 2 or Drive 3 (higher rpms for hills or snow), and press the gas pedal . . . lightly. James had been offering Kate driving lessons ever since he learned that she didn't know how to drive, but recently he'd become more insistent. He provided a series of relatable doomsday scenarios to persuade her that one day she might forestall a disaster with this ordinary skill.

He started with relatively realistic situations. "What if you're on a road trip with a friend and your friend becomes incapacitated?"

"Incapacitated like how?" Kate asked.

"Do I really want to list all the ways a person could become incapacitated?"

"It would be impossible for you to list all the ways."

"Drunk," James said. "You're on a road trip with Anna and she gets tanked."

"She usually waits until the driving is

done to start drinking."

"What happened to your parents was tragic, but you're not doomed to the same fate."

Kate's parents had died in a car accident, her father at the wheel. Toxicology reports came back negative, but he'd driven straight into a tree and there were no skid marks to indicate he'd tried to stop. Kate wasn't worried about driving into trees, although the extreme avoidance of trees could cause someone to drive into something equally immovable, like a concrete barrier. The thing was, because her father was driving, he was ultimately responsible for his wife's death. He could never have lived with that fact. Kate, too, could never have lived with that fact. Or what if she wasn't paying attention and accidentally hit a pedestrian? Or what if a pedestrian wasn't paying attention and Kate ran into him? Technically, it would be the pedestrian's fault, but Kate would still be the means of execution. And so, for years, Kate had remained a passenger, which was metaphorically a little too apt.

It was a Sunday morning and they were in an empty mall parking lot. The stores didn't open for two hours. Kate started the engine, put the car in Drive per James's instructions, and began circling the lot with increasing speed.

It was nice controlling something so powerful. She remembered how much she'd liked bumper cars at the county fair that one time she went. Although she hadn't particularly enjoyed the bumping, which Anna did relentlessly. But she liked the idea that she could turn a wheel, and the car would turn. Not many things in life were quite as trustworthy.

"What exactly is the nature of your relationship?" Anna impatiently asked after patiently listening to a play-by-play of Kate's driving lesson.

"We're friends and neighbors," Kate said.

"That's it?"

"Yes."

That was it. Now. Before, it was something else. Kate had felt that heady flush of attraction that very first day she met James in the hallway, when he'd gallantly dispatched Anna's lingering houseguest. It was Kate's habit, when emotions overtook her, to vanquish them by focusing on intellectual matters. That was why she never went anywhere without a book in hand.

She was currently reading about salt, a subject James once made the mistake of asking her about before she started the car. She was more than glad to put the driving lesson on hold and provide some highlights: *Did you know that salt was used as currency up to the twentieth century? The Afar tribe in Ethiopia traded it in one-pound bars called* amoleh. *It's possible to kill yourself by eating too much salt. Forget years of hypertension: one gram per pound of body weight will do the trick. Suicide by salt was apparently common among Chinese nobility, since salt was so expensive. Sodium chloride is the only form of rock that humans regularly consume.*

The day Kate met James she was reading a book about Pythagoras, which created an enduring connection in her mind between James and the Greek philosopher and mathematician. This association eventually extended to any philosopher or mathematician or Greek person. Finally, she came to realize that she was thinking of James all on her own without any prompts. She could be reading about the invasion of Normandy, and James would come to mind for no reason at all, and she'd feel a blast of heat on the back of her neck and wonder how quickly James could undo her buttons with just one working hand.

James thought of her too. He also thought that maybe she was too *something.* He didn't have the word for it. She looked so young and innocent, but he knew that she was harder than most people and immovable in some ways. Once, when he questioned her lack of ambition in light of her obvious intelligence, he'd received a long-winded complaint about the sickness of the American dream, the ubiquitous desire for money, recognition, and power without any true respect for the simpler things in life. When Kate went on these tirades, she thought she was invoking the spirit of her *deda,* but her *deda* didn't mind American ambition. It was only the greed he objected to.

And so Kate and James continued to think about each other, and James made what he believed were obvious overtures. At least, they'd worked in the past. His leg would brush against hers at the movie theater. Sometimes a quick shoulder rub. A soft kiss on the cheek, his lips waiting for an invitation. But Kate was useless that way. From a distance she could dissect the soul of a complete stranger, but there were glaring things she missed when her subject was too close.

A few days after the driving lesson, James and Kate crossed paths in the laundry room. Kate was sitting on top of a washing machine with a book, as usual.

"What are you reading?"

"Your book."

Kate held up the book so he could see the cover. Le Carré's *Little Drummer Girl.* A battered paperback at least ten years old. It was James's book. He'd lent it to her a month ago.

"You're finally reading a normal book," James said.

"All books are normal books."

"You don't seem to indulge in fiction much."

"I indulge in fiction all the time. I'll be done in about twenty minutes and you can have it back."

James took the book from her hands, slipped a dryer sheet inside to mark the page, and put it on a high shelf.

"Can I have your book back?" Kate asked.

Kate was about to jump off the washing machine, but James stopped her. She would have trouble avoiding eye contact if their eyes were on the same level.

"Do you like being alone, Kate?"

"I don't dislike it."

"That's not what I asked."

"I'm not afraid of it."

"Do you want me to leave you alone?"

"I don't know," Kate said. What she meant

was that she didn't know how to answer the question. Being alone was easy; emotions could be regulated like operating a crane. Once you add someone else to the mix, you hand over some of the controls.

"Let me know when you decide."

She decided exactly eight hours later, after watching a horror film late at night, then going to bed and being woken by the sound of a windstorm outside; tree branches lashed against her window. The wicked whirl of disturbed nature had a ghostly sound. Kate got out of bed, searched the apartment for Anna, and remembered that she was in the anatomy lab. Kate walked over to James's apartment, knocked on the door. She entered without saying a word, took off her clothes, and crawled into bed. James didn't have to mess with any buttons that night.

They were the same as before. Friends and neighbors, only they also had sex and sometimes slept in the same bed. Often James had nightmares and thrashed violently in his sleep, startling Kate awake, which was like taking her into his nightmare. Once, in the predawn hours, Kate was returning from the bathroom and James shot up in bed and shouted, his hand closed into a fist, *"Get the fuck out of here."*

James had no recollection of saying what he'd said. She tried to stay the night a few more times but found herself incapable of sleep, anxiously awaiting his night terrors. When she stopped sleeping over, she thought things could remain the same. They didn't. James no longer dropped by, and whenever Kate knocked on his door, she always seemed to be waking him from a nap.

A few weeks later, he woke up from the nap. Really woke up. He offered Kate more driving lessons. He fixed the girls' leaky faucet and tightened the screws on the deadbolt that were loosening. He even put insulation on their windows, which was a job for the landlord. Kate knocked on his apartment door one day and found James packing most of his belongings in boxes. She asked if he was moving and he said that he realized that he had too much stuff and was downsizing. Kate, a true minimalist, thought nothing of James's desire to rid himself of the burden of possessions.

Anna, however, thought something. On a number of occasions, she'd caught sight of James lugging boxes to Goodwill and trash bags down to the garbage bins. When she returned home in the early hours of the morning and passed by his apartment, she sometimes heard him rattling about inside. She knew a few things about him, had seen the bruises on Kate from his night terrors.

Anna knocked on James's door one evening when Kate was at the library.

"Anna, what are you doing here?"

"I could use a cup of coffee. Do you have any?"

"Sure. Come in."

While James prepared the brew, Anna roamed his near-empty apartment and noticed an antiseptic odor — that cloying hospital smell that gets stuck in the back of your throat.

"Can I use your restroom?" she asked.

"Sure," James said.

Her presence was making him uneasy; her visit was unprecedented, the request for coffee inexplicable. He knew for a fact that Anna kept a stockpile of coffee in their pantry. They never ran out. Ever.

Anna slipped into James's bedroom and slid open the top drawer of his dresser. Just a few pairs of jeans, T-shirts, socks, and underwear. The second and third drawers were empty. The walls were bare except for the shadows where framed pictures had once hung. She went into his bathroom and checked the cabinets. Only the essentials remained — toothbrush, toothpaste, a shaving kit, and aspirin. Baby shampoo and a bar of soap in the shower. She flushed the toilet, ran the taps, and returned to the kitchen.

"Are you going somewhere?" Anna asked.

"Wasn't planning to."

Anna sat down at his kitchen table.

"What are you planning?" she asked.

"Excuse me?"

"Who is your closest relative?"

"Why are you asking these questions?"

"You've reduced your personal effects to almost nothing, which is very considerate. But still, someone is going to find the body."

"I don't know what you're talking about."

"Do you have a gun in here? Is that how you're planning on doing it?"

James tried to pour a mug of coffee, but his hand shook and he had to rest the carafe on the sink.

"I'd like you to leave," he said.

"I can't let her find you like that."

"She won't."

"Well, somebody will."

"Anna, mind your own business."

"I'm going to drive you to the hospital and you're going to check yourself into the psych ward and you're going to tell them the truth. And then they'll help you get better."

"And if I don't?"

"Why didn't you tell me before you took him to the hospital?" Kate asked when Anna explained James's sudden departure.

"I didn't know for sure until I saw his apartment," said Anna.

"How did I miss that?"

"He didn't want you to know."

"How did *you* figure it out?"

"I don't know," Anna said. "I had a feeling."

"He was acting normal. Happy, even."

"Because he'd decided. He had a plan."

"How do you know that?"

"He admitted it, when I asked."

"But how did you know *before*," Kate said. She was becoming agitated, angry that Anna knew more about James than she had.

"I wouldn't want my friends and family to have to clean up after me. And I definitely wouldn't want them going through my stuff," said Anna. "I would do exactly what he did."

Kate visited James just once at the Metropolitan St. Louis Psychiatric Center. He was on a cocktail of meds that dulled his senses and made him appear, like before, as if he had just woken from a nap. It seemed to Kate that James's treatment protocol was designed to extract all emotions so that James had no urges, dangerous or otherwise.

"Do you need anything?" Kate asked.

They were in a sitting room with other patients roaming about, some agitated, some catatonic. Others played games or worked on art projects or sat quietly, staring out the window.

"I don't need anything," said James.

"How about a book? I bet you have a lot of time to read in here."

"It's hard to concentrate," said James.

"Why?"

"The medication makes me tired."

"Oh. Maybe they should adjust your meds."

"Kate?"

"Yes?"

"You should go."

2008
BOISE, IDAHO

"Where are you going, Carter?" George asked her six-year-old son, who had just tied each of his shoes with a double knot and was marching toward the front door.

"Out," Carter said.

Her son had adopted the cagey manner of her third husband, Kyle. Kyle was like Anna in college, unwilling to divulge his recent or future locations. The difference was that George had a good idea of where Kyle was going and where he had been. Slowly, like she was waking up from a deep sleep, she was coming to terms with the simple fact that she would soon be divorced for the third time.

"If you want to play outside, you can go in the backyard, and take Miller with you," said George.

She shoved Velcro-strap sneakers onto Miller's feet. The boys marched toward the back door. It was early spring, and the light snow had finally melted, which meant the grass was brown and hideous, but the air was crisp and just the right temperature for running wild without overheating.

"If you find something you want to put in your mouth, let me investigate it first. And don't sword-fight with the tree branches. We've been to the emergency room two times already this year. What did I tell you about eyeballs?"

"Mom," Carter said, impatiently stretching the word beyond its single syllable.

"You only get two eyeballs," Miller chimed in. "Just two."

"Thank you, sweetie. Four eyeballs are walking out of this door, four eyeballs are coming back. Do you hear me?"

"Yes. Goodbye," Carter said, trotting outside.

Miller followed in his wake. George watched her sons through the kitchen window. Carter climbed their giant oak tree, and Miller hopped on the tire swing and spun so fast she was relieved he hadn't eaten lunch yet.

George picked up the phone and dialed Kyle. She knew he wouldn't answer and that he couldn't listen to a voice-mail message that was longer than two brief sentences.

"It would be great if you came home soon;

I think our house is falling into a sinkhole. Take care."

With the divorce decision made, she felt free again, just as she had during those last few weeks with Mitch. She watched her boys through the window, feeling that familiar aching love, even though Carter had directly defied her and was flagrantly wielding his stick sword at his brother. They were growing so quickly. She tried to picture the kind of men they would become, and all she could see were variations of her husbands.

George phoned Kate, who she knew had Thursday off from the library.

KATE: Hello.

GEORGE: I'm raising boys.

KATE: Did you just figure that out?

GEORGE: They will be *men* one day.

KATE: That's usually how it works.

GEORGE: I'm probably getting divorced.

KATE: I'm sorry to hear it.

GEORGE: You're not sorry to hear it.

KATE: Well, I'm sorry that you married him. And I'm sorry you're sad, because you're probably sad now.

GEORGE: I didn't call to talk about that. I called about my sons.

KATE: Yes. The sons that will be men.

GEORGE: Right. Here's the thing. I raised them the way I was raised, the way I would raise girls to make sure that they weren't shackled by their gender. If I had a daughter I would encourage wildness and fearlessness, and if she scraped her knee, I'd tell her to suck it up and not to cry, just like my dad said to me. But I have boys. And they're different. So I think I should be doing something differently, but I don't know what. I'm responsible for what they're going to become, the men they will be one day. It's up to me to make sure that I don't raise assholes. I love them, but when I look into the future, sometimes I think Carter might be just like his father, minus the chilling nature phobias. And if there is anyone who can properly be described as an asshole, it is Mitch.

KATE: I can't argue with you on that one.

GEORGE: I watch Carter on the playground with girls. He looks at them as if they're aliens, the enemy. There's this divide, like two countries at war.

KATE: Isn't that an age thing?

GEORGE: I don't know. I feel like I've been at war with men for years.

KATE: Those are two different wars.

GEORGE: I need to raise sensitive men who

like women.

KATE: That's an excellent goal.

GEORGE: How do I do that?

KATE: If I find a book with a blueprint, I'll buy it for you. But I don't have the answer off the top of my head.

GEORGE: There's dissension in the ranks. I'll call you later.

Outside, Miller had joined the sword fight. Carter responded to his parry with a riposte that tumbled Miller onto his back, disarming him. Carter stepped forward, asserting his dominance, and pressed his stick against Miller's heart. George walked outside, picked up her own stick, and fenced with Carter until she had him pinned against an old metal shed. George stole Carter's sword and threw it across the yard, then held the tip of her stick against his throat.

"Do you accept defeat?" George said, her voice low with gravitas.

"Yes," Carter said, honorably.

George threw her sword aside. "No more stick swords today. We're going to do something completely different."

When George was pregnant with Miller, her mother had become convinced that the second child would be a girl because George was violently sick during the first trimester and carried the baby high during the last. Vivien had George's old dress-up trunk delivered just a month before she gave birth. Before her weedy growth spurt, before her father became her beacon, and basketball her passion, George had done what the other girls did. The trunk carried the signature costumes of the early years of Madonna's reign: tulle skirts and halter tops, bangles and headbands. George also came across a few of her childhood dresses, special ones that Vivien had saved. A Halloween costume or two had also found their way into the trunk.

Her experiment involved candy and video-game bribes, but eventually Miller found himself running around the house in a flowing periwinkle-blue dress that his mother, age nine, had worn to a cousin's wedding (he said he liked the way the satin fabric felt against his skin, and the breeze beneath him). Carter, more reluctant, wore a witch's robe from a Halloween George couldn't remember, and he let his mother paint his nails purple.

And then Daddy came home.

On the surface, Kyle had been an appropriate choice. George had met him in Boise, Idaho, on vacation with her boys. He

35. Q. Who were you in love with?
   A. A ghost.

But Matthew had just three questions, and he'd gotten three tightfisted answers. Over the next few weeks, he pressed for more, only to have Anna tighten the screws on her box of secrets. If she had been smart, she would have parceled out bits of information, feeding Matthew's starving-dog curiosity. Since she didn't, he scavenged on his own.

With his vast collection of associates, investigators, and databases, Matthew quickly amassed a healthy dossier on Anna. Her arrest and conviction were in the system. He was able to confirm with the medical board the circumstances under which her medical license had been revoked. He tracked her addresses since then and realized that she had been living in Mr. and Mrs. Blackman's vacation property for almost four years. She had her own family. Still alive. And yet she lived in the Blackmans' vacation home. The only thing he couldn't figure out was what her connection to Max was. And Matthew wasn't about to come out and ask.

Matthew lost and found case files the way

was the guide on a river-rafting trip. A man who liked nature as much as she did. A man who scooped up spiders in the shower and released them to play their role in the universal food chain. He could stare at the stars all night, sleep on the ground, and go for days bathing only in a swimming hole. He had the kind of tan that would never fade, skin that felt like rawhide — handsome now, but one day it would kill him, as Anna remarked when she first saw a photo. That was one thing that George and Kyle did well together: they would take the boys on weeklong camping trips, bathe in icy ponds and creeks, and hike for hours at a time. It was when they returned home, when Kyle faced the realities of domestic life — laundry, shopping, cleaning, chauffeuring children to and fro — that their relationship lost its luster.

"What's going on here?" Kyle asked as he gaped at Carter blowing on his purple nail polish, and Miller putting on a tutu. George had adorned herself with a simple pink feather boa.

"We're getting in touch with our feminine side," George said.

Kyle grunted disapprovingly.

"I need a shower," he said, which George always took to mean that he had just been with another woman. At some point she began to wonder what was wrong with the shower at his girlfriend's place.

George followed Kyle into their bedroom.

"Where have you been?" she asked. George had come to loathe that question, having asked it so many times.

"What difference does it make," said Kyle, who also had a low opinion of that particular interrogative. This was his first marriage and he hadn't quite grasped the idea that it involved a tether of some kind.

George wasn't going to engage in one more battle. The war was over and no one had won.

"You should move out," she said. "Oh, and I'm pregnant."

She swiftly departed; the pink boa danced in her wake. Kyle didn't pursue her. He took his shower, and the next day he was gone.

Two boys and the exhaustion of pregnancy quickly turned George's nerves into sandpaper. She had managed to make only a few friendly acquaintances in Boise, mothers of her boys' schoolmates, friends by convenience, occasional babysitters. Children as a common interest was something, but it couldn't compensate for history, for remembering that time you dove naked into the water just as Russian tourists traversed what you'd thought was a secret trail.

If Bruno were still alive, he would have been on a plane while Kyle was still packing his bags. George wanted to call Anna, but she was still punishing her for her most recent betrayal. She considered asking Kate to visit, but sympathy wasn't something that Kate did very well. So George dialed her mother. She spoke in teary hiccups, told her mother that a divorce was inevitable, asked for help with the boys. Vivien responded in soothing tones and promised to book the next flight.

When she arrived, the nurturing mother became the relentless commentator, like the kind you find on cable news. No thought in Vivien's head went unspoken.

Have you seen the dirt under Carter's nails?
They're having cereal for dinner?
Why is Miller wearing that ridiculous scarf?
When was the last time you cleaned the trash bin?
Don't you have eye cream?
Boys shouldn't wear nail polish, I don't think.
Have you gained weight?
You might consider choosing less attractive men. Studies have proven that relationships

do better when the woman is considered more attractive.

What happened to the ceramic vase I sent you last Christmas?

Miller, blow your nose.

Carter, do you have any long pants?

When's the last time you ran a comb through your hair?

George had to think about that last one, and while it might have been a reasonable question, George decided she couldn't stand to hear one more word from her mother. She went online, booked Vivien's plane ticket, packed her suitcase, and told her mother it was time to go home.

"I'm here for you, darling. I'll stay as long as you want."

"I think I should be on my own. If this is how it's going to be, I better get used to it."

With her mother gone, George was lonely again, although she didn't miss the soundtrack. George phoned Kate, who on occasion could provide a helpful perspective.

"I have two kids, another on the way, and I'm about to be divorced for the third time. Can it get any worse?" George asked.

"It can always get worse," Kate said.

It did. Mitch, out of the blue, decided to fly to Boise to visit Carter. He had a new

366

girlfriend who'd expressed interest in meeting his son. As George said when she phoned Kate, he was trying to impress her with a show of his humanity.

George hadn't seen Mitch in two years. The idea of coming face to face with her flawless-looking ex-husband in her current state was mortifying. Bloated from pregnancy, her skin blotchy from hormones, she looked worse than she had in years. She was still attractive to people who passed her in the grocery store, but Mitch would note every single flaw.

She took two hours to get ready on the day he arrived, so preoccupied by her own appearance that she almost forgot to dress Carter. With ten minutes to spare, she put her son in a pair of size 6 corduroy pants and a rugby shirt, an outfit Mitch had sent for Carter's birthday two years ago, when his son was four. It finally fit.

George peered out the window when she heard a quiet engine idling in front of her house. Mitch got out of the rental car and strolled up the walkway. He had the decency to make his girlfriend wait in the car.

When Carter put on his jacket, George said, "Do you have your gifts for Daddy?"

Carter gently patted his pocket.

"Good," said George. "I think he'll really

like them."

The doorbell rang. George's heart raced like a caged jackrabbit.

"Mitch," she said, as she saw Mitch in the foyer. He had a few more gray hairs, but nothing else about him had changed. George was ashamed to admit that the sight of him made her flush. Hate was the first emotion to surface, but a suffocating attraction came next.

"George," he said. "You look . . . well."

He sized her up, like he always did. She could sense that her attempts at camouflage had failed.

"Carter, say hello to your father."

"Hi . . . Dad."

Mitch mussed up Carter's hair. The gesture appeared laughably unnatural.

"Ready to go?" said Mitch.

"He's ready," George said, a slight grin edging onto her face.

Mitch turned back to Carter.

"Carter, empty your pockets," he said.

Carter turned to his mother for instruction.

Mitch repeated his directive. "Carter, please empty your pockets."

"It's okay," said George. "You can give Daddy his gifts now."

Carter reached into his jacket pockets and

withdrew four snails, two in each hand.

Mitch grunted, closed his eyes, and stepped outside. He took a deep breath, and she saw him try to choke back the nausea bubbling in his esophagus. His sick expression made him decidedly less attractive, which pleased George.

"Carter, give the snails to your mother," Mitch said from outside.

Carter dropped the snails into George's open palms.

Mitch stepped back into the foyer and said to Carter, "Wash your hands and then we'll go."

When Carter was out of earshot, Mitch glared at George and said, "That was really mature. What, no grasshoppers available this time of year?"

"I can always find a grasshopper," George said. "But their legs would break in his pockets. Doesn't seem right. Snails are sturdier. They could even survive a plane flight if Carter was careful."

"Don't threaten me," said Mitch.

"Your son wants to share his interests with you, that's all."

"No, you just want to torture me."

"If I wanted to torture you, there would have been snakes in his pockets."

2012
SAN FRANCISCO, CALIFORNIA

"That wasn't so bad, was it?" Anna asked as Matthew cradled his recently beaten wrist in his uninjured hand.

There was a glow about Anna that Matthew found startling. She felt a rush of excitement so heady it made her feel almost sick, a reminder of the past, her need to push the limits. There was that monster she'd banished again and again, returning.

"Are you a sadist?" Matthew asked.

"Not in the traditional sense. But I like all forms of experimentation, which sometimes requires that you be ruthless with your subjects."

Matthew held up his wrist and studied the location where the tumescent form had been. It looked like a molehill had been tamped down with a shovel. Anna noted his look of surprise and approached, taking hold of his arm.

"It worked," she said, trying to stem the

enthusiasm in her voice. "I'd love to see this written up in a medical journal. Can you imagine soliciting subjects for the study?"

"No," Matthew said, pulling his arm away. His wrist still ached from the impact.

"You all right?" Anna asked.

Matthew picked up a gift bottle of bourbon wrapped in a bow and uncorked it. He poured himself a drink.

"Do you want one?"

"No, thank you."

"I've never seen you drink."

"That's an accurate statement."

"Do you drink?"

"Is that your first question?"

"No," Matthew flatly said. He took the bottle and his cordial glass over to the leather sofa and sat down.

"Three questions only," Anna reminded him.

Kate had always believed that secrets would one day become an endangered species. Loyalty and silence were the two things Kate and Anna had most in common. Matthew was outmatched in this game, and yet he proceeded.

Q. Why aren't you a doctor anymore?
A. I lost my medical license.
Q. Why did you lose your medical license?

371

A. I was a substance abuser and I got caught doing things that doctors aren't supposed to do.

Q. How long have you been clean?

A. Three years, four months, two days.

"Do you miss it?"

"You already asked your third question."

"I let you smash a book on my wrist," Matthew said. He felt like he knew less about her now than he had when the questioning began.

If this were discovery, Matthew would have had thirty-five questions to get to the bottom of Anna. And the answers would have had to be the truth because the testifier would be under oath. It would have gone something like this:

1. Q. What is your legal name?
   A. Anna Lee Fury.

2. Q. Do you have any siblings?
   A. I have a brother. Colin Fury.

3. Q. Are your parents still alive?
   A. Barely.

4. Q. Did you have a happy childhood?
   A. I found ways to be happy.

5. Q. Have you ever had a romantic relationship with Mr. Blackman?

A. Of course not.

6. Q. How do you know him?
A. He's a family friend.

7. Q. Have you ever been married?
A. No.

8. Q. Engaged?
A. No.

9. Q. What do you do when you're not here?
A. I read a lot.

10. Q. What kind of books do you read?
A. Crime.

11. Q. Why?
A. Because in the books, people do things far worse than I have ever done.

12. Q. What is your favorite book?
A. Whatever is currently distracting me.

13. Q. Do you mind working for someone seven years younger than you?
A. Sometimes.

14. Q. What do you think of me?
A. I think you ask too many questions.

15. Q. What have you got against questions?
A. Sometimes answers don't help us.

16. Q. Why don't you drink?

A. Because I'm a drunk.

17. Q. Is that why you lost your medical license?

A. No.

18. Q. Why did you lose your medical license?

A. It happened in parts.

19. Q. What was the first part?

A. I prescribed drugs for patients and took them for my own use. I was caught. Sent to rehab and put on probation.

20. Q. What was the next part?

A. I prescribed drugs for patients I didn't know, who were most likely addicts, and gave the scripts to a local drug dealer in exchange for other drugs. I was caught again; I begged for mercy, was sent to rehab, and put on probation one last time.

21. Q. What happened next?

A. Six months later, I bought heroin from an undercover cop.

22. Q. What were you thinking?

A. I was thinking how smart I was buying street drugs under the radar.

23. Q. Did you go to prison?

A. I went to rehab and was sentenced to thirty days in the

county jail. Served two weeks. One
year community service. Medical
license permanently revoked.

24. Q. When did that happen?
    A. Six years ago.
25. Q. What did you do for those five
    years before you came to work here?
    A. I repented.
26. Q. What is your biggest regret?
    A. I have many.
27. Q. Pick one.
    A. Leaving a door open.
28. Q. What was your most cowardly
    act?
    A. Lying.
29. Q. What did you lie about?
    A. That maybe I did more than
    leave a door open.
30. Q. What's the worst thing you've
    ever done?
    A. I killed a man.
31. Q. Was it in self-defense?
    A. No.
32. Q. How did you kill him?
    A. I made him be at the wrong
    place at the wrong time.
33. Q. Do you believe in God?
    A. No. But I talk about Him a lot.
34. Q. Have you ever been in love?
    A. I have.

senile old ladies lost and found their glasses. They'd scurry about like mice in a maze only to discover them hanging around their necks, and Matthew's missing files were often similarly close at hand. But case files vanished on Matthew on a daily basis and he seemed at times willfully incapable of finding them himself. He also habitually accused other people of misplacing them.

The ritual repeated like a skip on an old record.

"Anna, do you have the Smith file?"

"No. Is it on your desk?"

"It's not in my office. Will you please look on your desk?"

Anna would then fake-search her workplace for the file that she knew was not in her possession.

"I'm sorry, it's not here. Let me check to see if it's been misfiled."

She would hide out in the file room drinking coffee for five minutes and then return to her desk and report that it wasn't there. She'd wait for Matthew to leave his office, and then she'd search for it herself. Invariably the file was hidden under another file on his desk or misfiled in his right-hand drawer when it should have been in the left, or vice versa. She'd leave it on his chair, and he would never ask where she'd found it.

It was during the final phase of their ritual one day that she found the Anna Fury file and got to briefly relive some of her grimmest biographical details. Matthew came upon her as she was reviewing the plea agreement she'd made after her arrest. The file was a different color than the others so that he wouldn't accidentally misfile it.

Matthew shut the door and closed the blinds.

"What is this?" Anna asked.

"Let me explain."

"What is this?"

"You never answer any questions."

"I do my job."

Matthew approached her carefully, as he would a large dog baring its teeth. He gently pulled the file from her hands and put it in the shredder.

"That's an empty gesture. You've already read the file."

"I just wanted to understand you," Matthew said.

"You don't need to understand me. I just work for you."

"It's more than that and you know it."

"I think we should swap back."

"I already made that request to Mr. Blackman. He refused."

"What did you tell him?"

"I told him I had feelings for you."

"What did he say?"

"He said I should tell you."

"If that's all, I'm going to go home now," Anna said.

Matthew slid his arm around her waist and kissed her. It was the kind of kiss you saw coming so if you really wanted to evade it, you could. She didn't.

"You shouldn't have done that," Anna said, focusing her gaze on the worn industrial carpet.

"I think you liked it," Matthew said.

"Most things I like aren't good for me."

2005

BOSTON, MASSACHUSETTS

"Anything to drink?" the waiter asked.

This was the kind of restaurant where you were expected to drink something expensive, so Bruno ordered the most expensive water.

"A bottle of sparkling water, please."

"Anything else?"

"No, thank you," Bruno said.

The waiter didn't bother hiding his disappointment as he watched 50 percent of his tip vanish with just three polite words.

Anna turned to Bruno. "You can drink in front of me. I can handle it."

"I can handle not drinking, and the waiter can handle one dry table tonight."

"I don't think he would agree."

"I'm sure you're tired of the question, but I'll ask anyway. How have you been?"

"I'm great."

"You look healthy."

"One of the side effects of not poisoning

my liver every day."

"Is it hard?"

"Not too bad," Anna said.

There were sputters to Anna's sobriety. The official line was two years, but in truth, the longest stretch had been six months, and the most recent stretch, after her second stint in rehab, was only three months.

Bruno thought she was lying when she told him rehab had been easy, but she wasn't. For Anna, rehab had been a breeze. Six weeks of no stress, plenty of rest, and not a single brutal hangover to mar her next day. She went for walks in the woods and smelled fresh air, and because she was doing what she was supposed to be doing, she could sleep at night. Her conscience took a vacation. She had been back to work only a few weeks now, but the palliative effects of her forced internment raised the bar on her coping skills. She was cured. The problem was in her past, like a childhood humiliation that dissipated behind the thick fog of time.

But she was taking shortcuts now and again. She wouldn't always sit through every AA or NA meeting. Other people's troubles could be so dull. She bounced around locations, never being loyal to one group, looking for stories that intrigued her rather than resonated with her. Sometimes all she did was prowl for the meetings with the best coffee and cookies.

Anna and Bruno talked about George with a guarded familiarity. In the restaurant, Anna was carefully attuned to the mild attentions of strangers. Did they think Bruno was her father or her date? A geneticist would have known in a flash. She wondered if Bruno cared what people thought of them. Not that anyone knew the truth. In fact, the worst truth these strangers could imagine was that he was an older man on a date with a much younger woman. It was the other detail that snagged on Anna's conscience.

"How has George seemed to you?" Bruno asked.

It had been a while since Anna had heard from George. Sometime after she drugged herself up and flew to Chicago to help George deal with Jeremy's betrayal, which turned out not to be a betrayal at all, their communication slowed. Anna could tell there were times in their relationship when George was being deliberately distant, rebuking her for some unknown slight. Anna was so accustomed to disappointing people that she never took these silences very hard. She simply waited them out, phoning or writing every few months until they passed.

"I haven't talked to her lately, to be honest. Is the divorce final?"

"Yes. They tried counseling, but Jeremy couldn't forgive her. She's thinking about moving to my lake house for a while with the boys."

"I'll call her," Anna said.

The last time they'd spoken, George asked about rehab and Anna pretended it was a paid vacation. And Anna would vaguely inquire after the family, never saying Jeremy's name so as not to remind George of her last drug-fueled encounter with Anna.

"Did she talk to you about her marriage?" Bruno asked.

"She did. But she told me it was great, until she called me that time and it wasn't."

"Seems a shame to end an entire marriage because of a misunderstanding."

"Marriages have ended for less," Anna said.

Bruno pulled his rental car in front of Anna's apartment. He wasn't looking for a parking space, Anna noticed.

"Don't you want to come inside?" Anna asked.

She had assumed that Bruno would spend the night, as he had in his past visits.

"I don't know if that's wise," Bruno said.

"Why?"

"Because as much as we like each other's company, when it's over, we always feel a little bit guilty. I want you to take care of yourself."

"I would really like it if you came upstairs," Anna said.

She had spent the last ninety days of her life alone in bed. It was another form of sobriety, one that she had planned to end that night.

"So, that's it? The last time was the last time?" Anna asked.

"It's for the best."

"I would have liked to have known then that it was the last time. Not months later."

"Does it make a difference?" Bruno asked.

"It does to me. I really want you to come upstairs."

She could sense his resolve weakening. She had an animal instinct for that kind of thing. Bruno drove through the narrow side streets, lined with cars parked so closely together they looked like toys that had required a giant hand to fit them in place.

"There's no place to park. It's a sign," he said.

"There are no signs," Anna said. Although there were always plenty of signs when it suited her. "My neighbor is out of town," she said. "Park in her driveway." She was lying, of course. The neighbor was an elderly woman who was usually asleep by ten and took her car out only to go to the beauty shop and the store. She was unlikely to notice anyone in her driveway. Although if she did, she had the towing company on speed-dial.

Bruno followed Anna into her apartment. It was clean and orderly, since she had been expecting a visitor. Earlier that afternoon, plates covered with congealed food had towered in the kitchen sink, dirty clothes were strewn across the floor, and her trash and recycling hadn't been removed in more than a week. An odor of trash lingered, which Anna tried to mask with incense.

Bruno followed Anna into her bedroom without protest. He sat down on the bed, and Anna unknotted his tie. He cradled her face in his hands and said, "This is wrong."

"I. Don't. Care," Anna said with a shadow of a snarl.

It was then that Bruno knew she wasn't better, but his shirt was undone and Anna was kissing his neck and he wanted her more than he wanted to do the right thing.

Anna could sense that Bruno was thinking again and fumbled with the button on his pants and the zipper. She threw her dress over her head, slipped out of her panties, and climbed on top of him before he could do any more thinking. It was only when he was inside her that her thoughts, that constant nagging commentator that lived in her head and told her how awful she was, clicked off. For a few minutes, she felt at peace.

Bruno held her in a boa-constrictor embrace for eight and a half minutes. Anna watched the clock, willing him to stay as long as possible. When he unfurled his arms, it felt like her body was falling apart, her organs and limbs and flesh disconnecting, as if Bruno himself had been holding her together.

"Forgive me," he said.

"I wish you wouldn't say that," Anna said.

"I'm going to go now," he whispered.

"So that was the last time?" Anna asked.

"That was the last time," Bruno said.

Anna remained in bed, curled up in a ball, while she listened to the rustle of clothes as Bruno dressed. The bed creaked as he climbed next to her to say goodbye. He kissed her on the neck. Anna never turned to look at him. She didn't even say goodbye.

She listened as Bruno walked slowly down the hall and let himself out the front door.

Tears streamed down Anna's face until she decided that she wouldn't cry over a man, especially one she was never supposed to have been with. She crawled out of bed and splashed her face with icy water, which softened some of the ruddiness. She tossed on a pair of jeans, boots, a sweater. Grabbed her overcoat and left her house.

She wanted a drink but reminded herself that she didn't do that anymore. Or take drugs or fuck strangers. She had to bat away a wild variety of impulses. She walked briskly in the cold fall air and focused on putting one foot in front of the next until she reached Downtown Crossing and found the alluring fluorescent lights of a used-book store in the distance.

She entered the bookstore and was engulfed by the central heat. It was like a warm bath. She strolled the aisles, which were overtaken by overstuffed bookshelves, kind of like untended ivy. Her eyes followed the stacks, assembled with a loose sense of alphabetical order. She had all night, so she started at the beginning, turning her head at ninety-degree angles that followed the horizontal, then the vertical stacks.

A tattered paperback caught her eye. *Sixty*

Stories, by Donald Barthelme. She drew the book from the shelf and crouched in the corner, leaving room for other patrons to pass, even though there were none.

The book had an itchy familiarity and yet Anna couldn't place it. She skimmed the pages for an hour. The surreal dialogue and disjointed narrative felt oddly comforting. And then she came upon a passage that she knew. It drove her back fifteen years and her memory clicked in so vividly, it was like she was watching a movie of herself.

— What did you do today?
— Went to the grocery store and Xeroxed a box of English muffins, two pounds of ground veal and an apple. In flagrant violation of the Copyright Act.

It was no longer the silent voice in her head reading these words. She heard Malcolm speaking as if he were there, tucking her into bed, that time she escaped to the Princeton dorm. Age fifteen.

Anna got to her feet and ran out of the store, unwittingly committing her first crime of the night — a misdemeanor for stealing a two-dollar book. She sprinted four blocks at top speed until the icy air burned her lungs. She stopped, gasping, and doubled over

388

until she could breathe without struggling.

She was helpless against a flood of tears. She sat down on the curb and let herself crumble and wondered how long she could live with that feeling. Then she realized she didn't have to feel anything at all.

1998

Kate had been in a television stupor for seven hours straight when Detective Russell rang the doorbell. Kate climbed the stairs from the basement and peered through the peephole. A man stood in front of the door, eyes cast downward. She could see only the thick wavy hair surrounding a bald spot at the top of his head.

"Who's there?" Kate asked.

Russell lifted his head and answered, "Detective Russell."

It had been four days since Roger Hicks had walked into the High Street home and attacked George in her sleep. It had been four days since Kate had hit him over the head with an empty vodka bottle and put him in a coma.

Kate opened the door and hovered in the foyer, inadvertently blocking the detective's entrance. It was past noon, but the detective noticed that she was wearing pajamas.

390

The top was the same one she'd been wearing when he'd interviewed her. Sheep jumping over stiles. It looked like she hadn't changed out of those pajamas since he'd seen her last.

"What happened?" Kate asked.

"Can I come in?" Russell asked. He didn't wait for an invitation but slipped past Kate and found his way to the kitchen. He had been there before. He pulled a chair from the table and took a seat.

"Sit down, Kate."

"He's dead, isn't he?"

"Please, sit down," the detective gently said.

"Are you going to arrest me?"

"Why do you ask?"

"I was going to offer you coffee or some other beverage, but if you're going to arrest me, that would be weird."

"A cup of coffee would be nice."

"So you're not going to arrest me?"

"Should I arrest you, Kate? Is there something you're not telling me?"

"Like what?"

"Did you know the intruder?"

"I told you, Detective. I didn't know him."

"Have a seat."

"But I thought you wanted coffee."

"Right. Coffee. Then sit," Russell said. He

had interrogated and interviewed all kinds in the ten years he'd been on the force, but something about Kate Smirnoff completely derailed his process.

Kate poured the detective a cup of three-hour-old coffee and nuked it in the microwave. "It's not going to taste good. Do you want milk and sugar?"

"Sure," the detective said. "Where are your roommates?"

"George's parents wanted her to come home."

"Is she okay?"

"I think so. The whole thing happened so fast."

"And Anna. Where is Anna?"

"I don't know. She left early this morning. Maybe studying."

"Do you have family nearby?" Detective Russell asked.

"No. Why?"

"Maybe you should go home too for a while."

"This is my home," Kate said. She set the mug of coffee on the table with a carton of milk, a box of sugar, and a spoon. Then she pulled out a chair and sat. Russell poured milk into the stale coffee and then added two teaspoons of sugar.

"Do you have family?"

"When did he die?" Kate asked.

"Last night. This morning. Around 2:00 a.m. The swelling in his brain didn't go down."

"So I killed him," Kate said. She wasn't looking for confirmation; she was merely stating a fact, a fact that she was going to have to get used to. She felt a deep wave of nausea followed by a hot and prickly sensation in her neck.

"I killed someone," Kate said. Her eyes started to water, but she kept them open until they dried out. No tears fell.

"It was justified," Detective Russell said.

"I shouldn't have hit him the second time."

"You were scared."

"Does he have a family?"

"An ex-wife. A daughter. A sister. We've notified them. His parents are deceased."

"Is there something I'm supposed to do?"

"No. We'll keep your name out of the papers. Try not to think about it."

"That never works. In fact, you just made it more impossible by saying that."

"Memories fade."

"I know. But they just fade. They never go away."

Anna, too, tried not to think about it. She

393

went to the library, to the park, to the movies, even to an arcade, where she played several rounds of Skee Ball with a pair of preteen boys, trying not to think about it. But all she did was think about the night she couldn't remember. An insidious guilt took hold inside her stomach and wouldn't let up. The refrain she silently spoke — *I don't know anything; I was asleep* — became more and more of a lie every time she repeated it. She hadn't slept in the four days since she'd slept through the night in question. While Detective Russell was at her home telling Kate that she had just become an unwitting killer, Anna went to the police station and found his partner, Detective Rose Williams.

"I'm sorry to bother you, Detective," Anna said as Rose led her down a corridor with winking fluorescent lights.

"It's no bother. I'm glad you came by. Did you see Detective Russell?"

"No. Why would I see him?"

"I think he was dropping by your house this morning."

"I left early this morning."

Rose knew that Anna's next question would be *Why was Detective Russell visiting my house?* Rather than play her hand, she waited to see Anna's first.

"What brings you to the neighborhood?" Rose said, sliding out a steel-framed chair for Anna and taking a seat in a plush leather chair she'd brought from home. She actually had to chain it to her desk, it was so coveted among the relics in a twenty-year-old squad room.

"I was asleep when it happened," Anna said as she sat down.

"I know. That's what you told me when I questioned you. You were still a little sleepy at the time."

"I had been drinking."

"I could smell it on you."

"Sorry. I had had a test that day. I had been studying around the clock leading up to it. I'm premed. But, um, I'm not as good at it as most of my classmates. Anyway, I was drunk and so I didn't hear George scream."

"Your friend is okay, that's all that matters."

"Right."

"Is there something else? Something you want to tell me?"

"I saw him, the intruder, when he was being taken out on the gurney."

"You told my partner at the time you'd never seen him before. Have you changed your mind?"

"No. I don't know. I was tired. Can I see him? Do you have a picture of him?"

Rose sifted through files on her desk. She had a hospital photo, but it wasn't the best likeness. Fortunately, Hicks had a record. She found a two-year-old mug shot in her case file. She slid it across her desk.

Rose's telephone rang as Anna picked up the photo. The detective missed the two-second flash of recognition that crossed Anna's face. There were four hours that Anna couldn't recall. But what she did know was that Roger Hicks sure looked familiar. Maybe she'd seen him in the bar that night. Maybe she'd talked to him; maybe she'd invited him home. She couldn't remember any of that, but that didn't mean it didn't happen.

Anna placed the photo back on the desk as Detective Williams ended her call.

"Do you know him?" Rose asked.

"He might look familiar. Maybe I've seen him around, but I can't say for sure. How is he doing?" Anna asked.

"He died early this morning."

After a long and nail-biting application process, Anna was finally accepted at a medical school in St. Louis. George was leaving in a few months for a forestry post in the Russian River Valley. Kate had no plans. If pressed to come up with one, she said that her plan was to stay put. Kate had a stubborn streak, no doubt, but if Anna set her mind against someone else's mind, Anna won. And Anna, after learning that she had had a hand in turning Kate into a killer, wasn't going to leave her alone in a giant house in Santa Cruz in front of a television set.

On the drive home from the police station, Anna solidified her plan.

Kate was on the couch watching television, as predicted. George once commented that TV was Kate's cocktail. And Anna told George that men were George's cocktail. Anna had held her vodka on the rocks aloft and said proudly, "And my cocktail is a fucking cocktail."

Anna entered Kate's basement abode carrying several moving boxes and silently began packing Kate's belongings. It wasn't until the commercial break that Kate even noticed Anna's presence and activity.

"What are you doing?" she asked.

"I'm packing," Anna said.

"But those are my things."

"I know. You're coming with me."

"I'm not going anywhere," Kate said. "I'm

staying. Not only in this house, but on this couch."

In fact, it was Kate's inertia that made what seemed an insurmountable task — making a grown woman move from Santa Cruz, California, to St. Louis, Missouri, against her will — possible. While Kate munched on dry cereal and watched one program after the next, Anna took her study pills and continued packing. She packed for almost three days straight with just a few hours of rest when her body physically couldn't lug another box.

She phoned a moving company and made all the arrangements. She packed all of Kate's personal effects that were not in her direct line of vision, and she'd wait for Kate to take a shower or use the restroom or sleep, which Kate still managed to do, and then pack more of Kate's belongings. Anna even crushed a sleeping pill into Kate's cocoa the last night. By morning, virtually all of Kate's worldly possessions were sealed up in boxes beneath a sound barrier of packing tape.

Anna phoned George as soon as her plan had taken shape. George supported the unorthodox scheme since she had decided to move home for the summer. She hadn't known what to do about Kate, and now that problem was solved. George returned to the High Street house to pack up her own belongings, offer Anna any backup she needed, and say her goodbyes. She arrived the night Anna roofied Kate and helped finish packing Kate's room.

"Are you sure about this?" George asked, suddenly realizing how extreme a measure they were taking.

"I'm not leaving her alone."

When Kate awoke, disoriented by her barren room, she wondered if she was dreaming. Just then the moving truck arrived, and Anna began barking orders. When Kate protested, Anna informed Chuck, the senior member of the crew, who seemed in charge, that he should ignore Kate. She was her mentally ill cousin with postconcussion syndrome, which caused her to forget everything that had happened the day before. Anna explained that while she had been telling Kate for months that they were moving to St. Louis, Kate was incapable of remembering it the next morning. George echoed Anna's directive.

"That's my box!" Kate would shout. But Anna had had the foresight to label every single box with her own name.

"Poor thing," Chuck said as he gingerly ducked out of the way when Kate lunged for the box he was holding.

Anna noted that he was remarkably light on his feet for a man his size and reminded herself to tip him extra well, since Kate was likely to become even more erratic as the truck started to leave.

"You won't get away with this," Kate said.

As with so many things, Anna did.

2002

BOSTON, MASSACHUSETTS

"Wake up, Anna. Wake up."

A woman's voice and a firm hand shook Anna awake. She'd meant to put her head down for just a minute, but she'd been up for twenty-four hours without a moment of rest, and she'd fallen asleep. She couldn't place where she was at first, didn't even recognize the woman roughly jarring her out of unconsciousness. But then she sat up and looked at the nurse. Her name was Betty, Anna reminded herself. Betty. Anna said it in her head again. She was having trouble remembering names lately, and she knew better than to refer to any of the nurses as just Nurse.

There was a problem. Anna could see it in Betty's eyes once she was able to focus on them.

It was a Tuesday night. Not a holiday, no full moon, and yet the emergency room was overflowing with patients. Only a gunshot

401

wound, heart attack, head injury, or compromised breathing would get you within spitting distance of a doctor. One patient with a superficial knife wound had caught a cab and gone to another hospital.

"Did you write this order for Louise Walters?" Betty asked.

Anna didn't respond. She was trying to remember which patient Louise Walters was. The heart attack? Head injury? Pneumonia?

Anna got to her feet and followed Betty to the patient's bed. When she saw her, Anna was able to connect the face with the disease, even though the face was partially concealed by an oxygen mask. Louise Walters, fifty-eight, had presented to the emergency room four hours ago with a high fever, vomiting, and severe neck pain. Anna suspected bacterial meningitis and had performed a lumbar puncture to confirm. She wrote out an order for antibiotics and was whisked away for another patient's emergency. The nurses needed an order for a 5250 shot (5 milligrams of Haldol, 2 milligrams of Ativan, 50 milligrams of Benadryl), a monster sedative cocktail, for a monstrously belligerent homeless man suffering from gangrene.

Betty, a nurse with twenty years on the

job, had seen the antibiotic order and intercepted Deana, who had just two years of experience, before she gave it.

"What does this say?" Betty asked.

" 'Twenty grams of ampicillin,' " Anna said, reading her order. "Shit. That's supposed to be *two* grams of ampicillin."

"That's not what the order said," Deana, who'd almost delivered the toxic dose, told her.

"I'm sorry," Anna said to Betty. "That was a good catch."

Anna had only a few hours left on her shift. She went to the hospital's outpatient pharmacy with a script she'd written for pain meds for Bernard Kent, who had kidney stones: eight 40-milligram OxyContins. Bernard was being discharged, Anna explained to the pharmacist, and she'd volunteered to pick up his prescription for him. On her way back to Kent's bed, she pocketed four of the pills. She wrote in Kent's chart that he'd been discharged with a script for four 40-milligram OxyContins. She waited until an hour before her shift was over before she took the first pill.

"I have to work late tonight," Anna said.

"But you've already been there over twenty-four hours," Nick said. "I even made you dinner."

"I'm sorry. I got behind on some paperwork."

"It can't wait?"

"No. I won't be too late," Anna said.

She hung up before any more questions could be asked.

Anna had never believed that whispers could be about anyone other than her. She was aware that this line of thinking was utterly narcissistic. Still, whispers always shamed her, even in a crowded movie theater.

It was 2:00 a.m. on a Wednesday, not that the day of the week made any difference anymore. The fluorescent lights flickered on in the previously blacked-out call room. She saw green scrubs in her peripheral vision as her pupils adjusted to the light.

"Five minutes. In my office," a male voice said, and then the splash of green disappeared.

Still flicking away nagging messages from her subconscious, Anna sat up on the cot and tried to identify the voice so that she could arrive at the appropriate office.

Dr. Gregory North made eye contact just once during their ten-minute meeting. When he spoke, he gazed through his venetian blinds. The view through the slats was all neon and traffic lights, but he focused on something nonetheless. Like most people, Anna supposed, he didn't want to look at her anymore. When the nurse who would remain anonymous informed North of her suspicions, he had finally taken a careful inventory of Anna's physical being and wondered how he could have missed it. But his job was to observe his patients, not his residents. Anna also stared through the blinds, not sure where else to look.

"It has been brought to my attention that you have often doubled the orders for some of your patients' meds — pain meds and sedatives mostly. However, not all of these meds have been administered to the patient. I have a partial list of the discrepancies. If necessary, I can do a more thorough investigation. Will that be necessary?"

"Excuse me?" Anna said.

Anna wasn't sure what Dr. North was saying to her. She knew she was caught, but what she couldn't comprehend was the consequence. Were police stationed outside the door? Was her career over? All those years of work. Was it all for nothing?

"If you deny this," North continued, "I'll commence a complete investigation. If you admit you have a problem, we can get you help. Once you complete rehab, you can return to work under probation. I've seen people recover from this. It doesn't have to ruin your life."

Then he looked at her.

"Do you have something to say to me, Anna?"

"What am I supposed to say?"

"You need to tell me that you have a problem."

Even then, caught, like a thief holding the goods, Anna didn't believe it. She felt like a liar when she spoke next.

"I think I have a problem," Anna said.

"Good. Then let's take care of it. Go home now and get some sleep."

Anna sat down at the bar and ordered a vodka and soda. If you'd asked her why she was there, she would have said she didn't know, and it might have been true. Anna could keep secrets from anyone, including herself. The exact moment she passed through the hospital doors, she knew where she was going; she just didn't know why. She had showered and changed into respectable clothing, still not admitting her plan. She put on makeup to hide the dark circles under her eyes and applied lipstick the color of blood.

Her eyes searched the cavernous bar. She knew what to look for; she had figured that out long ago. She knew what to say and what not to say; mostly, she didn't say anything. That always worked best. She tried not to remember their names, the men she met. If she couldn't identify a man, she could pretend it hadn't happened.

His name was Miles, he said. (You couldn't stop someone from introducing himself.) He was a musician and a bartender. How original, Anna thought, but she bit her lip to make the comment go away. Miles wasn't working that night, had just come into the bar out of habit. He'd seen her there before, he thought, or maybe she just had that kind of face. Anna didn't confirm or deny. He bought her another drink, even though she hadn't finished the one in front of her.

"Do you have a name?" he asked.

"Doesn't everyone?" she said.

"I'm not asking for your phone number or even a last name. Just give me something to call you," he said.

"I'm Kate," Anna said.

She smiled at her little joke. Miles thought the smile was for him. She had done this before, given Kate's name. She did it because she was doing something Kate

407

would never do.

"A pleasure meeting you, Kate."

"Is it?"

An hour later, she was in Miles's studio apartment. It was exactly what she expected. Furnished with a high-end stereo system and a thrift-store couch. Clothes were strewn about the four hundred square feet, and dishes were piled in the sink, but his records and CDs were all filed in alphabetical order.

Miles unbuttoned her shirt as she was studying his particular brand of housekeeping. He unsnapped her bra with one hand. She had a moment to be amused and impressed, and then she was distracted by hands working on the buttons of her jeans. He pushed his hand down her pants, and his fingers were inside her. She gasped and fell back on the bed. It was all moving too quickly. Anna's internal narrator couldn't keep up. It wasn't that she wanted conversation or foreplay. It just seemed that a few minutes ago, she was in a bar having a drink, and now every stitch of her clothing was on the floor. And this complete stranger was standing in front of her, taking off his belt and unzipping his fly.

"Condom," Anna said.

He pulled a string of them from his nightstand. Anna was thinking, *You'll only need one.* He put his mouth on her breast and bit hard. The pain didn't bother her, but he couldn't leave a mark. She had the presence of mind to think of that, at least.

"Stop," she said.

He turned her over, slid the condom on, and fucked her. She wanted to be somewhere else. Though she couldn't say where. Not home. Not the hospital. But definitely not pinned down on Miles's sandpaper bedspread getting a rug burn on her left cheek. She couldn't feel anything inside of her. Maybe it was the drugs, she thought. Or the stranger. She wanted it to stop, but it seemed impolite to do anything at that moment. Later she would wonder why her manners had kicked in just then. Maybe it was just easier; maybe she liked being punished, or the rush of fear she had in the stranger's presence. Or maybe this was what she deserved. He was fucking her harder and it hurt. She moaned in pain but knew he interpreted it differently. When he was about to come, he shouted the name she'd given him.

"Oh. God. Kate."

1995

SANTA CRUZ, CALIFORNIA

"Vat is de rush, Kate?" Ivan said. "Slow down and digest yur food. Anna and George, you too. You eat like starving dogs."

The women had convened at Smirnoff's Diner after George's basketball game. She had scored thirteen points, including a three-point winning shot at the end of the final quarter. Kate and Anna watched from the bleachers, both experiencing awe and envy. Kate marveled at George's mastery of her own body; she often felt like she was stuck inside a glove that didn't fit properly. Anna's experience was more directly jealous. She found George's legs so goddamn perfect, it hurt her to look at them.

Anna had always believed that envy of another woman was one of the basest emotions a woman could possess. Kate's envy was more cerebral, a sense of bafflement at the imbalance in the universe. She didn't feel any self-pity, since all her limbs worked

410

just fine, and her brain had served her well. But she wished that, just once, she could know what it was like to score a three-point shot.

Three now-empty dinner plates — once the home of meatloaf, chicken-fried steak, and Ivan's special buffalo burger, respectively — were scattered about the table. Ivan checked that his food had been consumed to his satisfaction and nodded in approval as he and Kate cleared the table.

"*Miláèku,* come to office. I vant to chat for a minute."

Kate followed her grandfather into his cluttered back office, no bigger than some walk-in closets, and sat down on the edge of the desk.

"What's up?" she asked.

"I'm old," Ivan said.

"I didn't know. Thanks for telling me," Kate said. "Good talk."

"American sarcasm. It's not so funny as you tink."

"I don't think you're that old."

"Vell, I'm old enough to start to tink about the tings I haven't done. Since I came to dis country, I have not traveled. Or taken a vacation. Elena can handle the business for two weeks over Christmas. I vould like to take a cruise to the Caribbean with my lady friend. I like you to come too."

Ivan had been spending time with a very nice bookkeeper who had also come to this country too late to lose her accent. She was from Portugal. Seventy-one years old, recently widowed. Their relationship, as far as Kate could tell, involved handholding and watching television together. Kate liked Marina just fine but had no desire to take a vacation with the two of them. Perhaps in Kate's absence, they could feel free to do more than hold hands. Not that she wanted to think about that all that much.

"I don't want to cramp your style," Kate said.

"I haf no style," Ivan said.

"I think I'll pass. But don't worry about me. I'll be fine."

"You don't vant to go to Caribbean?"

"No, I'm good."

"Dis would be first Christmas you'd spend without me, *miláèku.*"

"It was bound to happen sometime," said Kate.

In truth, their intimate Christmases under the four-foot plastic tree that Ivan collected from the basement and decorated with her mother's old ornaments always made Kate miss her parents more. She never quite got used to seeing just two stockings hung on the mantel. It would take ten minutes to open her presents, and then they'd eat leftover fish soup and gingerbread and go back to their usual activities. Kate would read a book and Ivan would clean the kitchen. It was a holiday that lasted no more than two hours. Kate was happy to skip it this year.

Ivan marched out of his office and over to the table where Anna and George were sucking out the last drops of their chocolate and strawberry shakes.

"I'm going on cruise for Christmas. Von of you must take Katia for the holiday. Vich one?"

"Dibs!" Anna shouted first. George was about to protest, but she figured that Anna needed the backup more.

"Very good. It's decided," Ivan said.

"Mr. Fury, Mrs. Fury, thank you so much for your hospitality," Kate said before any hospitality had been delivered. She shook Donald's hand first, a strong businessman's grip that he didn't lighten up for anyone. Then she shook Lena's hand. The corpse handshake, as Anna called it. The hand barely moved in Kate's grip, fingers cold. It sent a tiny shiver through Kate.

Lena looked Kate up and down, inspecting the young woman's secondhand sweater, scuffed sneakers, and baggy blue jeans with a look of distaste that made Anna want to stand in front of Kate like a human blockade.

"We have to go," Anna said, grasping Kate's arm, dragging her upstairs.

Anna gave Kate a brief tour of the house, ending in Colin's bedroom. Anna entered without invitation.

"What is it about knocking that you find so offensive?" Colin asked.

"The door was open."

"The door was ajar. There is a difference."

"I assume if you were whacking off you would lock it," Anna said.

"Hello, Anna," Colin said, kissing his sister on the forehead and then punching her in the arm before turning to her friend. "You must be Kate."

"Hi," Kate said, stretching out her hand.

She was pleased to discover that Colin had a normal handshake, not bone-crushing, not dead. Anna flopped down on Colin's bed. Kate stood awkwardly by the door. Colin pulled out his desk chair for her and then sat next to Anna. The siblings fell into their usual debriefing session as Kate played silent observer.

"Where's Malcolm?"

"You're so transparent," said Colin.

"No, I'm just trying to be hospitable. I want to make sure he's offered more to eat than tuna and melba toast."

"That's just what the women get. He's having Scotch and mixed nuts with Dad."

"Why?"

"Dad wants to share his wisdom or his Scotch. I don't know. Can we talk about Mom for a minute?"

"If you insist."

"What is wrong with her face? It looks almost like she had a stroke, but it's affected the wrong part of her."

"Have you heard of botulinum?" Anna said.

"The food-borne toxin?"

"She's having it injected into her forehead," said Anna.

"Why is Mom having a food-borne toxin injected into her face?"

"So she won't frown and get more wrinkles."

"You're joking."

"Look it up. It's the latest nonsurgical cosmetic treatment. It's relatively safe, as far as I can tell."

"I don't understand women," said Colin.

"Your last girlfriend had fake boobs and you had no problem wrapping your head around that, so to speak."

Colin shoved Anna off his bed with his feet. She landed with a thud on the ground.

"Okay, time for you to go," he said.

"What's on the agenda tonight?" Anna asked.

"Malcolm and I are going to a poker game," Colin said. "I don't know what you're doing."

"Take us with you," Anna said as Colin twisted her arm behind her back and police-walked her out of his room.

Anna wriggled out of Colin's grasp, faked to her left, and launched herself back onto his bed.

"Please," Anna said, hands meeting in prayer.

"No. This game is important. We're playing with these Harvard pricks. Bradford Marsh always wins. I just want to see him wiped out for once. I don't care who does it."

"If you want someone to beat him, take us."

"I've played poker with you, Anna. You're good. But not that good."

"Not me," Anna said. "Let Kate play. She's a human lie detector."

Kate felt like a performing monkey. Her

audition was a poker game with Anna, Malcolm, Colin, and some guy named Jack. Jack was famous in Colin's circle of poker buddies for not having any tells, kind of like Lena's Botox face. As far as Anna was concerned, Jack was about as dead as a person who was technically alive could be. And he wasn't the still-waters-run-deep kind of reserved. You actually got the feeling that there was nothing more than a puddle there.

Three hours in and Kate and Jack were the last players standing in the practice game. Unlike Jack, Kate had dozens of tells vying for attention. One of her tricks was to roll them out in random sequences, like drawing a name from a hat. The lip bite, the furrowed brow, the tongue click, the squint, the half cough, the gaping yawn, the shoulder twitch. Even Kate didn't know if she had any *real* tells anymore. Flat Jack gave Kate nothing to read, so she read only his game. In the end, it came down to luck. In her hand she held a jack and queen; the flop came seven, four, ten. Both players checked, and the turn was an ace.

"All in," Kate said, shoving her pot of peanuts to the center of the table.

Jack called. The river was a king.

While Anna, Colin, and Malcolm discussed strategy for the evening, Kate retired to the corner with a book. Malcolm glanced over curiously.

"What are you reading there, Kate?"

Kate held up the book. Malcolm read the title, adding a question mark to the end.

"The Fluxion Debate?"

"Is that a science fiction novel?" Colin asked.

"I wish," Anna said, having already gotten an earful about its contents.

"No, it's about Sir Isaac Newton and Gottfried Leibniz's war over who invented calculus."

"Can I see that?" Malcolm asked, extending his hand.

Kate reluctantly passed him the book. Malcolm took a seat on the floor next to Kate.

"Newton called calculus the fluxion method, right?" Malcolm said.

"Right," Kate said.

"Didn't Newton send a letter to Leibniz with an anagram expressing the fundamental theory of calculus, and then after that, Leibniz claimed to have invented calculus?"

"No," Kate said with a long sigh, stealing back her book. "I mean, yes. Newton sent the stupid anagram letter because he was a paranoid asshole. Here's the thing: It's perfectly possible that two men discovered calculus at the very same time. But Newton was buried like a king, and Leibniz, who was an all-around great thinker whose philosophies have made major contributions to modern geology, psychology, computer science — he was buried like a pauper."

"So you're on Team Leibniz, I see," Malcolm said.

"She always goes for the underdog," Anna said.

"What's the point in rooting for a winner?" said Malcolm.

Kate decided she liked Malcolm. He was different. He stayed put on the floor, continuing to read Kate's book over her shoulder. Anna watched them out of the corner of her eye, wondering what it was about Kate that drew Malcolm's attention. Maybe Malcolm, too, liked the underdog.

The buy-in for the game was one grand. Kate tried to make a run for it when she heard the price, but Colin chased after her and clumsily abused the only information he had to persuade her.

419

"Think of it this way. Bradford Marsh is Isaac Newton. You, you're Gottfried Leibniz."

Kate found no logic in Colin's argument, but there was an undeniable charge in the air and she didn't feel like being the person to neutralize it. Besides, it wasn't her money.

"How old is this chick?" Bradford Marsh said after introductions were made. Two of his fraternity brothers, Jameson Walsh and Patrick Reed — both ringers for Bradford — were already seated at the table, doling out chips.

"I'm twenty," Kate said.

"You look like you're twelve."

"I look like I'm sixteen," Kate said. A fair assessment.

"Would you like some candy, little girl?" Patrick or Jameson said.

"If you have any," Kate answered.

"You're serious about this?" Bradford said to Colin.

"They have the money. They want to play. You're not scared of some little girls, are you?" said Colin.

"Deal," Bradford said.

Anna went out first, her impulsiveness and love of the bluff getting the better of her. Colin shook his head in disappointment.

"You need discipline, Anna."

Over time, Kate got a clear sense of the men she was playing. Jameson wasn't as bad as he first seemed. Kate noted that he had a southern drawl that he tried to hide through hard Yankee edges in his voice. He regarded her with curiosity, not disdain. Patrick seemed vacant, harmless. But Bradford needed to lose. She felt a visceral distaste for him. Containing it, she knew, would mess with her game, so she let it spill out whenever the urge hit.

"I see you and I'll raise you two hundred," Bradford said.

Malcolm and Patrick folded. Kate had a feeling Colin had a decent hand. She sat with two tens.

"He's bluffing," she said.

Bradford chuckled casually, but his eyes narrowed.

"You sure about that, sweetheart?"

"I'm pretty sure," Kate said. "Check." She tossed her chips in the pot.

"Check," Colin said, adding to the pot.

Bradford looked at his hand one more time and tossed his cards face-down on the table.

"Cunt," he whispered.

"What did you say?" Malcolm said, getting to his feet.

Then Colin stood. Then Bradford and Jameson and Patrick stood, only because everyone else was standing. Even Anna got up. Kate stayed put.

"He said *cunt,*" said Kate. "Now, if you could all sit down again, that would be great. Because I'd like to finish this game. It's way past my bedtime."

Anna had always thought of Kate as buttoned up and restrained, but in sharp relief to the roomful of testosterone, with her towers of chips piled high in front of her, Anna saw, Kate had a stunning coolness. Unlike Anna, Kate could control her urges; she wasn't in a constant battle with herself. Her discipline gave her power. Days later, it occurred to Anna that Kate had orchestrated the near brawl to knock her opponents off balance.

Three hands later, Bradford went all in on a pair of fives with Colin holding two kings. A third king came on the turn, cementing Bradford's fate. Bradford threw his cards on the table and looked Kate over one more time.

"Why don't we call it a night," Bradford said. "You two can duke it out later."

Kate collected her winnings as swiftly as possible. Obligatory but strained handshakes followed. As she was leaving,

Kate approached Bradford and offered him her hand.

"Good game," she said, perhaps a little too cheerfully.

Bradford accepted her hand, gripped it a little too hard. He drew her close to him and whispered in her ear, "I'd like to fuck that smile off your face."

"Is that generally your goal when fucking?" Kate said.

Malcolm quickly ushered her out of the apartment. Outside, the temperature had drifted below twenty. The chill only energized the winning crowd. Malcolm and Colin hoisted Kate onto their shoulders and sang a song that Anna had never heard before, taught to Malcolm by his granddad, who often sang it for his grandmother Kathleen.

K-K-K-Katy, beautiful Katy,
You're the only g-g-g-girl that I adore;
When the m-m-m-moon shines,
Over the cowshed,
I'll be waiting at the k-k-k-kitchen door.

The song was so cheesy, it made Anna cringe, but watching Kate on Malcolm's and Colin's shoulders, celebrated and admired for all the things she wasn't, Anna felt an envy so deep it shamed her.

2004

BOSTON, MASSACHUSETTS

Drenched in a cold sweat, Anna changed her pajamas for the third time in the last eight hours. She yanked off the sheets, threw some towels on the couch, and wrapped herself in a bathrobe until she overheated again.

The vomiting had eased up, at least. Nothing was left. The first time she got clean she was in a clinic, mainlined with sedatives and antiemetics. It wasn't pretty, but it wasn't as ugly as this. She'd been dodging bullets, slipping up and getting clean and playing Russian roulette with drug tests. She told herself this would be the last time. It felt like her body was in a brawl with itself, or like she was being punched in the gut by an invisible fist. Sometimes she welcomed the sickness because it shoved away the shame. Another twenty-four hours and she'd go back to work. Maybe this was the last time.

The phone had been ringing, but Anna

thought the ringing was paracusia. She often had auditory hallucinations of telephones, doorbells, and alarm clocks, especially during half sleep. On her way back to bed, she saw that her message light was blinking. She pressed the button and heard George's voice, soft and clear, on the other end.

"It's me. Please call me back. I need your help."

Anna rested another hour or two. The phone rang again. She was close to the machine and heard the message in real time.

"I tried you at work. He's gone. I don't know what to do."

A baby was crying in the background.

Anna sat up on the couch, sipped a glass of water, gagged, and made the call.

ANNA: George, it's me.
GEORGE: Where were you?
ANNA: I had a long shift. I was sleeping. Didn't hear the machine.
GEORGE: My mom's out of the country.
ANNA: Did something happen?
GEORGE: If I tell my dad, he'll kill him.
ANNA: What happened?
GEORGE: Can you come here? I know you have to work. Just for the weekend.
ANNA: Have you called Kate?
GEORGE: I need you. Not her.

426

ANNA: What happened?

GEORGE: I kicked him out.

ANNA: What did he do?

GEORGE: He fucked the babysitter. She was fifteen. In the guest room. I called the cops. He was arrested. I need help. Miller and Carter. It's too much.

ANNA: It would probably be a lot easier for Kate to get her shifts covered.

GEORGE: Not her. I need you.

As soon as Anna hung up the phone, she placed another call.

"It's me. I need something. Willing to trade. How soon can you get here? See you then."

Anna ransacked her closet and found a single Valium trapped in the seam of an old pea coat. She snatched her suitcase off the top shelf and began packing in a desultory haze. An hour later, the doorbell rang. At the door stood a guy wearing a cashmere sweater over an oxford shirt; his hair was boyish and straight, and his bangs flopped over his eyes. He looked like a prep-school kid who'd refused a much-needed trim.

He reminded Anna of one of Colin's old college buddies. He was the same type — privileged, Ivy League. Maybe a guy whose trust fund had run out but who'd found a new way to survive. Only the glassiness in his eyes and the grayish pallor of his skin gave him away.

"What do you need?" Grant asked.

"Heroin and coke. Enough for a week. Any Oxy if you have it." Anna never used the sly nicknames for the serious stuff. As if she weren't really part of that world if she didn't speak its language.

"No Oxy," Grant said. "I got the street drugs. It's the scripts I need."

Anna unlocked her prescription pad from her desk drawer. "I need legitimate names, and I'll have to postdate some of these so they're not all written today."

They haggled for an hour over dosage and pills per script.

"Schedule two and three prescriptions are carefully monitored. I can't write more than a thirty-day supply, and there are no refills on schedule two drugs. Prescribing a high dose to someone without a history of chronic pain could be a red flag. I lose my license, and you lose me."

"I never really had you," Grant said, winking. "Until now."

Two hours until her flight to Chicago, and Anna was contemplating ways to disguise heroin to pass through security. Terrorism had put drugs on the back burner, but it was still a risky undertaking. She figured she could get needles from a pharmacy in Evanston. She found a vial that held powdered vitamin C and swapped it out for the H. She tossed into her Dopp kit a mess of skin care and cosmetics and perfume as camouflage. The cocaine she put in tinfoil that she folded up like a giant gum wrapper and slipped into her reading-glasses case. If caught, she had no plausible deniability. But she wouldn't get caught.

Men had devastated George before and likely would again. But Anna found the sight of her, clothed in pajama bottoms and a sweatshirt spattered with things that erupt from an infant, her hair matted down into a greasy sheen, unsettling. George had always managed effortless beauty, even after a weeklong camping trip. Anna used to think it was one of the most despicable things about her. But her beauty was now camouflaged by life. Her belly was still swollen from giving birth, but her face was drawn from crying and not eating. Her eyes, rimmed in red, stood out against the hollow shadows beneath. A crease from her last nap drew a long slice across her face. She appeared years older than the last time Anna had seen her. The baby was crying in her arms, tracing more worry lines on George's already worried brow.

Anna had snorted a line of cocaine in the bathroom stall in O'Hare Airport. She left a message for Kate while she was waiting for a cab.

"It's me. I'm in Chicago. What I want to know is why *I'm* here and not *you*. I'm on probation and in the middle of residency. Your only responsibility in life is to serve people coffee," Anna said, and she disconnected the call.

It was forty-five minutes in a cab to George's stately Colonial home in Evanston. White and pristine, gated and groomed, belying the chaos inside. Anna dropped her bags in the foyer and washed her hands in the powder-room sink, a ritual she would never quit, before she found George in the den. She kissed her friend on the cheek and took the baby. Miller. Anna had tried to talk her out of it. Last names as first names were always a pet peeve.

Anna walked into the kitchen. The sink was piled high with dishes, the floor covered with coffee stains and crumbs. Cereal boxes, spent milk cartons, and empty soup cans crowded the counter.

"Don't you have a housekeeper?" Anna asked.

"I fired her," said George. "She knew what was going on."

"Who paid her?"

"Jeremy."

"She thought she was going to lose her job. And you don't know what she knew. Give me her number."

George reluctantly scribbled the digits on a scrap of paper. Anna called from the landline. It went to voice mail. She phoned again from her cell phone, and Gloria picked up. Anna explained all the things that needed explaining and threw in the hormone excuse, sealing the deal. Gloria would get a pay jump and resume her duties that day. Anna returned to the den, where George was doing her best to make a permanent ass mark in the couch.

"Take a shower," Anna said.

"I can't," George said.

"Why not?"

"Because I don't want to look at myself naked."

"Then don't look. I do that all the time."

Anna gave Miller a bath in the downstairs bathroom and found a onesie in the nursery. She had done a pediatrics rotation, but caring for babies still put her on edge; she touched them as if dismantling a bomb.

When George resurfaced from the shower,

scrubbed raw with a shower brush, as if she could clean away more than dead skin and dirt, Anna put the baby back in her arms.

"Where's Carter?" Anna asked, remembering that George had another child.

George stared blankly at Anna.

"Where's Carter?" Anna said again.

"He's next door with the neighbor's kids. I told them I had the flu and didn't want Carter to get it."

"It's time to get him," Anna said.

"Will you go over there?" George asked.

"And say what? 'Hey, you got some toddler named Carter over here, I'll be taking him.'"

"I'll call them and give them a full description of you."

"You can walk next door, George."

While George collected her firstborn at the neighbor's house, Anna put the baby in the bassinet and snorted a line of cocaine in the bathroom. She then washed the tower of dishes in the kitchen sink. She emptied the swelling trash bin and collected the recycling. She threw a load of baby clothes and rags in the washing machine.

"You work fast," George said when she reentered her home.

Carter was cradling something in his hands. He'd take a peek every few seconds to check on it.

"This is your auntie Anna," George said.

"Hi, Carter," Anna said. "You don't remember me. I haven't seen you since you were a baby."

"Anna got you that ant farm for your last birthday. Do you remember?" said George.

Carter smiled and nodded his head.

"What have you got there?" Anna asked, crouching down.

Carter opened his palm and revealed an earthworm he had just captured from the neighbor's yard.

"Does he have a name?" Anna asked.

Carter shook his head. Anna had heard many stories of Carter eating small creatures, and while Carter's mother found it amusing, mostly because it tortured Carter's father, Anna thought it might eventually brand him as a weirdo.

"You should name him," Anna said. She figured anthropomorphizing the worm would make Carter less inclined to swallow it.

"It took like two weeks to name his goldfish," George said.

"Are they still of this world?" Anna asked.

"He doesn't like seafood."

433

"I like the name Ralph," Anna said.

"You don't like the name Ralph."

"I like it for a worm, not a person."

"Carter, why don't you take Ralph upstairs and put him in your terrarium?"

Carter took off with Ralph, and George returned to the couch and turned on the television. The baby was still sleeping soundly in the bassinet.

"Thank you for coming," George said. "I didn't know who else to call."

"I'm happy to be here. But why didn't you call Kate?"

"Because I need someone who is on my side. Not an objective observer."

"You should sleep," Anna said.

"When I close my eyes, I see them. Can you give me anything?" she asked, training her eyes on the television.

"Like what?" Anna asked.

"Something that will make me stop seeing them. I know you have a pharmacy on you."

"I just have a few sleeping pills," Anna said. She wasn't sure what she could spare. "I can write a script."

George went to the store with Carter to pick up her prescription and more baby formula while Anna stayed with the baby and attempted to make dinner from the ice-charred boxes in the freezer. Gloria arrived in George's absence and scrutinized the mess that had accumulated in the past two days.

"Thank you so much," Anna said.

Gloria gazed at Anna, sizing her up. "You friends with Mrs. Adler?"

"Who?" Anna briefly forgot that George had taken Jeremy's name. "Yes. Old friends."

"Hmm," Gloria said.

"Is there something you want to tell me?" Anna said.

"What she says Mr. Adler did, no. He didn't."

"Are you sure?"

"The police talk to the girl. She drink too much. She pass out, and Mr. Adler was just trying to wake her up. Mrs. Adler was wrong."

While George sat in the parking lot of the pharmacy and popped two Valiums, Anna phoned the police, and they confirmed the maid's story. When George returned home, she was so sedated that Anna didn't have to plead Jeremy's case as hard as she had planned. George admitted that she might have been mistaken. Anna suggested an apology was in order. George phoned her husband and begged for his forgiveness. She asked him to come home. George was never one for apologies, but narcotics improved her contrition. Jeremy, who had no idea that his wife was heavily sedated, found the transformation miraculous. There was a softness to her voice he had never heard before. He returned home. They had sex that night, the first time in over three months. Jeremy didn't mind that his wife fell asleep in the middle of it.

Anna booked her flight out of Chicago the next morning, leaving the Adler family in a domestic calm: George was cooking eggs for her husband while Jeremy poured cereal for Carter. Miller, the baby, was sound asleep.

Anna called Kate on her way to the airport.

"Why didn't George ask you to come?" Anna said.

"Maybe because I strongly suggested she shouldn't marry him."

"He's not that bad."

"Is that a reason to marry someone?"

"It still doesn't explain why she called me instead of you. She likes you better," Anna said. "Always has."

"I can't prescribe her drugs," Kate said.

George and Jeremy's reconciliation lasted

less than a month. A single apology couldn't compensate for being falsely accused of statutory rape. When George began questioning Jeremy's whereabouts yet again, he realized that he had nothing left. He went to work at eight thirty one morning, filed the papers, and never stayed another night in his house.

George fully owned the fact that the demise of the second marriage was her fault, and in an attempt at self-improvement, she entered into therapy. After several weeks of discussing her two marriages, she moved on to new topics. She rambled for a while about her idyllic childhood and those perfect parents of hers who'd turned out to be a mirage. Eventually, she landed on *that* night. With the clarity of hindsight, sanctioned by a mental-health professional, George finally had the answers to all of her problems, the reason why she was the way she was: Anna had left the door open. A man almost killed her when she was alone in bed. Therefore, she could never be alone in bed again. The breakthrough arrived during her fifth session with Dr. Langley. George called the only person who would understand.

Kate listened patiently as George presented her case, mapping out her emotional landscape. George paused, awaiting a sympathetic confirmation of her analysis.

"You couldn't be alone before that. Remember?" Kate said.

The next therapy session was dedicated entirely to Kate.

After that, George turned back to the subject of Anna. She talked about Anna's visit after the incident with Jeremy. "You know, she was high the entire time," George said.

"How could you tell?" Dr. Langley asked.

"You can just tell with Anna," said George. "I let a drug addict watch my children."

George knew that she wouldn't have survived that week without Anna. She also knew that Anna wouldn't have helped her unless she was high, but she never mentioned that part to her shrink.

What she did mention was Anna's constant judgment, the way she acted as if she were the final arbiter of good taste. It seemed that Anna was always cutting down the things George liked.

Top-forty music: *You listen to that?*

Romantic comedies: *They should have quit after* The Philadelphia Story.

Men: *Overrated.*

Shopping: *Surely there are better things to*

do with one's time.

Teddy Roosevelt: *Arsonist, if you think about it.*

As George recounted these proclamations to her therapist, they lost their power. Except the part about Teddy Roosevelt. George would always regret telling Anna about his reforestation policy.

"You can't *live* here," Colin said.

"Why not?" said Anna.

"Because it's so uncivilized."

"There are bathroom facilities up the hill. Showers, toilets. They're cleaned at least once a day. There's fish in the lake. The Appalachian Trail is just over there."

Anna reached into her tent and pulled out a folding chair, offered it to her brother. She sat on a rock a few feet away from him. Colin merely stared at his sister, unsure how to proceed. She seemed entirely rational and clear. He couldn't recall the last time he had seen her eyes without the glassy redness that he'd once believed was perfectly natural. It took him a while to notice it was gone, since he'd gotten out of the habit of looking. He couldn't remember when he had stopped looking, but it had been a long time. It was easier that way.

"You've been sleeping," Colin said. It

wasn't a question.

"Yes." Anna smiled.

Her days were full of physical labor. She had forgotten about all the effort involved in maintaining a campsite, keeping a fire going, cooking meals, washing dishes. And then there were the hikes and the fishing. Sleep came easily. It had been years since she'd been so well rested, waking without an alarm clock, easing into consciousness. Hadn't her entire life up until now been on the clock? Every night since that very first night in the campground, she'd slept nine hours straight. She was not herself here. Or not like that person who had inhabited her physical being for so many years. It was like she was in a reverse sci-fi film: a friendly invader had taken over her body. Still, history would dictate that the old Anna was lurking nearby.

"Are you coming to my wedding?" Colin asked.

"Of course, Colin. I'm not being held prisoner. I can come and go as I please."

"Right. I just want you to be there," he said.

"I'll be there," she said.

"I'm going to be a father," Colin said.

"Madeline is pregnant?" Anna asked. This explained some things. Like the wedding.

"It's not what you think," Colin said. "I love her."

Anna knew the comment was a bad omen. Wasn't love a prerequisite for marriage?

"I'm going to be an aunt?" Anna said.

"It's always all about you, isn't it?" Colin said.

"Yes."

Anna smiled and suddenly didn't care about anything else. She was going to be an aunt, and if Colin had decided to endure a loveless marriage for it, that was his choice. Of course, she didn't say any of that.

"Why don't you stay for dinner?" she said. "I'll fry up some bass."

"It doesn't fit," Lena said, circling her daughter in her old bedroom.

Anna struggled to close the zipper on the knee-length powder-blue bridesmaid's dress.

"No, it doesn't. I need a size six. I told you that," Anna said.

"You used to be a four," Lena said, sounding disappointed.

"I also used to be a drug addict and an alcoholic. Sometimes that helps keep the weight off."

"The wedding is in six hours," Lena said. Whenever she was stressed, a tremble lapped over the vowels in her voice.

"This dress is off-the-rack, Mom. I'll just run to the store and get it in a bigger size."

"This had to wait until today, Anna? You couldn't have arrived a day earlier and had your hair done and maybe a thing or two waxed?"

"I'm going to shave my legs and armpits, Mom. And for the record, I have no plans to lift up my skirt tonight, so no other landscaping will be required."

Anna's mother winced at the indelicate reference. "You'd better get to the store."

Lena's worst nightmare came true, though she would never hear about it. The dress was no longer available in a size six. Anna tried on the eight and it was loose, but a sympathetic shop clerk with amateur-seamstress skills was able to make a few quick alterations to keep the dress in place. When Anna returned to her car, she sat in the parking lot, took several deep breaths, and realized now was probably a good time to call her sponsor.

"I've been expecting your call. Cracked yet?" Leticia said.

"Almost. My mother was angry that I gained a dress size."

"Rich white women," Leticia mused. "Only satisfied when they look like they need to be hospitalized."

Anna laughed. "Sometimes not even satisfied when that happens."

"So are you ready for your first sober wedding?"

"I don't know."

"The first sign of trouble, just get out of there. You go to a meeting, you call me, you do what you have to do. Promise?"

"Promise."

"How are you doing?" was the catch phrase of the night, spoken in a tone that was sympathetic and meaningful. By the third query of the evening, Anna began counting; the tally reached forty by night's end. Despite her mother's desperate efforts to keep Anna's "weakness" a secret, that kind of secret could not be kept for long.

Anna knew that hiding wouldn't change anything. In fact, she was fine with her troubles exposed for everyone to see. It was the sticky-sweet delivery that got under her skin, the way ten people could duplicate the exact same overearnest expression. She blamed film and television for providing the world with an emotional blueprint. What if no one had ever seen actors perform the specific facial contortions representing sadness, embarrassment, fear, anger, remorse.

Would those expressions look different in real life now?

Mr. Conklin, a colleague of her father's, approached her early in the evening, holding his own glass of club soda. He didn't have a look he had to practice before he spoke.

"Heard you got sober," he said plainly.

"Yes," Anna said.

"It gets easier," he said. "Some days you don't even think about it."

But Conklin had been sober twenty years. Anna figured she had a long way to go. The whole night she was thinking about it. The whole night she was imagining how fun it would be to lose herself in something. Anything. But she wasn't lost. She was so present, her skin felt the prickle of every sensation. She could feel every muscle on her face as she smiled appropriately, playing the proud sister.

Max Blackman didn't ask how Anna was doing. When he saw her, he drew her into a bear hug, the kind of hug that you just had to go along with. Her father never hugged like that. No one in her family did. Max's hugs took some getting used to for Anna.

Whenever she saw Max or his wife, Abigail, she always thought, *Shouldn't they hate me?* One drunk night she'd almost asked

445

but caught herself in time. They never blamed her.

Max loathed small talk. One of the many things about him she adored.

"I hear you're living in a tent" was the first thing he said to her. His tone was more amused than judgmental. His eyes twinkled with delight.

"Word gets around fast," Anna said.

"You have no idea."

"It's not as bad as it sounds," Anna said in her defense.

"It sounds ideal, if you like camping."

"I do," Anna said.

"I think you like camping more than you like living at your parents' house."

"Perhaps, but that doesn't negate my love for camping," Anna said.

"You should have been a lawyer, not a doctor."

"Either way, I'd still be an addict."

"You're stubborn."

"Have you always known that, or is this a new observation?"

"Anna," Max said, shaking his head with mock disappointment. "You're a grown woman. You need a place to keep your stuff. Women have stuff. That's one thing I know about them."

"Don't marginalize my gender like that."

"I have a proposition for you," Max said. "We have a vacation home in the wine country. Well, forget about that part. It's in the middle of nowhere. Lots of trees, ponds, that sort of thing. Just like a campsite, only there are gamekeeper's quarters a hundred yards from the house. It's a nice cottage. Empty now. We could use someone to keep an eye on the place, take care of the main house. Abigail would like to have a garden, but we need someone there to maintain it. It's a short drive from civilization. But if you're looking for a break, I think this is a better long-term solution than living in a tent."

"I don't know what to say," Anna said.

The idea appealed to her, but she wasn't sure if the offer was too generous or if she was ready to be responsible for anything but herself.

"The cottage has a bathroom, if that sweetens the deal," Max said jovially.

Anna laughed for the first time that night.

Max leaned in and whispered conspiratorially, "It's also three thousand miles from your mother."

"I've never gardened before," Anna said. But she had already made her decision.

"I think you'll like it there," Max said.

"It's very peaceful in the country. Quieter than you could ever imagine."

2007

The animal that had kept her up for two weeks straight had finally shut up. When she first heard the scratching noises, she'd hunted alone at night, following the sounds behind the drywall, knocking on the spot where she imagined the creature poised, like her, with its ear against the wall, waiting. She named it Ralph and tried, briefly, to pretend it was a pet. During daylight, Anna climbed into the crawlspace and looked for signs of squatters. Abigail Blackman had told her that might happen. The raccoons, the squirrels, the coyote, they were here first; humans were the true trespassers. The Blackmans' visits became rarer and rarer, but when they did come, Abigail could sit on her Adirondack chair and watch the squirrels scurry around for hours. She dotted her yard with bird feeders, as if trying to lure all the song sparrows from the neighbors' property to hers. She was an

449

ornithological Pied Piper.

As soon as Abigail and Max departed, Anna hid the bird feeders in the shack. She found their songs grating, repetitive. In summer they were her alarm clock, chirping before the crack of dawn.

"Who doesn't love birds?" a neighbor once asked, dropping by with a holiday gift of a hummingbird feeder for the Blackmans.

Anna talked about her bird-hate only with her therapist.

"Why the fuck does everybody love birds? I get vultures. I like them; they clean up the roadkill. I feel like when they're squawking, there's probably a point to it. Maybe they're alerting other vultures to new meat."

"There's likely a biological imperative to bird songs as well," Dr. Goldstein said. "You've been talking about birds your last three sessions. I'm concerned that birds might be a stand-in for something else."

"There's an animal living in the walls," Anna said.

In truth the noise had ceased a few days ago, but the smell of a small death soon became so powerful that Anna had to move out of the guesthouse and into the main house. She called an exterminator, which struck her as ironic.

"It happens all the time," Grady, the pest

specialist, said. "Once the body is desiccated, the smell will go away."

"What do you think it was?" Anna asked. That was all she'd ever wanted to know during those two weeks it was living with her. A raccoon, a squirrel, a large rat, maybe?

"Something small enough to fit in the walls," Grady said.

Anna had made a recording of the animal and played it for Grady. It sounded as if it were digging through the wall, trying to get to the other side.

"Busy devil," Grady said.

"Can you tell what it is?" Anna asked.

"A small animal."

"No kidding."

Anna called Kate and questioned the exterminator's qualifications.

"Seems to me he should be more informed," Anna said. "It's his job."

"He's an exterminator," Kate said. "Not a zoologist."

"Maybe George would know. I could play her the recording."

"It might be time to come back to civilization," Kate said.

Anna phoned George. They hadn't spoken in six months.

ANNA: George, it's Anna.

451

GEORGE: Anna. Everything okay?

ANNA: Yes. I'm fine. Things are good. Mostly. Something died in the walls.

GEORGE: Put the cookie down.

ANNA: Hello?

GEORGE: What did I tell you? After dinner, Carter.

ANNA: Ah, you're talking to your kids.

GEORGE: Carter, don't make me say it twice.

ANNA: Should I call back?

GEORGE: No. What's up?

ANNA: Well, I wanted to see how you were doing and —

GEORGE: Put the gun away.

ANNA: Wow. Things escalate quickly.

GEORGE: If you shoot me, I will take a hammer to your Xbox 360. You think I'm bluffing?

Max and Abigail came for a visit on the heels of the Ralph incident.

"You sure you're doing all right?" Max asked.

Anna was still catching up on sleep. Every new sound, every quiet creak in the house, was a potential new Ralph.

"I'm fine. I'm good."

"Maybe you should get a dog."

"No. No pets," Anna said, thinking the

Ralph episode provided a reasonable simulation of how she would respond to a pet.

"You've been here six months. Maybe it's too much solitude," Max suggested.

"It keeps me out of trouble," Anna said.

During Max and Abigail's visits, Anna felt best. She could pretend they were her parents. Anna and Abigail spent the afternoon in the garden. The squash blossoms were in bloom.

"Have you ever had a fried squash blossom?" Abigail asked.

"No."

"They're exquisite. But if you harvest the blossom, the squash won't grow," Abigail said. "It's nature's Sophie's choice."

Max and Abigail were having company that night. Not a single squash survived that season.

Bruno died of a heart attack at his home on Lake Huron on a Sunday. He was discovered Monday morning by his housekeeper. On Tuesday, Kyle — husband number three, as Kate always ungenerously called him — phoned Anna and Kate and informed them that the funeral would take place on Saturday. On Wednesday, George and Kyle flew to Michigan and stayed in Bruno's home to make funeral arrangements and start packing up his personal effects.

After Mitch, George thought nothing of invading anyone's cyber-privacy. Kyle had spotted her boundary blindness early on in their relationship and set up a password on anything that would allow for one, going so far as to use a different password for each device, which occasionally, when his memory failed him, locked him out of his own property.

It never occurred to George that there was a difference between logging into her father's computer to access contact information for his friends and reading his e-mails. That's where she found dozens of e-mails from Anna. The subject lines tended to reference a specific date or a visit. *Last Week. Tomorrow. Next month.* She randomly clicked on an e-mail.

TO: Bruno Leoni
FROM: Anna Fury
RE: Saturday

I miss you. Is it okay to say that? Give me more warning the next time you're in town. That wasn't enough time.

xo,
Anna

George opened another and then another e-mail. And while there was nothing tawdry in any of them, they were clearly written between two people who shared an intimacy that ran deeper than what should exist between one's friend and one's father. George's jittery agitation as she read the letters turned angry. Her tears ran hot, burning her cheeks. She was pacing the small cabin, trying to contain her ferocious energy, when the phone rang.

"Are you okay?" Kate asked. "That's a stupid question, but you know what I mean."

"I will be all right."

"I just got my plane ticket. I'll see you on Saturday."

"Okay," George said in a monotone.

Kate chalked up the dullness in her friend's voice to grief.

"Has Anna called?" Kate asked.

"She left a message," said George. "I haven't had time to call her back."

"Do you want me to call her?"

"I'll take care of it," George said.

Instead, George sent an e-mail from her father's account.

TO: Anna Fury
FROM: Bruno Leoni
RE: Funeral
May 3, 2007

Anna,
   You shouldn't come. It might be too
hard on you and I don't want you to risk
a relapse.

                              Take care,
                              George

When Anna saw the e-mail from Bruno in
her inbox, she took a breath so deep her
chest hurt. Her heart beat as if she were
running wind sprints. Explanations jumped
to mind, from ghost to spam, and she
calmed herself, until she looked at the
subject line. *Funeral.* How would spam be
that savvy? Finally she read the message.
Her face flushed red and her hands balled
into fists. She phoned Kate when she could
finally breathe.
   "George knows," Anna said. "About me
and Bruno."
   "You didn't tell her, did you?"
   "No. But she knows."
   "Are you sure?"
   "She sent me a message from his e-mail
account telling me not to come to the

456

funeral."

Kate wasn't sure what to say, so she said nothing.

"Are you there?" Anna said.

"She knows."

At the same time Bruno was being put into the ground, Anna had her own private wake. She went to the store, bought a bottle of his favorite Scotch, and drank it to the bottom. She spent the next day hovering over porcelain, and the following morning she started again at day one.

2005

BOSTON, MASSACHUSETTS

Colin knocked on Kate's door. She opened as his knuckle was about to make contact again.

"Where is she?" Colin asked as he entered.

"Shhh, she's finally asleep," Kate said, backing away from the door.

The entirety of the apartment could be seen from the threshold. It was a four-hundred-square-foot studio, sparely furnished with few personal effects. The word that popped into Colin's head was *Dickensian.* Everything was repurposed. A trunk as a coffee table. An old door as a desktop. A milk crate as a chair.

"In the bathroom," Kate said.

"Why is she sleeping in the bathroom?"

"Because it's the closest place to the toilet."

"How bad is it?"

"She's been sick all night."

"Why didn't you call me sooner?"

"Because she was awake and told me not to and threatened to bolt if I did."

"I see."

"Have a seat," Kate said, pointing at a thrift-store easy chair. It was Kate's chair, unless she had guests. Then she always relinquished it and took a seat on a milk crate.

Colin studied Kate's stolid expression.

"You look tired."

"That's because I haven't slept."

"You live here?" Colin asked. It was a rhetorical question and yet there was that upturn at the end of the sentence as if he was hoping it wasn't true.

"No. This is just my crash pad for strung-out junkies I bail out of jail."

"It's a closet," Colin said scornfully.

"It's called a studio."

"You got any coffee?"

Kate started the kettle and scooped grounds of bulk organic espresso roast into a French press. They could hear faint sounds of Anna's heavy breathing in the bathroom. No one said a word until Kate walked three steps back to the milk crate and handed Colin his cup.

"Black, right?"

Colin couldn't think how she would know that, but it was correct. He took a sip.

"This is really good coffee."

"I'm a barista, remember?"

Kate tucked herself into a corner of the room, wrapping her arms around her legs. Anna had had a fever the night before. Kate, who was famously stingy with heat, had turned it off completely.

"I found a rehab facility for her. They'll hold off the court date until she's out," Colin said.

"What will she tell the hospital?" Kate asked.

"It doesn't matter what she tells them. It's over, Kate. She's been on probation twice during her residency. She was caught stealing drugs from patients and writing phony scripts. Two stints in rehab already. And now she vanished for ten days and went on a heroin binge and bought drugs from an undercover cop. She has no business being a doctor. If she stays out of jail, we'll be lucky. Trust me. I've looked into the matter from every angle. She will lose her medical license. She will not be able to legally practice medicine anywhere."

"Are you going to tell her?"

"She knows, Kate. When the undercover cop identified himself, she knew it was over."

■ ■ ■ ■

An hour later, Anna woke in a cold sweat in the bathroom. She bent over the toilet and dry heaved for another hour. Colin waited it out while Kate went to Anna's apartment and packed a suitcase full of clothes. Colin found a pricey and peaceful rehab facility in the Berkshires. The pamphlet boasted of daily hikes and natural surroundings. He secured Anna in the back seat of his BMW and gave her a plastic bin and strict vomiting instructions. They drove two hours, which wasn't ideal considering the condition she was in, but he wanted her safely ensconced in the facility before Lena or Donald got wind of the news. He knew that the first few weeks, no one was allowed to make contact, and keeping his parents away from his sister was now the only thing he could do for her.

Anna freely signed the admission forms. In the past, there was always some corner of her brain that thought she was okay. She could fix it. Only now did she realize that something was wrong with her, though she couldn't tell what.

Colin dropped by Kate's apartment a few

days later. He walked inside and sat down on the good chair without an invitation. He put a bottle of quality bourbon on the trunk/coffee table. Kate obeyed the unspoken instruction and collected two small shot glasses from the kitchen. One had cost a quarter at a thrift shop and was adorned with a four-leaf clover. The other had the letter *K* on it. It had been a gift from Anna on Kate's twenty-first birthday, as had a bottle of Smirnoff vodka, of which Anna was the primary consumer.

Colin poured two shots. They clinked glasses and he toasted: "To rehab."

Colin took his medicine without expression; Kate grimaced and shivered as she always did when drinking booze neat. Colin poured two more shots and took another slug.

"You hoping to join her?" Kate said.

"I just told the folks. My mother pretended she didn't hear me, and my dad immediately got on the phone with his lawyers. He seems to think he can buy her out of this mess. He was still on the phone when I left."

"I'm sorry," Kate said. She sipped her drink and then took a few steps into the kitchen to collect a jar and some ginger ale. She mixed the bourbon and ginger ale in the old jelly jar.

Colin studied her with a combination of amusement and gut-twisting sadness. He had never noticed it before, but Kate had a gift for drawing out a peculiar medley of emotions. On this occasion, the combo was pity, bafflement, and reverence.

"Why do you live like an immigrant during the Great Depression?" Colin asked.

"If that were the case, I'd be sharing this room with at least three other people."

"You know what I'm asking."

"Some people like to spend money. Some people like to not spend it."

"You still have that nest egg tucked away," Colin said. At Anna's urging, Kate had spoken to Colin about what to do with her *deda*'s money. Colin got her in touch with an old Princeton friend who was horrified that Kate's long-term plan was a 1 percent yield savings account. She'd since invested wisely, and the money Ivan had left her had doubled.

"How did you forgive her? After what happened."

"After *what* happened?" Kate asked.

Colin sighed and poured himself another drink. Like his mother, he sometimes preferred speaking in veiled references. *That hot summer in 1988; that horrible visitor from*

Europe; after the surgery. Colin figured *what happened* was enough.

"I've never killed anyone, Kate. And I know what you did was justified. But I also know you enough to realize that it couldn't have been easy to live with that."

"It wasn't. I couldn't move. I couldn't breathe. Anna got me out of there, out of that house, so I didn't constantly have to be reminded of what I did."

"But she's probably the reason it happened," Colin said.

Kate felt a chill so deep it was like stepping into an ice bath. She saw spots in front of her eyes, felt as if she might faint.

"How do you know about this?" Kate asked.

"Anna said something to me when she came home a week later. She was out of her mind — well, that's all relative —"

"What did she tell you?" Kate asked.

"She told me that she'd blacked out that night. But she went to the police station later and saw a picture of the intruder and he looked familiar. She figured he'd followed her home and she'd left the door open, or worse, she'd invited him over. She didn't know exactly what happened, but she knew she'd done something."

Kate filled the jelly jar with bourbon and

took a healthy gulp. She wasn't a crier and when emotion took hold, she would fight it like a bull, but tears streamed down her face. For years she had guarded a very simple secret — *Anna forgot to lock the door* — to protect her friend from sharing the guilt. But now she understood that Anna had known much more than she ever admitted. She knew she'd made Kate a murderer and she'd never thought to tell her the truth.

Colin got down on the floor and crawled next to Kate. He put his arm around her, took the drink out of her hands, and sat silently while she cried on his two-hundred-dollar cashmere sweater.

A week later, Colin dropped by again.

"I'm fine," Kate said when she opened the door.

"Invite me in."

"I don't feel like company."

"Me neither. Invite me in."

Kate stepped away from the door and Colin entered the apartment. When he sat in the good chair and noticed that it was warm, he finally realized that it was Kate's chair. He thought about moving to the milk crate, but Kate had already settled on the floor.

"How are you doing?"

465

"Okay," Kate said.

"Anything new?"

"Actually, yes. I was fired today. Why do I have a feeling you had something to do with it?"

"I don't know what would give you that feeling," Colin stiffly said. There wasn't much heart in his protest. He wanted Kate to know that he could do that kind of thing. "What's next for you, Kate?"

"I'll find another job."

"No, Kate. You're going to leave."

Colin got to his feet, reached into his pocket, and set the keys to his seven-year-old BMW on the trunk/coffee table.

"You know how to drive. So drive. Pack a bag and get out of here and have a life. For ten years I've watched you do nothing on your own. You read books in this closet, you serve coffee to people for a living, and when Anna's sober, maybe you take a trip with her. I had the oil changed, the tires checked, and there's a tank full of gas. Pack your bag tonight and go."

"What if I don't?"

"I'll make your life very difficult." Colin pulled a brand-new mobile phone from his pocket and wrapped Kate's hands around it. "You'll call me once a week and text every day so I know you're okay. You won't drive at night, and don't get too friendly with strange men. There are maps in the glove compartment. Go wherever you want to go."

"I want to stay here," Kate said. She said it without much conviction, and she felt even less.

"No, you don't," Colin said, giving her apartment one last disparaging glance.

He kissed Kate on the cheek.

"Leave, Kate."

1997

SANTA CRUZ, CALIFORNIA

"Come in, *miláèku,*" Ivan said from his office. He rolled a chair out for Kate. "Sit down."

Kate took a seat and spun back and forth in semicircles like she had when she was a child.

"Sit still," Ivan said, like he had when she was a child.

Kate braked with her feet and made eye contact with her *deda.* He wore his serious face, which prompted immediate concern.

"Are you sick?" Kate asked.

"Ven haf I been sick in my life?" Ivan asked, with a spark of outrage.

Kate didn't want to contradict him, but her *deda* had had shingles just three years earlier. The rash started on the right side of his neck and traveled to his jawline. He wore a turtleneck and worked through the illness, despite uncomfortable stares from customers and employees. Ivan had also had his share of colds and flus, which also never sidelined him. He once told Kate that germs were an American invention.

"You're doing that thing with your eyes," Kate said.

It was a kind of hybrid between a furrow and a heavenly glance, although the glance seemed more pleading than serene. Kate remembered the first time she'd seen it. She was eight years old. In the middle of the night a man (her *deda,* she always assumed, but she never saw his face) rolled her up in blankets and put her in the back of his car. The nautical-level shock absorbers in the Cadillac had lulled Kate back to sleep. In the morning, she woke up in the guest bedroom of her *deda*'s house. She'd heard him on the phone, speaking in rushed Czech whispers and then in slow and loud English, trying to be understood. She crawled out of bed and into the kitchen and overheard Ivan say, "Ven can I see my son?"

He'd rushed the end of the call and then sunk two slices of hearty brown bread into the toaster.

"Sit down, *miláèku.*"

His eyes were rimmed in red, his voice hoarse and crackly like an old radio show replayed on the wrong equipment.

Kate had sat down on the chrome-andpleather kitchen chair. This one didn't spin.

"How did I get here?" Kate asked.

"I take you in the middle of the night."

"Where are Mama and Papa?"

"They are not here."

"Where are they?"

"There was an accident. Last night. It was very bad. Your mama and papa are with God now."

All of Kate's memories were categorized by whether they'd occurred before or after that moment. But all memories shift over time, like a story rewritten again and again. When she was older, the memory was dusted with suspicion. She'd always felt that there was something her grandpa wasn't telling her. Maybe because that was the only time he'd ever mentioned God. For an hour she'd sat on his lap and cried. Ivan said, "I am your papa now. I vill take care of you." Kate never went back to the house she'd lived in with her parents. Her clothing was gathered in a rush, her parents' belongings either sold or donated to charity. Ivan paid a waitress named Doris three hundred dollars to take the day off and turn his guest room into the perfect domain for an eight-year-old girl. Kate returned home from school to find her new bedroom transformed into a princess's chamber. The smell of fresh paint stung Kate's nostrils, but it was the light pink walls that offended her senses the most. The ruffled curtains in a darker rose shade, Doris explained, were an accent, as decorators called it. Atop the twin bed was a frilly white duvet and ivory dolls with locks of tight blond curls. Kate's unfinished-wood dresser from home had been painted white and decoupaged with butterflies and fairies. Ivan and Doris looked so pleased with themselves that Kate could only force a smile and thank them. It took Kate three years before she had the heart to tell him that she missed the bare wood of her old room and the checked flannel comforter on the bed. She had never wanted to be a princess.

Ivan had come to the United States with his wife and ten-year-old son. Two years later his wife died of cancer. Ivan was a kind father and then grandfather, but he had little interest in anything but work. He had come to this country for a better life, a life he could pass on to his child. Kate could recall very few leisure activities with her *deda*. He took her to the movie theater once. She slumped in her seat, shrinking in embarrassment, as he commented his way through *What About Bob?* The next time

Ivan asked her if she wanted to see a movie, she told him she wasn't a fan. Of movies in general. Smirnoff's Diner was the glue that held them together. That was what they did together. They didn't need anything else.

The tone of this conversation in her *deda*'s office was unlike anything that had previously transpired between them. Kate noticed an odd formality in Ivan's voice, as if he were trying to calmly deliver an unfortunate piece of information.

"I haf news, Katia. I tink it good news. I hope you agree."

"You don't look like someone with good news," Kate said.

"It is good news," Ivan firmly stated.

"Spill it," Kate said.

"Spill it?" Ivan repeated with a mocking tone.

"It means 'lay it on me,' " Kate said. She liked to define colloquialisms for her *deda* with even more obscure colloquialisms.

Ivan rolled his eyes with vaudevillian theatrics.

"I haf sold the diner."

He leaned on his desk. Kate felt a knot in her stomach and adrenaline heating the back of her neck.

"Is it sitting on an oil well?"

"Vat? No, did I say oil vell?"

"No. But why would you sell the diner?"

Kate began swiveling the chair, making its joints squeak rhythmically. Ivan circled his desk, took both arms of Kate's chair, and steadied it.

"I don't vant this life for you. You are smart. You are smarter than anyone in the family. You could be anything," he said, sitting down again.

"And I want to be the owner of this diner," Kate said. "We had an understanding. I was going to take over the restaurant when you retired."

"It is too late. I haf already signed papers."

"Why? Why would you do that?" Kate stood. She was almost shouting. She rarely shouted, especially not at Ivan. He got to his feet again, alarmed by her anger. Kate had never been this angry with Ivan before. And now she was furious, incapable of modulating her response.

"I haf put some money aside for you. You vill be fine. You vill do something else vith your life. Now, you go home and you calm down. Do you understand me?"

"No," Kate said. "I don't understand you."

She turned on her heel and walked briskly out of the restaurant.

The 2.4-mile walk home did little to dull

Kate's anger. Kate couldn't remember a time when she hadn't known her future and embraced it. Her mother and father had worked at the diner until they died. Kate remembered years of her childhood spent sitting at the counter eating cherry pie and reading library books while her family hustled around her, seating customers, serving customers, patting her on the head as they passed by. She began working at Smirnoff's at age twelve and learned every aspect of the family business. She had big plans for the diner when her *deda* retired. For example, the Czech delicacy furry dumplings would be excised from the menu, and she would hire a chef who made comfort food that didn't taste like it came out of a box. She'd always wondered how the restaurant managed to stay afloat.

Kate's ability to spot a poker tell extended to everyday life. Her grandfather was lying about one thing: the papers hadn't been signed. There was still time to reverse this trajectory. The house was empty when Kate returned home. She found Anna's address book by the kitchen phone, picked up, and dialed.

"May I speak to Colin Fury," Kate said when Colin's receptionist at the law firm of Galey and Furst answered the phone. "Tell him it's Kate Smirnoff. I'm a friend of his sister."

Colin picked up the phone immediately, his tone rushed and edgy. "Is Anna all right?"

"She's fine. She's fine. I'm calling about a legal matter," Kate said.

"A legal matter? Related to Anna?"

"No. A personal legal matter, related to me."

Colin quickly regrouped once he realized his sister wasn't in prison or worse.

"What can I do for you?"

"I think I want to sue my *deda* — my grandfather. Ivan Smirnoff."

"What do you want to sue him for?" Colin asked.

"Breach of contract."

Colin asked Kate to take a week to cool down and then revisit her response. Meanwhile, Ivan solicited the help of Anna and George to talk some sense into his potentially litigious granddaughter. Both roommates diligently advocated for the elder Smirnoff, baffled that anyone would want to stand on her feet twelve hours a day running a greasy spoon. Ivan understood that it was Kate's last connection to her parents, but he wanted to break the link. The diner was part of the past. Kate needed to look forward. Ivan called the house repeatedly, leaving angry, ranting messages on the answering machine for Kate. He could shout for five minutes and yet he always signed off the same way:

"I love you, *miláèku.*"

Despite Kate's repeated phone calls to Colin, Anna convinced him not to take the case. She also suggested he be prepared to provide legal precedent when he turned Kate down. Colin told Kate that the statute of limitations on a verbal contract was two years. Kate couldn't recall the last time they had had an explicit discussion about her role in the business, but she had a letter exchange from her freshman year in college conveying the same sentiment, and since the statute of limitations on a written contract was four years, Kate believed she still had a case. Colin told her he was unfamiliar with California law and was not equipped to take on her lawsuit.

Kate promptly sought out local attorneys and soon concluded that she couldn't afford one without the money she would receive upon the sale of Smirnoff's Diner. In the midst of finals, just a week before graduation, Kate spent all of her usual restaurant hours in the law library learning how to write a legal brief. She drafted a three-page complaint against her grandfather citing the numerous occasions on which they'd discussed her future in the business and the many sacrifices she had made over the years to ensure the success of Smirnoff's Diner. She filed the document with the circuit court in Santa Cruz, California, right after completing her Managerial Economics final.

When Ivan was served the complaint, by an eighteen-year-old skateboarder with a pierced lip, he phoned the Fury/Smirnoff/ Leoni household and started hurling what Anna could only assume were Czech invectives at Kate. Anna attempted to mediate between the two, but Kate refused to speak to Ivan about it, and Ivan refused to speak about it in English. Ivan also refused to seek legal help and hoped that in the thirty days he had to respond, his granddaughter would come to her senses.

As the thirty days ticked away, Anna and Kate prepared for graduation. The event was anticlimactic in the household, since George wouldn't graduate until the following year and Anna was still taking courses to try to ramp up her mediocre GPA. Before all the legal maneuverings commenced, the roommates had arranged for a graduation party at Smirnoff's Diner with a small flock of family and friends in attendance. Anna asked Kate whether they needed to find a new venue, considering the brewing conflict, and Kate said, "Of course not. One thing has nothing to do with the other."

Kate received her diploma, tossed up her hat, and walked down the procession line into her grandfather's arms.

The diner hosted a crowd of twenty or so people. Ivan had kept the buffet simple, at Kate's request. She explained that the Furys had no taste for goulash. Sandwiches and salads would suffice, although Ivan, believing the Furys to be descendants of early colonists and thus WASPy to the core, couldn't refrain from attempting a few high-tea recipes he'd found in his research. He baked a couple dozen doorjamb scones and served what he thought was clotted cream but that was really just whipped cream, which deflated the moment it hit the reheated scone. Every time Kate breezed past the table, she'd pocket a scone and later toss it in the bin. By the end of the day, only three scones had touched anyone's lips. Ivan assumed they were a great success. The cucumber sandwiches were acceptable, as Lena said. Then again, how hard is it to pull off white bread, cucumber, and butter?

Like cliques in a schoolyard, the families didn't mingle much at the party beyond the preliminary introductions. Although Colin, unable to turn away from a pretty girl, made his way over to George and chatted with her about the negative effect of commercial forestry on rivers and catchments.

"When you plant trees," George said, "rainwater runoff in rivers increases the sediment and can also cause floods downstream. There are plenty of methods to mitigate the impact, and commercial forestry still has some environmental benefits, but it has to be done responsibly."

"Of course it does," Colin said, taking a thoughtful glance downward, furtively memorizing the outline of George's hipbone jutting out from her dress.

Anna briskly walked over and bulldozed her brother in the direction of Lena and Don. There were occasions during which Anna believed Colin's sole purpose was to be in the domestic trenches with her. If she had to endure small talk with her folks, he did too.

And across the room were Kate and Ivan. She sat on his lap after he insisted. He whispered how proud he was of her. He told her how proud her parents would have been. He said, "I love you, *miláèku.*" She said "I love you" back. He gave her an envelope, a graduation gift. A tacky card with flowers and glitter and a whirling calligraphy font.

Colin watched the exchange from across the room and nudged Anna with his elbow.

"Isn't she planning on suing him?" Colin asked.

"She already filed the complaint. Drafted it herself."

"But he looks so proud of her, like there's nothing wrong."

"He is proud of her. He's also angry with her. After he was served the papers, he called her up and shouted for fifteen minutes and then he told her he loved her," Anna said. "They're fucking crazy, right?"

"I don't get it," Colin said.

When Kate opened the card, a check dropped onto her lap. As a child, she had been instructed not to look at the money until later, so she slipped the check back into the card and kissed her *deda* on the cheek.

"Thank you, Deda."

"Look at it," Ivan said.

Kate opened the card and unfolded the check. She had never seen so many zeros. Two more zeros than she had ever seen on a check with her name on it: $50,000. At first she thought Ivan had made an error. His eyes weren't what they used to be. It's easy to mistake a comma for a decimal. But then she reread the amount. Fifty thousand dollars. And she knew he had signed the papers.

"Blood money," Kate said, getting to her feet.

"You vill get over dis," Ivan said instructively.

Kate's voice took on a formal register: "You have thirteen days now to respond to my complaint. If you do not do so, the court will rule on my behalf."

It turned out that Ivan had only five days. He died of a heart attack while cleaning out his office. He had spoken to Kate just two hours earlier. They argued, and she threatened to sue for damages. And still, when they ended the call, they both said in sharp, angry tones, *I love you.*

"What do you say?" George said to her three-year-old son when she gave him a cookie.

"I love you?" Hudson said.

When Anna got the birth announcement, she'd exclaimed, for the third time in a row, "What the fuck is up with the last-name first names?" But Anna was pleased to have heard from George at all. It was a sign that their relationship was continuing its glacial thaw. A month after Bruno's funeral, Anna began phoning George. Once a week, without fail. At first George didn't answer the phone. Anna left messages, long, rambling, one-sided conversations, mostly about her life off the grid. Eventually George picked up. They stayed on safe subjects — children, creatures in the walls — with one exception.

"Do you want to talk about it?" Anna

asked at the end of the first call.

"No," George said. "I don't *ever* want to talk about it."

They never did.

"Normally, you say 'thank you.' But I think 'I love you' is better," George said to Hudson.

"Thank you. I love you," said Hudson, who was now the sweetest of her boys. Carter, ten, wanted only his Game Boy or George's smartphone to occupy him. He had no interest in her beyond the power she wielded over his electronics. Miller, eight, lived to be outside, to ride his bike, play baseball or soccer, and climb trees. His mother was nothing but transportation to locations where these activities could be pursued. She still occasionally tried gender-role interventions and encouraged playdates with girls, and when Hudson had lost his shit in the barber's chair, she let him grow his wavy brown hair well past his shoulders.

Other than a few relationship sputters and whiplash breakups, George had been single for four years now. Some days she enjoyed not having a man around, having the option of serving pancakes for dinner or leaving the dishes until the morning or not even thinking about shaving her legs. She liked ruling her boys by whim — *Go ahead, eat the worm,* or *jump off the roof onto your old mattress,* or *set the raked leaves on fire (just make sure you've laid the rocks for a fire pit as I taught you)* — but some nights in bed, the same old need returned, and it felt so ugly. She wondered if it was what Anna had felt that day when she got herself arrested.

These days, human contact could be simulated on one's computer, and George would sometimes spend hours online, reading what her distant acquaintances were up to through their mundane posts.

Shari is enjoying a latte.

Jonathan just scored fifty points on Brain Game.

Francine likes white wine.

John wonders if it's okay to eat two burgers in one day.

Sometimes George would share pictures of her boys in midair. Lately she had stopped including photos of herself with her online posts. As far as George was concerned, she'd become middle-aged overnight.

It was always when the house was so quiet that the creak of the floorboard under her feet sounded like a legato stroke on a violin that she'd creep into her office and try to connect with the world. George had looked up old friends before. Mostly old boyfriends. Occasionally after she drank a couple glasses of wine, she'd make clumsy contact. She hadn't searched for Edgar but saw his profile turn up on the page of another acquaintance from college who had tracked her down just a year ago.

Edgar Dalton. Apartment 3A. She remembered their one dreadful night together. She remembered how he'd looked at her, that unabashed adoration, a look she should have been seeking from every boyfriend and husband since. *That's the kind of man I should be with,* she thought. She drank a glass of wine and ran a search on her old friend.

Edgar Dalton had been busy in the intervening years. He had apparently made quite a name for himself in Silicon Valley. Photos of him, in tuxedos, no less, were littered over the Internet. He looked different these days, impeccably groomed, at ease, sure of himself. George drank another glass of wine and composed a message.

Dear Edgar,
George Leoni here from Santa Cruz. Do you remember me? It's been almost twenty years. I'm not sure why I'm writing. I saw your picture online and it

brought back memories and I wanted to see how you were doing. Although it's clear you're doing well. I had a feeling great things would happen for you.

I just thought I'd say hi. Write back if you have the chance.

Best,
George

George turned off her computer after she sent the message and went straight to bed. By morning she had received a reply.

Dear George,

Of course I remember you. How have you been? A brief survey of your online profile informs me that you live in Chicago and have three boys. That must keep you and your husband very busy. Are you still working in the forestry service?

I hope your life has turned out well. Are you still in touch with Anna and Kate?

I've thought about you now and again over the years. Tell me what you're up to these days.

Warmest regards,
Edgar

George, elated to receive such a prompt response, immediately replied.

Edgar,

It's rare to make contact with someone you want to hear from when trawling these sites. Maybe it makes up for the slightly dirty feeling you have when you realize you wasted an hour (okay, two) of your life reading about the banal details of acquaintances' lives. Most of the time I wonder what draws me to this cheap form of communication. I'm still in touch with Kate and Anna. I'm not sure what to say about either of them. I'm surprised how Kate turned out, and Anna's story — I'm not sure that it's mine to tell. Maybe I'll answer those questions another time. Just so you know, Anna uses a nom de plume to spy on her friends. She goes by the name of Kate Mirnoff as a less-than-subtle mockery of Kate's blind resistance to all forms of cyber-communication. (Kate still doesn't know a parody of her is online reporting regularly about the lunch she ate or the lecture series she recently attended or the bad vacuum cleaner she purchased.)

As you know, I have three boys. All

wild animals and I can't deny that I prefer them that way. I was a forest ranger for all of one year and then I married (more than once). I'm not married now. I no longer work as a ranger. I consult for environmental groups. But it's not the same. We camp as much as we can. Only one of my husbands shared my love of the great outdoors and even that one didn't work. Can you believe I have ex-husbands, plural? That's enough about me.

Tell me what you've been up to. Married? Children? Career? I suppose those are tedious questions. So middle-aged. Is that what we are now? Anna says she will admit to middle age only when she turns fifty. She says she's going to live to be one hundred. I believe her.

George

A few polite but staid e-mails passed over the next few weeks, and then Edgar suggested a phone call. George put the boys to bed, took a bath, threw on a pair of an ex-husband's sweats, wrapped herself in an old musty family quilt, and poured herself a glass of wine as she waited by the phone. Edgar had said he would call at ten on the dot. The phone rang at 9:59 p.m.

George's experience with men was that, after the initial courtship, they showed little interest in what she had to say, and even during the courtship phase, that interest was theatrical. She could spot the well-timed head nod, the radio-delayed canned laughter at something amusing she might have said — often stories about her children or an old forestry anecdote. Like the time she'd found a throng of Deadheads lost on a hiking trail in the Russian River Valley. When they couldn't find their way out, they saw it as a sign that they were supposed to live off the land. There was enough water and fishing for basic survival (one of the Deadheads had been an Eagle Scout). They thought they'd start their own minicivilization, believing they were miles deep in the Sierras.

"Dude, we thought we were like the Donner Party. But we made a pact not to eat each other," a white guy with dreadlocks and a tie-dyed T-shirt said. "Some of us are vegetarians," he added.

George pointed the Donner Party Redux onto a trail and explained that a thirty-minute walk would bring them back to civilization. There was only one holdout (the Eagle Scout), and he'd lasted just a few minutes.

George couldn't count on her fingers and toes how many times she'd told that story. It was her go-to anecdote. Most men expressed mild to moderate amusement. But Edgar liked the story best.

Edgar was different. Religiously curious. It was as if he were trying to siphon intelligence, as if it were a scarce resource. He listened intently and interrupted to ask questions only when he felt the information provided was inadequate — and it was always inadequate. She had said so much about herself during that first phone call that, when it was over, she wondered if she had a single biographical detail left to reveal.

While George spoke, Edgar managed to absorb the information while summoning a vivid image of the beautiful, leggy college girl he'd met at that very strange party he'd been conned into hosting so many years ago. The sharp sting of her rejection was now a soft memory. They spoke until well past midnight, until the battery on George's phone began to die. Edgar told her that he'd call her next week.

That night George started to think of Edgar in ways she hadn't thought of him before. More specifically, she began forcing herself to think of Edgar in those ways, since the feelings didn't come naturally. George had always been attracted to a certain type of male. The type who didn't speak much, or listen much, for that matter. The kind of man who didn't ask if he could kiss you good night but just did it. The men George liked didn't ask her any questions at all.

That night Edgar masturbated to a mental picture of a twenty-year-old George.

Edgar sent George an e-mail the following morning. She responded that afternoon. He e-mailed again the next day and they spoke on the phone two days later and then two days after that. The balance of the early conversations, so heavily in favor of George, began to shift after the third phone call, when George noted how often she heard the sound of her own voice. She couldn't recall Edgar saying more than *Yes; That's true; I see; How unfortunate.* She had gathered only a few details of his life after well over two hours of phone conversations. He lived alone in Silicon Valley; he had a cat named Squirrel; he owned a tech company called Axiom Inc. that specialized in creating renewable energy for personal electronic devices. While George was curious about how a cell phone could charge itself, she was far more interested in Edgar's personal life.

"You never married?" she asked. It was

her first question beyond the passport-application-type inquiries.

"I came close. Once," Edgar said. And he told the story of Amy, whom he had met in graduate school in Texas. They moved in together after dating only two weeks — compatible in mind and spirit. They could spend hours discussing renewable energy and the relative merits of biofuel and wind, solar, and nuclear power. Amy was wildly against the last, but Edgar remained open to all possibilities. A year into their relationship, Edgar proposed, and they began preparing for their nuptials. And then a few months before the wedding, Edgar realized he wasn't in love anymore. What Edgar didn't tell George was that sometimes he thought of George when he was having sex with his fiancée. As the wedding drew nearer, he decided he didn't want to spend the rest of his life fucking one woman while thinking about another.

Three months after George first made contact, she flew to San Francisco to meet Edgar for the weekend. He sent a limo to pick her up at the airport. He didn't want their first encounter after almost twenty years to be a quick roadside embrace followed by fumbling with luggage and narrow escapes from minor fender-benders and the stress of traffic. He had been told on more than one occasion that he drove like an old man. Their reunion had to be perfect.

Edgar was standing on the porch of his three-story Colonial in Palo Alto when Edgar's driver pulled George's chariot along the circular driveway. George noticed the house first, not Edgar. The plantation-manor-size structure took her aback. George immediately thought of what Kate might say: *Six thousand square feet for one man. That's environmentally irresponsible. Let's say he doesn't even use the heat or air condition-ing — the water required for that half acre of lawn is three hundred and twenty-five thousand gallons per year, approximately. That's the equivalent of over two hundred thousand toilet flushes.* Then again, Kate would have been happy living in a closet. And George had researched the common lawn on her own; there were some environmental benefits.

Edgar waved, which pulled George's at-tention away from lawn-care statistics. He looked the same, but fleshier — in a good way — and he still had most of his hair. He wore a flattering, pressed white shirt and designer jeans, which led George to the quick and accurate conclusion that someone else bought his clothes for him. They were too on the nose for Edgar to have chosen them of his own accord. She wished he had looked a little more scruffy and unfettered, like his old self.

He opened the car door for George. They embraced. The driver grappled with her heavy suitcase while Edgar led George on a twenty-minute tour of his home, which showed no evidence that it was inhabited by him. Any rich man could have lived in that house. One room contained a massive flat-screen television, several video-game consoles, and shelves loaded with alphabetized comic-book collections and a few Batman figurines from the 1950s that were worth more than some people's cars. Everything with color, with memory, with a tie to the owner of the home was trapped in that single room.

As George was leaving, she saw a large, expensively framed set of mushroom sketches on the wall. Roughly drawn with colored charcoal and labeled in a scrawl that looked as familiar to George as her own hand.

" '*Amanita muscaria,* also known as the fly agaric.' Why do I know that?" George asked, staring at the picture with an unnerving sense that she'd seen it before, a picture that felt utterly wrong in this house.

"Kate drew that," Edgar said.

"You saved it for all of these years?"

"I was sorting through stuff when I moved two years ago," said Edgar. "I always liked that picture. It reminded me of a different time. I think I sent the fake Kate a message telling her about it. I didn't hear back."

"I forgot all about the mushroom phase," George said wistfully. The memory did not serve to remind George that Kate liked Edgar first. It merely reminded her that time was passing her by. She was thirty-seven years old with three children and no husband, and her forehead carried worry lines that didn't disappear when she stopped worrying.

Edgar did everything right. Or at least, he did everything he could think of to make the evening perfect. He had hired a chef to teach him how to make pasta puttanesca and a flourless chocolate cake. He made the meal for George that night, attempting to radiate smooth culinary certainty. A few hiccups with sauces bubbling over and an obvious lack of familiarity with how the oven worked gave him away, but George didn't let on. She offered her assistance, but he refused, ordering her to sit and drink, which she did prodigiously. By the time dinner was served, she'd killed almost an entire bottle of red wine on her own.

Edgar was easy to talk to, but it's always easy to talk to someone who is captivated by your every word. In the three hours it took Edgar to prep the meal and serve it, the subtext for George remained the same: *I should feel something.* But Edgar had enough feelings for the two of them. He tried to wait until dessert was on the table to kiss her, but he slammed her against the refrigerator when she got up to refill a glass of water. George returned the kiss because it was the polite thing to do and she wanted to feel something. The cake burned. Edgar turned off the oven and opened the window.

"I'll make you another cake," he said.

"Let's go upstairs," George said. She still wasn't feeling anything but thought that she might feel something if they had sex.

The middle-aged couple disrobed with adolescent speed, as if racing to copulate before someone's parents returned home. Edgar tried to do all the right things. Things he had learned from the five women he had been with; things he had read in men's magazines; things he had seen in porn. George seemed to respond. Her moans and breathing quickened, but George was skilled in the art of sexual performance. She had gotten almost too good. After George fake-came and Edgar really did, she still thought, *I should feel something.* She comforted herself with the knowledge that Edgar did feel something, and, for now, that was enough.

On Monday, when Edgar returned to work, his colleagues required a full report on his weekend. Edgar provided the gentleman's version and was about to send George a bouquet of flowers when Rufus, his CFO, intervened.

"Dude, you've got to play it cool. Chicks don't like it if you seem too needy."

"Rufus, grown women aren't interested in men who play games," said Edgar.

Cathy, a grown woman, said, "But we also don't like men who seem desperate. You have to figure out how to strike a balance."

"How do I do that?" said Edgar.

"Wait five days, then you can call her," Rufus said.

Edgar waited three days until he sent flowers. The first day after George returned home, she felt ambivalent toward Edgar. The second day, when the phone didn't ring and there was no message in her inbox, she began to feel a stew of emotions that she interpreted as longing. By the third day, she was so desperate to hear from Edgar that when the bouquet of red roses arrived, she convinced herself she was in love.

Edgar would eventually notice the consistent and reliable push and pull in their relationship. If he withheld emotion or attention, George came alive. When he showered her with affection, she would first accept it hungrily, and then withdraw. Edgar often felt like he was tending an extremely temperamental garden.

"She's barking like a dog," Colin said. He was referring to his three-year-old daughter, Zooey.

"I don't see the problem," Kate said.

Kate had been working at the West End Branch of the Boston Public Library going on three years. She took the job when she finally returned from Operation Bankruptcy, as Colin called it. As Kate saw it, she'd merely come home from her travels with much less money and a little less guilt. It was that simple. Kate never regretted that first swing of the bottle on the intruder, but she'd always wondered if the death blow had been necessary.

It had taken Colin all morning to track Kate down. He knew she worked part-time at a library, but she had never mentioned which library. So he had his secretary call every single one in Boston proper.

At that very moment, while Colin was

speaking in hushed tones to Kate behind the stacks of biographies (Dewey 900–999: history, geography, biography), Zooey was barking and crawling on all fours in his office while his secretary chased her around, shushing her.

"The *problem* is that my nanny quit because my daughter has been barking like a dog for a week straight. Mrs. Kline says that she doesn't have a dog of her own for good reason."

"Allergies?" Kate asked.

"I've been through three nannies in the past year. If my ex-wife hears that I took my daughter to work again and left her in the hands of my secretary, she will use this against me in court and file for full custody. Don't you have any vacation days coming?"

Kate agreed to nothing at that first meeting. She dropped by Colin's office after work and picked up Zooey.

"Zooey, do you remember Kate, Aunt Anna's good friend?"

"Arf!"

"Good doggy," Kate said, patting Zooey on the head.

"Don't encourage her," Colin said.

"Why not?" Kate asked. "She's three years

old. When else will she have a chance to be a dog?"

Colin didn't have time to argue, at least not with Kate. He had a brief to write. Kate drove Zooey straight from Colin's office to the dog park, where Zooey raced around with the medium-breed canines, having quickly abandoned the dedicated but cumbersome four-legged approach. Most people assumed that Kate had an animal in the mix of ecstatic hounds. But a few dog owners were suspicious. A woman approached Kate, who was standing leashless by the sidelines, and said, "Which one is yours?" Kate pointed to Zooey and said, "That one."

The woman clarified: "Which dog?"

Kate pointed to Zooey again. "*That* one."

The woman did not make any further attempts at conversation.

After the dog park, Kate took Zooey to the pet-supply store and let her pick out a dog bowl and a few balls, which Kate made sure could bounce and therefore would be useful when the Fido phase ended.

"This was a mistake," Colin said when he returned home and caught sight of his daughter eating oatmeal out of a dog bowl on the floor. He sat down at the table and rubbed his temples. "My mother would have a heart attack if she saw this."

"And your mother is the gold standard for good parenting?"

"Point taken."

When Zooey lifted her head from the dog bowl, Colin took a napkin and wiped the oatmeal from her face.

"Arf."

"Good dog," Kate said.

Colin winced. "I'm not sure this is the approach I would take," he said in hushed tones.

"I want ice cream," Zooey said, her first human words in forty-eight hours.

Colin was about to remind Zooey that they had sweets only on the weekend, a rule instituted by Madeline, whose fear of her daughter becoming fat had started when Zooey was an underweight baby.

"Dogs don't eat ice cream," Kate said plainly.

Zooey regarded Kate for a long stretch, the child's giant brown eyes boring into the eyes of this tiny woman in her home.

"I don't want to be a dog anymore," Zooey eventually said.

"What do you want to be?"

"A girl."

"Girls eat ice cream," Kate said.

There was no ice cream in the house, but

the trio walked hand in hand to a shop around the corner. Zooey got a scoop of rocky road on a sugar cone and devoured it under the fluorescent lights of the pastel-colored parlor. When she was finished, she said "Arf" for the last time.

The next phase she stuck to a bit longer. Zooey ransacked her costume trunk one afternoon (dress-up was an activity Kate wildly encouraged) and donned a white tennis skirt, a black cape, and sweatbands and called herself Swinger Girl, an unfortunate moniker that referenced her high-flying acts on a swing set. Swinger Girl's primary objective was to have the cape afloat in her wake. When she wasn't on a swing, she was racing through the house shouting, "Swinger Girl is on the loose!"

"Zooey, please sit down for dinner," Colin said three nights into the Swinger Girl era.

"How long is this phase going to last?" he asked.

"A long time, I hope," Kate said. "Swinger Girl eats her vegetables."

Colin was working seventy-hour weeks and had little time to vet potential nannies. He delegated the responsibility to Kate, who interviewed five women and one man but found no acceptable candidates. Candidate number one kept referring to Zooey as a *young lady,* emphasizing *lady* and loading the word with old-fashioned notions of gender roles — or at least, that was how Kate interpreted it. Candidate number two spent five minutes talking about how children needed routines and consistency; Kate didn't have a problem with the concept, only with the degree to which it was underscored. Candidate number three was clearly anorexic. Candidate number four appeared unduly concerned when Zooey scratched her head, and she inquired repeatedly about lice. Candidate number five mentioned her fondness for porcelain figurines. Candidate number six, the one male, arrived forty-five minutes late for the interview.

For almost a month Kate managed to work her library schedule around the half of the week that Zooey spent with Colin. Three days a week she'd tuck Zooey into bed, go home, read, sleep, return to Colin's house at 7:00 a.m., and get his daughter ready for school. Every other weekend, when Colin had Zooey but could care for his daughter on his own, Zooey would ask after Kate. Sometimes she would call her and tell her about her day. When Zooey was with her mother, she asked for Kate. Madeline phoned Colin in a rage.

That was when Colin offered Kate the job. Kate turned it down at first, but Colin appealed to her sense of thrift. He offered her more money than she made at the library, free rent, and three and a half days a week in which she could kill as much time as she wanted among shelves of books without having to actually shelve them. Kate immediately gave notice and moved out of her three-hundred-square-foot apartment into Colin's three-thousand-square-foot home.

A few weeks later, after Kate served breakfast to Zooey while Colin read the newspaper, she choked on her coffee as she recognized the comically domestic tableau. She was even wearing a chef's apron (to hide the fact that she wasn't wearing a bra). Zooey ate Cheerios laced with white chocolate, which would have been forbidden on most school mornings, but Zooey and Kate had brokered a deal the day before when Zooey had strict instructions to clean her room and found herself lost under toddler flotsam, unable to even begin to comprehend the task. Kate sat on the bed and bribed and coached until the room was suitable for the housekeeper to clean — a concept Anna once told her she thought was hilarious. *Clean your room before the housekeeper gets here,* Lena used to say every Thursday morning for almost ten years.

Zooey hunched over her cereal like a convict protecting her food. She was mostly trying to hide the dead chocolate weight at the bottom so her father wouldn't catch on. When Colin did check his daughter, he grimaced at her rounded back and elbows on the table.

"Sit up straight, like a nice young lady."

Kate's expression tightened into a cold stare.

"Zooey, sing the bath song for your dad," Kate said.

Zooey put down her spoon and launched into a loud rendition of a tune she'd heard in Kate's car that later became the theme song for bath time.

Ain't nobody dope as me, I'm just so fresh
    and clean
Don't you think I'm so sexy, I'm just so
    fresh and clean.

Kate approached Colin and whispered, snakelike, in his ear, "I'll teach her every swearword in the book if you *ever* say anything like that to her again."

■ ■ ■ ■

Neither Kate nor Colin informed Anna of their new living arrangements. Kate and Colin discovered this fact when Anna arrived at Colin's house during an unscheduled trip to the East Coast. Don had recently been diagnosed with stage 1 esophageal cancer and insisted that Anna come home to consult. Two years before, he had received a diagnosis of early Alzheimer's. Most of the time he remembered that his daughter was no longer a resident at Boston Medical Center and that she lived three thousand miles away and worked as a paralegal. But when the diagnosis came in, the trauma of the word *cancer* seemed to choke out the hard facts he had come to accept.

Anna arrived in the middle of the afternoon and took a cab from the airport to Colin's house. Kate answered the door.

"What are you doing here?" Anna asked as she dropped her bags in the foyer.

"Didn't Colin tell you?"

"Tell me what?" said Anna, leaping to a conclusion that felt disquietingly unnatural.

"I live here," said Kate. "I thought he told you."

"Why didn't *you* tell me?"

The women had spoken at least a few times since Kate's move, and many things had come up in conversation: the origin of Brillo pads, the decline of the seersucker suit, the gradual disappearance of phone booths, dangerous ingredients in sunblock, those crazy motherfuckers who didn't believe in global warming, Kate and Anna's mutual fondness for turtles, and how to sanitize kitchen sponges in the microwave.

"I guess it never came up," Kate said.

While that statement was true, Kate had known that whenever she spoke to Anna, she was omitting an important piece of information.

Anna remained in the foyer, slack-jawed, glaring at Kate with an alarming expression of disappointment.

"It's not like I robbed a bank, Anna."

"If you robbed a bank, I'd know what to do."

This was no time for a conversational detour, but Kate was curious what Anna's response to that particular event would be.

"So what would you do?"

"I'd help you lie low for a little while, then I'd secure you a new identity and get you out of the country."

"Really?" Kate said. "You'd do all that for

508

me, even if I committed a felony?"

"Sure. Although I would make you give the money back."

"That's pretty swell of you."

"Can we get back to the subject at hand? What the hell were you thinking, moving in here?"

"I was thinking free rent."

"Huh."

"You remember I'm cheap, right?"

"Does my brother know this?"

"That's how he lured me here. By telling me to think of all the money I'd be saving."

"How romantic," Anna said, parking her bags at the bottom of the stairs and making her way into the kitchen. She promptly turned on the kettle, a marginally satisfying substitute for pouring a drink. Her friends marveled at the ridiculous number of herbal beverages Anna could consume in a day. The hot liquid was soothing going down, but there was no lasting effect.

"I think you have the wrong idea," Kate said.

"What idea should I have?"

"I'm Zooey's nanny. The last one quit and all the others were going to cause permanent psychological damage. He offered me a handsome wage and free rent. I have the maid's quarters all to myself. More square footage than my last apartment. And it comes with a bathtub."

Anna drew Kate into a bear hug and said, "Thank God."

"Did you really think —"

"Yes."

"That would be very . . . odd," Kate said.

When she said it, it sounded like a bluff, like she was hiding something. On occasion, Kate had caught herself looking at Colin in ways that would complicate her role as domestic help. But she knew his history, his reputation, and she had more than a few times witnessed his schooled flirtations. That gave her an excuse to subjugate her desires, and Kate hardly needed an excuse to do that. Most days she could shove the nuisance thoughts aside; some nights she couldn't.

Anna visited her father after his first chemo session. Lena had hired and fired two nurses before she found Alvita Bailey, a Jamaican woman with green-card issues, an impenetrable accent, and the remarkable ability to make virtually anyone do her bidding. She rarely used the imperative to elicit a desired response. She was a master of the judgmental interrogative.

To get Donald to put his clothes on: "Are

ya going to sit around all day in your pajamas like a schoolboy home with da cold?"

To encourage Donald to eat his untouched plate of food: "Are you on a hunger strike?"

To make him exercise: "Will I have to carry you or will you walk on your own?"

She would even use the same tack with Lena: "Will you be eating lunch with your husband or going out with your girlfriends again?"

And to anyone who was visiting Donald, Alvita would offer a variation on the following: "He's in a mood t'day. It's best to ignore it."

When Anna visited, he was most definitely in a mood.

"I need you to call in a prescription for Ambien. I can't sleep. If I can't sleep, I can't work."

"You're retired, Dad. Remember?"

"I consult," Donald said. Sometimes he did call his old colleagues and offer suggestions on the stock market. Sometimes the research was current and sound. No matter what state his mind was in, Donald always read the morning's business section. Whether it stuck was another story. Donald could read today's news and then pick up the phone and remark on conditions five years past. *You should consider adding some environmental funds to your portfolio. That global-warming talk isn't going away.*

"I think it's best if you take the meds your doctor prescribed," Anna said.

"I'm not demanding Vicodin. Although my knee is still giving me trouble. I just need a prescription for sleeping pills, and I don't have the energy to go in to the doctor today."

"I can't do that, Dad."

"Why not?"

"I don't write prescriptions anymore, remember?"

"What kind of doctor doesn't write prescriptions?"

"I'm not a doctor anymore, Dad. I haven't been for four years."

"Why did you quit?"

"I didn't quit. I had a problem with drugs. I lost my medical license. Four years ago."

"You're weak," Donald said, his face burning red. That was the standard attack in his Rolodex. Nothing was worse than weakness. "How did I raise a drug addict?" Donald said. This was the second time Donald had learned that his daughter had been an addict and destroyed her career. It would not be the last.

Anna had seen enough shrinks to know

how easy it was to blame her parents. She blamed them for many things, but not for who she had become. She took full credit for that.

"Go. I don't want a druggie in my house," Donald said.

"I'm clean now."

Anna left the house and drove straight to a meeting. The following day she had a brittle lunch with her mother in a restaurant on the top floor of a department store. Lena offered to buy Anna a new outfit for work. She didn't mention the incident at the house, although when Anna ordered French fries, she said in a warning tone, as if her daughter were stepping into heavy traffic:

"You should be careful with that."

Then Lena nibbled at her salade niçoise for five minutes while remaining uncharacteristically mute. Even under circumstances more dire than these, Lena could usually manage polite conversation. The weather, gardens, charity organizations, other people's failed marriages, the inedible food served at the last dinner party, the relative weight gain or weight loss in her circle of acquaintances who passed as friends.

Anna let herself enjoy the quiet and didn't try to fill the space. She devoured her hamburger and French fries and didn't click her eyes upward to check Lena's expression.

After the waitress cleared the plates, Lena ordered a cup of decaf coffee, which she doctored with skim milk and fake sugar. She then spoke with more bluntness than Anna had thought she was capable of.

"Why haven't you ever married?"

"I was busy. Medical school and drugs are very time-consuming hobbies."

"Colin said —" Lena quit on the sentence, thinking better of it.

"What did Colin say? Go ahead."

"He said you were in love with Malcolm. Were you?"

"Yes."

"You still think about him?"

"All of the time."

"Is that why you're like this?"

"No, Mom."

"Then why? Did we do this to you?"

"It's not one thing. Maybe it's nothing. Even if Malcolm lived, I might have derailed this train the exact same way. I know I didn't turn out like you or I expected. But it's not as bad as it looks. I'm going to be okay."

That was the first time Anna said that and meant it.

The next morning, Kate, Anna, Colin, and Swinger Girl ate pancakes together before Kate drove Anna to the airport. As Anna was leaving, Colin gave her a wonderfully suffocating embrace. She had to wonder where he'd learned such things. Perhaps it was fatherhood. He lifted Swinger Girl out of her booster seat, spun her around, and landed her facing in the direction of the staircase.

"Shoes," he said, knowing that she would return wearing lace-up pink Converse high-tops that finished off the superhero outfit.

Colin placed his hand on the back of Kate's head, said, "No Sex Pistols," and left.

Anna turned to Kate for an explanation.

"I had my iPod on random in the car. 'God Save the Queen.' Zooey liked it and asked me to play it again. Then she started singing it around the house. 'God save the queen, she ain't no human bean.' She comes up with some really good lyrics. But Colin does not approve of my music. I don't approve of children's music. But he wins."

"How long are you going to live here?" Anna asked.

"Until there's a reason not to."

Anna couldn't remember a time in her life when she didn't want more of something. Now it was a constant struggle to be satisfied with what she had. It had taken years to feel at peace when she introduced herself to someone and couldn't tell the new acquaintance that she was a doctor. Even now, admitting her occupation sometimes embarrassed her. And yet she remembered the days when Kate would proudly announce at a party full of high achievers that she was a barista. As she grew older and older, Anna found more and more things to envy in Kate.

"Is this enough for you?" Anna asked.

"Less than this would be enough for me."

Anna departed, and life returned to normal for Colin, Kate, and Zooey, although Colin could never assign that word to it. Every night, when he walked through the front door, a new, bizarre activity greeted him. There was the day that Zooey made cookies from scratch with her own personal recipe — inedible, of course; baking is a science, and no cookie recipe on earth calls for three packets of cherry Jell-O mix. There were forts in his living room made from blankets and chairs — a common childhood activity, but done with a grasp of military defense tactics. There were lessons on code breaking and surreptitious communications, and secret languages that would change from week to week. There were books, not just the current trends in children's picture books but the brutal old fairy tales that had fallen out of fashion. Kate would argue that they hadn't caused *her* any permanent damage, although Colin couldn't be sure of that. He had failed to understand the recipe that made up Kate.

The one time Colin argued against Kate's brand of literary entertainment was when Zooey woke from a nightmare about a witch wanting to bake her in an oven.

"People have nightmares," Kate said.

One night Colin returned to an empty house. A few lights were still on, and the second car was in the driveway. He saw a reflection of flames in the living room window and raced into the backyard to find a campfire burning in a pit surrounded by landscaping rocks. A tent was pitched nearby, and Kate and Zooey were toasting marshmallows on twigs over the flames.

When Zooey saw her father, she jumped to her feet and ran toward him with the marshmallow stick outstretched like a lance, missing only the horse. Colin disarmed his daughter as she leaped into his arms. He took a bite out of the burned marshmallow as Zooey protested.

"That's mine, Daddy. You can make your own."

Colin changed clothes and returned to the campsite. Kate silently handed him a stick with a fresh marshmallow while Colin inspected the newly dug fire pit. Kate, anticipating some protest, said, "You mentioned you were going to have new sod in spring, and, since it's almost winter, the snow will cover the hole."

Colin let his marshmallow catch fire and then blew out the torch.

"You could have called and asked," he said, unperturbed.

"You would have said no," Kate said.

"True."

Kate proffered a graham cracker and a chocolate square as a peace offering, and it was accepted.

The sky was clear. Zooey rested on her back and looked up at the stars and named the constellations for her father. "That's Ursa Major, that's Ursa Minor. I keep looking for Ursa Medium, but Kate said there isn't one."

"Why should there be an Ursa Medium?" Colin asked.

"*Ursa* means 'bear' in Latin, Daddy."

"Very good. But still —"

Zooey passed the marshmallow torch to Kate, who blew it out.

"Can I have two pieces of chocolate?"

"Sure," Kate said, breaking a square in half.

"That's cheating."

"You have school tomorrow," Colin said. "Now finish up and then you need to brush your teeth for twice as long as usual."

Zooey ran back into the house. Colin turned to Kate. "What was she talking about with the bears?"

"Goldilocks and the Three Bears. There are only two bears in the constellations. She was looking for a third."

"Why?"

"Because we were talking about patterns in stories and life and how everything is just a variation of something that has already been."

That got Colin thinking of patterns. Sometimes Zooey reminded him of Anna as a child, fearless and independent with so many ideas. He wondered if that pattern would repeat.

Colin followed his daughter into the house and supervised her dental hygiene, having noticed her habit of staring into space without moving the toothbrush in her mouth. Anna had done the same thing as a child.

"Circular motions, Zooey."

Zooey obeyed her father but believed that the task was in vain. When she'd learned that she would lose all her teeth and get an entirely new set, it occurred to her that she could neglect the originals. When she asked Kate whether her assumption was correct, Kate couldn't argue with her logic.

"Why do I brush teeth that are going to die?"

"Practice. So you know how to keep the next set alive."

Zooey insisted that Colin read her "Rumpelstiltskin" as a bedtime story. Colin changed the ending and didn't let Rumpelstiltskin split himself in two in a fit of rage. Instead, he saw the error of his ways.

"Daddy, you changed it."

"There's always more than one ending, Zooey."

From the window Colin watched Kate tend to the fire, letting the embers burn to their final death. Then she poured a bucket of water over them and returned to the house.

Colin and Kate sat on the couch in the living room in front of the gas fireplace. Colin picked up the remote control and pressed the On button. Flames burst out of rocks, casting shadows around the room. He flicked the fireplace off and on again, for effect. "You can, however, roast them over the gas stove and eat them in front of a gas fireplace."

"You want everything to be easy," Kate said, getting to her feet.

She kicked his legs, which were resting on the coffee table, blocking her exit.

Colin took her hand and said, "Not everything."

Colin understood very little about Kate, but he knew to tread cautiously. When Colin reached for Kate, she'd felt her skin flush and wanted to believe it was a delayed reaction to various fires. Colin tugged on the bottom of Kate's shirt, pulling her toward him, waiting to see how she'd respond.

Kate straddled him on the couch and kissed him, tasting marshmallows again. She admonished herself by repeating this refrain: *This means nothing to him.* She pulled her shirt over her head and struggled out of it, wrestling with the shirt in a childish manner. Colin thought, *This means nothing to her.* They continued to disrobe, misreading each other's minds.

2013

YELLOWSTONE NATIONAL PARK, WYOMING

George and Anna threw off their clothes by the watering hole. Kate couldn't help but stare at George's natural breasts, which sagged slightly from the weight of time and the loss of silicone.

Anna had noticed that the implants had been removed when she met George at the airport, but she didn't say anything until they were laid bare for observation.

"Hey, your fake boobs are gone," Kate said enthusiastically.

"Edgar prefers things natural."

"Huh," Kate said, the enthusiasm entirely drained from her voice. "What do you do if you find a guy who likes big tits again? Can't be healthy going back and forth like that."

"I'm getting married, Kate. There isn't going to be another guy."

Anna jumped into the water to signal the end of the conversation.

"How did you find this place?" George asked Kate. George, Anna, and Kate, after months of planning, had found a pocket of time in June to gather for a medium-dry bachelorette weekend before George and Edgar's August nuptials. George chose Yellowstone Park and Kate remained mum about her previous visit, although she couldn't resist urging them toward that one private hot spring she'd found eight years earlier.

Kate guided her friends by faking a sense of the geography. She said, "Let's go this way. I have a good feeling about this way." And the hot spring miraculously appeared.

The trio swam for an hour and then gathered their belongings and climbed up to the road to watch the sun set in a cloudy tangle of purple and yellow. Kate ranked the sunset against a few others and it came up short, but sunsets were like pizza, she thought; they were all pretty good. (Except the kind in the frozen-food section and one that she'd had in Kansas.) George wished her boys were with her. Then she remembered Edgar. Engaged now for three months, she worried that she had to remind herself to remember him. For a brief moment, Anna thought how nice it would feel to have a cold beer in her hands. The women returned to the car and drove to the campsite.

Kate held the flashlight and timed George as she pitched their tent in the dark. Three minutes and fifty-five seconds. Each step so rote, she could have been loading a dishwasher. Before George could take on the coveted job of fire starter, Kate had collected kindling and lit a match.

Just twenty minutes after they landed at the site, the three women were warming their hands by the fire. George uncorked a bottle of wine and drank straight from the bottle. She offered it to Kate, who declined. No matter how many times Anna had told her she was fine with people drinking in her company, Kate never partook when Anna was around.

George took another swig. She had had a proper boozy bachelorette party the weekend before with girlfriends from Chicago and Boise and a few wives of Edgar's colleagues, whom she was encouraged to befriend. All of the women, without exception, were desperate to get away from their husbands and children and have a weekend of sheer debauchery in Las Vegas.

There was a wild disparity in the manners in which George's new friends indulged in their brief freedom. Amanda played blackjack for twelve hours straight. Whitney insisted on going to a male strip show. She had a hundred singles in her pocket and stayed for the second performance. Rebecca drank mojito after mojito and ordered two desserts. They all flirted whenever possible. Loretta let herself be groped by a banker with a greasy head of Jersey-thug hair, and Shelley, the clear winner of the trophy-wife award, disappeared with a twenty-three-year-old first-year law student at his own bachelor party. All of them slept until noon and played nickel slots for hours so they could drink for free. There was a shopping excursion and a few glittery shows. One involved an illusionist whose entire act, it seemed to George, consisted of disappearing in a ruffled shirt and reappearing bare-chested. George wished Kate were there just so she could hear her say something like *I wonder where all the shirts go. Do you think he gives them to Goodwill?*

As the weekend wore on, there were several moments in which the antics of the women seemed not only tasteless but dull. It was then that George longed for the old Anna, the Anna who elevated reckless behavior beyond the vulgar or mundane. If she could have had the old Anna for just one day and then return her safe and sound, like a prison release, she would have done it. Because, once again, she wanted a professional guide into complete oblivion.

The campfire burst with satisfying crackles, and the smell of burned wood was better than any perfume George could think of. She took another swig of wine.

"You might want to slow down," Anna said. "I think that's the only bottle." Sober for years, Anna still had the software of a drunk in her system, always aware of the amount of booze and planning accordingly.

"I got another in the car," George said. "I have to use the bathroom anyway. I'll get it on the way back." George corked the bottle and tucked it into a groove in the dirt. She clicked on the flashlight and headed down the trail.

When the sound of George's footsteps had faded under the chorus of crickets, Anna spoke.

"Is she okay?"

"I don't know," Kate said.

"Edgar isn't like the others," Anna said. "Let's wait and see. Just casually bring up the topic and go from there. Could just be wedding jitters."

"You're right," said Kate. "Edgar isn't like the others."

"Whatever happened between you and

Edgar?" Anna asked.

"I thought you didn't even remember him."

"I remembered when I saw the pictures," Anna said. "I thought his name was Ernest. He used to visit you all the time. I figured something had happened between you two, because one day he stopped coming around."

"He wasn't visiting me."

"But you liked him, didn't you?"

"Yes. But he liked George."

"Huh. Were they together back then? I don't remember that."

"She slept with him once," Kate said. "Regretted it. That's why he suddenly dropped off the radar."

"Did she know you liked him?"

"I never told her."

"Why not?"

"It wouldn't have changed how he felt," Kate said.

"You sure know how to lock it down when you need to."

As George trudged back to the campsite, Kate mumbled to Anna, "We don't mention this again. *Capisce?*"

"Yes, Godfather," Anna said.

George settled next to the fire and leaned back against an ice chest covered with an ancient wool blanket.

"I hate camping when I have my period," George said. "It's such a pain in the ass."

"When I was in Girl Scouts," Kate said, "the counselors used to freak us out and tell us that grizzly bears were prone to attack women who were on their period. In fact, I think they used to have us sign a waiver or something."

"It's bullshit," George said. "The only kind of bear known to be attracted to menstrual blood is the polar bear, and we're not likely to run into any here."

"My grandmother told me that you shouldn't wash your hair when you have your period," Anna said.

George choked on her wine. "I've never heard that one. Is there a premise behind it?"

"I don't remember. She also thought you could get rid of warts if you got someone to buy 'em off you," Anna said, shaking her head in disbelief.

As Anna watched the fire crackle, another recollection took hold and she began chuckling to herself.

"Something on your mind?" George asked.

As Anna's new memory took shape, she

528

felt like she was watching an old movie of herself.

"When I was sixteen or so, visiting Colin at college, I woke up on the floor of his dorm room and I was bleeding through my underwear. I raced to the bathroom. It was a coed dorm, and I thought I could catch a woman alone. It was empty and I was too embarrassed to say anything. So I used a wad of toilet paper as a stopgap measure and returned to the room and reluctantly told Colin of my predicament. He promptly started roaming the corridor, knocking on women's doors and shouting, 'My sister has her period. Anybody got any tampons to spare?' I swear, he was *shouting* it at the top of his lungs. I was beet red and begging him to stop. Finally, Malcolm told him to shut the fuck up and give me a break. He got some tampons from a friend of his.

"Later we had to go to the drugstore so I could get a full supply, and he kept shouting the same thing in the store. 'Where are the tampons? My sister has her period.' He was so evil."

Kate said, "At least he got you tampons. My *deda* would buy me those horrible giant pads. I was teased relentlessly in PE until a teacher took pity on me. I had to use my allowance money to buy tampons because I couldn't talk about it with my *deda*."

"My dad always cooked me steak," George said wistfully. "I don't know how he knew, but he always knew."

"Because you're a crazy bitch for the week before," Kate said.

"So that's how he knew. Anyway, I always got steak."

"Typical," Anna said. "We endure emotionally scarring humiliation and you get *steak*."

"So, will you be serving a choice of steak or seafood at the wedding?" Kate asked.

Anna turned to Kate. "That might have been one of the worst conversational transitions in the history of man," she said.

"Doubt it," Kate said. "So, steak or seafood, or will there be a vegetarian option?"

George drained the first bottle and uncorked the second. Anna bit the inside of her lip. Kate took the open bottle from George's grip and took a swig for the sole purpose of lessening the amount of alcohol that George could consume.

"We will have three options. Steak, salmon, and pasta. We even have a gluten-free cake alternative for dessert. But with three hundred guests, there will still be a few who will leave unsatisfied."

"Have you picked out a dress?" Anna asked.

"Yes. It's white. Shut up."

"I didn't say anything," said Anna.

"You didn't wear white at your second wedding," Kate said.

"I know. But this is Edgar's first wedding. So he wanted the whole she-bang. Or perhaps it was his mother. I can't really tell."

"You were happier before your other weddings," Kate casually commented.

"And look how those turned out."

George took the bottle of wine from Kate. She could tell other women the truth, but not them: She enjoyed the luxuries and the ease Edgar provided. She liked that her children had taken to him, and he to them. That she felt loved and respected and safe. She would never tell Kate and Anna that she believed this might be her last chance to find a decent man, and that she now mistrusted her instincts so thoroughly that she defied them completely.

As her wedding ticked closer, she began to think of other men in her past and the sick, desperate feeling their intimacies had evoked. She wondered what it would be like to live the rest of her life without that feeling. Sometimes, as in that moment, drunk on cheap red wine and with people who reminded her only of the past, she thought that maybe she couldn't.

Anna and Kate exchanged glances, a veritable conversation of eyebrow lifts, while George dug patterns into the dirt with a stick.

"That's a hell of a ring," Anna said, noting the seven-carat diamond on George's finger and comparing it to Kate's simple silver band.

"I didn't ask for it," George said.

"I'm sure you didn't," Anna said, noting the edge in George's voice.

"If you ever get mugged, promise me you'll hand over the ring," Kate said.

"Of course."

"Are you sure about this one?" Anna casually asked.

"I'm not sure about anything," George said. "I don't know that I ever have been."

2006

BISMARCK, NORTH DAKOTA

"Room for one," Kate would say. She'd said it now more times than she could count.

"Is this business or pleasure?" the motel clerk would ask.

Business.

Her ritual was always the same. She'd enter the room, try to decipher the layers of odors from previous guests. A scent that had been years in the making, like the bouquet of a fine wine. Only it smelled bad, typically an amalgamation of cigarettes, pets, the ghost of perfumes past, mildew, cheap shampoos, burned dust from the heating vent or dander rising from the blast of air conditioning.

Kate would check the drawers and the closets, first for people, then for forgotten items — most of which were worthy of immediate disposal. In six months the only real treasure she'd found was a stack of postcards left in the nightstand drawer with a Gideon Bible. Housekeeping must have missed it. But these postcards, unlike the others left behind, were not blank. They were drafts of the same note, which presumably the author had finally perfected.

Dear Mona,
I fucked up, okay? People fuck up, don't they?
If God can forgive, why can't you? You can't blame the whole thing on me. [Line scratched out.]
I want to come home. I promise it'll be different this time.
Is there any way we can forget?

Love,
Barney

Dear Mona,
I had a danish this morning and thought of you. I want to come home. Will you take me?
I know I don't deserve your forgiveness, but I don't know what I'll do if you don't take me back.
We're soulmates. You said it yourself thirty years ago when we got married.
One mistake can't change that.

Love,
Barney

Dear Mona,

I'm sorry. I'm really, really sorry. You won't answer my calls, and the letters return unopened. But a postcard, you don't have to open that. Now the mailman will know our business.

I'll do whatever you want. We can be happy again. I know it.

On the last card, Barney didn't even bother signing his name. Kate was hopeful that he'd sent off the perfect note and that Mona took him back. He certainly wasn't staying in this hotel room anymore. Maybe Mona didn't take him back, and Barney had to find a dingy apartment with a shag carpet that had seen as much traffic as the motel's. The postcards reminded Kate of Anna and the six letters she'd received from her in the course of her travels. If Mona could forgive Barney, Kate certainly thought she should forgive Anna. Kate was surprised to see this motel had its own stationery, and then she noticed it was from a competing motel chain. Kate tried three ballpoint pens before she found one that worked.

Anna,

I got your letters. And thanks. I was livid for a while, but I'm over it now. I know it's part of your recovery to revisit the past. But do we need to stay there? I hope you're doing okay. And that living with your folks isn't fucking up your recovery. It would fuck with mine. Seems like there has to be another way. Let me know how you're doing. How you fill your days.

Have you heard about the demotion of the planet Pluto? I, for one, am incensed. How do you go your whole life being a planet and then, suddenly, you're not a planet anymore. Correction: dwarf planet. What does that even mean? I see an idiom taking shape. Five, ten years from now, when someone gets dissed or demoted or loses his or her job, people will say, "He was plutoed." "Are you plutoing me?" someone will say when witnessing a snub. "That was some pluto, wasn't it?" Hmm, I'm not sure about the syntax of the last one, but I think you get the gist.

Do you think I should write NASA?

I've been hearing things about the Montana sky and I've been thinking I should see that, just so I can be that person who tells you one sky isn't so different from the next. I might stay put

536

and seek employment. I'll write more soon.

Kate

The librarian had had her hip replaced last year, and now her knee was acting up. She couldn't shelve books anymore. She could stamp the due date on the atavistic index cards and that was it. Kate was strolling through the town of Prairie Basin, looking for a coffee shop, angling for a job in her area of expertise. But then she saw the sign in the library window. *Part-time help wanted: assistant to librarian.*

Mrs. Popovsky wore tweed skirts and starched shirts with just the top button undone and sweaters and stockings in muted colors and sensible shoes. She even had those glasses that dangled around her neck from a chain. She explained the menial job duties to Kate and briefly summarized the Dewey decimal system, which Kate happened to be very familiar with. In fact, she had recently read a biography of Melvil Dewey. She expressed her appreciation for his dedication to spelling reform but stopped short of mentioning her shock at discovering that Dewey was an unrepentant womanizer. Kate remembered something Anna once said on the subject: *There are* two kinds of womanizers. *Those who love women too much and those who hate them.* Kate wondered what kind of womanizer Melvil Dewey had been.

Mrs. Popovsky was duly impressed by the job candidate but had to admit that she thought the young woman overqualified, based on her knowledge of Melvil Dewey and several other topics that arose during the interview. Kate told her that her primary occupation for the last ten years had been barista. Her unambitious employment history worked in her favor. She was hired on the spot.

After Kate spent a night in the town's official motel — the Prairie Basin Inn — Popovsky phoned and told Kate that she knew of a woman renting a room at her farmhouse, just a few miles out of the city. A single bed, a dresser, a writing table, and a twelve-inch television provided the entire décor. Mrs. Bennett, now in her late seventies, was slightly hard of hearing, so the entire interview sounded like a conversation held over the cheers of a ball game.

"Rent is two hundred a month. With a two-hundred-dollar security deposit!"

"Okay!"

"No male guests!"

"I don't know any males in town!"

"If you meet them, don't invite them over!"

"Okay!"

"How long do you think you'll be staying?"

"I don't know!" Kate honestly and loudly said.

"Me neither!" Mrs. Bennett said, punctuating the reply with a wink.

Kate paid cash on the spot and lugged in all her worldly possessions in two short jaunts from the car. Mrs. Bennett commended her on packing light.

Kate managed to shelve the books in a fraction of the time that Mrs. Popovsky expected. Sometimes Kate would hide the cart among the stacks and nestle herself in a corner, reading whatever struck her fancy. Occasionally Popovsky would come looking for her, but the brushing sound the heavy fabric of her clothes made gave Kate ample time to look busy. Although she wasn't certain that Popovsky would even care. Three weeks after she started, Kate didn't even bother looking over her shoulder when she heard Popovsky coming.

Kate knelt with her back against a warren of Nancy Drew mysteries and read a book on the history of wool, which included some surprising facts on the fabric that Mrs. Popovsky so favored.

For instance, wool was remarkably stain resistant due to the overlapping scales on the fiber's surface. Unlike some fabrics, it protected against body odor. *Although it still stinks when it's wet,* Kate thought. A coin toss. Wool could both absorb and release the sweat. Its resilient fibers could be bent close to 20,000 times without breaking; compare that to silk, the fibers of which had a lifespan of about 4,500 bends. More important, it was naturally flame resistant; it smoldered rather than flamed, and the burn products did not lodge in wounds, which was why it was used to clothe military personnel. And if you were concerned about the sheep that the wool came from, Australia had developed a revolutionary process that caused a sheep to shed its entire fleece at once so it did not have to endure what appeared to be the rather brutal shearing procedure.

She couldn't determine how this revolutionary system worked. A pill? A shot? Were there side effects? She would look into the matter later.

Kate felt her phone buzz in her pocket as she was reading. She was so unaccustomed to phone calls, it startled her out of her reading coma, and she snapped the book shut as if caught in an illicit act. She looked at the phone in her pocket and noted that the call was from George. One of her routine check-ins, she assumed. She would return the call later. Kate unfurled her legs and got to her feet, shaking her body out, like a swimmer before a race. She shoved the cart along the precisely maintained Dewey system and shelved a few more books at warp speed. Before she left for the day, she checked out a book on the history of soap.

In winter, Mrs. Bennett fed her fire from morning until night. She kept her thermostat at fifty-two degrees. She wore a wool sweater that she'd knit herself and sometimes a scarf and hat. A cup of weak tea warmed her hands.

Kate's bedroom was exposed on three sides, and the wood frame had little insulation. She kept a portable heater one foot from the bed and slipped under the covers the moment she returned home. She wore two sweaters and a skullcap at all times. In the evenings she read from whatever she had checked out of the library. She thought it was solitude that she needed, even though she had always felt alone. She sometimes saw flashes, like images from a slide show, of herself from the outside. Her ridiculous monastic existence. Thirty-one years old and she was sleeping in a twin bed on a foam mattress over metal coils. She spent her days studying anything that had nothing to do with her.

A rotary-dial phone sat on the floor of Kate's bedroom. It rarely rang, but when it did, the room vibrated. It rang now, and Kate's heart skipped a beat. It rang a second time, and Mrs. Bennett picked up.

"Hello. Hello. Who? Oh, yes. One moment, please."

Kate picked up the phone as she heard Mrs. Bennett's footsteps shuffling toward her door.

"I got it!" Kate shouted. "Hello."

"Kate, it's George."

"How'd you get this number?"

"I called the library."

"She shouldn't give my number out to strangers."

"I'm not a stranger."

"Mrs. Popovsky doesn't know that."

"I got a phone call from Colin."

"What happened to attorney-client privilege?"

"He doesn't think of himself as your attorney. He's just the treasurer of Golden Retrieval Inc."

"Still, he should use some discretion."

"I thought you were on a road trip," George said.

"I was," said Kate. "Now I'm not anymore."

"Colin said you were roaming the country impersonating a woman named Sarah Lake and then giving money to complete strangers under the corporate name Golden Retrieval Inc. It's too crazy for him to make that shit up. He said if you were related to him, he would have toyed with the idea of having you committed."

"I'm glad I'm not related to him."

"I pressed him for details, but there was one question he couldn't answer. As far as I know, the last time anyone saw Sarah Lake was ten years ago. Why are you using her identity?"

"I'm just using her name because I can't use my own."

"Next question: Why are you giving your money away?"

"It makes me feel better."

"It made you feel better to give close to fifty thousand dollars to a woman named Evelyn Baker?"

"It did."

"Who is she, Kate?"

"She's the daughter of the man I killed."

Until that moment, Kate hadn't admitted to anyone what she was doing. But now that her business was done, she could say it.

For years George had tried to banish her memories of that night, eventually relenting and accepting that they would never go away. It was with her forever, and now she realized she could live with that. But she'd always thought of that night as hers alone. It happened to her; his hands were around her neck. But Kate's hands were on the vodka bottle. George never thought of it as murder; she hadn't realized that Kate had.

As soon as their call ended, George phoned the treasurer of Golden Retrieval Inc. and told him precisely what that business entailed. While Colin tried to get Kate on the line, George called Anna and explained the purpose of Kate's nine-month road trip. George's call was akin to Kate's seemingly redacted letters; words dropped randomly from the conversation because of the dodgy reception at the campsite Anna currently called home. But Anna got the gist of it, eventually. She got into her car and drove to civilization, or at least to a location where cell towers reached, and phoned her brother.

"Do you know what Kate's been doing?" Anna asked.

"I only just found out," Colin said, still stunned by the role he'd played in this enterprise.

"I don't understand," said Anna. "She was protecting George."

"Someone died at her hand. Not everyone knows what that feels like."

I do, Anna thought.

"She was also protecting you," Colin said.

"What are you talking about?" Anna said.

"She knew you'd left the door open, but she told George to keep it a secret. All of those years, she was keeping a secret that you already knew."

"When did she find out?"

"Right after you went into rehab. I told her what you said to me afterward."

"You told her that?" Anna asked.

"Isn't it true?"

"Yes. But it should have come from me," Anna said. "Why did you tell her?"

"Because I wanted her to leave you," Colin said.

Anna immediately phoned Kate, but the call went to voice mail. Anna drove straight to an Internet café and spent an hour composing and recomposing an e-mail.

Dear Kate,
    I just found out what you've been up

to. I wish I had known. There are so many things I would have done differently, if I had. I've only just started admitting to things and I suppose there are some gaping holes in my confessions. Honestly, I thought if I brought it up, it would just be to ease my conscience. It never occurred to me that you've been revisiting the past on a regular basis. So this is what you should know: I went to that bar, Pete's Emerald. I remember talking to an old man and ordering a few drinks and then being woken by sirens and ambulance lights. I went to the police station a day or two later and I looked at a mug shot of Roger Hicks. He seemed familiar. Our back door was open. I'm piecing together the night the same way anyone else would. I don't remember talking to Hicks, but I might have. I don't know if he followed me home, or if I invited him. I don't remember leaving the door open, but I'm sure I did. It wouldn't have been the first time. It's hard to apologize for something you don't remember. I should have told you at least what I thought I knew. I understand now that the worst thing I could have done was lie about it, but I never knew exactly what the lie was.

I thought it would be easier if we all just forgot. I'm sorry. I know that will never be enough.

Love,
Anna

Kate sent Anna a postcard after she got that letter. Anna was able to decipher every word.

Anna,
    I think I'm ready to forget.

Kate

Kate swiveled back and forth in the plush leather chair designated for clients. She had returned to Boston three days earlier after being gone almost a year. When Colin asked her why she was back, she said that her business was done.

"You were kind of like a traveling vacuum salesman," Colin said. "Only you gave all of the vacuums away."

Kate noted and ignored the impatience in his voice. "And now all sorts of people have vacuums who wouldn't have had them otherwise."

"Do you know how much money is left in

your account?" Colin asked.

"You do know that I'm really good with numbers."

"In my book, good with numbers means you hold on to the numbers."

"I have seven thousand, four hundred and twenty-two dollars and sixty-four cents in my account."

Colin looked at his spreadsheet. "Close enough. You had seven thousand, four hundred and forty-three dollars and eighty-five cents this morning."

"I had to gas up the car," Kate said. "I thought I should return it with a full tank."

"It's your car," said Colin. "Maybe you should sell it. You won't need one in Boston."

"I borrowed it. That's all. Now I'm returning it."

"You should have talked to me. You should have told me what you were doing."

"How's Anna?"

"She's good. She's a country girl now. Hasn't had a haircut in a year. She drives a truck. She's always covered in mud. My mother is terrified that she'll meet a farmer and raise a brood of children who'll be educated in the public-school system."

"Congratulations," Kate said. The mention of children reminded her that Colin had recently had a daughter.

"For what?"

"You're a father now, no?"

Colin spun a picture around on his desk. It was a close-up of a baby in a woman's arms — presumably the mother, but she was not the subject of the photo.

"She looks like a healthy baby," Kate said. She'd never found infants attractive and never bothered gushing in the socially acceptable fashion.

"She's got a set of lungs on her," Colin said.

Kate got to her feet. "I won't take up any more of your time."

Colin circled his desk and gave Kate a warm embrace. She returned it with a businessman's pat on the back.

"Don't give away any more of your money, Kate."

"I've settled the debts as best I could."

"That's good, because you're just about broke."

"I have over seven thousand dollars and not a single debt. That's not broke in my world."

"What will you do now?"

"What everybody else does. Wake up in the morning, drink coffee, read the paper,

549

go to a job, come home, live my life for as long as I can."

1998

SANTA CRUZ, CALIFORNIA

When Anna was a child, every morning her father sat in complete silence reading the business section of the newspaper. Her brother tackled the sports section, and her mother gazed at the style section, occasionally trying to draw Anna into some discussion of the latest fashion trend. Anna read the backs of cereal boxes and milk cartons, and when the milk was gone and the kitchen empty, she'd steal the discarded container and slice out the data on the missing person. She kept an album in her room and tried to memorize their faces. She noticed how her family poured their milk and didn't give the lost boy or girl a second glance. This was why people stayed missing, Anna thought. And when she was out in public, she clocked the faces of strangers and consulted the memory of the file she kept in her room. Lena was searching Anna's bedroom for a peach cashmere sweater that Anna claimed to have lost when she discovered the missing-person photo album in the back of her closet. She promptly tossed it in the trash and did her best to ignore the nauseated feeling it summoned in her.

Anna always knew when her mother had been in her room, because she left sharp heel dents in the rug and Chanel No. 5 in the air, which offended Anna's senses more than rank body odor. Anna promptly checked the garbage, salvaged her scrapbook, and secreted it away with more stealth. Eventually Anna stashed the album in her hideaway.

Anna stopped collecting the milk-carton ghosts when she was seventeen, but she never quite shook her quiet obsession with the vanished. She read every article in the newspaper about a missing person or a found body; she carefully read the signs on telephone poles with MISSING in a giant font. And she followed the stories until they faded like newspaper print left in the sun and she wondered where on earth all those people could be.

BODY OF FEMALE HIKER FOUND IN WILDER RANCH STATE PARK

The body of a female hiker was found a few miles off a trail in Wilder Ranch State

Park on Friday. Jane Doe, approximately 5'11", blond hair, blue eyes, slim build, died of exposure sometime between Saturday evening and Sunday morning, according to the coroner's report. Police found a tent and camping equipment three miles away that they believe belonged to the hiker. Record-low temperatures hit Northern California last week and the authorities surmise that the woman was attempting to find shelter when she succumbed to the elements. No identification was found on the woman or at her campsite. If you have any information, please contact the Santa Cruz County Coroner's Office.

Anna cut out the article, staining her fingers with newspaper ink, and stuffed it into her purse. She attended class, her focus on the lecture as fleeting as that of a teenager in love. She left class in a haze and drove off campus to the Ocean Street address of the sheriff's office. She waited patiently at the administration desk and showed the article to the staff.

"I think I might know her," Anna said.

Without any paperwork or other evidence of official business, the officers took Anna to the hospital and into the bowels of the morgue.

The body of Jane Doe was on what looked like a rolling metal cot. Some kind of administrator in scrubs pulled the sheet back to reveal Sarah Lake's face. Anna had been to her grandfather's and great-aunt's funerals. She knew that dead people didn't resemble the living, but in someone so young, death was particularly startling.

"Do you know her?" the administrator asked.

"Not really. But her name is Sarah Lake. She used to work at Pete's Emerald. The owner might be able to tell you more."

"Is there any other information you can provide?"

"No," Anna said. Which was the truth and a lie. Kate might know something, but Anna wasn't sure she was going to tell her what she'd discovered.

Anna returned to Pete's Emerald to have a private wake for the woman she'd kicked out of her house.

Anna sat down at the bar and ordered a whiskey with a beer back. Within the hour, she was draining her second round.

A lanky male wearing a flannel shirt, beaten denims, and work boots on their deathbed took a seat next to Anna. He tossed a twenty-dollar bill on the bar.

"Can I buy you a drink?"

"No."

"What kind of woman turns down a free drink?"

"The kind who knows that nothing is free."

Kate had cooked trout the night before, and the carcass sat rotting in the overflowing trash bin.

"It stinks in here," George said.

"Take out the trash," Kate said. She hadn't been able to smell anything since the pollen count had risen two months ago.

"It's Anna's night. She never does her chores. You have to take a stand. The smell is nauseating."

"Remember, most wars begin when someone takes a stand. Taking stands isn't all it's cracked up to be," Kate said. Then she hoisted the garbage out of the bin and tied the plastic bag into a knot.

"I'll do it," George said.

"Why? So you can pick a fight later?"

"I feel like getting some air."

"In the alley, with the rest of the trash?" Kate asked, relinquishing the bag.

George needed leverage in the showdown she was eager for. Anna never abided by the household rules. One week she'd do nothing at all. Then, when she could sense

George's fuming tension or Kate's passive-aggressive reproach (sometimes she'd put the trash bin outside Anna's bedroom door), she'd compensate by knocking back a pot of coffee and some NoDoz or something stronger and then scrubbing the house from top to bottom.

George took out the trash, returned to the kitchen, and grabbed the recycling bin. The telephone rang. Kate picked up.

"Your dad's on the phone," Kate said.

George put the recycling bin down by the back door and took the phone. Bruno called every week without fail. The first few weeks after his confession about the other woman, George wouldn't take his calls, but George was an unrepentant Daddy's girl and he was the only man who offered her the unconditional affection she craved. It didn't take long for father and daughter to fall back into old habits. An hour on the phone with Bruno was nothing out of the ordinary for George.

"What do you talk about for an hour?" Anna would ask. Her phone calls with Donald Fury could be as brief as a handshake:

You're well?

Yes.

Good. Stay that way.

George often described her basketball

practice in such detail that sometimes it seemed to Kate that the account lasted longer than the practice. On this particular phone call, George grumbled about Anna's irresponsibility. Bruno had learned to not play adviser with his daughter. Long ago, he'd decided that women didn't want answers even if they seemed to be posing questions. "What am I supposed to do?" George asked. Bruno said, "That's a tough one." The phone call ended exactly fifty-seven minutes and thirty seconds after it had begun. Kate had gone to bed. George took a bath. The recycling bin sat by the unlocked back door.

Roger Hicks bought Anna a drink anyway. She was drinking well whiskey, so he opted for a middle-shelf blend to show he had taste.

"For the lady," he said to the bartender, who slid the drink six inches in Anna's direction.

Anna glanced at the drink but didn't touch it, knowing that making contact with the glass would somehow be taking owner-ship.

"The lady can pay for her own drinks, and the lady really hates the word *lady*," Anna said.

"The lady is kind of a bitch," Roger said.

"Do we have a problem here?" the bartender said.

"I don't," said Anna. She shifted a few stools down and sat next to one of those pickled regulars who move into the bar on the first of the month and move out when their disability checks are spent. Anna bought the guy a drink. His name was Herb. Herb, she thought, might have dementia, or maybe he was just drunk. Herb struck up a conversation about the universe expanding. He'd read it somewhere, he told her.

"Does that mean just the universe is expanding, or is everything inside the universe also expanding? Maybe that's why we're fatter than we used to be," Herb said, looking down at his gut.

"Maybe," Anna said. She liked talking to the older barflies. They wanted nothing from her except maybe another drink, but they were fine with just the company and the peripatetic conversations.

Roger Hicks had had his share of rejection, but usually when a pretty woman turned him down, it was for a prettier man. Herb had a gut that hung low over his belt and a greasy mop of brown-gray hair, and his face had the veiny marks of a career alcoholic's. Plus everyone knew that Herb was as mad as a cut snake. And that bitch was chatting away with him, laughing at his nonsensical patter. Hell, maybe she was just playing hard to get.

The girl could hold her liquor, he'd give her that. She'd drained five whiskeys and two beers since he'd arrived. But now she was on the move. She set a few more bills on the bar and made her way, weaving ever so slightly, down the galley to the door. She was drunk. Maybe drunk enough.

Roger Hicks closed out his tab, waited a minute or two, and left. He saw her at the end of the block making a right turn, and he followed her home. He almost quit after the second mile, but then he saw her reach for her keys as she turned onto High Street. He watched her unlock the front door. He sat by a tree, waited for the lights in the house to be extinguished, and then checked the front door. Even these days, some people forgot or still thought they were living in a different world. The door was locked. Hicks checked the windows. Closed. There was one that might work in a pinch, but he'd need to find a milk crate or something. He walked around to the back door, gripped the doorknob, and it turned, just like that.

Some people, he thought, *still trust their* neighbors.

2014
BOSTON, MASSACHUSETTS

Lena Fury died in her car on her way to lunch. She had a stroke at a stoplight, slumped over the wheel, and was pronounced dead at the scene. Colin was the emergency contact; Kate answered the call. She phoned Colin and spent the rest of the day being the messenger of death.

Anna got the news at work. Matthew saw tears streaming down her face as she spoke to Kate. Later, when she thought about it, Anna knew those tears were not for herself but for her mother, for the ugly truth that an entire life could be wasted on appearances.

She stepped into Matthew's office and asked for a week off. He said yes, of course. Then he approached her cautiously. He had been cautious with her ever since that night they'd kissed.

She'd gone home. They never spoke of it again.

561

"I'm going to hug you now," said Matthew. "Take it up with HR if you have a problem with it."

He put his arms around her. Anna didn't tense up, like he'd expected. She just fell into the embrace and let someone comfort her. He hugged like Max Blackman, she thought.

At their boozy office Christmas party, Max had tried to encourage the relationship.

"Matthew is a good man," he said.

"He's my boss," said Anna.

"I've seen you two together," Max said. "You're the boss."

"That's not a good idea."

"You have become so boring, Anna."

"True. But nothing bad has happened."

"Is that going to be the litmus test for your life?" Max said. "My stepson is never coming back. Besides, what are the odds that you and he would have made it anyway? You probably would have forgotten about him by now. You were always too —"

Max let a handwave finish his sentence.

Although Anna thought it made more sense incomplete. She was too something, but even she didn't know what. Years of therapy, rehab escapes, and meeting after meeting, and all she could tell you was that she was too something. And Max was right about Malcolm. When Anna was being honest with herself, she knew exactly how that relationship would have played out. She would have worn him down, gotten him, and then fucked it up.

It had been more than five years since she'd last lost control. Five years of every morning and evening exactly the same. She imagined her life as the readout of a healthy EKG, her heart beating slow and steady.

Lena's death threatened Anna's equilibrium. Whenever serious emotions fought to surface, Anna watched herself like a prison guard. She reminded herself again and again of what she was capable of.

Anna and Colin wrote the eulogy in one coffee-fueled night, agonizing over every word, trying to find the balance between respectful and honest and still manage to fill five minutes, which they'd decided was the absolute shortest acceptable length of time. Colin was saddled with the job of delivering it, so he expected Anna to pull her weight in words.

"Lena Fury was a principled, disciplined woman who dedicated her life to charitable endeavors," Anna said. "She was a devoted wife and mother who . . . something,

something."

"I need the something, something," Colin said.

"What did Mom like?"

"She liked shopping."

"You can't say that in a eulogy."

"Frame it differently. She had a love of fashion — no, she was a champion of artistic expression," Colin suggested.

"You got that from 'She liked shopping'?" Anna said. "Remember, her friends are going to be there."

"What did Mom love?"

"Order," Anna said. And as she said it, she realized that she too had come to love that condition. Here she was, finally on the same side of the fence as her mom — unless you considered the line between life and death a fence. Which it kind of was.

Colin delivered the eulogy in four minutes and forty-nine seconds. He rushed it when he was at the podium. He spoke of Lena and Donald's fairytale romance, of how she'd stood by his bedside until the very end. He talked about her love of animals and her endless charitable work. He mentioned her humor without using the word *biting* at any point. He spoke of her warm embrace, from the memory of one hug thirty-two years ago when he'd lost a soccer match. He mentioned bedtime stories and never revealed that they were delivered by Agnes, their nanny.

A single anecdote was the centerpiece of the brief tribute. Colin told the story of when he was in high school and one day decided to ditch class and go to the movies. *Midnight Run* was playing. He sat in the third row and ate an entire box of licorice and drank a Coke. When the movie ended, after the credits rolled, he walked up the aisle and right into his mother, who had been sitting just a few rows back.

They regarded each other for a long, awkward moment until Lena finally said, "I won't tell if you won't." Then she bought him an ice cream cone and wrote him an absence note for the day. The anecdote was the only really true thing in the eulogy, but it had happened to Anna.

George had flown out with her three boys for the funeral. Edgar had business but sent the most obscenely enormous flower arrangement. Everyone stayed at the old Fury mansion. On the last night, the sky was clear, and George suggested they pitch tents and sleep outside.

Kate dug another fire pit.

Zooey sang.

God said to Abraham, "Kill me a son."
Abe say, "Man, you must be putting me
    on."
God say, "No."
Abe say, "What?"
God say, "You can do what you want, Abe,
    but
The next time you see me comin' you
    better run."

"Sweetie, what are you singing?" Colin asked Zooey while staring directly at Kate.

Zooey answered by singing the next verse.

Abe says, "Where you want this killin'
    done?"
God say, "Out on Highway 61."

"Kate, you have to stop playing music like this in the car," Colin said.

"You said you wanted her to learn the Bible," Kate said.

Anna said to Zooey, "Why don't you go help Hudson do whatever he's doing."

"He's foraging for snails," George said. "Do you know if your mother used pesticides on this lawn?"

Carter surfaced from his tent briefly and handed his mother his Game Boy.

"Battery is dead. I need your phone."

"How about you get some fresh air. Go play with Miller. Where is he?"

"Up there," Carter said.

Miller was twenty feet in the air, straddling a long branch on a hundred-year-old oak tree.

"Miller, it's time to come down," George said.

Zooey ran inside the house and returned wearing last month's Halloween costume. She wore a black cape and hood and was carrying a cardboard scythe.

Colin gaped at his daughter. "On the day of my mother's funeral. This is so inappropriate."

"It's just a costume," said Kate.

"That's what you always say," said Colin.

"It's just a job; it's just a house," Kate had said when Colin lost his job and the house. He found a new job and a smaller house. It was still too big for Kate.

"It's just a piece of paper," Kate had said when he'd asked her to marry him.

Colin was ashamed to admit this, but it wasn't until Kate turned him down that he knew what it felt like to be in love.

"It's not just a piece of paper to me," he'd said.

"Courthouse," Kate said, bargaining for the smallest nuptials.

"Backyard," Colin countered, and won.

The wedding was too simple for Lena, but since she didn't approve of the bride, she could hardly complain about the lack of fanfare over the ceremony.

When Colin phoned Anna to tell her the news about his relationship, Anna first thought he was joking. Then, after he convinced her otherwise, she hung up on him and called Kate to remind her of his two failed marriages. It never occurred to Anna that Colin would be different because Kate wasn't like the others.

"He could break your heart," Anna said.

"Or I could break his," said Kate.

"I prefer that scenario," Anna said.

Anna phoned her brother after she ended the call with Kate.

"Try not to fuck this one up," she said.

Two months later, Anna received an invitation to the wedding. Anna thought it was the kind of wedding that you had when you had nothing to prove, and this time she believed her brother when he said, "Until death do us part." Kate had tried ardently to get that bit excised from the ceremony, but the preacher was old and forgetful and ignored the red line Kate sliced across the vows.

■ ■ ■ ■

In the Fury backyard, after the funeral, Colin kissed Kate on the lips in front of all the company. Sensing Kate's discomfort with the public display of affection, he pulled her into a full embrace and then dipped her in a movie-star smooch.

"I'm going to bed. Inside. Like normal people," Colin said, shaking his head at the collection of tents in his mother's backyard. Lena would have been furious.

"That's nothing to be proud of," Kate said.

Colin returned to the house but didn't go to bed. He started his own fire in the civilized living-room hearth. Kate had finally taught him how to build a fire, and he'd gotten pretty good at it. After twenty minutes it was a beautiful blaze. Colin sat down on the couch and opened up a biography of a now-deceased movie star that Kate had recommended after noting he only read books on business or politics.

Hudson found eight snails in the grass and proudly delivered them to his mother. George asked for butter and a skillet so she could fry them up over the fire.

"Are you going to eat those snails?" Anna asked.

"We eat them at home," George said, "once I stopped the gardener from using pesticides. They're the same kinds you get in a French restaurant."

"I'm sure my mother used pesticides."

"Sorry, Hudson," George said. "These are poisonous snails. I'll fry you up a batch as soon as we get home."

Hudson shoved his hands in his pockets and bowed his head in disappointment, like a child actor playing sad. He snapped out of it when Kate fetched a bag of marshmallows from the pantry.

Zooey showed Miller the two bears in the sky and told him not to look for a third while Anna stabbed marshmallows on chopstick stakes.

The group held their wands over the flames.

"Not as good as snails," Hudson declared.

"Better than snails," Zooey countered.

The conversation repeated seven times until Kate interrupted: "Zooey prefers marshmallows; Hudson prefers snails. There is no universal truth."

After the children were tucked into sleeping bags in their tents, Anna, Kate, and George returned to the fire, fueling it with another log.

The women regarded one another silently.

Is this as good as it gets? George thought.

Nothing is better than this, Kate thought.

And Anna thought how peaceful it was to think about nothing at all, to simply sit by the fire and enjoy the snaps and cracks and the smell of burned wood and the ghostly swirls of smoke dissipating into the cold night air.

When the fire died, the women crawled into a two-man tent, knowing that only one of them would sleep well that night.

Kate woke shortly after 2:00 a.m. when George kneed her in the ribs. She curled into a ball in the corner and tried to go back to sleep. The smell of burned embers lingered in the air. She'd been sure the campfire was dead when they went to sleep, but she crawled out of the tent to check again. The bonfire was indeed a cold, damp pile of charred wood.

The Fury mansion, however, was alight with flames, the entire bottom floor engulfed. Kate rushed to the back door as the kitchen window burst out. She raced back to the campsite and found George's coat in the mouth of the tent. She rifled through her pockets, picked up her cell, and dialed.

"Wake up, wake up, wake up," she repeated.

He woke up and answered.

"What?" Colin said groggily.

"The house is on fire. Climb out of the bedroom window and onto the trellis."

"What?" Colin said again.

"Wake up, Colin, and get the fuck out of the house. Now," Kate said. It was the loudest she had ever spoken to anyone.

Kate rushed toward the house and willed the bedroom window to open. Colin unhooked the latch, wondered why there needed to be a latch on the top floor, and opened the window. He fumbled with the fastener to the screen and shoved it loose. Colin straddled the window and thought that maybe he should go back and get a coat and slippers.

Kate saw him hesitate and shouted, *"Whatever you're thinking is wrong."*

Colin climbed onto the aging trellis, feeling the sharp wood dig cornered grooves into his bare feet. He descended the lattice like a grownup on a jungle gym, the distant tactile memory returning. He jumped the last few feet to the ground and landed on a rock.

He hopped over to Kate, wincing in pain. The sole of one foot was covered in blood.

"I think I need to go to the hospital," he said.

"Better than dead," Kate said, dialing 911. She passed the phone to Colin. "Tell them we need a fire truck."

Anna and George, hearing Kate's raised voice, emerged from the tent and took in the blaze. Before anyone could think unthinkable thoughts, Kate unzipped the children's tents and made sure all four were safe. Carter was still in a dead sleep; the faint bass sounds from his earbuds could be heard as he curled into a ball. Children could sleep through *anything,* she thought. Kate breathed for the first time in hours, it seemed.

As more windows burst into the air, raining glass onto the Fury lawn, Kate realized the fire had spared her the trouble of cleaning out Lena's home. She also realized that Colin had no idea how to properly extinguish a flame. George stared at the violent blaze and could think only of her children safely zipped up in their tent. She wished just for a brief second that Edgar's house would burn to the ground so she and her boys could set up camp in his backyard and live under the stars.

Anna thought that she should feel more, watching her childhood home burn to the ground. The idea that all the memories the house contained would turn to dust somehow released her. Her secret room, her mother's letters, the pink gown she wore to Colin's wedding and the black dress from Malcolm's funeral, all tucked away behind those doors. Soon they would be gone forever, and maybe, with the physical memory in the form of dust, her own memories would fade. And she thought the flames were breathtaking. How could nature come up with colors so fantastic, like that Montana sky Kate had once told her about. She also thought it was a miracle she hadn't dabbled in arson as a child. Then she wondered how the fire started. And she remembered the man responsible for all fires.

"You know whose fault this is?" Anna said. *"Teddy Fucking Roosevelt."*

ACKNOWLEDGMENTS

I wrote the first few chapters of *How to Start a Fire* at the beginning of 2006, right before I sold my first novel, *The Spellman Files*. While the Spellmans took over my universe for the next several years, I never forgot about this book. I'd revisit it in small doses until I finally had the chance to dedicate myself to it full time. I can't claim that I spent nine years working on this book, but it's the novel I've lived with the longest, and I am indescribably grateful to finally see it published. Along the way, many people read drafts, provided research, or inspired me. My goal here is to not forget anyone, but I'm sure that I will. I apologize in advance.

To begin, I must thank Andrea Schultz, my amazing editor. Your dedication, humor, and relentlessness made this novel so much better than I thought it could be. You always seemed to know which direction would get me out of the woods.

Stephanie Rostan, my agent, Madam Forewoman. I owe my career to you. There's nothing else to say.

There are many more amazing people to thank at HMH. In no particular order: Naomi Gibbs, Lori Glazer, Carla Gray, Liz Anderson, Michelle Bonanno, Laura Giannino, Beth Burleigh Fuller, Brian Moore, Lauren Wein, and Chelsea Newbould. You have all been amazing. And thank you, Michaela Sullivan, for the phenomenal jacket design.

My wonderful agency, now Levine Greenberg Rostan: I love you all. Thank you, Melissa Rowland, Elizabeth Fisher, Monika Verma, Miek Coccia, Daniel Greenberg, Jim Levine, Tim Wojcik, Jamie Maurer, Kerry Sparks, and Shelby Boyer. Meet me at the Brigadoon bar in seven years.

A *huge* thanks to my doctor/copyeditor Tracy Roe. I cannot believe my good fortune in having you on board. Your advisement was invaluable.

There are two friends/copyeditors I must single out for the cruel number of drafts I forced them to read over the last few years. Clair Lamb and David Hayward, I am very grateful for your wise counsel and your restraint in mocking my limited grasp of the English language.

Thanks to all of the other friends who beta-tested my book: Anastasia Fuller, Julie Ulmer, Steve Kim, Morgan Dox, and Ronnie Konner.

Kate Golden, thank you for your obsessions.

Lisa Chen, thank you for your illegible letters.

No doctors were injured in the writing of this book, but several were troubled repeatedly. I would like to thank you all for generously answering my questions: Drs. Josh Bazell, Jonathan Hayes, Sarah Lewis, and Julie Jaffe.

I would like to thank my family for being awesome and present and for other things too. Especially my Aunt Beverly, but also my Uncle Mark, Uncle Jeff, Aunt Eve, and cousins Dan and Lori and Jay Fienberg.

I would also like to thank the awesome community of crime writers that I'm fortunate enough to be a part of. There are too many people to list here (and it would probably seem like name-dropping). You know who you are. I am very lucky to know you people.

Lastly, I'd like to thank all of my friends, especially the female ones, the weird friends, the ones who inspired the book by being unique and strange and completely *of themselves.* I won't name names, but some of you are even weirder than I am, and that has always brought me great comfort.

ABOUT THE AUTHOR

Lisa Lutz is the *New York Times* bestselling author of *The Spellman Files, Curse of the Spellmans, Revenge of the Spellmans, The Spellmans Strike Again, Trail of the Spellmans, Spellman Six: The Next Generation* (previously published as *The Last Word*), *Heads you Lose* (with David Hayward), and the children's book, *How to Negotiate Everything* (illustrated by Jaime Temairik). Her latest book, *How to Start a Fire,* will be published in May 2015. Lutz has won the Alex award and has been nominated for the Edgar Award for Best Novel.

Although she attended UC Santa Cruz, UC Irvine, the University of Leeds in England, and San Francisco State University, she still does not have a bachelor's degree. Lisa spent most of the 1990s hopping through a string of low-paying odd jobs while writing and rewriting the screenplay *Plan B,* a mob comedy. After the film was made in 2000, she vowed she would never write another screenplay. Lisa lives in a town you've never heard of in upstate New York.